MANIPULATED

Lauta,

Thank you For your
interest in Manipulated.
I hope you enjoy it.

John Ford Clayton

ISBN: 0999548204
ISBN 13: 9780999548202
Library of Congress Control Number: 2017916423
John Ford Clayton, Harriman, TN

ACKNOWLEDGEMENTS

To my editors Deckie and Linda, first of all, thank you for the reminder that I really should have paid more attention in high school English. Secondly, I promise I actually listened to some of your advice. You both made the book a better product.

To my cover designer Barbie, thank you for your patience with my many edits. Your work helped me tell the story to prospective readers.

To my doctors McColl, Pardue, Midis, and Foust, thank you for helping me to be cancer-free. Without you this story would never have been finished.

To my friends Tanya, Matt, Tyler, and Bob, thank you for reading early versions of the book and providing consistent encouragement. Your feedback help me to keep pushing to "the end".

To my kids Ben, Eli, and Christina, thank you for putting up with years of "I'm going to write a book." Believe it or not, I finally did.

To my beautiful (inside and out) wife Kara, how many times did your gentle nudges keep me going? I wanted to quit after 77 pages, you said to keep going. I wanted to quit after 150 pages, you said keep going. I wanted to quit with just a few chapters to go…you get the point. Even after the book was done and I was ready to put it on the shelf and not pursue publication, you wouldn't let me drop it. Although I may have written the words, this project is truly a partnership that would never have become a book without you. To the moon and back!

To God, my Creator, Sustainer, and Savior, I am nothing without You. Despite my daily failings You still love me. It is my prayer that this book would somehow bring You glory.

PROLOGUE

"Hey, Babe, I'm on the way home. My cell phone is almost dead, so I can only talk for a minute. Yeah, I finally had the conversation with Victor. It went a lot better than I expected. He actually seemed OK with it. Yeah, I know; I guess I was worried about nothing. Tell Shelly and Kendall I'll be home in 30 minutes and I've got Savano's, two large pepperonis. See you soon. I love you, too."

Bryce Dunn had expected that his boss, Victor Youngblood, would be upset about his submitting his resignation. He had heard many stories—apparently most of them urban legends—about Victor refusing to allow associates to leave the firm, especially those like Bryce who worked on Mouse Trap. But that wasn't the type of reaction Bryce experienced. He had made his case for leaving; and at the end of his plea, Victor simply extended his hand, said "I understand," and wished Bryce the best of luck.

His first eight years with Mouse Trap had been exhilarating. Bryce had a direct hand in guiding many of the country's daily headlines, although he had accepted that no one would ever know about his accomplishments. His research led to the rise and fall of the highest profile politicians, movie stars, and athletes. He was responsible for the bankruptcy of some companies and the record profits of others. He often had the benefit of knowing what the next day's headlines would be, even before they had been written.

He didn't mind that he couldn't talk about his job outside of his Mouse Trap circle. He was OK with simply telling friends and family he was a project manager. He was delighted that his salary and generous bonuses had swelled his Cayman Island bank account to $2.5 million by age 31. But something just no longer seemed right. Maybe it was his transition from the single guy he was when he first joined Mouse Trap to a full-fledged family man with a wife and two young daughters. Maybe it was his growing Catholic faith tugging at his conscience. It could have even been the recent death of his father, who had been his closest confidant. Whatever it was, Bryce felt compelled to step away from the only employer he had ever known. He had been working up the courage for almost a year to have the conversation with Victor. After it went so smoothly, he now regretted not having it sooner. He felt great. He felt exhilarated. And for the first time in years, he felt like a free man.

With his newfound liberty, he couldn't wait to get back home to his family. During the rural Maryland evening commute, he glanced in the rearview mirror and noticed a set of fast-approaching headlights. "Who is this crazy guy?" Bryce thought. The curvy road followed the banks of the Potomac River, and there was no easy place to pass. Instinctively Bryce sped to give the tailgater some room. Another look in the mirror and the lights were now only a few feet away and still closing ground. Then Bryce felt the impact. The large SUV had rammed his BMW X1 with a glancing blow that caused it to slide sideways. As Bryce tried to regain control of the skidding vehicle, a second impact struck the small car squarely on the passenger side. With the second blow, the SUV again accelerated, pushing Bryce down the road, rapidly approaching a curve leading to a steep cliff, straight down to the river. Bryce tried again to steer his way out of the crash, but the undersized car was no match for the force of the 9,000-pound SUV.

The tandem approached the edge of the 40-foot-drop. With its brakes fully engaged, the SUV, screeched to a halt a few feet short of the precipice. Bryce's car was not so fortunate. The weight of the engine pulled the car careening down the hill, first striking a jagged rock outcropping before flipping three times on the journey down the hill, ultimately coming to rest on its top at the edge of the frigid Potomac, cooled by the runoff of the thawing January snow.

The SUV sped away but was followed closely by a black sedan that pulled over to the narrow shoulder. Two men climbed out of the backseat of the car and rapidly navigated down the steep hill as the sedan hurried away from the scene. Reaching Bryce's car, they looked inside to find him badly bruised and beaten but somehow still clinging to life. One of the two men hand-signaled his partner, who responded with a nod of the head. The first man reached into the car, grabbed Bryce by the neck and executed a sharp twist, breaking Bryce's C-2 and C-3 cervical vertebrae. As Bryce Dunn breathed his last breath, he thought, "The rumors about Mouse Trap must be true; it really is a job for life."

1

January 7, 2015
671 Days Until the 2016 U. S. Presidential Election

"No More Hate! No More Hate!"

The chants echoed through the Quad from the two dozen protesters assembled near the campus's main pedestrian intersection. Situated in the middle of the sidewalk was Dr. Molly Jefferson, the leader of the rabble. Dr. Jefferson's pride swelled as she admired the growing assembly, who had numbered only six the day before.

"What do we want?!" she shrieked through the bull-horn borrowed from the track coach.

"Justice!" came the reply.

"When do we want it?!"

"Now!"

Dr. Jefferson, dean of the College of Religious Studies at Richfield College, had spearheaded this protest.

"Is hate speech welcomed at Richfield?!" Dr. Jefferson asked the crowd.

"No!" came the compliant response.

Dr. Jefferson felt a great sense of pride that a protest she launched only the day before was beginning to gain traction.

The protestors felt they were part of a larger, important, maybe even historic movement. Little did they know they were all simply being manipulated.

In the Winchester Library, just off the Richfield College Quad, Jeremy Prince had found a table where he could observe the growing protest. He peered through the leafless branches of the Bradford pear trees that stood guard just outside the tinted window. The sun was giving way to the early January sunset, and he suspected the protestors' resolve had not yet grown to a level warranting a stay past dark in temperatures expected to dip into the low 20s. As Jeremy watched the marchers, he couldn't withhold the grin that grew to a smile, ultimately producing an unconscious chuckle.

"Shhh," objected the students sitting at the tables nearby. "Please be quiet."

"Oh, sorry, my bad," Jeremy raised a hand of apology. "Won't happen again."

Finding the fortitude to suppress his audible excitement was almost achievable, but losing the grin was asking too much. After all, a plan he had hatched two short weeks ago in a fraternity house 275 miles away was now unfolding right before his eyes. Not just unfolding, but thriving. And to imagine he was just getting started. He knew he had to channel his energies to his laptop for the next step in his diabolical plan.

Richfield Bible College was founded in 1956 by the Southern Baptist Convention. It was situated in a rustic valley in East Tennessee, just outside the small town of Bard's Ridge, 30 miles from the city of Knoxville. A local farmer donated 60 acres to get the college started. With the donation came a two-story hay barn, which served as the classroom for Richfield's initial enrollment of 27.

Growth would come quickly to Richfield, as in four short years the freshman class of 1960 swelled to 80. By 1972, the college had grown to occupy over a dozen buildings, including the newly christened Winchester Library. Richfield enjoyed its peak enrollment throughout the 1980s. By 1988, Richfield Bible College's enrollment rose to 927.

As much success and growth that Richfield had experienced in the 40 years since its founding, the 90s would usher in a decade of turmoil, challenge, controversy, and ultimately profound change.

Pinpointing the exact catalyst for the transformation is difficult, but many point to a seminal series published in 1992 by Knoxville's largest newspaper, *The Knoxville Chronicle*. The series ran four consecutive days, each highlighting a Richfield Bible College transgression.

Day one of the series focused on the lack of quality education the Richfield students received. Comparing a Richfield bachelor's degree with those of other area colleges, the article noted that in a 120-hour bachelor's degree program at Richfield, students took 90 hours of Bible classes. That first day's headline read RICHFIELD OFFERS SUB-STANDARD EDUCATION.

The second day's article focused on equality and diversity, hot topics in the early 90s. Noting that of Richfield's 875 enrollees, 780 were men, *The Chronicle* led with the headline RICHFIELD COLLEGE: WOMEN AND MINORITIES NEED NOT APPLY. The article blasted Richfield's racial uniformity, remarking that after spending three days on campus *The Chronicle* staff could find only two non-white students.

The third day's headline read RICHFIELD LEADER-SHIP DISCONNECTED AND UNQUALIFIED. The article blasted Richfield's leadership, noting that its president had no advanced degree. A similar criticism was levied at Richfield professors with accusations of a chronic lack of experience and qualifications. The article's most biting criticism was of the Board of Trustees, composed of seven men—most of whom had no educational experience and who had rarely been to Richfield. By the time the third article was printed, national publications were beginning to ask for permission to reprint the series.

The last day focused on Richfield's foundational belief system. Running on Sunday to guarantee maximum readership, its headline read RICHFIELD: VOW OF PURITY REQUIRED, referencing a "covenant" all students were required to sign as a condition of their college admission. This covenant required that students submit to the authority of college educators and administrators and that they commit to 60 hours of ministry service (with emphasis on UNPAID service). Having to accept the Protestant Bible as the inerrant Word of God, students also had to acknowledge that Jesus Christ is the way, the truth and the life, and that no one would go to heaven except through Him.

The Chronicle noted other practices it considered Puritanical, such as a prohibition on students engaging in sex and a ban on homosexuals. *The Chronicle* even included excerpts from an interview with a former Richfield student who claimed he had been dismissed from school after admitting his homosexuality to his college advisor in what he thought was a private conversation.

The series won *The Knoxville Chronicle* and its author, Delores Jenkins, three Tennessee Press Association Awards, as well as significant national acclaim and attention. It brought Richfield Bible College scorn and ridicule throughout the country as the articles were printed in over 100 U. S. newspapers.

After the series was published, Richfield Bible College was never the same. In just a few months, the president resigned from office. Not long afterward, a mass exodus of faculty followed as enrollment began to plummet from 875 enrollees at the time of *The Chronicle* series to 550 in just over a year. The snowball continued as the Southern Baptist Convention decided to divest its sponsorship of Richfield, leading to a loss of all seven members of the Board of Trustees. Richfield Bible College was in freefall. Were it not for an anonymous donor, who for three consecutive months made payroll for the remaining staff and faculty, the college might have been forced to close.

In these most difficult times, a handful of remaining faculty members and staff assembled in an emergency session to determine how to pick up the broken pieces of the college they all loved. They knew if Richfield were to survive, a new beginning was required. They decided to hold their initial planning meeting symbolically in the still-standing hay barn, which had been converted to a Richfield museum. Many options were thrown on the table, all involving keeping the college alive. Not a single voice suggested closure as an option.

In times like these, natural leaders tend to emerge; in this case, that leader was the Dean of the fledgling Business College, Joe McArthur. Mac, as everyone called him, listened to the various opinions before writing down a few common concepts he was hearing. After two days of meetings, a consensus emerged of how to move

Richfield forward. As frustrated as most were with *The Chronicle* article, they all admitted some valid concerns needed to be addressed. The first was that the college should broaden its educational offerings and drop the word *Bible* from its name. Efforts were also made to diversify the college in both the student body as well as in the administration and teaching staff. A new Board of seven trustees consisted of three women, including one African-American, and four men.

Once seated, the trustees selected a new president, a PhD who had over 20 years of educational experience, and who was not affiliated with the Southern Baptists.

Throughout the 2000s, the Richfield College transformation was remarkable. The student body was now 55% female with a growing multi-cultural population. Tattoos and piercings were commonplace at Richfield, which now reflected the diverse culture of most college campuses across the U. S. The curriculum was completely overhauled to be more aligned with that of similar size colleges. Most Bible classes were dropped and were replaced by the Religious Studies Department, which Dr. Jefferson was hired to chair in 2012.

With the most recent cheer, Dr. Jefferson sensed the crowd begin to lose energy. Knowing they didn't have the experience she did with protests, she recognized this moral stand would be a marathon, not a sprint. She decided it was time to send the crowd away but not before a final word of inspiration.

Stepping up on a park bench, she reactivated the bullhorn, drawing all eyes and ears in her direction. "I hope you all have an appreciation for the historic action that you have started today...and I do mean *started*...because we are just beginning to let our voices be heard." Cheers sprang up around her as the original two-dozen protestors had been joined by 30 curious onlookers, not all of whom were fully invested in the movement, at least not yet.

"We all know the sordid past of this institution, a past of exclusion, hate, and intolerance. Do we want to return to those days?!"

"No!"

"That's right; none of us want to go back to those dark days. And we're not going to let that happen!" Again, enthusiastic applause filled the Quad.

"If it is the last act I do at this college, I will stop the bigoted, close-minded, hatemonger Elijah Mustang from speaking at this institution! We're going to bring today's protest to a close, but I'm going to ask—no, I'm going to plead with—those of you on the periphery listening to my voice to join us tomorrow at noon to resume this movement. We don't want to go back. We only want to move forward! I truly believe that together we are doing God's work!"

As she stepped down from the bench, she was greeted by hugs and cheers. She could tell she had reached a new constituency. She prayed that tomorrow's crowd would be even larger than today's; the same for the next and the next and the next, until justice was served.

Among those standing in the periphery was Jeremy Prince thinking to himself, "I can't believe this is actually working." Again unable to suppress the smile that consumed his face, he took a step back toward the library thinking, "Now, let's see if the next bait is swallowed as voraciously as the last." Would he be so lucky?

As Dr. Jefferson unlocked the door to her apartment, she didn't remember the three-mile drive from campus. She wondered if she had driven or just glided on the winds of change. She had been part of many protests in her career. She joined a movement that kept the ladies' swim team going at Delaware State, picketed for gender equality pay at the Connecticut State Transportation Department, and was among the throng who successfully got a fraternity shut down for a pattern of abusing its little sisters. However, the Richfield College movement was her maiden voyage as the leader of a protest. She quite liked it and felt she was a natural. In fact, she felt a special calling to this important undertaking. She was a true social justice warrior!

As a single, 30-something college professor with degrees in philosophy and religion, Dr. Jefferson knew the stereotype many would foist upon her: a shrill, angry, unattractive female—a stereotype that many of her colleagues unfortunately reinforced. However, she worked diligently to establish her own persona. She was known as kind, professional, even deferential to her peers. While she had strong opinions, she didn't eagerly share them. She chose her opportunities wisely for when and with whom to make her thoughts known. At 5' 2" with a petite figure, she was not an imposing physical presence. She was also a Christian, a fact that brought derision from many of her university contemporaries. Her Christian beliefs were the primary inspiration for her seeking a Richfield faculty position.

She also considered herself significantly out of the mainstream of American conservative evangelical Christian orthodoxy. While she believed that Jesus Christ offered a path to a heaven-like afterlife, she did not consider that the *only* path. She considered the Protestant Bible a mix of theology, history, and fantasy, much like other holy books such as the Koran and the writings of Confucius and Buddha. In general, she considered herself open to new ideas and teachings; and she read voraciously, always seeking a deeper truth.

Although she normally led with her gentle spirit, Dr. Jefferson held great passion for where she saw injustice and unfairness, especially if a Christian institution was involved. This passion was driving her voice of leadership in the Richfield protest. She knew the history of Richfield's injustice and how hard those who came before her worked to correct it. Thus, she felt obligated to pick up the baton from the trailblazers who worked for almost a decade to make Richfield the more open, diverse campus it was becoming. The more she learned about Elijah Mustang, the more she was convinced that inviting him to speak at the graduation ceremony was a step backwards from the significant progress already enjoyed. His speaking there could even usher in a return to the college's dark past. This would be a battle to which she was willing to give everything she had to win.

Receiving her B. S. in religious studies from Vermont State University in 1990, Dr. Jefferson had studied the country's religious journey from the growth of the Christian Conservative Movement as a political power in the 80s to the backlash and decline during the Clinton years of the 90s. She had even written a paper on Jerry Falwell titled "The Immoral Majority," making her case for how the Christian Conservative Movement had blurred the lines between church and state, causing major damage to the country in the process. In her doctoral thesis written at the University of North Carolina, she chronicled the Southern Baptist Convention's rise and decline with a particular focus on Southern Baptist colleges. Now finding herself a professor at Richfield College seemed surreal to her. The notion that she was at the center of such a protest seemed implausible.

Walking through the door of her small, one-bed-room apartment, she instinctively popped a vanilla ha-zelnut decaf cup in the Keurig and took a seat at the kitchen table. Flipping open the cover to her laptop, she began perusing social media as Anthony, her rescue cat, navigated a figure eight around her outstretched legs. Twitter was her first e-destination, and she was delight-ed at what she found: "Awesome day on the Richfield Quad." "Actually doing something to make a differ-ence." She even found that a hashtag #Richfield Protest had been established. Her movement started a hashtag! Although she knew it wasn't "her" movement, she felt a sense of profound satisfaction.

Next came Facebook, with similar results: a half-doz-en statuses from students with inspired posts, positive comments, and many "likes." Not a single negative com-ment or snarky retort was found. As she scrolled through her posts, she found what she was hoping to see: a new post from Dr. Jocelyn Rosenberg, a women's studies pro-fessor, who had befriended her on Facebook a month prior. Although they had only been acquainted a short time, they were obviously kindred spirits. Dr. Rosenberg was the first to bring Elijah Mustang's transgressions to her attention. This new post was linked to an article in *The Chattanooga Observer* that included excerpts from an interview Mr. Mustang had given to a reporter in 2011. In this interview, Dr. Jefferson found even more bigotry and hatred. When the reporter asked Mustang about his stance on gay marriage, he stated, "It is my belief that marriage is between a man and a woman. That's not just my opinion, but I believe the Word of God is clear and consistent on that point."

"So now he's deciding what the Word of God is?" she asked her cat, Anthony. Dr. Jefferson had found even more fuel for her passionate protest. She felt her heart race as she quickly typed three e-mails: one to Dr. Rosenberg thanking her for the link to this article and for her inspiration to pursue this issue; another to the president of Richfield College detailing her concerns about Elijah Mustang; and a third to an old acquaintance, Delores Jenkins, now *The Knoxville Chronicle*'s assistant editor. She sensed what started as a modest protest was about to hit it big. However, she couldn't begin to predict what the next three days would bring.

2

As she started most days, Delores Jenkins strode into her office, flipped on the lights, and powered up her computer to see what e-mails came in overnight. Her desk was spotless, without a single pile of paper. The walls of her office were adorned with over 20 journalism awards, won as much for her tenacity as for her writing. As assistant editor of *The Knoxville Chronicle,* she often received over 100 e-mails from the time she walked out of the office at 6 p.m. until when she returned at 7 the following morning. On a normal day, her inbox would include complaints, praises, donation solicitations, meeting requests, and myriad advertisements. She even received the occasional hot news tip, as would be the case this day.

She was turning 70 next month but only those closest to Delores knew her real age. Her appearance suggested she was still in her 50s, and her health was that of a 30-something. At 5' 11" and a lean 135 pounds, she was still a striking figure. Her close-cropped salt-and-pepper hair only served to magnify the respect that she commanded from all she encountered.

In the past ten years, she had hiked all 84 trails in the nearby Smoky Mountains, recording over 1,000 miles. On her 65th birthday, she had even climbed Mount McKinley, the U. S.'s highest peak. Married to Gerald, the love of her life for 45 years, she was a woman content with who she was. To many, she was the most interesting woman in Knoxville.

In her 42 years at *The Chronicle*, she had done it all. Starting as a junior writer, she quickly displayed a penchant for taking on the toughest assignments. Her stories brought down a federal judge addicted to painkillers, revealed the leaders of the city's most notorious street gang, and exposed widespread corruption in the county school system's contracts division, just to name a few.

Delores caught the attention of *The Chronicle*'s leadership team, leading to her rise through the ranks of senior writer, news director, and ultimately to assistant editor. In fact, she had all of the qualifications for editor, except dealing with the day-to-day corporate bureaucracy and glad-handing with the self-important whom she disdained. She knew she had reached as high as she was going to, and she had made peace with that reality several years prior.

Through her years at *The Chronicle,* her most satisfying assignment was the Richfield Bible College exposé. She won awards and acclaim, but her greatest satisfaction was in knowing she had a hand in the monumental changes that had taken place at Richfield and had impacted thousands of student's lives through the years. This satisfaction made the e-mail she had received overnight from Dr. Molly Jefferson even more intriguing. Although her duties did not provide the time or opportunity to write very often, this could be an exception she would consider. Grabbing her coat and keys, she was back out the door to make the 45-minute drive to Bard's Ridge to see for herself what was really going on.

"Dad, when are you leaving for Costa Rica?" asked Rachel Mustang over the sounds of eggs crackling in the cast iron skillet.

"It's actually Honduras," replied Elijah Mustang, fastening the last button on his shirt. He was making one last trip to the office before leaving the country for the next two weeks.

"I thought you went to Honduras last time, Dad," Rachel asked.

"I did, but I didn't get everything done."

"It should be just like you like it." Rachel gently slid the omelet on her father's plate as she did each Wednesday morning. At 21, Rachel was the youngest of three daughters and the only one still living at home. She loved making her father happy; and preparing his favorite omelet with bacon, provolone cheese, and jalapeno peppers would always bring a smile to his face.

A true rags-to-riches success story, Elijah Mustang was CEO and founder of Promise Transportation, one of the largest trucking companies in the Southeast. Headquartered in Knoxville, Tennessee, the company had offices in 23 cities and operated over 2,000 trucks. But that wasn't always the story.

With both parents out of the picture by the time he entered first grade, Elijah was raised by his grandparents. What they lacked in material wealth, they more than made up for in the love they showered on Elijah. They also instilled a determined work ethic that yielded Elijah a solid "B" average in high school. With meager resources available to Elijah, college was out of the question; so he took a truck driving class right out of high school. He was in the driver's seat of an 18-wheeler by age 19.

Knowing he was capable of more, Elijah set aside enough savings to begin taking a few classes at Richfield Bible College, which had recently started a business curriculum. By age 21, he was taking 12 hours of college credits while driving a truck as many miles as he could. The pressure on Elijah was crushing, but he went to great lengths to keep up the hectic pace. He started innocently with coffee, then caffeine pills, then stronger and stronger "helpers" until he was hooked. It all came to a crashing end when Elijah fell asleep at the wheel after 54 straight waking hours. It was, thankfully, a one-vehicle crash, but his semi-truck left the road, skidded down a 15-foot embankment, only stopping when the trailer wrapped around a tree. The paramedic said Elijah was lucky to be alive. Both arms and his right leg were shattered. Broken ribs had punctured his lungs. His pelvis was fractured in three places.

All told, his stay in the hospital and rehab was seven months. During that time, Elijah found what he would often say was the greatest gift he had ever received. He found God; or as Elijah often confessed, "God found him."

After what his doctors called a miracle recovery, Elijah renewed his college pursuits, enrolling in a few hours per semester and eventually earning his bachelor's degree in business by the time he was 26. Upon graduation, Elijah was a new man with a new passion for life. Applying what he had learned from Richfield's business curriculum, he purchased four semi-trucks and founded Promise Transportation in 1982. One decree that Elijah issued with those first four trucks was that all Promise Transportation trailers would have the following words painted prominently on the side:

"For God so loved..." John 3:16

Elijah hoped that the verse was so well-known that those reading it would be bound to finish the verse in their heads: "...the world, that He gave his only begotten son, that whosoever believes in Him would not perish, but have everlasting life." The thought of hundreds of motorists mentally reciting this verse every day brought a smile to Elijah's face. This was a decree he continued to maintain with now over 2,000 trucks on the road.

"So, when did you say you were leaving, Dad?"

"Tomorrow morning, first flight out of Knoxville."

At age 59, Elijah was beginning to feel his years. A chronic 20 pounds overweight, Elijah carried most of the excess as his spare tire. He ate fried foods most days for lunch and seldom sought intentional exercise. His work and ministry commanded a frenetic pace, and he inherited a high metabolism from his parents; otherwise, he'd likely be tipping the scales at 350 pounds. Despite a nervous habit of running his hands through his hair, he somehow managed to retain a full head of snowy white hair that he wore combed straight back with just a touch of gel.

One core belief that Elijah Mustang fostered while at Richfield College was that everything he had, and ever would have, was a blessing from God. As an acknowledgement of those blessings, Elijah vowed to honor God through giving back a portion of his material gains.

Many Christians strive to devote 10% of their earnings to the church. In Christian terms, this is called a *tithe*, which translates from Hebrew to *a tenth*. Elijah started by giving 10%, but he vowed to increase his giving every year by 5% until he reached giving 90% and living on 10%.

For many years, meeting this lofty target was a struggle; and in 1997, when he was planning to donate 45%, he fell just a bit short. In every other year, he met his goal, reaching 90% giving in 2002 and maintaining that level of giving ever since. In fact, for three years Elijah gave away 100% of his personal earnings.

Early in his career, Elijah accompanied a friend on a trip to El Salvador. It was a trip that changed his life. He was moved by the love and warm spirit of the Salvadoran people but was heartbroken by the conditions in which the poorest citizens were forced to live. In much of the country, poverty was widespread and medical care was almost non-existent. But what affected Elijah the most was the number of children living on the streets without parents. A little girl named Maria first stole his heart. Only seven years old, she carried the filth and odor from the nearby garbage dump that she called home, which she shared with her ten-year-old brother Hector. Maria was drawn to Elijah immediately and climbed into his lap. He found a book and started to read.

Before he knew it, two hours had passed. Somewhat embarrassed that he had lost track of time, Elijah responded, "I am sorry. Where are the parents of this child?" People were silent at first; then most heads turned away, to avoid eye contact with Elijah. Finally, someone simply shook his head. Unsure of the gesture at first, Elijah asked, "What... what are you trying to tell me?"

A local priest finally responded, "Like many Salvadoran children, Maria does not have parents, any other family members, or even a home."

"But, where does she live?" Elijah asked.

"She lives on the street."

"What?!" Elijah was floored. "But, she's what, four years old?" Elijah was told Maria was actually seven, her growth stunted by malnutrition. Maria was one of many Salvadoran children who were dependent on the scraps from garbage cans for their daily sustenance. It was an encounter that would change the course of Elijah's life, as well as the lives of many Salvadoran people. Before he returned to the U. S. from that first visit, he vowed to do something about the deplorable living conditions he had encountered. He wasn't sure what he could do, but he knew he had to do something.

Over the next 30 years, Elijah did more than just "something"—and not just in El Salvador. As Promise Transportation grew exponentially, so did Elijah's ability to serve the people of Central America. Shortly after that first trip, he started Promise Ministries. Now thriving, with a presence in El Salvador, Honduras, Guatemala, Nicaragua and Costa Rica, Promise Ministries has built a dozen medical clinics, over 30 churches, and more homes than anyone could count. Elijah's proudest accomplishment was the construction of nine orphanages, which provided homes for many of the region's neediest children. He called them Promise Homes.

While his time and dedication to Promise Ministries were most rewarding for Elijah, four years in the 90s were the worst of his life. During this time, he stepped away from Promise Transportation for what he considered a genuine calling to enter the contact sport of American politics. He was later quick to admit it was the worst decision he ever made.

The midterm elections of 1994, coined the Republican Revolution, saw the GOP gain 8 seats in the Senate and 54 seats in the House of Representatives, one that Elijah Mustang won, representing Tennessee's Third District. The election was historic because it was the first time in 40 years that Republicans held the House majority. It was heady times for a then 38-year-old Elijah.

He had little interest in politics but had an unabashed love for his country and was concerned about its direction as both a citizen and business owner. This concern led Elijah to meet with influential Tennesseans who quickly saw political potential in his genuine nature and sharp intellect. They convinced Elijah that the best way to remedy the issues he had raised was to run for office himself. After no small amount of coaxing and stroking, Elijah reluctantly agreed. To his surprise, he won his first election, unseating an incumbent by a comfortable 10-point margin.

Within a month of being sworn in, Elijah began to have doubts about his decision to run. He quickly realized his new Tennessee "friends" had encouraged him to run for office so they could profit from his power, a *quid pro quo* relationship that he detested. He also realized that the only thing dirtier than politics was a politician. Except for a few of his fellow freshmen, most colleagues were out for themselves and were working to accumulate as much power as possible, regardless of the cost. To the intrinsically humble Elijah, this mentality sickened him to the pit of his soul.

Despite his early misgivings, he decided he would focus on his primary objective: to truly represent his Tennessee constituents. He would do everything within his power to avoid the quagmire of party politics. This approach didn't sit well with his Republican leadership, who expected him to toe the line. He quickly gained a reputation as a contrarian and was given junior roles on mundane committees. He was being marginalized.

He did his best to wade through the Washington morass but after reluctantly running for and comfortably winning a second term, he decided he couldn't stomach another year in Washington and ended his political career after four tumultuous years. He told anyone that tried to convince him to run for a third term that our nation's capital was a steaming cesspool of corruption and that he hoped to live long enough to forget everything he encountered there.

After his time in Washington, he happily returned to his post as CEO of Promise Transportation and redoubled his efforts to grow Promise Ministries to the thriving charity it is today. Promise Ministries now employs 30 staff members whose primary responsibility is to coordinate the acquisition of equipment and materials needed to construct homes, clinics and churches. Another staff role is to partner with churches throughout the U. S. who provide both funding and labor for operations and maintenance. Maria, now age 36, serves as liaison to the work that Promise Ministries does in her home country of El Salvador, improving the lives of the Salvadoran people.

Among Elijah's most rewarding projects is Promise Connection. Started in 2010, Promise Connection is a ministry that works to connect couples in the U. S. who are unable to conceive with children in Central America who have no parents or extended family members to provide for their care. Since starting, Promise Connection has successfully placed over 40 children with loving parents in the U. S.

"Best omelet ever." Elijah was pointing to the empty plate with his fork, mumbling as he chewed the last bite of his breakfast.

"Yeah, Dad, you say that every Wednesday."

"And I'm right every Wednesday." A huge smile came across his face. It was an easy smile felt most deeply in the wrinkles around the corner of his eyes—wrinkles that had grown more prominent with each birthday.

"What are you doing back in Honduras?"

"We are acquiring land for a new..."

"Let me guess, a new orphanage," Rachel interrupted, knowing her dad's passion had shifted in recent years to providing homes for Central American children.

"Yes, but you know I don't like the term orphanage. It conveys a lack of hope for these kids and suggests that they will never find a home. So we're just calling them Promise Homes."

"Promise Homes. I like it."

"You know, if I were forced, I could probably choke down another omelet."

"Dad, you're going to be late for work," Rachel warned.

"One of the perks of being the boss."

Playing along, Rachel asked, "Hey, Dad, would you like another omelet?"

"I thought you'd never ask. Maybe a few more jalapenos this time."

Reaching for the last two eggs in the carton, Rachel announced, "Omelet number two, coming up."

"Love you, Rachel."

"Love you, too, Dad."

"Next on the agenda is the matter of the basketball trip to The Bahamas." Richfield College President Richard Curtis involved himself in the minutiae of everyday decision-making, a habit that frustrated most of his staff. Barely a year in the position, Curtis saw his hands-on approach as a means to both educate himself about the college and leave his fingerprint on the overall culture of the campus. Most others simply saw it as micro-managing.

"What is there left to discuss? I thought we decided the trip was a go in the last staff meeting," responded an irritated Chip Collier, who served in the dual role of athletic director and basketball coach.

"We agreed to sponsor the trip with a budget of $24,500, but we did not finalize who would be accompanying the team on the trip." President Curtis was renowned for his encyclopedic memory of the most insignificant details, and that's how most of his staff viewed the details he retained—insignificant.

"The trip is still seven months away! Why is that something we have to decide today or even something that has to be decided at all in the president's staff meeting?" Chip was clearly exasperated.

Richard Curtis was the first Richfield president who was both a PhD and an attorney. Hired by the Board of Trustees to tighten the reins on the razor-thin budget, Curtis was a pure administrator who had never spent a day in the classroom as an educator. For most of his life he was a corporate attorney. He entered the education profession only within the last decade. There was much he didn't understand, a fact he failed to fully grasp.

"Chip, I know you sent me a list of personnel you'd like to accompany you on the Bahamas trip, but I'd like to have another month to review it before we take action; so let's table that until the next meeting."

Chip had no verbal response, but his body language and deep sigh spoke volumes.

"Next on the agenda is graduation. It is less than a month away, so hopefully everything is in order." Something in Curtis' makeup called for, even demanded, order.

"Everything is in place. The chairs are ordered, the caterer is under contract, the caps and gowns have been received, the gym is reserved, and the speaker is confirmed." Victoria Melendez had been dean of academic affairs for just under a year, coming on board with President Curtis. She had worked with him in his two prior jobs, providing her an understanding of his penchant for detail.

"Is everyone aware of the dust-up that the graduation speaker Elijah Mustang is causing with some of the faculty and students?" asked David Lanter, dean of students.

"What do you mean?" Curtis had not heard of the growing protest. As he asked the question, his assistant Anna sorted through a stack of papers pulling out a printed copy of the e-mail Dr. Jefferson sent the previous night.

Dean Lanter continued, "It apparently started modestly a couple of days ago but grew yesterday to over two-dozen students. Dr. Jefferson in the Religious Studies Department appears to have spearheaded it. The group is protesting against Elijah Mustang. They don't want him to be the graduation speaker."

Fidgeting nervously in his chair, President Curtis asked, "What is their primary grievance with Mr. Mustang?" Before anyone could answer, he noticed the e-mail his assistant had placed on top of his reading pile. "Wait, Dr. Jefferson sent me an e-mail last night. She says, and I quote, 'Elijah Mustang would be an inappropriate choice to represent this college at graduation. He is very much out of the mainstream of widely-held higher education beliefs. He's not inclusive, does not embrace diversity, and is opposed to gay marriage. His speaking would signal a return to Richfield's dark past, setting back decades of progress that so many fought so hard to achieve.'"

"That is the most ridiculous thing I've ever heard!" exclaimed Joe McArthur, dean of the Richfield College of Business. The man most people called Mac had a 35-year tenure, was the longest serving dean on the leadership team, and was a friend of Elijah Mustang. "Elijah Mustang is none of those things! He's a wonderful man who is among the most supportive alumni we have!"

"Am I right that you were on faculty here when Mr. Mustang was in school?" asked Natasha Hagood, Richfield's general counsel, fresh on the job for only six months. Natasha had become Curtis' most trusted advisor on almost every issue that arose.

"You are absolutely right; I know Elijah very well!" an enthusiastic Mac responded, not aware that he had scrunched to the front edge of his chair and raised his voice to a level that was making some people uncomfortable. Mac was among the true gentlemen at Richfield, and it took a lot to get him excited. He was loyal, trusting, and always sought the best in people. Unfortunately, this trait would not serve him well because he failed to recognize the path down which Natasha was mercilessly leading him.

"Weren't you Mr. Mustang's faculty advisor during his time here?" Natasha continued.

"Why, yes, yes I was." He was a bit surprised she would know that kind of detail.

"Didn't Mr. Mustang attend Richfield Bible College…" (adding the word *Bible* intentionally) "in the late 70s and early 80s?"

"Yes, he graduated in 1982, third in his class. It took him seven years to graduate as he worked full time while taking classes when he could but in the end his hard work paid off and now…."

Before Mac could continue, Natasha interrupted, "The late 70s and early 80s, wasn't that a period of significant turmoil for Richfield Bible College?"

Finally realizing Natasha's questions weren't so innocent, "What are you getting at, Counselor?"

"The staff is attempting to have an open conversation about the appropriateness of having Elijah Mustang speak at the graduation ceremony; and I believe your relationship with Mr. Mustang renders you unable to be objective on the matter."

Now as animated as anyone remembers seeing the normally mild-mannered Mac, he responded, "Objective!?!

You gotta be kidding me! I'm the only one at this table that even *knows* Elijah Mustang. How can any of the rest of you even have an opinion on the matter?!" he exclaimed, emphasizing the word *matter* as a retort to the counselor.

Attempting to diffuse the growing hostility, Dean Lanter interceded, "I am afraid this discussion is my fault. I brought up the concerns a few students and faculty raised, but this protest really didn't have much traction as of yesterday. Why don't we just let the next couple of days play out and see where it leads? More than likely it will all blow over by the end of the day, and we can forget about it."

Everyone in the staff meeting agreed that patience was in order and that this protest would likely be a flash in the pan. They couldn't have been more wrong.

3

With her Religious Diversity class scheduled to start in less than a minute, Dr. Jefferson knew her parking spot was a full five-minute walk to the classroom. She was going to be late. Although students rarely made it on time for the 9 a.m. class, she still felt obligated to be positioned at the head of the class as scheduled. However, the night before, she had tossed and turned in bed, taking hours to finally fall asleep as she was excited for the day of civil action awaiting her in the Quad. By the time sleep finally came, her alarm failed to wake her, and she arose only 20 minutes before class started. She hastily dressed, ran a brush through her hair, sloshed a mouthful of Listerine for a few seconds, and headed out the door.

Finally bounding through the door at 9:06 a.m., she entered talking, "I know, I know I'm late, but I...." As she crossed the threshold of the door, she was taken aback by what she saw or more by what she didn't see—her students. No one was there. Where 27 fresh faces were supposed to be ready to learn, there were only vacant desks. Her mind quickly cycled through the possible explanation for the emptiness. Was it the wrong day? No, a quick look at her phone confirmed it was Friday. Was it a holiday? No, just a normal day in January. Were classes cancelled for some reason? No, she could hear other classes down the hall. Then the most dreaded explanation came to mind. Was she fired for inciting the protest? She hadn't checked e-mail that morning due to being late, and maybe she had a message to come to the president's office. Just as she opened the cover of her laptop, she heard a voice.

"Dr. Jefferson." It was Candace Lindsey, one of her brightest students who had just walked into the classroom.

"Candace? What's going..." Before she could finish her question, Candace interrupted.

"Dr. Jefferson, can you come here a second?" Candace walked to the second-story window.

"But, what...?" Dr. Jefferson asked.

"Just come over here." She gestured with both hands.

As Dr. Jefferson looked out the window, she could see a group of students—her students—lining the sidewalk, through the pine and oak trees, winding around the building. "But I don't understand; what's going on?"

"Dr. Jefferson, that's your class. We've made a human chain from this building all the way over to the Quad. We think there could be no better lesson in religious diversity than for our class to kick off the day's protest with you."

Stunned, Dr. Jefferson struggled to piece together a coherent sentence, "But, the protest...is supposed to start at noon, not..."

"You don't know what's happening, do you?" Candace chuckled, knowing she had the honor of informing Dr. Jefferson.

"I'm not sure what you mean," a still confused Dr. Jefferson mumbled.

"Dr. Jefferson, you've started something huge! Word of the protest has gone viral, and people were at the Quad all night. Over 100 students are probably already there, plus your entire class. All they need now is a leader."

"Over 100? Really? But how?"

"People know injustice when they hear it, and having Elijah Mustang speak at our graduation is the absolute definition of injustice. Dr. Jefferson, your army awaits." Candace pointed out the door as both headed for the Quad for what would be a most memorable day.

Delores Jenkins pulled into the Richfield College Student Center's parking lot in her silver 1994 Mercedes Benz E320 whose odometer had recently surpassed the

300,000-mile mark. With the top up, as most crisp Tennessee January mornings would warrant, she stepped
out of the door and paused to survey the campus that
had meant so much to her career as a journalist. She
was taken aback at the conflicting senses of familiarity and change. A few new buildings had been constructed and the trees were much taller, but what made
the most impression was the color. Color was everywhere. Her memory of Richfield was a drab, gray, nondescript collection of mundane buildings and, more
importantly, monochrome students. She wondered if
her memory was accurate or if the image was conjured
from the negativity she had retained from when it was
still called Richfield Bible College. She knew her nos-
talgia would have to wait. She was here on business.

Following her class to the Quad was intoxicating. Dr.
Jefferson felt like a star athlete entering the field of
play with a throng of fans cheering her on. When she
finally arrived at the center of the protest, over 150
students had assembled. The picnic table, which the
day before had been her perch, had been replaced
by a wooden stage with an actual podium. No one
was quite sure where either had originated, and most
were afraid to ask. Even a microphone stand wired for
electricity and large speakers were at the corner of
the stage. Yes, day three would be many times beyond

the humble beginnings of the protest's first two days and way beyond anything Dr. Jefferson ever dreamed could happen at Richfield College.

"We want Dr. Jefferson!" a voice yelled from the crowd, inspiring a cacophony of cheers until Dr. Jefferson relented and took the stage.

Before she spoke, she paused to see the faces—so many faces—staring back at her. Was this real? Was she still back in bed in her small apartment, dreaming of this moment? She took one last look around, breathed a large sigh, and then gave the students what they wanted.

"Wow! That's my first reaction, wow! You are truly amazing! Do you know that? I am both humbled and inspired. I am humbled that you would join me in this movement to protect and defend Richfield College's bright future from Richfield Bible College's dark past - a past that seems intent on regaining a foothold in this beautiful institution. And that's why I'm inspired. I'm inspired to walk...no, not walk...march arm-in-arm with you to make sure that doesn't happen. I see many new faces in the crowd, so I want to remind everyone why we are here. This college's leadership has invited Elijah Mustang, a symbol of the old close-minded Richfield Bible College, to speak at this year's graduation. Elijah Mustang graduated in the early 80s and retains that era's flawed core belief system. Let me remind you what the 60s, 70s, 80s and even part of the early 90s were like here."

She scanned the crowd to find a representative female face. "You! You wouldn't be welcome here! Richfield

Bible College was almost exclusively male. And you," pointing to an African American man in the crowd, "you wouldn't be welcome here. Richfield Bible College was lily-white, so sorry." Pointing to a young man in the crowd with dreadlocks, both ears pierced, and tattoos on both arms, she used her best faux Southern accent, "And you, oh mercy me, good heavens, you might have even been arrested." The crowd roared in laughter.

Feeling the energy from the crowd, she spoke with an old-time revival preacher's fire and zeal, "Well, is this the 1980s?"

"No!!" Roared the students, drinking in the moment.

"That's not what those guys think!" Dr. Jefferson gestured in the direction of the Administration Building, which housed the college president as well as most of the leadership team. "Those guys want Elijah Mustang to drag you back to those days. You know, one of the most refreshing things about this college is your spirt of acceptance and your embrace of diversity. Unfortunately, Elijah Mustang doesn't share that same spirit. Last night I read an article in which Mr. Mustang was quoted as saying that marriage is supposed to be between a man and a woman only and that's the way God commanded it. Hey, Mr. Mustang, the 80s called, they want their bigotry back!" Again, the students bellowed.

It would be a heady day for Dr. Molly Jefferson, and it was just getting started.

Elijah Mustang had asked his executive team to meet him in the board room for a 10 a.m. meeting. Although he still retained the title of CEO, he had delegated almost all of his day-to-day responsibilities to members of his leadership team, most notably, to Beth Hope, Chief Operating Officer. Beth had been with Promise Transportation for the past 20 years, rising through the ranks from a logistics analyst to her current post as second in command. In recent years the leadership team had seen Elijah's passion slowly shift from Promise Transportation to Promise Ministries. In 2014, Elijah had spent over 20 weeks in Central America tending to ministry needs. The team also knew his new focus, Promise Connection, was driving him even farther away from the business.

As he started most such gatherings, Elijah brought in three-dozen donuts to keep his team energized. "Good morning, everyone. I appreciate your taking a few minutes out of your busy day. I'll be quick. I'm going to be out of the country for a couple of weeks, starting tomorrow morning; and I wanted to see if there were any burning issues that needed to be addressed before I left."

With a business as large and complex as Promise Transportation had become, there were, of course, many pressing issues; however, the leadership team had things well under control and knew Elijah's attention was elsewhere anyway.

"Anyone?" Beth asked the leadership team. She only received head nods and a few "nos."

"Elijah, it looks like we have everything under control." Not dismissive, the response of the leadership team did not indicate that they failed to trust Elijah. They all knew about the 80-hour weeks he worked for so many years building Promise Transportation to what it was today. Their lack of response was out of respect. They knew his heart and accepted that he had found his new calling. They felt he had deserved his time away from the office, and most of them recognized the important contributions his ministry was making to the lives of Central Americans.

"Glad things are under control. I will be out of reach of cell phone and e-mail coverage for most of the time, so plan accordingly."

Elijah was the first person out of his chair and out the door to make final arrangements for his trip.

Arriving at the Richfield Quad just as Dr. Jefferson began speaking, Delores Jenkins captured the entire discourse on her camera phone. She was now in the Richfield Student Center seated at a table watching the speech again, this time on her phone, listening to the audio through her ear buds. She wanted to make sure she had captured everything accurately.

Her duties as assistant editor were heavy on administration and light on writing; so three years ago she started Delores' Doodles, a blog in which she wrote about everything from hiking in her beloved Smoky Mountains to activities in the Middle East and even the best way to prepare quinoa. She used Doodles as an outlet to feed her unfulfilled love of writing. While *The Chronicle*'s website was sometimes linked to her blog, it was totally freelance and not considered part of her official duties as assistant editor.

This morning's entry would be among the hardest hitting and personal that Delores had written in months. She knew there were many angles to this emerging story, and she wanted to make sure she correctly prioritized them. First, there was Elijah Mustang. As CEO of one of Knoxville leading employers, she knew the name and may have even met the man but really didn't know much about him. Her writing about Elijah would center on his representation of everything that was wrong about Richfield Bible College's history and how his invitation to speak sent conflicting messages about the past decade's hard-fought progress. She hyperlinked this blog entry to her original series on Richfield to give new readers some historical perspective of what was transpiring at the Quad today. She wrote about Dr. Molly Jefferson and her courageous leadership of the protest. Saving her highest praise for the Richfield student protestors, she focused on how they represented the bright and optimistic future of, not just East Tennessee but the entire country. She didn't realize how furiously she was typing until she noticed it was almost noon. She had been working on the blog for two hours straight without looking up from her keyboard. With a quick read through and a few minor edits, she was ready to publish. Just settling into Richfield with no plans to leave any time soon, she hoped this would be the first of several blog entries she would post throughout the day.

As the protest continued growing in strength, Dr. Jefferson slipped away to her office for a short lunch break and some much needed rest. She hadn't realized how exhausted she was until she took a moment to exhale and relax. She was obviously running on adrenaline from the excitement of the morning. Having overslept, she just realized in her rush out the door that she had failed to prepare her lunch. She rummaged through the drawers of her office and found a package of ramen noodles, a bag of roasted peanuts, and a package of skittles for dessert. As she quickly consumed the makeshift lunch, she opened her laptop to again find social media abuzz about the protest. A short three days before, she had 237 Twitter followers. Now she had over 2,000, a number that was growing rapidly. Quickly checking her email, she found a message from Dr. Rosenberg, who had some news about Elijah Mustang that thickened the plot:

> *Dr. Jefferson,*
>   *I have been following with great admiration your progress at the Richfield protest. I can't*

believe what a groundswell you've been able to generate in such a short time. Very impressive!

I have discovered some new and interesting information about Elijah Mustang. There are still some dots to connect, but I wanted to get this information to you as quickly as possible. The subject is a 501c3 charitable organization that Mr. Mustang started a few years ago. It is called Promise Connection. With this charity, Mr. Mustang will take children from Central American countries and place them in homes in the U. S., where these children are adopted. This arrangement seems very suspicious to me! First of all, how do we know these children really are orphans? It could be they have been taken from their parents. Even worse, perhaps their parents are selling them to Mr. Mustang's organization. Secondly, how are the U. S. homes where they are sent selected? How does Mr. Mustang confirm they are safe? How does he ensure they are not human traffickers? How much do the U. S. families pay Mr. Mustang's organization to have these children uprooted from their native countries? Who is to say that these children are better off in the U. S. than in the country in which they were born? Isn't it arrogant for us Americans to assume everything is better here?

As I noted, some of the facts need to be checked, but there are enough troubling issues that I felt compelled to pass them along.
Take care, keep the faith, and press on!!
Your friend in the struggle,
Dr. Rosenberg

Wow! Are things with Mr. Mustang possibly even worse than she originally thought? Maybe even human trafficking? She had to get back to the protest and share this incredible new chapter in the story.

The Richfield campus was situated like a town square with four main thoroughfares running north, south, east, and west with a large, five-acre grassy area in the center known as the Quad. The Quad had many large oak, maple, and hackberry trees to offer shade to students who curled up to study, throw football, and hang out. Along each major thoroughfare, streets and sidewalks meandered off in all directions providing access to classrooms and dormitories. The normally peaceful roads were now buzzing with activity. President Curtis, concerned about the growing protest, ordered the entire security force—all three of them—to the campus. He also called the Roane County Sheriff's Department, who sent two deputies just to ensure the situation didn't get out of hand. To add to the excitement, three Knoxville-based television stations had just arrived with news crews and satellite trucks to capture the emerging story for their live evening news broadcasts. Richfield was certainly getting its 15 minutes of fame. The excitement was just getting started.

Dr. Jefferson hurried back to the scene of the protest, finishing off the last few skittles during the brisk walk. She could see the crowd had not dissipated, but she sensed the energy waning ever so slightly. Perhaps the students were nervous about the police or the television cameras. She assumed responsibility for reigniting the flame, and she felt very much up to the task.

At first she made the rounds to personally interact with the pods of students congregating in the Quad. She told them she had some important information to share. She then slowly climbed the three steps to the stage and strode toward the podium. She could sense every eye was on her as a hush came over the crowd.

"Friends, I have some disturbing news to share about the subject of our noble gathering, Mr. Elijah Mustang."

Boos rang out from the crowd as the name was spoken.

"It would seem that our friend Mr. Mustang runs a charitable organization." She used air quotes while uttering the words *charitable organization.* "Its primary purpose is uprooting children from their home countries in Central America and shipping them all the way to the

U. S." Now almost quoting directly from Dr. Rosenberg's e-mail, she groaned, "This seems very strange! How do we know these children are orphans? Were they ripped from their parents' arms? Were they sold by their parents? How can we know if the U. S. homes are safe or even if they are homes at all?"

After much internal deliberation, she decided using the words *human trafficking* would be irresponsible without any substantiation but felt there were enough suspicious circumstances to warrant sharing this new information and to continue questioning Mr. Mustang's already shaky reputation.

"In fact, who is to say that these children are better off in the U. S. than in the country in which they were born? Isn't it arrogant for us Americans to assume everything is better here?"

She had succeeded in inspiring the crowd. They were at a fever pitch by the time she finished.

"You can check this out by doing a simple web search for Promise Connection, the name of Mr. Mustang's new charity" (using her most sarcastic voice on the word *charity*). "So many unanswered questions. And this is the guy that is supposed to be an example to Richfield students at graduation? I don't think so, Mr. Mustang. Go sell your hate somewhere else because we're not buying it!"

She continued, "To call even greater attention to our worthy cause, we need to hit Mr. Mustang where it hurts the most—right in that swelled bank account of his. Today, I am asking for corporate America to join our struggle and boycott Promise Transportation until Richfield College disinvites Mr. Mustang or until Mr. Mustang does the noble thing and steps down himself. How about it? Are you with me, corporations?!"

A compliant crowd cheered their approval of Dr. Jefferson's latest call for action.

As Delores Jenkins furiously penned her latest blog entry, she felt a bit conflicted. She was convinced this latest information Dr. Jefferson shared was terribly troubling. However, the journalist in her knew that she didn't have all the facts. A quick web search confirmed that Promise Connection existed and that the organization's mission was to pair children from Central America with U. S. families. Otherwise, the search results were short on details, with only an e-mail contact for more information. She found a blog written by a mother in Iowa who had adopted a child from Nicaragua through Promise Connection. It described the process in general and even showed pictures of the child's first trip to Iowa but again lacked facts and didn't address any of the concerns Dr. Jefferson raised. How was this family selected? How much money did they have to pay? What was the story behind the child? Did she have a family in Nicaragua? How was this family selected over the thousands of other families hoping to adopt?

The competitive spirit of Delores was also piqued as she knew her Knoxville television and radio counterparts had arrived on the scene and would certainly be sharing this story live during the local evening newscasts. The last thing Delores wanted was to be scooped by this group of talking heads on TV! Besides it was Delores who first put Richfield on the map with her seminal series 24 years ago. Thus, she decided she would simply report what she'd heard Dr. Jefferson share with the crowd. She wouldn't editorialize or sensationalize because she saw herself as above such journalistic mischief. She would simply tell the story.

4

January 10, 2015
668 Days Until the 2016 U. S. Presidential Election

Ramesh Patel was responsible for searching the web for emerging stories around the U. S. He read local newspapers, watched local television reports, scanned trending videos on YouTube, and subscribed to over 500 blogs. Weekly, and sometimes each day, he received a list of topics of interest to the leadership of the National News Service, one of the U. S.'s leading cable news networks. His assignment was to find stories that fit within those topics.

When he came across Delores Jenkins' latest blog, it seemed to check all the boxes. It was a protest. It was on a college campus. It seemed to involve corruption. It centered on a one percenter CEO. Yes, this would be a story that would get Ramesh noticed by the brass at NNS. He compiled the information, including links to dispatches from the Knoxville television stations and sent them to his superiors. Stories that analysts such as Ramesh found particularly appealing would be flagged as Priority Red. Ramesh knew this was just such a story.

Jeremy Prince entered the Richfield College bookstore looking for a memento of his epic week. He had never been to Bard's Ridge, Tennessee and wasn't sure he'd ever come back; so he had to find some tangible artifact to remind himself years down the road that this week had actually happened. The bookstore was fairly modest with the usual variety of mugs, cups, t-shirts, mouse pads, and pennants all sporting the maroon and gold of the Richfield College Eagles. After a few rounds through the store, he opted for a Richfield College hoodie, the quintessential college apparel. Greeting the clerk with a smile, he handed her his debit card to complete the transaction. Although he would never know it, this routine transaction would lead him right to Mouse Trap, which would change the course of his life.

As one of the domestic news' assignment editors at NNS, Courtney Mackenzie had the responsibility of reading analyst reports on emerging stories around the country.

Courtney was trained to pay particular attention to stories flagged as red. Her first response to such stories was usually one of skepticism because she knew analysts liked using the flag to make a name for themselves. This story seemed different, which is why she found herself standing outside the door of the NNS executive producer, waiting to have a moment of his time.

"What is it, Courtney?" One of the greatest skills a cable news network executive producer must have is the ability to sort through a mountain of information and find the few nuggets that have the potential of attracting the largest audience. Opinions varied widely as to whether Dane Newton had this skill. Nevertheless, he definitely had the position.

"There's a story emerging in Tennessee...." Courtney would explain the growing protest, a brief background on Richfield College, and the local coverage in both print and on television.

After listening to Courtney's account and scanning the report written by Ramesh, Dane knew that he had a priority story emerging and immediately took action.

"OK, Courtney, great job. Have news put together a short piece to run on the air within an hour and a full story within two hours. Have the online team put a link on the first page of the website. Get Tyler Edison on a plane to Knoxville tonight. I want NNS to be the first network to get this story in the mainstream."

"I'll get right on it," Courtney excitedly replied, heading out the door even more quickly than she entered.

As Dane Newton read the notes Courtney had left, one name was of particular interest to him. He flipped through a worn-out address book, found the number he was seeking, and dialed it in hopes it was still in service.

"This is Delores Jenkins."

Bingo. It was still she. Dane Newton spent three years in the Nashville bureau of NNS and had worked with Delores Jenkins on a number of national stories that were based in East Tennessee. He even considered her a friend at the time but hadn't spoken with her in close to a decade. "Delores, this is Dane Newton with NNS."

"Well, this is a voice from the past. I didn't know you were still alive." Delores joked.

"Barely. How is life treating you these days, Delores?"

"Life is good, I'm good, husband is good, everything is good," she responded in rapid fire. "Now that we have the small talk out of the way, what can I do for NNS?"

"You always like to get right to the point, Delores. One of the many things I loved about you."

"Wow, you must want a huge favor to start with the flattery this early in the conversation."

"Not really a favor but something that can serve our mutual interests. We're getting ready to jump on the Richfield College protest story as a feature. We're going on air and online within the hour. I'm dispatching a reporter who should be there in a few hours. I've read your blogs, and I think this could be big. We'd like to interview you as well as seek your consultation on some of the background. You interested?"

"Wow, NNS is going to follow this little Tennessee story?" She spoke with surprise in her voice, but this was exactly the kind of attention she was hoping to attract. Not much excited Delores Jenkins, but at this moment her heart was beating out of her chest. She was hoping her excitement didn't come through in her voice. "Sure, if there's anything I can do to help NNS, I'm happy to do so."

"Great! We'll be in touch. Keep those great blog entries coming. For now, you are the eyes and ears of the nation on this story. Great to catch up with you, and I look forward to talking again soon."

The afternoon progressed quickly for the Richfield College protest story. NNS ran its first mention of the story at 3 p.m. By 4 p.m., a three-minute feature was in the rotation. The story opened with an enterprising news reporter who found a truck stop in Brooklyn with a Promise Transportation truck refueling. The reporter stationed herself just in front of the trailer and started the story:

> "If you've traveled the U. S. interstate system with any regularity, you've probably seen one of these trucks emblazoned with the opening words of the well-known Bible verse John 3:16. It turns out the man behind the company finds himself embroiled in controversy and scandal…"

The story went on to discuss many of the issues raised during the protest, including Elijah Mustang's connection to Richfield's "dark past," his reported intolerance for alternative lifestyles, and the many unanswered questions about Promise Connection's Central American adoption program. The report included video highlights of protest speakers, including Dr. Jefferson, filmed by Knoxville television stations. Excerpts from Dr. Jefferson's most recent speech, calling for a boycott of Promise Transportation, were included prominently in primetime newscasts.

When the story was posted on the NNS website, it received the most comments and shares of any story over the previous 10 days.

Both broadcast and cable news networks had staff dedicated to watching the competition; and when a story went viral, as the Richfield College story had, other networks followed quickly. By the time the evening news aired on broadcast networks, the Richfield story was featured prominently.

"This is probably not the best time for Elijah to be leaving the country." Promise Transportation's Public Relations/Communications Director, Kyle Swafford, nervously paced in Beth Hope's office, anxious about the growing protest against the company's CEO and the burgeoning boycott.

"And why would that be, Kyle?" The always calm Beth tried to temper her fretful colleague.

"At the last count, over a dozen companies had signed up for the boycott. How much more of this can we stand? We're not a huge corporation; we're a family company. We're not accustomed to this kind of negative publicity."

"Kyle, I have some good news and some bad news. The bad news is that yes, we have a list of companies that have signed up for the boycott." Beth pulled a list out of her portfolio and began to read, "An apple orchard in Washington, a dairy in Illinois, a solar energy farm in New Mexico, six colleges in the New England area, three non-profits, two florists in California, and there's probably a partridge in a pear tree here somewhere."

"I can't wait to hear the good news."

Beth chuckled as she laid the list on her desk. "Kyle, none of these bozos use us to ship right now. We aren't losing any business; they are just trying to gain some publicity for saying they are boycotting something they don't use anyway."

An astonished Kyle couldn't believe what his boss was telling him. "Really? None of them?"

"None of them. I've reached out to our ten biggest customers. They all think this boycott is silly and are sticking with us. Just give this a couple of days. It will blow over."

Kyle walked out of Beth's office, finally managing a smile. "They're boycotting—nothing; now that's crazy!"

Although the truck accident was a traumatic event in Elijah's life, nothing had tested his faith like the loss of his wife, Becky. He had asked the questions asked by most spouses left behind after the death of their loved one: Why her? Why him? What did she do wrong? What did *he* do wrong? Why couldn't it have been him? He knew these were emotional questions and not intellectual ones; but they still needed to be asked, even if he knew a satisfactory answer would never come. Becky had been gone five years; some days it seemed like five weeks, others like 20 years. On this day she came to Elijah's mind more than usual, perhaps because he had left work just after lunch to pack for the two-week trip, a task she had always helped him with.

Elijah took a break in the middle of the packing and walked out with the company of his dog Clyde to his patio, which provided him a stunning view of Watts Bar Lake. When Promise Transportation put its 500th truck on the road in 1998, Elijah allowed himself and Becky a rare indulgence and purchased a six-acre tract on a peninsula in Ten Mile, Tennessee, offering a 180-degree view of the picturesque lake. They built a modest but well-maintained 3,400-square-foot house, which was Elijah's retreat from the hectic pace of the transportation business. The Mustangs loved bird-watching and would regularly spot bald eagles, great blue herons, ospreys, and kingfishers soaring above the lake. On this day the sky was empty, offering Elijah a time of reflection and prayer before he was to leave his beloved home the following morning.

As technology continued encroaching on the daily life of American businesses, one of the things Elijah loved most about his lakefront home was the spotty cell phone coverage. On this particular day, this was a blessing that Elijah wasn't even aware of, but it was a blessing nevertheless as news reporters throughout the country were trying to get quotes from the now infamous Elijah Mustang. None would succeed.

"Where is everyone?!" President Curtis was frantically pacing the floor of the executive board room.

"It's only 6:50; the meeting doesn't start until 7:00." Anna was trying to provide a calming influence, but this behavior was unchartered territory for the usually unflappable president.

"Don't they know how important this issue is?!" Curtis exclaimed. He was clearly starting to lose control.

"You only gave them less than an hour's notice, so I'm sure some of them had to rearrange their schedules to make it here."

Thankfully for Anna, she was saved by the entrance of the first attendee, Dean of Students David Lanter. "It's getting pretty hairy out there. Screaming students, security, police, the media---you'd think one of the

Kardashians was here, maybe even the one with the big..."

"Do you think this is funny?! Do you think this is a joke?!" President Curtis uncharacteristically snapped at his dean of students, catching him off guard.

"Uh, no, just trying to lighten the mood a bit, I, uh..."

"The mood doesn't need to be lightened; this just needs to get fixed!"

During the dust-up, General Counsel Hagood had slipped into the room. "There is a pretty clear path out of this mess. We just need to find another speaker for graduation."

President Curtis whirled around and pointed, "Yes!! That...that's exactly what we have to do! We have to get another speaker!"

"That's the worst possible answer that you could ever come up with." Mac had walked into the room and seemed ready to join the battle with President Curtis.

"What are you talking about?!" President Curtis was frustrated with the prospect of someone trying to grasp defeat from the jaws of victory.

"Giving in to a crazy, unmerited protest is no way to solve a problem."

"*Crazy*?! You want to know what's crazy? *Crazy* is having over 500 unread e-mails in my inbox, most of which I am sure I don't want to read!" Curtis grabbed a stack of paper and held it up in his right hand shaking it at Mac. "*Crazy* is having 20 messages from media all around the country asking my opinion of Elijah Mustang!"

"Well, what is it?" Mac countered, continuing to challenge the boss.

"What is *what*?" Curtis snapped back.

"What is your opinion of Elijah Mustang?"

Surprised by the question, Curtis realized he didn't really have an answer. "Well, I, uh...my opinion right now is that I want to move beyond this chaos and get back to running the college, whatever that takes."

"Here's an even better question. Have you ever even met Elijah Mustang?" He turned to the rest of the staff, who had assembled. "Has anyone here met Elijah Mustang?" There were no audible replies, but the lack of eye contact spoke volumes.

"Well, I have. In fact, I consider Elijah Mustang a friend, not just to me but to the college." He was now standing and walking among the team as a lawyer would make closing arguments to a jury. "Do you know what he's done for Richfield College?" Mac looked up to the ceiling, knowing he was about to betray a confidence but feeling that circumstances warranted it. "He swore me to secrecy on this, but this is as good a time as any to break a promise. Back in 1992 when all hell broke loose and we lost the president, half the faculty, the Board of Trustees and the Southern Baptist Convention's support— all in the span of a few weeks, Elijah Mustang personally met the payroll for the entire Richfield staff for three months!" Pointing out the window, "You see that nice business building out there?! You know how we got that? Elijah Mustang donated $2M to fund a large portion of it! Those misguided students out there don't know Elijah Mustang any better than you do; they are just sheep, just followers. All this talk about his being intolerant, a hatemonger, and whatever other ridiculous things they are saying about him are just 100% wrong."

Mac continued, "Do you know how stupid this whole protest is? We don't agree with a guy who has an opinion about gay marriage or whatever; so we fire him on the basis that he doesn't embrace diversity? Let that marinate for a minute. We don't accept his viewpoints because he doesn't accept other people's viewpoints, so we tell him he can't come to our party because he won't let other people come to his party—even though none of that's true!" Mac was now at full volume.

A few awkward moments of silence followed Mac's treatise until Hagood decided to try bailing out her boss. "It sounds like Elijah Mustang loves this college."

"Exactly! With everything in his soul he loves this college." Mac was hoping his pleas had found a sympathetic ear.

"Would he want all of this chaos and turmoil? Wouldn't he want to step down from the graduation speech if he knew it was causing this much pain?"

Realizing he was being played by the counsel, his frustration returned. With a renewed steely resolve, he lowered his voice to a dramatically deeper tone, "He's also a man of courage, honor, and principle. And to answer your question, he would consider it an abomination to give in to these kinds of unfounded protests."

Throwing up his hands, a frustrated Curtis blurted out, "How was he even selected to speak at the graduation?"

"Don't pretend you don't remember," Mac retorted, now fully invested in defending his friend. "You...," now pointing at the exposed president, "thought it would be a 'neat idea'—those were your exact words, a *neat idea*—to select a successful, distinguished alumnus to speak at the graduation. I gave you the bios of three candidates, and you selected Elijah. I wholeheartedly agreed with the selection; but this was your guy, too."

Hoping no one remembered that little decision, Curtis made the "courageous" resolution to deflect and defer. "OK, there's obviously a lot of emotion both outside and inside this board room, so maybe it's best that we don't make any decisions tonight. Let's see how the evening goes and reconvene tomorrow morning at 10 a.m."

All but Mac agreed with the decision, but even Mac knew it was the closest thing to leadership President Curtis had displayed all evening; so he allowed his objections to have a night of rest. None of them knew it, but the protest would unfold exponentially the following day; and the situation would become much, much more volatile.

Both exhilarated and exhausted, Dr. Jefferson unlocked the door to her apartment at 10:45 p.m., certain that she had just experienced the best day of her life. Flipping on the kitchen light, she saw the flashing number 18 on her answering machine: 18! She really had 18 phone messages? It was not unusual for her to go an entire week without a single message and now 18 in one day! She could only imagine what her e-mail inbox would look like. Just as she was about to hit the play button, the phone rang again. She decided to screen the call. "Molly, honey, this is your mom; pick up if you're there."

Quickly reaching for the phone, Molly answered, "Hey, Mom, I'm here."

"Honey, where have you been? Your dad and I have been trying to get in touch with you all day."

"Things are getting interesting here on campus, I..."

"I know, Honey. Turn on the TV, turn on NNS," her mother frantically urged.

"OK, but why?"

"Just turn it on."

She fumbled for the remote control, turned on the TV, and saw a familiar face—her own. "Really, I'm on NNS?"

"You've been on TV all evening and not just on NNS but almost every other channel as well."

Yes, this would be the best day of Molly Jefferson's life. But, that's only because tomorrow hadn't happened yet.

Cedar Lassiter was certain he heard the chirp of an incoming text message. The only problem was he wasn't sure where his cell phone was. Truth be told, he wasn't even sure where he was. After an evening of chain bong hits, Cedar was feeling no pain. He fumbled around the cushions of the tattered couch and retrieved his iPhone 6, which had been pinched between the springs. Tracing his finger over the security picture, he saw one new text message, which simply read; *ACTIVATE: Richfield College, Bard's Ridge, Tennessee, ASAP, forward to Level 3.*

Cedar was one of 100 to receive the same message. He dutifully sorted through his contact list; found a contact named "Level 3"; pecked out a text message similar to the one he had received; and hit "send," forwarding the message to another 100 recipients.

His most challenging act would be stumbling through the house to awaken his compadres, hoping one would be lucid enough to drive the van.

"Hey, lads, wake up! We got a gig!"

Within 30 minutes, Cedar and six of his closest friends were on the road to make the six-hour journey to Bard's Ridge. With any luck, they'd arrive just before sunrise. It was going to be a great day.

"Are you watching this?" Victor Youngblood asked his Chief of Staff Colin Burrow, who had entered his office to drop off the evening's reports. The north wall of

Victor's office was covered by nine 50-inch high-definition TV's, each tuned to a different channel.

"Yes, we've been monitoring this situation all evening. It has unfolded very quickly."

"Just to be clear: we didn't do this, did we?" Victor asked.

"No, we didn't."

"You understand why I'm asking, don't you?"

"It sure looks like our work; but I can assure you, this isn't us," Colin replied.

"What do you know so far?" Victor pressed.

Without notes Colin responded, "It started four days ago and was led by Dr. Molly Jefferson, Chair of the Religious Studies Department at the college. She's 35 with a PhD from the University of North Carolina. She's been department chair since 2010. Seems she's been motivated by Facebook messages and e-mails she's been getting from a Dr. Jocelyn Rosenberg, who seems to have significant insight into the subject of the protest, Elijah Mustang. It isn't clear what Dr. Rosenberg's motivation is. The protest started with a handful of students on the first day, grew to a couple of dozen on day two, and now you see what's happened."

"We need to find out who is really behind this and why, and we need to find out tonight," demanded Victor.

"Already on it. We will have an update early tomorrow. There's one more thing," Colin continued. "CivDis was activated." CivDis is the Civil Disobedience network, a loose collection of mostly young, unemployed, disenfranchised, and disgruntled individuals who are at the ready when a protest needs their for-hire services.

"What? By whom?"

"Not us. We're still trying to confirm; but it looks like someone saw the college protest on TV, assumed they were supposed to be there, and initiated the chain."

"Interesting," pondered Victor.

"Do you want us to stop it?"

"No, let's see where this leads. And get me more information about how this protest all came about. I'm intrigued."

5

January 11, 2015
667 Days Until the 2016 U. S. Presidential Election

As she had done the day before, Delores Jenkins started her morning at Richfield College, by-passing her office at *The Knoxville Chronicle*. On this day she would be joined by three other *Chronicle* writers, who recognized the significance the story was gaining nationally and wanted to ensure all angles were covered.

Although Delores still maintained the blog, her stories had landed on the front page of *The Chronicle* because the public's appetite for information about the protest had not yet been satisfied.

Before leaving her condo, she published a short blog entry about her anticipation for the day:

What's wrong with kids these days? It's a question posed by every generation of adults about every generation of youth that comes after them. That's certainly no exception in this era. Today's youth have developed a reputation for being addicted to social media, having their faces stuck in their smart phones, taking selfies, being obsessed with video games, and being self-absorbed and disconnected from the larger world around them.

What I've witnessed at Richfield College over the past two days has been the exact opposite of that stereotype. I have been watching inspired young people take a stand for an issue that is larger than their own self-interests. They have arrived in larger numbers every day to rally against hate, intolerance, and bigotry. In the process, they have been getting a firsthand lesson in what it means to live in a free society where they have not only the right but also the obligation to let their voices be heard when they encounter injustice.

The missing player in this emerging drama is the Richfield administrators, who have been deafeningly quiet thus far. This silence is particularly disturbing as the new leadership is supposed to present a fresh perspective compared to that of so many failed leaders who came before them.

This writer not only hopes but also expects things to change today as the groundswell call for action continues to grow, demanding that these young voices be heard. I'm expecting a big day at Richfield College. Stay tuned...

Cedar Lassiter's van had just pulled off I-40 onto exit 347 in Roane County, Tennessee, as the morning sun crawled over the horizon formed by a series of thickly-forested ridges in the Cumberland Plateau's foothills. The group had almost made its goal of arriving at Richfield College by sunrise, missing only by the remaining 10-minute drive down Highway 70.

Sage Reynolds had chauffeured during the last three hours of the trip because she was deemed the most co-herent member of the crew. Nevertheless, navigating the curvy rolling hills proved challenging as she had her own battles with a shortage of sleep and a surplus of chemicals in her bloodstream. The trip was complicated even more by the unusual traffic load on this normally peaceful stretch of road.

As she topped the last rise leading up to their final destination, Sage knew she was in the right place as she was greeted by the familiar combination of satellite news trucks and a field full of tents, all erected in the last four hours.

The crew unloaded from the van and immediately saw at least a dozen familiar faces that had joined them on previous demonstrations. They knew they were in the right place and were anxious to get the day started. Things were about to get real.

Tyler Edison got the assignment at 5:45 p.m. the day before. His instructions were to book a flight to Knoxville, Tennessee, arriving as early as possible the following morning. In the limited time he had, Tyler was to become an expert on the subjects of Richfield College; Bard's Ridge, Tennessee; Elijah Mustang; Promise Transportation; Promise Connection; and any other ancillary topics he could dig up.

By 7:30 that morning, Tyler had completed his checklist and was deplaning in Knoxville. He found a Ruby Tuesday's at the end of the concourse that offered a hot cup of coffee, just what he needed to start his engine after a night of only two-and-a-half hours of sleep. He was in a rush to get to his rental car and make his way to Bard's Ridge; however, as he reached for his wallet, something appeared in his peripheral vision that would change the course of his morning and perhaps his entire trip. He noticed a briefcase with Promise Transportation's logo emblazoned on the side. It belonged to a gentleman dining alone. Tyler couldn't leave without at least asking a couple of questions to see where the conversation might lead.

"Excuse me, sir, but would you happen to work for Promise Transportation?" Tyler asked, hoping to get some inside scoop on one of his assignment's main subjects.

"What is going on today? You're the fourth—or maybe the fifth—person who's asked me about Promise Transportation this morning. I normally can go a month and not get a single question," he responded, more curious than agitated.

"Well, I just…" Tyler was caught off-guard, hoping he hadn't stirred up a hornet's nest.

"I'm sorry; I didn't mean to be rude. It's just been an unusual morning already, and I'm not sure why. To answer your question, yes, I work for Promise Transportation."

"That's really interesting. Would you mind if I joined you for a couple of minutes?" Tyler asked hopefully.

"Certainly, have a seat." He gestured for Tyler to take the open seat opposite his. "I just found out my flight is delayed 90 minutes, so I'm in no hurry and would appreciate the company." He was attempting to recover from the uncharacteristic terse tone with which he started the conversation.

Taking a seat, Tyler extended his hand. "I'm Tyler Edison." He made a spur of the moment decision not to reveal that he was a member of the media so as not to cause any undue alarm.

"Nice to meet you, Tyler; my name is Elijah, Elijah Mustang."

Tyler hoped he had successfully suppressed the astonishment that was fighting to overtake his face. He worked to stay calm as he mentally inventoried everything he had learned in the last few moments. First, here was the guy, right in front of him, whom he had researched the night before. How did he not recognize him? To where was he flying? Was he trying to escape all of the controversy? He couldn't blame him if he were. On the other hand, he appeared to be oblivious to the storm that was engulfing him, making him the subject of every newscast in the country. Was such oblivion even possible? How could he not know? Tyler decided he would play along.

"Nice to meet you, Mr. Mustang."

"Let's just go with Elijah."

"OK, Elijah. So, what do you do for Promise Transportation?"

"Well, Tyler, you probably wouldn't believe it seeing me dressed like this, but I'm actually the CEO." Elijah had worn jeans with holes in the knee, not the type of holes a fashion designer intentionally created but the kind resulting from hundreds of hours of hard work. He was dressed for his final destination in the countryside of rural Honduras.

It's him! It's really him! Tyler couldn't believe it. "Elijah, you look just fine. I haven't met many CEOs, so I'm not even sure I know what one is supposed to look like. Where are you headed this morning?"

He pulled his itinerary out of his pocket and began reading, "Knoxville to Atlanta; Atlanta to Miami; Miami to Tegicigalpa, Honduras. Then a taxi, a bus, and a truck until I reach my ultimate destination of Yuscaran, a small town in Southern Honduras."

"Wow, that sounds like quite a journey!" Tyler knew he was onto something. In his research the night before – and into that early morning, he'd read about a new project, an orphanage, which Promise Ministries was building in Honduras. He had to know more. "I don't mean to sound overly intrusive, but what is going on in Honduras that would call for the services of a CEO? Do you have some transportation contracts you're working to secure?"

Elijah chuckled a bit and then replied, "No, no transportation contracts in Honduras. I'm not going as a CEO; I'm just going as me."

"Then I'm curious. What's going on in Honduras?"

"It's a bit of a long story, and I'm sure you are on your way to…"

A long story?! A long story is exactly what Tyler was looking for, but he couldn't seem too anxious for fear of tipping his hand. "You know, Elijah, I'm actually not in a hurry at all. I'm in town for a few days, and I'm not on a schedule this morning; so I'm up for a long story."

Not totally convinced Tyler really wanted the long story, Elijah decided he'd start with the abbreviated version. "OK, well, I am going to Honduras as part of a ministry that we started a few years ago as an offshoot of Promise

Transportation. We unimaginatively named it Promise Ministries. We seek to improve the lives of people in a number of Central American countries including Honduras, Nicaragua, Costa Rica, El Salvador, and Guatemala."

"That's it? That wasn't such a long story," hoping to coax more out of Elijah.

"I was trying not to bore you."

Tyler was now almost pleading, "You're not boring me; I asked you about it."

"OK, well, here's a bit longer version, if you're really interested."

"I'm interested!" Tyler blurted out impulsively, hoping he didn't seem too eager.

"When I started Promise Transportation in 1982, I made a commitment to myself and to God that I would give back as much as I could, recognizing how blessed I was. I made a trip to El Salvador when I was 28, and it really opened my eyes to the needs in that country; so we started our first Promise Ministries project there."

Tyler made a mental note that when Elijah talked about the charity work he always used the word *we*.

"We started with medical facilities, then built a few churches, and ultimately a home for children who didn't have family. We worked with other ministries and churches in the U.S. and really felt like we were making a difference. Some doors opened for us to expand the ministry to other Central American counties, so we basically repeated the process there. We now have churches, medical facilities, and kids' homes in five countries. The most recent door that God seems to be opening is to help kids without families. We have been finding permanent homes for them here in the states."

"So, I've noticed that you use the phrase *kids without homes*. You mean orphans, don't you?" asked Tyler.

Elijah chuckled, "That's just a little quirk of mine. I don't like the term *orphans*. It seems to have a permanent connotation that we're working to overcome. We want these kids to have homes and a family, even if our facilities provide that home."

Tyler thought that this guy was either the most genuine man he'd ever met or one hell of an actor. He continued prodding in hopes of finding out. "So, tell me about the process of sending these kids to be with families in the states. How does that work?"

"The first thing we have to do is to make sure the kids have no family in their home country. They have to truly be—and I don't like this word—*orphaned*. Even if they have parents who have deserted them, we hold out hope that their circumstances will someday change and that the parents may want back in their children's lives. In those situations, we work to make the children's lives as good as they can be in our Promise Homes. We feed them, clothe them, provide them medical care, and education. For those where we can confirm there's no family at all, we make them a candidate for adoption."

Tyler again made a mental note. If this information proves to be true, that would dispel one of the most damning accusations in the case against Elijah

Mustang, an accusation being adjudicated throughout the American media landscape.

Elijah continued, "The other side of the equation is finding a suitable home in the U. S. Literally tens of thousands of U.S. citizens are hoping to adopt; and hundreds, maybe thousands, of adoption services are working to help them find adoptable children. Our desire was to devise something different from what everyone else was doing. When we did our research, we found one of the greatest barriers to adoption was cost. Most adoption agencies charge tens of thousands of dollars to complete an adoption. That cost excludes many loving and deserving people. So we challenged ourselves to come up with a way to make the adoption process free to the adoptive parents. We knew legal costs, travel costs, and other costs would be involved; but we wanted to find a way to cover them in Promise Connection. That's the name we gave the service. I know, not very original."

If this guy was telling the truth, the allegations about him were beyond untrue. How could this story have gotten so distorted?

As he finished speaking, Elijah checked his watch and realized that time had gotten away from him. "Oh my, I didn't realize it was so late. I'm going to have to head to my gate. I'm praying it isn't delayed any longer, or I won't make it there until tomorrow. It was nice meeting you, and I hope your stay in East Tennessee is a pleasant one."

"Elijah, it was truly an honor. Thank you for sharing your story with me."

The two shook hands, and Elijah headed down the terminal. Tyler found a quiet area of the airport to make a few phone calls. He thought he was about to have a bombshell story for which no one was ready. He would soon learn how right he was.

Dr. Jefferson was surveying her closet to find just the right outfit for the day's events. On normal days she didn't make much of a fuss about what she wore, but she had to admit that she did look a bit frumpy on TV last night. If she was going to be on again, for all her family and friends to see, she was going to make a bit more of an effort this morning. Her search was interrupted by an unusually early 7:30 a.m. phone call.

"Hello."

"Dr. Jefferson, come down to the Quad right now!"

"Calm down, who is this?"

"It's Candace from your religion class. Please, come down to the Quad!"

"OK, I will; but what's going on?" Dr. Jefferson asked.

"Just come now!"

As Delores Jenkins crested the last hill leading to Richfield College, she could tell things were going to be different today. At the edge of campus, she was stopped by a Tennessee State Trooper.

"Good morning, ma'am, can I help you?"

"I'm with *The Knoxville Chronicle,* and I'd like to get to campus. I've been here the last two days covering the protest."

"Can I see some ID?" asked the trooper.

"Certainly." Reaching for her license, she asked, "What's going on? I didn't have to go through this the past two days."

"This isn't like the past two days," he said dramatically. "OK, ma'am, please be careful."

"Thank you." Taking her ID, she wondered what she had to be careful about. She would soon found out. Once the campus came into her field of vision, she counted over 20 TV trucks set up in the University Center parking lot, taking up the parking spot she had secured each of the past two days. Driving toward the Quad, she quickly saw the most striking new dimension of the protest. In what was normally a sprawling open field, the Quad was now sprinkled with tents, consuming over half of the five-acre space.

She also saw a new breed of protestors, the angry mob. While students had been persistent the previous days, they had been calm and peaceful. This protest was very different. Cars passing by the Quad, including her own, were greeted with screams and shouts. Her convertible Mercedes seemed to draw the ire of two young men shouting in her direction; she wasn't really sure why.

Her keen eye noticed a peculiarity in the signage the new protestors were carrying. They included the normal "No more hate" and "We want change" slogans but upon her closer inspection, the Richfield messages were painted over faint leftovers of previous protests. On one sign the words 'We are the 99%' could be seen faintly in the background; on another, a more ominous "Eat the rich" was barely visible. She could tell these were no longer Richfield students; these were professionals.

"Courtney, this is Tyler!"

"Tyler? You're supposed to be in Tennessee."

"I am. I'm still at the Knoxville airport. I stopped to get a cup of coffee, and you're not going to believe who I ran into; Elijah Mustang! He was actually at the airport on the way to Honduras."

"Honduras? You gotta be kidding me. Trying to get away from the controversy, I assume. Please tell me you got to interview him."

"I did, and I initially had the same thought, "Here's a guy that's running away." But I really don't think that's the case."

"What do you mean?"

"I think we've got this guy all wrong. I think everyone has the story all wrong. I had a fairly long conversation with him here in the airport. I don't know where this storyline about his taking kids from their families for adoption in the U. S. originated but there is no merit in it. And the notion that he was charging U.S. families big adoption fees is an illusion. His charity actually seeks out needy but deserving families looking to adopt and pays for everything."

"And you know this because he told you?" Courtney was suspicious as this version of the story contradicted what everyone was reporting.

"That's where it started, but I actually made a number of phone calls to confirm what he told me. I called the Honduran Embassy, whose representatives were very familiar with Mr. Mustang and corroborated everything he said. Through a web search I found a family who adopted a child through his organization and was able to talk to them on the phone. They confirmed everything as well. And lastly, I made a call to our guy at everyone's favorite government agency that starts with *I* and ends with *RS*. Get this: Elijah Mustang made $1.3 million in 2013; so you're thinking rich guy, right? Well, he gave away over a million dollars to his charity! A million dollars!" Tyler's tone was conveying excitement about this newfound truth. "And get this: I think this guy must live in a cave because somehow he didn't know that half of the country was talking about him! I think we now have the real inside story that no one else has! This guy isn't a racist *or* a hatemonger *or* whatever else people say. I think he is legit. I know I'm throwing all this information at you quickly, but I should have it together for a spot within the next hour. Or if you'd prefer, I can report from the college; make it two hours."

"Tyler, I was going to call you shortly anyway. The story has taken a significant turn, and we've actually dispatched Peter Robbins to report." While Tyler was the religion correspondent, Peter Robbins was an emerging feature reporter who got many of the network's sexiest assignments. At first Tyler felt insulted, but he repressed that instinct and recognized the gravity of the information he now had to share. "That's fine, I'm happy to work with Peter."

"I'm sorry, Tyler, but Peter is going solo on this. Go ahead and send me the information you gathered, and we'll get it over to research and have them do some background checks," Courtney said.

The feeling of insult quickly became anger as Tyler not only felt himself pushed aside, he felt the truth about to be covered up. "You're kidding right? You're *really* not going to report this?"

"Tyler, I told you to send me the information. I have to run. This story is emerging more quickly than anyone expected, and we have to get the story together. Great job!" Courtney ended the call.

Great job? Yeah, right. He had heard about this type of marginalization happening to others but this was his first time, and he didn't like it.

૭

Candace was waiting in the faculty parking lot for Dr. Jefferson to arrive. It was one of the few parking lots free from the media or protestors because of its small size and location, tucked away between the business building and the chapel. As Dr. Jefferson pulled her Prius into the parking spot, Candace rushed to meet her before she even put the car in park. "Dr. Jefferson, things have gotten crazy!"

"Now calm down. What do you mean?"

"The Quad…it's full of protestors from out of town. They've put up tents, dozens of them, maybe more!"

Now walking quickly in the direction of the Quad, Dr. Jefferson wondered, "Tents? Why?"

"I don't know; it's just gotten really crazy!"

As she made the last turn, her rapid pace came to an abrupt halt when she saw a campus she no longer recognized. Tents were indeed erected throughout the Quad but now trash was everywhere. And as she looked to the south end of the Quad, she could see a Richfield College van pushed on its side. She heard chants but they were in the most angry, hateful voices, ironically screaming, "No more hate!" Without thinking, she approached the fray.

"What are you doing?!" She screamed at a protestor who was tearing down azalea bushes that formed a beautiful hedge around the Quad.

"We don't need your hate! No more hate!" came the angry reply.

"What are you talking about? I'm not hating anything. I *started* this protest!?" A frustrated Dr. Jefferson replied.

The dust-up attracted more of the protestors who now encircled Candace and Dr. Jefferson. At least a dozen protestors were now shouting in their faces, "No more hate!" Quickly realizing they were going to get nowhere with reason, Dr. Jefferson and Candace retreated as quickly as possible, sprinting toward the Religious Studies building. As they entered, both breathing heavily, they noticed a broken window in Dr. Jefferson's classroom.

"How did this get so crazy?" Candace asked, now even more frightened.

"I have no idea."

6

"This is Peter Robbins reporting live from the campus of Richfield College in Bard's Ridge, Tennessee. This is day four of a campus-wide protest against this man, Elijah Mustang." NNS displayed a picture of Elijah Mustang's face on the screen with a Promise Transportation truck in the background; a video zoomed in on the excerpt from John 3:16.

"Mustang, Promise Transportation's CEO and a Richfield alumnus, is scheduled to speak at this year's graduation ceremony but many of his views are intolerant, and, some even say racist. The largest firestorm appears to be the accusation that a charity he heads, not coincidentally named Promise Connection, removes Central American children from their home countries and pairs them with U. S. families through an ambiguous process. There is even an allegation that Mustang may profit from this international adoption scheme.

This allegation doesn't sit well with many of the Richfield students."

Next was a video of a student interview in which the student said, "I just don't understand why anyone would think it's OK for the college to have a man who holds the racist, intolerant, views that Mr. Mustang holds to speak at our graduation."

The camera returned to Peter Robbins, live on campus. "We heard from several on campus that controversy is nothing new to Richfield College. Earlier today we caught up with *The Knoxville Chronicle*'s assistant editor, who has written extensively about Richfield College." The screen showed Delores Jenkins speaking with her name and position in the caption. "Richfield College has a very dark past. Until just a few years ago, its name was Richfield Bible College. The administrators' policies discouraged women and minorities from attending. An unwritten rule excluded the LGBT community. A few years ago, I interviewed a young man who had his dreams of going into the ministry crushed because he made the mistake of telling a Richfield administrator that he was gay. The next day he was told to pack his bags because he was no longer welcome on campus. This type of discrimination actually happened in the United States of America, just a few years ago. So, these young people are being so vocal because they don't want to see those policies reinstated at Richfield."

The camera returned to Peter Robbins. "There are certainly some strong feelings on this campus. We have tried to secure an interview with the campus president, Richard Curtis; but thus far we have been unsuccessful. Also, calls to Elijah Mustang's office have not been returned. Reporting live from Bard's Ridge, Tennessee, this is Peter Robbins."

Still winded from the sprint back to her building, Dr. Jefferson opened her laptop to see if she could find any answers for what was transpiring at her previously peaceful demonstration. Maybe a new e-mail from Dr. Rosenberg would provide some insight. A scan through her inbox came up empty, so she decided to email her.

> *Dr. Rosenberg,*
>
> *If you've been in front of a TV the past 24 hours, I'm sure you've seen how the protest has grown. I'm not sure if this is coming across on TV this morning, but the protest has taken an ominous turn. Most of the protestors have come here from out of town. They've erected tents and are actually living in the Quad. Have you had any experience with this type of protest? If so, what suggestions do you have for dealing with it? Need some quick advice!*
> *Thanks,*
> *Dr. Jefferson*

Moments after hitting the send button, Dr. Jefferson got a strange reply:

> *Your message was not delivered to the intended*
> *recipient. User unknown.*

"That's weird," she thought. She doubled-checked the e-mail address and confirmed it was the same one she'd previously used to communicate with Dr. Rosenberg. As plan B, she sent a Facebook message because that's how she originally connected with Dr. Rosenberg. That approach also yielded a peculiar result. Dr. Rosenberg was no longer listed among her friends.

She did a quick search to see if perhaps she was "unfriended" but couldn't find Dr. Rosenberg's page. Thinking this must be a strange coincidence, she decided to search for Dr. Rosenberg's university e-mail address. She went to the University of Wisconsin website and found the faculty search engine, but a search for Dr. Rosenberg yielded no results.

Next, she called the campus. "Hello, my name is Dr. Molly Jefferson. I'm a colleague of Dr. Rosenberg. It seems I have misplaced her contact information. Could you please provide her e-mail address and phone number?"

"I'm sorry, ma'am, but we don't have a Dr. Rosenberg on our faculty."

"There must be a mistake. Would you please look again?"

"Yes ma'am. Sorry, no luck. I even searched faculty over the past ten years and didn't find a Dr. Rosenberg."

"OK, thank you."

Her thoughts came quickly but provided no satisfactory answers. "This made no sense. Why can't I find her? It's like she has disappeared from the planet. It's like she doesn't even exist." Just then, a crushing feeling came over Dr. Jefferson. "Surely not," she thought. Returning to her laptop, now with an increased sense of urgency, she went to *The Chattanooga Observer* website and in the search window typed "Elijah Mustang." She scanned all 17 articles that came up, but they were mostly mundane business stories. There was no mention of gay marriage or anything remotely controversial.

Her heart was now pounding out of her chest, her hands were cold and clammy, and she was sure her face was losing its color. Surely she wasn't this wrong about something this important. She would continue digging.

As he often did when he faced difficult decisions, President Curtis relied on his general counsel as his primary sounding board.

"Natasha, we have to make this problem go away. Have you seen the Quad this morning?"

"It's out of control. Richard, I'm going to stick by the advice I gave you yesterday. You have to find a different speaker for graduation," urged Natasha.

"What do you think about Mac's argument, that Elijah Mustang has done a lot for this college and it wouldn't be right to cancel his speech?"

"At this point, it doesn't really matter. If Elijah Mustang really loves this college like Mac says, he'd want us to do whatever it takes to restore peace and get back to being an educational institution."

Just as Natasha was speaking, Mac appeared at the door, clearly agitated at the discussion that he overheard. "*It doesn't matter*? After everything that Elijah has done for this college, all you can come up with is that it doesn't matter? "

Both Curtis and Natasha were startled by Mac's presence. "Now just calm down, Mac; we have to think about what's best for the college; that's what Elijah would want." The counsel spoke in what Mac considered a condescending tone.

"How do you know what Elijah would want? You've never even met him!" Mac screamed.

Just as Mac finished speaking, a crash was heard as a rock came hurtling through President Curtis' office window. Curtis dove to the floor as if under sniper fire, knocking Natasha to the ground as well. Mac, still standing, shook his head in disappointment as Richfield College's leadership lay spooning on the floor.

Recognizing the awkwardness of the moment, Curtis and Natasha stumbled to get to their feet as Mac simply shook his head in disbelief. Curtis murmured, his voice shaking, "OK, that's it. I'm calling a press conference for noon. We're putting an end to this chaos. Natasha, can you stick around and help me craft the statement?"

Disgusted at what his beloved college had become, Mac took this as his cue that he was dismissed. As he turned to walk away, he heard the door to the president's office close as Curtis and Natasha disappeared behind it. He couldn't help thinking that the many rumors about the two administrators had just been confirmed; they were both cowards.

"Courtney, this is Peter. Did you get the word about the noon press conference with the Richfield president?"

"Yes, we just got the announcement. Any idea what he's going to say?" Courtney replied.

"Rumor here is pretty strong that he's going with another speaker for graduation."

"Not surprising. Looks like things have gotten out of hand there."

"I wasn't here the past two days; but there's definitely a large, unsettled crowd gathering. I also wanted to mention I got a call from Tyler Edison. He was quite excited. He said that he had an exclusive interview with Elijah Mustang and that we had it all wrong. Any idea what that's all about?" asked Peter.

"Tyler shared his information with me earlier. We're doing some independent research here from headquarters. If anything comes of it, we'll let you know."

"OK. I assume we'll be going live with the press conference at noon?"

"You got it."

🐚

"I need to see President Curtis!" A frazzled Dr. Jefferson had hurried over to the president's office seeking an audience with him.

"I'm sorry, but President Curtis is booked solid throughout the day." As administrative assistant to the president, one of Anna's primary responsibilities was keeper of his schedule, an especially grueling task this particular week.

"I'm sure he's busy; but if he's in his office, I really need to speak with him."

As she was finishing her sentence, Curtis poked his head out of the office. "Anna, can you please—"

"President Curtis, I really need to speak with you!"

"I'm sorry, Dr. Jefferson but now isn't a good time. I want you to know that I have a press conference scheduled in just a couple of hours. I believe you will be pleased with what I'm going to say."

"That's just it, Dr. Curtis. I may have made a huge mistake."

"Richard, we really need to get back on this issue. The press conference is less than two hours away." A nervous general counsel gently grasped Dr. Curtis' arm, urging him back into his office.

Natasha interrupted, "I'm sorry, Dr. Jefferson; but we have to get ready."

"I know I'm the one who started all this, but I really think I may be wrong about Elijah Mustang," Dr. Jefferson insisted.

"Look out the window...the broken window, Dr. Jefferson. I think you may be a little too late." Natasha, was now speaking on behalf of President Curtis.

"But I really..."

"We'll schedule a meeting in the next couple of weeks to discuss your concerns, Dr. Jefferson but there just isn't time now." Dr. Curtis closed the door and disappeared with his general counsel to put the finishing touches on what would be the defining speech of his tenure.

7

Constructed in 1986 at the height of Richfield Bible College's growth, the Harrison Administration Building was an impressive three-story red brick neoclassical edifice. Its most prominent feature was a collection of six large white columns framing the front of the building. A series of granite steps led from the ground up to the second-story main entrance. A 25-foot-deep landing halfway up the 16-step climb made a natural space for students to congregate. On this landing a podium had been placed with over two-dozen microphones now situated immediately in front. The maintenance department had stationed several large speakers around the stairs so that the president's words would be projected into the north end of the Quad.

Word of the press conference spread quickly; and most of the crowd, at least those still conscious, made their way to the grounds in front of the stairway. There was an eclectic collection of interested parties, including the original set of student-activists whom Dr. Jefferson first inspired, a small army of media from around the country, and a swelling number of outside protestors fresh for the fight—all escorted by Tennessee state troopers, county deputies, and the small Richfield campus security force.

As was his normal practice, President Curtis was punctual, walking out of the door at 11:58 a.m., striding confidently toward the podium. Because he had made a practice walk over a dozen times in his office, with the advice and encouragement of his general counsel, the short stroll seemed a bit more familiar. A few steps be-hind, most of his staff accompanied him, save for Mac, who chose not to attend the proceedings.

Curtis brought with him a portfolio, which he dra-matically opened to reveal his script. On this January day, a cold front had swept down from Canada bringing with it a 24-degree temperature and 20-mile-per-hour winds, which mussed the president's usually well-coiffed hair.

"I want to thank you for coming to Richfield College on this historic day..."

He took the first five minutes acknowledging the dignitaries present and the next ten minutes summariz-ing the history of Richfield College, emphasizing its early struggles. Another ten minutes were spent praising the Richfield students for their stand and singling out Molly Jefferson as the protest's leader—a gesture that brought applause from the students as they looked through the crowd hoping to see Dr. Jefferson. They were unaware that she had retreated to her apartment, searching for answers that would not come.

Now twenty-five minutes into the oration, Curtis was finally reaching a crescendo, a welcome sound to the shivering assemblage.

"This is a complex situation that made for a very difficult decision. It is moments like these that try men's souls. Moments where acts of courage are difficult to muster but are nevertheless required. Moments where personal comfort must take a backseat to doing what is right." An attentive observer spied Natasha's lips subtly moving in synch with Dr. Curtis' as she admired the words she had crafted only minutes before.

"So, this brings us to the ultimate decision for which you have all assembled. I have determined that in the best interest of Richfield College we will thank Elijah Mustang for his contributions to the college and his willingness to present the graduation address but then tell him we will be seeking an alternative speaker for this year's ceremony."

Cheers rang out throughout the campus—first by the students who had been protesting for the past four days, followed closely by the new outside protesters, many of whom were uncertain exactly why they were cheering. Television cameras panned through the crowd to capture the response for those watching from homes, businesses, and college campuses throughout the country. After a minute, the cheers gave way to chants of "No more hate";

but now the demanding tone was replaced by a declarative one, rejoicing with the president's announcement.

After giving the crowd time to settle down, Curtis decided it was his cue to continue. "Put simply, many of the viewpoints attributed to Mr. Mustang are inconsistent with the values and principles of Richfield College. There are also concerning issues related to Mr. Mustang that need to be further investigated but because of the serious nature of the allegations, allowing him to speak would be unfitting. A search committee, led by me, has already begun conferring to identify a qualified replacement for Mr. Mustang. We want to ensure all Richfield College stakeholders that a distinguished and appropriate replacement will be identified as soon as possible. I will not be taking questions this afternoon but will provide a forum where questions may be submitted in writing. Thank you for coming today, and thank you for the passion that you've shown over these past few days for the betterment of Richfield College."

Over the sound of shouted reporter questions, Curtis put the transcript back in his portfolio and turned to walk back into the Administration Building. As he passed by his general counsel, she whispered, "Great job." The deed was done.

"No more hate!" was heard one last time echoing through the tall oak and pine trees that stood guard over the Richfield College campus.

At the end of a dirt road in Southern Honduras, a white Ford F-150 pickup truck was parked at the edge of the small town of Yuscaran. The tailgate was down, and Elijah Mustang's feet dangled a few inches off the ground. From the bed of his truck, members of the village had just unloaded 30 boxes, including food, medicine, and school supplies. A large crate contained children's books, one of which Elijah was pleadingly urged to read.

"Read Papa Eli, read!" Years ago, the Yuscaran children had given Elijah the moniker *Papa Eli,* and it stuck. Before opening the book, Elijah took a moment to survey his surroundings. The landscape was barren and the village was poor, with no running water or electricity. A mountainous terrain several miles in the distance provided the backdrop. Ten-year-old boys Carlos, Daniel and Edgar had climbed onto the bed of the truck and were now looking over Elijah's shoulder with Carlos' arms draped around Elijah's neck. Sisters Sirena and Nadia were seated on either side of Elijah on the tailgate, while five-year-old Rosibel was snuggled on his lap. He drank in the moment and indulged himself with a deep sigh of satisfaction. There was no place on earth he'd rather be.

"Now the very blustery night turned into a very rainy night. And Pooh kept his lonely vigil, hour after hour, after hour—until at last... Pooh fell fast asleep—and began to dream..."

Delores Jenkins stared at her keyboard knowing she had to report on this climactic turn of events but felt somewhat conflicted about what to write. She knew the simple, linear storyline was that Richfield College had selected an inappropriate individual to speak at the graduation ceremony, that this mistake was identified by brave Richfield students who mounted a protest to get that decision reversed, and that a concerned administration recognized this error and took the bold and courageous stand to correct it.

But Delores knew that there was much more to the story and that other factors made the narrative considerably more complicated.

First, the influx of outside protestors who changed the tenor of the demonstration. They transformed a student-led, non-violent protest to one with broken windows and overturned vehicles. But, if Delores emphasized the outsiders, would the storyline of the normal everyday students who took a strong stand for their college be diluted?

Secondly, there was the matter of President Curtis. Delores knew a weak anemic leader when she saw one. As a tough reporter she was always excited to encounter this type of man because she knew she could easily break him down and extract information from him. As she witnessed the press conference in person, she knew she was looking at just such a man. This was no courageous leader; this was a guy scared out of his wits who would do anything to get out of the crosshairs.

Lastly, there was a disturbing e-mail from Dr. Jefferson, which she saw as she logged on to her tablet. Dr. Jefferson raised a concern that perhaps she had acted hastily in condemning Elijah Mustang so quickly and that maybe he wasn't the evil guy she claimed he was. Delores thought, "What does she expect anyone to do with this information now?" In a moment of clarity, Delores had to admit that she personally knew almost nothing about Elijah Mustang. Does that mean he's necessarily a good guy? No! Does that mean he's necessarily a bad guy? No again!

If she included these additional detours in the otherwise straightforward story, would her readers be able to process all of the information, filter out the dross, and come to their own conclusions about the salient points of the story? Or, she could keep it simple and make sure they understood what was really important. In the latter approach, she would metaphorically chew their food for them.

After considering her options, Delores published this short blog:

> *Today, at high noon, I got to witness some of the greatest aspects of this wonderful country of ours as Richfield College President Dr. Richard Curtis made a bold decision to disinvite the controversial Elijah Mustang from speaking at the college's graduation ceremony. I won't rehash the many issues that have attached themselves*

to Mr. Mustang as those can be found elsewhere on this blog. Today I want to focus on the positives because there are many that we saw in action this week.

We saw the future of this country, and it is bright: Young people who took a peaceful stand for a cause they believed in and in the end saw it pay off.

We saw that the right to assemble and make our voices heard is alive and well. This right that so many of us take for granted is a gift that many other countries do not enjoy.

We saw real leadership as Dr. Curtis swallowed his pride; recognized that a bad decision had been made in inviting Mr. Mustang to speak; and reversed course, knowing the criticism that would result.

We saw that justice still can prevail in this country. We can all point to injustices that are still alive and well, but this decision should be a ray of hope to those still in the midst of the struggle.

Yes, today was a good day to be in Bard's Ridge, Tennessee and a great day to be in the United States of America.

Delores would follow up later in the evening with a more detailed story, which would run on the front page of the following morning's *Knoxville Chronicle*. She decided to omit some of the details that might confuse rather than enlighten readers. She would keep things simple.

Cedar Lassiter was the only member of his contingent to make it to the Administration Building for the press conference, as his comrades were crashed in or near the six-person tent that had been their companion on many such journeys.

With a gentle kick, Cedar uttered a not-so-gentle "Get up!" to each of his fellow travelers. "Time to head." Within 45 minutes, the crew had taken down the tent, packed up the van and headed back home. They had gone through this routine before and would again when the next text tolled.

In the living room of the Beta Epsilon Theta fraternity house at the edge of the campus of Virginia Tech University, Chip Braxton turned on the TV just in time to catch the end of the press conference.

"Guys! Come here!" Five fraternity brothers who had been playing pool in the rec room responded to the call.

"You're not going to believe this; he did it!" pointing to the TV. "The son of a bitch did it!" All stood in amazement as they watched the reporting of the Richfield College protest.

They knew they should have learned by now not to bet against Jeremy Prince, but this one seemed so far-fetched. In fact, some weren't even sure it was a bet but from the story they were seeing on TV, Jeremy clearly thought it was.

"Who wants to ride with me to get the keg?"

"We got the full story behind the college protest. You're not going to believe this." Colin Burrow had made hundreds of reports to Victor Youngblood, but this was among the most bizarre.

"Try me." Victor remained intrigued by what he saw unfolding on several of his nine TVs and was anxious to get the full story.

"The last time we talked I mentioned that the leader of the protest was Dr. Molly Jefferson." Colin clicked a remote, converting Victor's nine individual screens to a single large screen, now with the image of Molly Jefferson on display.

"Professor of Religious Studies at Richfield, wannabe feminist, just looking for a protest to join. Bachelor's and master's from Delaware State, PhD from Chapel Hill."

"Sounds like a target we would have picked." Victor's interest continued to grow.

"It does. You may also remember that we mentioned Dr. Jefferson had been inspired to start the protest by messages she had received from Dr. Rosenberg." Colin again clicked the remote, and the TV screens went black."

"What happened?" a confused Victor asked.

"There is no Dr. Rosenberg." Colin deadpanned, then paused for effect. "She doesn't exist. However, this guy does." Another click of the remote, and the image of Jeremy Prince filled the screen.

With looks that could land him the lead in a Hollywood blockbuster, Jeremy had a natural attraction that drew others to him and allowed him to easily gain their trust. The product of a Hispanic mother and a Caucasian father, Jeremy was the rare individual who had yet to find a situation in which he was uncomfortable.

"This is Jeremy Prince. Twenty-two years old; just graduated from Virginia Tech in December with a 3.9 GPA with a double major in business and philosophy."

"I get it; he's a smart kid. So what's the connection to Richfield College?" Victor asked impatiently.

"He loves to show off, and he loves to make wagers, especially with his fraternity brothers. Oh, by the way, he's the president of Beta Epsilon Theta."

"How much longer do I have to wait before you make the Richfield connection?" Victor asked rhetorically.

"He did all of this just to win a bet." Colin again clicked the remote. Each of the nine screens included a different image of the Richfield protest.

Victor smiled and pointed at the screen, now enthralled by what he was hearing. "I like this kid."

"We've been through the usual: e-mails, social media, everything he's stored on the cloud, family, close friends. There's absolutely no prior connection to Richfield College. In an e-mail this afternoon to his fraternity brothers, he told them he'd be back tomorrow to claim his keg." Colin again pointed to the screen. "He did all of this for a keg! He created the Dr. Rosenberg pseudonym, became an online friend of Molly Jefferson, somehow convinced her to start this protest, and continued to fuel the flames that ultimately got Elijah Mustang disinvited to speak at graduation!"

"I want to meet him." Victor opened the top drawer to his desk where he kept the names of the most promising prospects for joining his organization. He added one more name to the top of the list.

"He's got big stones too. Get this—he's actually on the Richfield campus."

"He's at Richfield?" asked Victor.

"Yep, he used his debit card at the bookstore. We used that to track him to a local hotel where he's been checked in for the past four days. I hope you're thinking what I'm thinking. He could be a candidate for Mouse Trap." Colin responded excitedly.

"That's what I want to find out. I remain intrigued." Victor drummed his fingers on his desk.

"OK, I'll use Savannah to get him here."

"That should work."

With that exchange, the wheels were set in motion that would change the course of Jeremy Prince's life. What was unknown to Victor Youngblood was that an introduction to Jeremy Prince would change the course of his organization and everything he'd spent most of his life building. It was going to be a wild ride, for which no one was fully prepared.

8

" **W** hat do you think about that college in Tennessee that told a guy he couldn't be the graduation speaker just because he's a Christian?" Jake Everman asked in a clearly frustrated voice.

"It wasn't because he was a Christian; it was because he's a racist stuck in a time warp from the 1950s. Plus he's shipping poor kids from Central America to live with rich families in America." Little brother Brad always countered his big brother's rants.

"OK, who wants some gravy on their chicken?" Edith Everman was ever the peacemaker, working hard to focus the family discussion on less controversial topics.

The Everman clan met for lunch every Sunday in Bronson and Edith Everman's home in Dayton, Ohio. They shared a meal, their victories and struggles, and inevitably their varying opinions about the hot topic of the week.

Bronson Everman was assigned to Wright Patterson Air Force Base in 1979 as a Lieutenant Colonel with the 4950th Test Wing. His group was responsible for designing a variety of aircraft, including transports, tankers, and helicopters. Early in his career, Bronson accepted the nomadic lifestyle of a military officer as he moved his family nine times in the first 18 years of service. However, his assignment at Wright Patterson was an opportunity to put down roots for a relatively long-term stay, an appealing prospect to the entire Everman family. At the time of the move, Jake was 14; Brad was 13; and Maggie, the baby of the family, was 10. For their entire lives, the Everman kids had lived with the reality of packing all of their worldly possessions, changing schools (usually in mid-semester), and the grueling process of making new friends every couple of years. Moving his family to Dayton had a profound effect on the Everman clan for generations.

Bronson was reassigned a few more times in his career, but Wright Patterson was large enough and diverse enough to allow him to stay on base until his retirement. Now at 76, Bronson enjoyed spending days with his beloved Edith, the love of his life; volunteering at the local Boys and Girls Club helping kids with math homework every afternoon; and keeping in touch with his Air Force buddies. But what Bronson looked forward to most each week was Sunday lunch with his family, as all three of the Everman kids had remained in the greater Dayton area.

Jake, now 50, was the superstar of the family. Quickly acclimating to high school life in Dayton, he went on to be a star linebacker for the Chaminade Julienne Eagles, leading the team in tackles and earning first team All-State. He continued his football career at the state's preeminent program, The Ohio State University. He started in both his junior and senior year as a Buckeye, earning Big Ten Conference Honorable Mention both seasons. His Aerospace Engineering degree put him on a path to success and ultimately led him to start Everman Aeronautics. Now at 125 employees, the firm had grown every year since its founding in 2005. Jake married Amy, a Buckeye cheerleader, shortly after college graduation. Their kids, Emily and Cameron—a sophomore and senior, respectively—followed in their parents' footsteps at Ohio State. At 6'3" and a solid 225 pounds, Jake worked hard to maintain his athletic build, running in four marathons and four half marathons each year. Always the apple of his father's eye and a success in both business and family, at age 50 Jake seemed to have life figured out. The only blemish in Jake Everman's otherwise spotless persona was that he never seemed happy. Some would say he lived on the edge of anger, seeming ready to snap at any moment. Jake called this characteristic "drive"; but to his wife and kids, his brooding nature kept him closed and distant—and although none would admit it in public, even a bit afraid. Their only respite was Jake's business travel, which was frequent, but a welcomed diversion for Amy.

While Jake was always the assertive man of action, Brad was much more of a thinker. He opted for hometown Wright State University, where he earned both bachelor's and master's degrees in history—degrees that Brad loved but for which neither his father nor brother could understand the utility. Brad's love of education was the cardinal point for his career as he had spent the last 23 years as a teacher at Dayton's Belmont High School. Brad was the stereotypical "cool teacher" with long hair that he often wore in a ponytail, a subject of ridicule for the always neatly coiffed Jake, who typically greeted Brad with a trademark question: "When are you gonna get a haircut?" Although Edith tried to hide it, Brad was her favorite with his calm and quiet demeanor; and even at age 49, he still was the subject of his mother's doting. The opposite of big brother Jake in so many ways, Brad never settled down, never married, was 5'9" with a slight build, and was content with his life.

College wouldn't be the path for Maggie. High school homecoming queen her senior year, Maggie was the beauty of the family. However, just as Jake seemed to be the fortunate son, hard luck followed Maggie at every turn. Pregnant at 19, she married her high school sweetheart while wearing a maternity dress. Unfortunately, that union lasted only 18 months, a foreboding sign of things to come. Pregnant again at 22, this time the father's identity was known only to God. Married for a second time at 24, she was sure this husband was the man of her dreams. Unfortunately, taking care of two stepchildren proved to be more than he bargained for, so the "dream guy" walked out on Maggie less than a year after the "I dos." A third try at age 30 would be the longest marriage for Maggie and produced a third child, her only daughter. She often laughed, thinking she was just like her parents with two sons and a baby daughter; but she knew that's where the similarities ended. After a mercurial six years in marriage number three, she again found herself a single mother, this time with three mouths to feed, not including her own. Now at age 46, she had not given marriage a fourth try; but she still held out hope that she would someday find the right guy. Her first son Cody, now age 27, left the house at age 21 but not before leaving behind a granddaughter who Maggie was now raising. The middle child, Shannon, had somehow found a stable life as an electrician. At age 24, he was the calming influence whom Maggie went to when she needed an ear. Her daughter Jasmine, a precocious 16-year-old, considered her mom the stupidest person on the face of the planet. Maggie worked a day job as an administrative assistant plus three nights a week as a waitress just to make ends meet. Unfortunately, they didn't always meet without occasional assistance from her father.

This eclectic assemblage met each Sunday at the Everman home. Those Sunday lunches were full of debates and discussion; fussing and cussing; and, as Edith ensured, laughter and love. This particular Sunday the table was full. Bronson was at his normal spot at the head of the table with Edith by his side. Brad was to her left, then Maggie, her six-year-old granddaughter Kendall, Shannon and his girlfriend, and Jasmine. Down the other side of the table were Amy; Emily and Cameron who usually made the one-hour drive down from college; and as always, Jake at the other end of the table.

"Oh, bull, if the guy wasn't a Christian, none of this would be a big deal. Every news report included a close-up of the Bible verse on the trucks, and the reporters just loved to emphasize that he was a Christian." As a business owner and elder at an evangelical megachurch in West Dayton, Jake embraced the conservative perspective, both socially and economically, on most topics. His thoughts were often buffeted by perspectives he heard on talk radio.

"Do you even watch the news? The guy hates gays, is a CEO one-percenter, and thinks the world revolves around the U. S. Does he even consider that life might be better for those kids if they were raised in their home countries away from the greed and waste of our American capitalistic society?" As far right as Jake tended to swing, Brad swung equally as far left. He was head of the teacher's union at school; was the faculty sponsor of Enough, the school's anti-bullying movement; and occasionally attended the local Unitarian church. He had his favorite blogs and cable news channels, which provided exactly the information he wanted to hear.

"What are you guys even talking about?" It was not an unusual response from Maggie. She had enough to worry about in her own life and didn't typically have time to dive deeply into the news or politics.

"How about we table the political discussion for a while and let Bronson and me hear about what's going on with the grandkids?" Ever the peacemaker, Edith had a way of knowing when a debate was about to get out of hand and brought the discussion back to family, her favorite topic.

Each member of the Everman family chose a source of news and information that reinforced their belief system. Like millions of Americans, the information they received was lacking one key element—the truth. It was a fact that Victor Youngblood knew well and designed into every facet of Mouse Trap.

9

January 13, 2015
665 Days Until 2016 U. S. Presidential Election

"**D**ouble cheeseburger, large fries, and a chocolate shake." It was a celebratory meal for Jeremy Prince at the American Eagle Diner in Kingston, Tennessee, just down the road from Richfield College. It was his last meal in Tennessee before he hopped on nearby Interstate 40 and headed east to Virginia to collect his winnings. He was enjoying the solitude of the moment until an unexpected visitor interrupted his peace.

"Jeremy? Jeremy Prince? Oh my gosh, what are you doing here?!"

As quickly as his brain could process, he was cycling through his memory to connect with the face that was in front of him. The initial search came up empty.

"Well, I'm just…"

The tall blonde quickly sat down at the empty chair opposite him and continued her rapid-fire reunion. "So, how have you been doing? Did you graduate? Do you live in Tennessee now? What's going on with you?"

Hoping his memory would eventually engage, Jeremy decided to play along and give it some more time to catch up. "I graduated in December, still trying to find the right fit for my skillset. I'm just passing through Tennessee from a visit with family out West." He was hoping she wouldn't pursue the "out West" storyline as his imagination had not fully developed it.

"I'm sorry; I know I sort of caught you off guard. Hopefully you remember me; I'm Savannah Lynch from speech class."

He still had no idea, but she obviously remembered him; so he'd continue the charade.

"Of course I remember, Savannah. How are you doing? What's going on with you?"

"I'm doing really well. After graduation I went with Youngblood and Associates in Washington D. C. I absolutely love it! It's a great company, and I really feel like I'm making a difference! But enough about me, how's your dad's hardware business going? I still remember that speech about how the business has been in your family for three generations. That was really interesting."

Victor Youngblood's "researchers" had access to just about anything stored on a computer anywhere in the world. Fortunately, Jeremy's speech professor required that speeches be recorded and placed on the Virginia Tech cloud for posterity. After watching a half-dozen of them, it was decided the hardware store speech was the most personal and would yield the strongest connection to fully engage Jeremy in conversation.

"The hardware store's doing OK, could definitely be better. You know how the big discount stores are killing small family businesses throughout the country, but dad's hanging in there." Still not sure how he didn't remember Savannah, he finally identified his memory loss as one of the casualties of fraternity life.

"So, you're not going to join your dad and make it four generations?"

Prince's Hardware Store had been a fixture in Abingdon, Virginia, for 67 years. Started by Jeremy's great-grandfather after he returned home from World War II, it had seen many years of success and had sent to college 17 kids, spanning three generations of the Prince family.

"Probably not. I'm looking for something maybe in a larger city."

Now in her most enticing voice, "Jeremy, I have an idea. Youngblood is in the midst of a staffing ramp. Would you be interested? The D. C. area is amazing to work and live in. I've been to Capitol Hill, the Pentagon, and even the White House."

Research had identified Jeremy's interest in being a mover and shaker, and the prospect of interfacing in the highest levels of government was thought to be appealing to him.

"Well, I don't know. What kind of positions are open?"

"Several Congressional liaison positions are available. Youngblood is looking for business majors and maybe sociology or philosophy majors to deal with the people part of the equation."

Jeremy responded, almost thinking out loud, "I did graduate with a double major in business and philosophy."

"Shut up! Are you serious? You know, Jeremy, I don't think it's a coincidence that we're meeting here." It was the only truthful comment she had made during the entire conversation. "Let me give you my card, and you give me your contact information. I'll call the office, and someone will be in touch."

"OK, I'm not sure I'm..."

"This will just be a get-to-know-you conversation to see if you might be interested. I still can't believe I ran into you here in Tennessee! What are the odds?! Well, I gotta run, but I hope to see you in Washington!"

As Savannah made her way out the door, Jeremy's mind was conjuring a new reality. "Maybe I do remember her."

Golden Poplar Farms was located in the green rolling hills of Central Kentucky between the towns of Paris and Lexington. It was named for the Goldenrod, the Kentucky state flower, and the Tulip Poplar, the Kentucky state tree. In 1938, Jesse Calvin purchased the original 500-acre farm with the proceeds from his profitable Eastern Kentucky coal mines.

As the Calvin Mining Company expanded its coal empire, it also acquired adjoining parcels; consequently the farm now totaled a sprawling 1,950 acres. The thriving farm was home to over 150 horses, including 35 stallions that were highly sought after for siring prospective racing champions. The spread included 12 horse barns, 3 practice tracks, 6 paddocks, and 5 guest homes ranging from 2,000 to 4,500 square feet. In the middle of the property, on the highest knoll, sat Goldenwind, the 18,000-square-foot Georgian mansion that was home to Cam Calvin, grandson of Jesse Calvin.

For the past hour, limousine after limousine made the 24-mile drive from Blue Grass Airport in Lexington, northeast on highway 68, through the Golden Poplar entrance gate, and down the half-mile driveway, leading its riders to the front door of Goldenwind.

The invitations stated that the event's purpose was to celebrate the 2014 Kentucky Derby, as a Golden Poplar stallion had sired this year's Derby winner. However, a call was placed to all invitees—except for one—to explain the real reason for the gathering. Each call was personally made by Cam, who at age 45, was now Goldenwind's proprietor as well as Calvin Mining's CEO. The content of Cam's call would now be revealed to the only attendee who thought he was at a Kentucky Derby party.

"If everyone would take a glass of our fine Kentucky bourbon, I would like to make a toast." Cam was the ultimate toastmaster. He had been blessed with the gift of gab and loved to be in front of a crowd. With this congregation at his beloved Goldenwind, Cam was euphoric. "I would like to recognize our Honorable Governor Bobby Lincoln. His tenure as governor has been historic. He has balanced the budget every year, brought over 200,000 new jobs to the Commonwealth, and reduced the unemployment rate to the fourth lowest in the country. To show his sincere concern for all Kentuckians, he's moved over 150,000 off the welfare dole and into well-paying jobs where they can be contributors to society. To you, Governor, we raise a glass."

All toasted the governor, who seemed surprised by being singled out. "Thank you. Cam. It is Kentuckians like you that have made this success possible."

Elected first in 2007, Bobby Lincoln won the governorship by a ten-point margin. In an already right-leaning state, his Republican candidacy was bolstered by unprecedented name recognition as a member of the state's beloved Kentucky Wildcat basketball team in the 1970s. Although Lincoln was a political neophyte, his ability to make deals with members from both sides of the aisle yielded considerable success in his first term as governor. When he ran for re-election in 2011, the Democrats only ran a token opponent, recognizing that unseating the popular governor was unlikely. Lincoln went on to garner 70% of the vote in his second and what he thought was his final election.

Because Lincoln was unable to run for governor again due to term limits, his successor would be selected in just nine months. As his final year in office wound down, Lincoln's political talents caught the attention of highly placed and highly influential Republicans from around the country, many of whom were in the Goldenwind ballroom at this moment.

"Governor, I have a confession to make. We're not here today to celebrate a horse, at least not a four-legged one." The feeble attempt at humor elicited heartier than called for laughter from the gathered dignitaries. "We're actually here for you."

A surprised Lincoln looked askew, not certain what he had gotten himself into.

"Take a look around the room, Governor. You should see many familiar faces: CEOs, athletes, movie stars, producers, and leaders of Wall Street. Governor, we're all here for you."

With an awkward chuckle, Lincoln tried a bit of humor, mostly as a defense mechanism. "Do I owe you all money or something?"

The room burst into laughter that seemed to go on for at least a minute.

"See what I told you all? The guy is oozing with personality." Cam gestured to the guests. "No, Governor, you don't owe us money. I'm just going to say it as bluntly as I can. Governor, we think you'd make a great president of the United States. Everyone in this room is here to encourage you to run for President in 2016."

Then it was Lincoln's turn to laugh until he realized he was the only one laughing.

"Bobby, we're serious. We think your work as governor here in the Commonwealth could translate throughout the country, and Lord knows we need it!"

"You gotta be kidding!" Lincoln exclaimed.

"I'm going to tell you how much we're not kidding. The 42 people gathered here today have pledged five million dollars to get your campaign started. There's plenty more once you get organized. I know we're hitting you cold with this idea, but what do you think?"

And thus began day One of the Lincoln for President Campaign, a campaign that would soon attract the attention of Victor Youngblood's Mouse Trap.

"Good afternoon, welcome to Prince's. What can we help you with today?"

"I've got this bolt, and I need three more exactly like it—same size, same thread pattern."

"Certainly, we can help you with that. It looks like an inch-and three-quarters carriage bolt. Let's go over to aisle 3…"

Friendly, personal, genuine customer service was the only thing keeping Prince's Hardware afloat. With the two large home stores operating in Abingdon, Prince's could no longer compete based on price. They had to differentiate on customer service and in offering unique merchandise that no one else carried.

Started by Samuel Prince in 1947, Prince's Hardware Store had been an institution in Abingdon for the past 67 years. It was located on West Main Street, just on the edge of what was now considered the historic district, a few blocks from the Barter Theatre and the Martha Washington Inn.

"Yes, these look perfect. Thank you."

"Great. If you'll walk over to the counter, I'll ring you up."

Exceeding customer expectations had always given the Prince family great satisfaction; and that was especially true of Walter Prince who, with his wife Rosita, now had the responsibility of carrying on his grandfather's legacy.

"That'll be eighty-nine cents." And therein was the challenge facing Walter Prince. Through the relationships that the Prince family had developed over the years, the store was usually bustling with activity but over thirty percent of the purchases were under ten dollars. With the narrow margins typical of most small businesses, Prince's couldn't survive on eighty-nine-cent purchases for very long. The fact that Prince's was not a typical small business compounded the situation.

A foundational principle since its opening was investing in the Abingdon community. For most of its existence, Prince's sponsored youth sports programs including baseball, soccer, football, and basketball. Prince's also employed at-risk teens who otherwise found securing a job difficult. Although most of them did not fully appreciate it at the time, Walter's compensation went well beyond a paycheck, as he personally invested in each teen, giving them lessons in both business and life. Walter also maintained a larger-than-necessary workforce as he wanted to give as many kids as possible the benefit of a job.

"Thank you, sir, and please come back to see us again." It was the same salutation Walter had heard his grandfather and father give thousands of times. As the customer walked toward the door, the creaking wooden floor echoed back a symbolic refrain signaling to Walter: "We're trying to make it, but we're struggling."

The only thing that gave Walter greater concern than the fate of his family's store, was the fate of his only child, Jeremy. On the surface Jeremy was a bright kid who was becoming a solid young man. Working at the hardware store throughout his childhood, Jeremy graduated first in his class from Abingdon High School. His recent graduation from Virginia Tech University with a 3.9 GPA should have given Walter and Rosita much peace and satisfaction; however, they often spent evenings discussing their feeling that something was missing with their son. Actually it wasn't *with* their son but more *inside* their son.

From the time Jeremy was born, Walter had secretly hoped Jeremy would represent the Prince family's fourth generation to run the hardware store. However, he never shared this desire with his son, wanting Jeremy to plot his own course in life. In the seventh grade Jeremy's vision for his future became crystal clear. The family was vacationing in Washington D. C., touring monuments and museums, when they decided to visit Maryland's nearby capital of Annapolis. This unplanned side trip inspired Jeremy to dream. The family visited the United States' Naval Academy, and Jeremy was immediately hooked. He often wondered exactly what caught his fancy, never getting a definite answer; but from that day forward, being a midshipman at the Naval Academy was his mission.

The walls of his room were covered with posters of aircraft carriers, battleships, and destroyers. His shelves held over 20 highly detailed models of U. S. Navy ships that he meticulously built. He read every book he could find about the Navy. By the beginning of his sophomore year in high school, he was writing his congressman and senators about his desire to attend the Naval Academy. With a 4.0 GPA and a 34 on his ACT as well as earning Eagle Scout and being involved in numerous other extracurricular activities, it seemed that Jeremy's dream was actually going to come true—until it didn't.

Early in his senior year, he received a short letter thanking him for his application but regrettably informing him that he was not selected for the Naval Academy. He went through the usual cycle of anger, denial, and depression, never quite reaching full acceptance. Adding to his dismay was that a classmate from his own Abingdon High School was admitted, a classmate who had a lower GPA and ACT, and far fewer extracurricular activities.

After a long period of disappointment, Jeremy finally decided to attend Virginia Tech and participate in the Naval ROTC program. Unfortunately, his ROTC career lasted only one year. To Jeremy, there was no comparison between ROTC and going to Annapolis.

Jeremy admitted to only his closest friends that he never got over the wound that the Academy rejection had inflicted. He could maybe accept it if superior students were selected, but in his mind that did not happen. He lost faith in the system and found himself slow to trust anyone or anything. He was angry, jaded, and lost.

Walter and Rosita supported their son the best that they could; but as Jeremy's college career advanced, they saw their son fade from their lives as he chose to spend every weekend, and the summer between his junior and senior year, away from home. His behavior was understandable, and his desire to become independent of his parents was natural; but there was something different about Jeremy's distance. He seemed directionless. He didn't seem happy; nor did he seem angry. His parents could have dealt with either of those emotions; however, he was disconnected. Their concerns were amplified when he didn't pursue a job after graduation. Walter queried one of Jeremy's high school classmates who followed Jeremy to Virginia Tech and who affirmed Walter's concerns. Jeremy had been invited to several interviews but never showed up. His professors encouraged him to pursue an advanced degree and even offered scholarships, but Jeremy didn't seem interested.

What was he going to do with the rest of his life? He didn't have a job and didn't seem to have any direction. Walter and Rosita were unaware that was all about to change in a matter of days.

10

March 30, 2015
589 Days Until 2016 U. S. Presidential Election

J eremy thought about turning around and heading back to his hotel. Why was he even here? It had been over two months since encountering Savannah at the diner. Their discussion was certainly intriguing and even she said it was a crazy coincidence that they'd met there. The Youngblood recruiter's follow-up calls solidified everything Savannah had told him. They made all of the arrangements, including his stay at the Crowne Plaza, by far the nicest hotel in which he'd ever stayed.

After researching Youngblood and Associates online, Jeremy found it to be a wide-ranging enterprise that included marketing, public relations, lobbying, consulting, and various other professional, service-based business units. He made notes of some of the basics, including 23 offices in 12 different countries, over 3,000 employees, and headquarters in Bethesda, Maryland. The CEO was a gentleman named Victor Youngblood.

He did research on Victor and found that a Washington magazine had done a profile of him a few months prior. The article noted that at age 74 Victor could easily pass for a man in his 50s. He was thin, tanned and always maintained a well-groomed appearance, aided by twice monthly haircuts and weekly pedicures and manicures. His fit build made his six- foot-four-inch frame seem even taller. Victor was known to be charismatic; some would say enigmatic. Jeremy even read a couple of articles Victor had written to get better insight into both the company and its leader.

Jeremy took the Dwight D. Eisenhower Memorial Highway, also known as I-270, from the hotel. He never dreamed it would take close to 45 minutes to navigate the six-mile drive to Youngblood and Associates' headquarters. Fortunately, he allowed himself an hour in case he made a wrong turn, so he was going to be right on time.

After parking in an adjacent garage, he approached the entrance to the building, double-checking to make sure he had everything he had intended to bring. He was surprised he felt a twinge of nerves as he couldn't remember the last time he was nervous about anything. Some of his fraternity brothers had even given him the moniker "smooth" because he was usually unflappable. But today he felt an unfamiliar quiver that unnerved him. That feeling was about to change.

"Hey, Jeremy! It is great that you could make it! Can you believe we're actually here? Imagine, this all started over a cheeseburger in Tennessee!" It was his "old" friend Savannah. Victor thought it would be best to start Jeremy off with a comfortable companion to make him feel at ease. He had quite a day planned for Jeremy and considered Savannah's pleasant greeting to be the calm before the storm. Victor was excited to get this day started and find out more about the intriguing Jeremy Prince.

"That makes me so mad!"

"Watching the news again?" Walter Prince knew every nuance, subtlety, and tone of Rosita's voice. He not only knew *when* his wife was angry, but he usually knew *why*.

"They act like we're this monolithic group of people who think alike and act alike." The "we" to which Rosita was referring were U. S. immigrants of Hispanic descent. Born in rural Oaxaca, Mexico, Rosita's parents were migrant workers who came to the U. S. every March to pick strawberries. They started with the Florida strawberry crops and worked their way up through the Southern U. S. picking strawberries in nine states before concluding the season in Ohio in June.

Starting at age ten, Rosita accompanied her parents and older siblings on these trips north into what she came to consider her dream land. On her first trip she was amazed at the stark contrast in living conditions between the U. S. and her Mexican home. Everyone in the U. S. had cars and homes with air conditioning. Most towns had movie theaters and most of the farms they visited were lush and green. For Rosita, the U.S. was almost too much to believe. By the time Rosita was 16, a growing desire that had been effervescing within her was finally taking shape as a real plan. She wanted to become an American citizen.

Her family had long-standing relationships with many of the farms where they worked, so Rosita had American friends throughout the Southeast. From these relationships she would ultimately learn to speak fluent English. The Garrett family from Mayfield, Kentucky, was one of the families with whom Rosita built a special bond. Garrett Farms was a large, diversified enterprise that included corn, tobacco, soybeans, apples, peaches, pears, and strawberries. The Garretts always needed labor to harvest their crops and saw an opportunity both to help Rosita and to access a broader base of migrant workers. They offered Rosita a year-round job to live with the Garrett family and act as a liaison/translator. Although her parents weren't initially supportive, Rosita convinced them to let her stay so at age 17 she was a full-time U. S. resident.

She spent the next five years with the Garrett family, working long but fulfilling hours during the day. She spent many evenings studying to become a U. S. citizen. Finally, at age 22, Rosita saw her dream come true when she passed her citizenship test and took the oath to become an American. That same year the Garretts hosted a summer visit from their cousins from Virginia, the Prince family. For Walter and Rosita, it was love at first sight. They were married within six months; and Rosita said her tearful goodbyes to the Garretts, who had been so kind and generous to her. They knew she had to follow her heart and her beloved Walter to Abingdon, Virginia, where she became a fixture at Prince's Hardware.

"One side just wants to load everyone up on trucks and ship them back to Mexico, even if they've been here with their families for 10, 15, or 20 years. The other side wants them to become citizens in hopes of getting their votes. Don't they understand that each person is different? Everyone is unique. Everyone is an individual."

It was a passionate plea that Walter heard on too many occasions to count but increasingly so in recent years as the undocumented Hispanic population became pawns in a polarized battle between two stubborn political parties. Rosita knew neither party truly understood (or really cared about) the Hispanics' hopes and dreams.

"Have you finished this week's column?" Walter asked.

"Almost. I am titling it "What is Home?"

"It has a nice ring to it."

In addition to Walter's willing ear, in the last six months Rosita had added another outlet for her passion: a weekly column in the Abingdon area's periodical, *The Washington County News*. She hoped to give an insider's perspective on Hispanic issues. Although she had been a citizen for over 40 years, she still felt a connection to her country of birth. She wanted to add a sense of humanity to the hollow rhetoric that most stories about the Hispanic community contained.

Her new article would focus on the importance of "home" to Hispanics and how most simply wanted to contribute to the country's fabric. Although she would not state it explicitly, her new article would also contain undercurrents of the struggles she felt in seeing her son Jeremy slip away from Walter and her over the past two years. How she wished he would come home or at least settle down in a home of his own.

As he always did, Victor Youngblood had a very specific plan to get to know his interviewee - in this case Jeremy Prince. Step one of his three-step regimen was to make him feel comfortable through his interactions with Savannah. She was instructed to chat with him for 30 minutes in the lobby, give him a tour of the office, discuss topics familiar to him, and ultimately lead him to the conference room where the interview would take place.

Step two was for Colin to do the initial interview. Questions would be asked to determine Jeremy's honesty or even better his skill at deception. At the conclusion of step two, three outcomes were possible. One outcome could be a determination that Jeremy would be a good fit for one of Youngblood and Associate's open positions in one of the regular business units. If that were the case, Jeremy would be shuttled off to the division that best aligned with his skills and talents. A second potential outcome would be to determine that Jeremy was not a good candidate, and the process would end right there. The obligatory "we'll get back with you" would be spoken but would ultimately lead to a letter thanking Jeremy for his time and informing him that there were no current openings that aligned with his skillset. A third possible outcome, and the one that Victor hoped for, would be that Jeremy was a potential candidate for Mouse Trap.

Victor would view Colin's interview from his office on his nine-screen wall of monitors. If Victor determined that Jeremy was Mouse Trap material, he would initiate step three of the interview process: walk into the interview room and personally query the candidate. As anxious as Victor was to find out, he knew the process and understood step two had to come first.

"Good morning, Jeremy, my name is Colin Burrow. I am one of the recruiters here at Youngblood."

"Nice to meet you, Mr. Burrow."

"Let's go with Colin."

"OK, Colin."

"I understand that Savannah showed you around the office."

"Yes, she did. Everyone I've met has been very friendly."

"Jeremy, I've heard a lot about you from Savannah. She said you two went to college together. Is that right?"

"Uh, yes, we were in speech class together."

"Yes, she mentioned that. Did you know her beyond speech class?"

Jeremy had decided before the interview that he'd stick with what he knew and not improvise, as he was often inclined to do. "We may have crossed paths a couple of times on campus, but we met mostly in speech class."

"I see." Colin pretended to write for a while to allow a few awkward moments of silence to marinate in the room as Jeremy did his best not to squirm.

"The only reason I asked about Savannah is that she has really been in your corner. She practically begged us to interview you. She said you'd be perfect for Youngblood. You must have really made an impression on her."

Not exactly sure what to say, he had hoped to avoid comment; but the second consecutive period of awkward silence screamed for him to respond. He decided he'd try to lighten the mood a bit. "It must have been a really boring class for her to remember me so well."

Colin wouldn't bite and didn't crack a smile. "I guess it was."

Two doors down, Victor was enjoying the show and was impressed with how calmly Jeremy responded to Colin's prods. He wondered if Jeremy knew that Savannah was never in his class or if he had been convinced by the power of suggestion that he actually knew her. If things kept going the way they were, it was a question that Victor would personally find out the answer to if he had his time in the barrel with Jeremy. But he wanted to listen a bit more before he made his final decision regarding step three.

"You have a very impressive resume, high GPA, a few extra-curricular activities; that's good. I see you were in Beta Epsilon Theta. I loved fraternity life. I was a Pike. Some of my best memories of college are some of the crazy things we did as Pikes. We used to come up with ridiculous stunts, and then we'd bet each other if we could pull them off."

Both Colin and Victor were curious to see how Jeremy would respond to this part of the interview. Would he squirm in his seat? Would he know something was up?

With a calm smile, Jeremy simply responded, "Yes, sir, my time with Beta Epsilon Theta was very fulfilling. We definitely had some enjoyable experiences, but the most impactful facet of fraternity life was the incredible people I had the opportunity to meet and the relationships I expect to maintain the rest of my life." It was the only part of the interview preparation that Jeremy had practiced in front of a mirror– four times. He knew the reputation that fraternities had and wanted to put up a strong defense if he were backed into a corner. He was prepared. He just hoped his response hadn't sounded rehearsed.

Victor pointed to the screens; and to no one but himself he uttered, "This kid is good; I've seen all I need to see." He got up from his chair and headed out the door. Jeremy Prince's interview was about to take an interesting twist.

11

On the wall facing Colin, a small light had just been switched on. He knew what that meant and had to wrap things up.

"OK, Jeremy, I think that's all the questions I have for you. We have one more interviewer who will be in shortly…"

Before Colin could complete his sentence, Victor burst into the room like a game show host kicking off the show.

"Jeremy Prince! It's great to meet you! I've heard so much about you! I'm Victor Youngblood!" Victor thrust a huge hand that Jeremy did his best to shake. At six-foot-four, Victor was an imposing figure; and his catcher's mitt hands engulfed Jeremy's in the greeting.

Jeremy stood uneasily, still trying to process that Victor Youngblood was actually standing before him. "Umm…nice to meet you, Mr. Youngblood."

"Come on, Jeremy, I'm sure Colin has already covered our first-name policy. Call me Victor!"

"Yes, sir, Victor."

In the exchange Colin had excused himself from the room to observe, via monitor, the next step of the Jeremy Prince vetting process. Colin never knew what to expect from Victor and stopped trying long ago to predict how he would approach an interview.

"Please, take a seat, Jeremy."

Since his office tour with Savannah and his interview with Colin, which included some unusual questions, Jeremy had suspected there was something strange about this day. With Victor Youngblood personally interviewing him, Jeremy's suspicion was confirmed.

"I've really been looking forward to this, Jeremy. Thank you for making the trip to D. C. I trust all of the travel arrangements and accommodations were acceptable?"

"Yes, sir, more than acceptable, really nice," Jeremy assured.

"That's great. So, Jeremy, I hear you are good friends with Savannah; is that right?"

"Yes, sir...well...not exactly *good* friends. We were in speech class together in college."

"Ah, speech class. I recall that can be a nerve-wracking class for a college student."

"Yes, sir, it definitely can be."

"There's just one thing that's somewhat confusing." Victor ran his hand through his close-cropped salt and pepper goatee. "You spent your entire college experience at Virginia Tech, is that right?" Victor was waving a long finger at Jeremy.

"Yes, sir," Jeremy replied nervously.

"You see, here's the confusing part – Savannah went to Georgetown for her undergrad and Penn State for her master's. She never attended Virginia Tech. How could you two be in the same speech class?"

Jeremy's first thought was "oh crap!" The lingering doubts that Jeremy had about Savannah were confirmed. He didn't have class with her! He would remember a tall blonde like Savannah. Why had he let himself be convinced otherwise? Why would she tell him they were in class together? Why would Victor Youngblood know this? Why was Victor Youngblood, the company's CEO, even in the room with him? Something was wrong—really, really wrong! After regaining a measure of control over his thoughts, he mustered an inner-voice pep talk: "OK…just keep cool, Jeremy; you can deal with this."

He started with his trademark chuckle. "OK, here's the story, Mr. Youngblood. I recognize that this is going to sound really strange. I ran into Savannah in Tennessee a couple of weeks ago. She recognized me as someone she went to school with and told me about this job. I guess I just allowed myself to believe I knew her. Apparently I was confused. I apologize for the misunderstanding."

Victor thought, "Not a bad response for a 22-year-old kid under pressure." He decided to see if Jeremy could maintain the charade.

"Tennessee? What were you doing in Tennessee?"

"I was just passing through and stopped to get something to eat."

"Oh, I see, just passing through. Where were you headed?"

"I was...," Jeremy stammered.

"Oh well, it doesn't matter. I apologize for getting us off track."

Wow, Jeremy thought. What a relief! The relief, however, would be short-lived.

"I noticed you included some solid references on your résumé, but one reference we received was unsolicited. It was from Dr. Jocelyn Rosenberg at the University of Wisconsin. She reported that you were quite an accomplished young man."

Recognizing that this was no longer a job interview and that he could be in significant distress, Jeremy decided to lighten the mood and play along with Victor. He determined that he didn't have much to lose at this point. What's the worst thing that could happen? That he doesn't get the job?

"That's great! Dr. Rosenberg and I are very close."

"She contacted us through Facebook. That seems to be Dr. Rosenberg's communications platform of choice, at least over the last few weeks."

Not knowing exactly where to go with the conversation, Jeremy opted for brevity. Nodding his head, he simply replied, "I see."

"You see? What exactly do you see Jeremy?" Victor was impressed by Jeremy's ability to diffuse a potentially explosive situation, but he wasn't quite ready to let him know it yet. He wanted to continue applying pressure to find Jeremy's breaking point.

Jeremy responded, "What do I see? I see that this is apparently no longer a job interview. I see that Youngblood and Associates has a fairly extensive research arm with far-reaching capabilities. I also see that, depending on whom you have shared this information with, I could potentially be in a troubling situation."

"Potentially?" Victor rose from his seat, conjuring his most dramatic persona while shaking his head disapprovingly. He walked to the window. "Do you know that this stunt you pulled could ruin someone's life? How much do you actually know about Elijah Mustang?"

Jeremy had to quickly process this information that was coming at him at fire-hose strength. He thought he had pulled off one of the greatest deceptions ever; and more importantly, he thought he had done so without anyone knowing. Now, somehow, for some reason, the CEO of a company in Bethesda, Maryland, was apparently aware of every detail. *How* and *why* were only two of the thousand questions coursing through his brain. He had tried humor to no avail. He had tried the short response, again without success. Success? He wasn't even sure what success was. This time he'd try something different; he'd go on the offensive. He got up from his chair and walked over in the direction of Victor Youngblood, stopping short of meeting him face-to-face.

"You've been peppering me with questions. Well, I have a few questions of my own! Why do you think I know *anything* about Elijah Mustang? How do you know about Dr. Jocelyn Rosenberg? Why did you have Savannah, or whatever her name is, entice me to come here? What do you want from me?"

Victor took two steps to close the space between them, put both his hands on Jeremy's shoulders, and peered directly into his soul. His eyes twinkling, he sighed deeply, then conjured his most sincere smile, and replied, "Jeremy...I want you to work for me."

"How's he doing?" Savannah had quietly entered the observation room where Colin was monitoring the proceedings. He hadn't heard her come in and was startled by the sound of her voice.

"I'm sorry; I didn't mean to alarm you."

"No worries. I just didn't hear you come in. I guess I was enthralled by another Oscar-worthy performance." Colin had observed many such encounters but few as entertaining as this one.

"By the boss, I assume?" Savannah asked.

"Good question. Actually by both."

"Both? The kid's that good?"

"He's that good."

"So, I guess we are about to have a new member of Mouse Trap."

"I'd say so."

Had he heard Victor correctly? This was beyond bizarre. Jeremy asked incredulously, "You want me to work for you? Doing what?"

"Now that, Jeremy, is going to take some time to answer. Tell you what. Let's go back to the table and hit the reset button. I'll tell you what I know, and I'm going to ask you a few questions about what I *don't* know. Deal?"

At this point Jeremy wasn't sure what options he had; so he replied, "Deal."

Jeremy took his original seat at the table, but Victor walked around and sat in the chair next to Jeremy, turning it 90 degrees so that the two were face-to-face. "OK, Jeremy, here's what we know; and I warn you, this revelation may be alarming at first." Victor read from a tablet. "Jeremy Prince, graduated from Virginia Tech with a 3.9 GPA with a double major in business and philosophy. Parents are Walter and Rosita Prince. They live in Abingdon, Virginia, where you were born and raised as an only child. Dad owns a hardware store that his grandfather started in 1947 after coming home from WWII. You are a member of Beta Epsilon Theta. Just a few weeks ago, you made a wager with some of your fraternity brothers with the stakes being a full keg of beer. How am I doing so far?"

Jeremy sat in stunned amazement. So far Victor was 100% correct, including the part about this knowledge of him being alarming. "So far, so good."

Victor continued, "I'm not even to the best part yet. The part that got my attention. The part that makes me want you as part of my team. *The bet*: you bet your fraternity brothers that you could get the graduation speaker cancelled at an obscure little college in Tennessee. It took some imagination and some large cojones to make that bet." Now Victor was again standing and pacing. "Oh and the best part? You won! You won that crazy bet!" He again took his seat adjacent to Jeremy. "I'm at the end of what I know about Jeremy Prince's wager, and I'm dying to learn the rest of the story. So tell me, Jeremy, why Richfield College and why Elijah Mustang? Did one of his big trucks try to run you off the road or something?"

Now nervous, he wasn't sure whether to spill his guts, make up a story, or simply make a break for it and run out the door. For some reason he opted for the transparent approach. He wasn't sure why.

"Well…I hope you aren't looking for some justifiably righteous story because there really isn't one. You see, one of the guys at the fraternity had a family member—a sister, brother, cousin, I don't really know who—graduating from that college. That person received a graduation invitation, which was on a table in the frat house's game room.

I saw it; and on impulse, I bet the guys I could get the speaker changed. I didn't even know who the dude was."

Victor laughed as hard as he'd laughed in months, almost falling over backwards in his chair. "Seriously? That's the story? You gotta be kidding me."

"I'm sorta known around the frat house for my bets. I haven't lost one yet. It's to the point that no one will bet with me anymore, so I have to come up with weird stuff like the graduation speaker to get any takers."

"OK, that's part of the answer I was looking for. Now, tell me *how* you did it."

Jeremy cocked his head to the side, perplexed. "So, why are you so interested in this little prank I pulled?"

"*Little prank?* Jeremy, rolling someone's yard is a little prank. Doing something that causes the entire U. S. media to show up is a major accomplishment!"

"I just don't understand why you're so interested."

"Come on, Jeremy, indulge an old man and tell me how you pulled this off. I'll explain my interest soon enough."

Realizing he wasn't leaving Youngblood and Associates until he told his story, he took a big breath and began to explain.

"You know I've already graduated, so that means I have time on my hands. I did most of it on the Internet. First I had to find out who the speaker was. I found out this Elijah Mustang guy was the CEO of the trucking company with the Bible-verse trucks that everyone had seen on the interstate. Once I found that out, I knew I had an easy target. Then I went to the Richfield College web-site and searched the faculty. I narrowed it down to three prospects based on some simple demographics. Then, I did an Internet research on each of the three. Molly Jefferson was the obvious choice. Her Facebook page was full of pictures of her at protests. She had also shared on Facebook some urban-legend type stuff that I knew wasn't true, so that told me she wouldn't really do any back-ground checks on information I would send her."

"Next, I created a Facebook page for Jocelyn Rosen-berg. By the way, Jocelyn Rosenberg was the name of my lunch lady back in Abingdon." Victor again chuckled. "From there it was just a matter of getting Dr. Jefferson to start the protest. Knowing what sheep most college stu-dents are, I knew it wouldn't be difficult for her to get a following. I definitely didn't count on nationwide press and the crazy protestors that last day. To be honest, it was kind of a rush when I saw all those cameras rolling when the college president announced he was not going to allow Elijah Mustang to speak at graduation. It actually worked!"

"Jeremy, what if I told you that Elijah Mustang was a very respectable family man and that all of these allega-tions about him unfairly impugned his character."

"Yeah...uh...I'm really sorry about that." Jeremy spoke the words but couldn't be less convincing.

"Sorry? You're really sorry?" Victory prodded in mock incredulity.

Jeremy didn't lack much; but if there's one thing that he was in short supply of, it was a conscience. "OK, you know most everything anyway; to be honest, I'm not really sorry. The dude's a former congressman, a CEO of a big freaking trucking company, no doubt a millionaire. I think he'll be OK."

"He'll be OK?" Victor repeated, then again burst out in laughter. He now spoke in the direction of the camera that was hidden in the sprinkler. "Did you hear that? He'll be OK! Have we got the right guy or what?!"

❧

"Not sure I've seen Victor like this before," Savannah stared at the monitor in disbelief.

"It's been a long time since he's acted this way. I think he's found his new apprentice," Colin declared.

"Hope the kid's up to it."

❧

"So, that's what my original question was. The right guy for what? You said you wanted me to work for you. What do you want me to do?" asked Jeremy.

"Jeremy, I'm sure you've done your research like a good college boy would. You undoubtedly know we have the usual lineup of D. C. business areas: lobbying, marketing, public relations, and the sort. But we have another area that's a bit more...clandestine."

"Clandestine? You mean like support to the CIA?"

"Not exactly. I understand that we're going to have to ease into this a bit, but I'm going to need you to get up to speed quickly because we have a lot of work to do and you are already behind."

"I'm sorry, but I'm totally lost."

"Jeremy, did you enjoy pulling this—we'll use your word *prank* to get the graduation speaker changed? Be honest."

For the first time all day, Jeremy felt comfortable—at ease; and he realized that he was smiling for the first time since he left his hotel room earlier that morning. "Enjoy it? No, I wouldn't say I enjoyed it. I would say I freakin' loved it. I know it's kinda weird; but when I saw all those protestors and the story unfold on TV, it was awesome. And I was standing maybe 50 yards away when that jackass college president announced he was pulling the plug on Elijah Mustang. It was a feeling like I had never felt before...in a good way."

Victor spoke enticingly. "Now imagine if you had a job where you were paid very handsomely to do that kind of prank every day but on a much grander scale. Would that be something that would be interesting to you?"

"Hell, yeah! I mean...yes, it certainly would." Jeremy tried to hide his exuberance.

"*Hell, yeah* is an acceptable answer, Jeremy; in fact, that's what I was hoping you'd say. Let me suggest the next step. I want to give you a week to think about things. In that week I want you to go to Abingdon and spend some time with your parents. Tell them that you have a job offer in D. C. and that you are seriously thinking about taking it. Come back here at 8 a.m. a week from today, and we'll talk."

"A job offer? I have a job offer?" a confused Jeremy asked.

"Yep, here you go." Victor reached into his jacket pocket and handed Jeremy a letter addressed to him. "Go ahead, open it."

A bit suspicious, Jeremy opened it slowly and read:

> *Dear Mr. Prince,*
>
> *I am pleased to offer you a position with Youngblood and Associates as a Project Manager in the MT Department. If you accept this offer, you will receive an annual salary of $100,000, which will be paid monthly. You will also be eligible to receive employee benefits including medical, dental, 401K, life insurance, and periodic performance-based bonuses.*
>
> *We believe you will find employment at Youngblood and Associates fulfilling and rewarding and look forward to your acceptance.*
> *Sincerely,*
> *Youngblood & Associates, Human Resources*

"Are you serious? A hundred-thousand dollars?" asked Jeremy.

"Plus bonuses."

"What's the MT Department?"

"We'll talk about that next time. And Jeremy, in the week before our next meeting, I'll give you just a small glimpse into some of our capabilities."

"What kind of a glimpse?"

"You'll see. Well, Jeremy, it's been a pleasure to meet you; and I am very much looking forward to working with you. I have to run to another meeting. Colin will be in shortly to see you out." Victor thrust his hand toward Jeremy to signal his exit with a parting shake.

"It was nice to meet you as well, Victor. I will see you next week."

As Victor exited the room, Jeremy was left alone. He got out his offer letter and read it again and again and again.

Victor walked two doors down the hall and joined Colin and Savannah in the observation room. Victor asked, "Is he reading the letter again?"

"Yep," Colin answered.

"We got him."

"Yep, we got him."

"Give him another 20 minutes alone before you lead him out. Let him soak it all in," instructed Victor.

"Will do. Do you think he'll do OK here?" Savannah asked.

Victor chuckled a deep laugh that seemed to come from the bottom of his lungs. "Yeah, I think he'll do *OK*."

As Colin entered the room, Jeremy was again looking at his letter, still in a state of disbelief.

"You ready to head back to the hotel?"

"Yes. Do you mind if I hit the head before we go?" asked Jeremy.

"No problem, come on and I'll show you."

Colin led Jeremy down the hallway to a large restroom.

"I'll wait for you right here."

As Jeremy finished his business, a young man in his early 30s entered the restroom.

"Here for an interview?" the man asked.

"What?"

"I just noticed your visitor badge and wondered if you were here for an interview."

"Oh, yes, I am…or I was," Jeremy responded.

"Hi, my name's Joseph." The employee extended a hand.

"I'm Jeremy. It's nice to meet you."

"How did the interview go?" Joseph asked.

"I think it went pretty well."

"Will we be seeing you around here soon?"

As a member of Mouse Trap, Joseph also noticed at the lower right corner of Jeremy's badge the inconspicuous

MT, a signal that this candidate was being vetted for his group.

"You're an employee here. How do you like it?"

"It's great!" exclaimed Joseph.

Just as he spoke, he dropped a pen on the floor. Jeremy instinctively stooped to help him pick it up. "Let me help you with that."

Joseph stooped to meet Jeremy eye-to-eye, quickly grabbed Jeremy's tie and whispered, "Welcome to the Hotel California." Then he quickly stood back up and resumed his regular volume. "Yes, I love working here; and I'm sure you will too. Best of luck to you."

12

"Good afternoon, welcome to Prince's. What can we help you with today?"

"I was hoping to speak with the owner."

"You're in luck; that would be me. Hello, I'm Walter Prince." Walter extended a hand in greeting, hoping, as always, to meet a customer's needs. "How can I serve you today?"

"I was hoping to speak with you for a few moments, privately if possible."

"Is there anything wrong?"

"No sir, nothing is wrong."

It was an unusual request, but it was clear to Walter that this was no ordinary shopper. A starched designer brand shirt, crisply pleated pants, and polished shoes were oddities in Prince's Hardware. Walter decided he would invest a few minutes of his time to see where this encounter might lead.

"Certainly, we can go into my office. It's in the back. I'm sorry, I didn't catch your name."

"It's Dan Thacker. Thank you for taking the time to meet with me."

It was the second time Thacker had been in Walter's office in the past 12 hours, with the previous visit being around 2 a.m. to case the store for security and surveillance equipment. After a sweep of the office, he was satisfied that a conversation in Walter's office would not be recorded.

Walter entered the office, closed the door behind him, and gestured for Thacker to take the seat in front of his desk. "Now, what can I do for you, Mr. Thacker?"

"Mr. Prince, am I correct in assuming that you have some commercial accounts?"

"Yes, sir, we have a number of commercial accounts."

"That's good. Mr. Prince, I represent an agency that I am not at liberty to disclose. I hope you understand," Thacker cautioned.

"Well, I'm not sure…"

"We have a business proposition that will be beneficial to both of us. We have a need to procure several items on a regular basis. Here is a list." Thacker handed Walter at least a dozen pages.

A very confused Walter Prince scanned the list and read aloud, "Generators, air compressors, chain saws, electrical supplies, lighting; yes, we certainly have all of these…"

"We need a source to place large orders of this type of merchandise on a monthly basis, and we think Prince's would be the ideal solution for us."

"I certainly want your business; but if you're with the government, won't you need to go through a lot of bureaucracy to make these purchases?" asked Walter.

"That's exactly what we think you can do for us, Mr. Prince. We want to bypass that bureaucracy. We will be doing business through private entities, who will then supply us with the equipment. Here's a list of five companies that will be purchasing on our behalf. When you receive an order from a company on this list, you will know it is from us. It is extremely important that these purchase are not traced back to us. After I leave today, you will not see me again. Do you understand, Mr. Prince?"

"Yes, I think I do," Walter responded in a hushed tone.

"Is this something that you are willing to do? I can assure you that it will be a great service to your country."

"Is this all legal? I certainly wouldn't want to put our business in jeopardy in any way."

"Completely legal. To the world, this will just be a group of businesses purchasing equipment and supplies. All the businesses are legitimate enterprises. There's no risk to you," Thacker assured.

Walter walked to the window of his office and saw his employees hard at work. He saw his beloved Rosita on her knees stocking the bottom shelves. He looked on the wall at a graph showing the store sales' trend declining each of the past five years. He took a moment to clear his mind before turning back to Thacker with a conditional answer.

"Yes, I am willing to do this, but I have some questions."

"Most of them I will not be able to answer. I can't stress to you enough the importance of security. We have to act as if this conversation never happened."

"Earlier you mentioned large orders. Exactly how large are we talking about?" asked Walter.

"Rosenberg Electric will place the first order in the next few days. It will be for $30,000."

"$30,000! And you'll be placing orders every month?"

"The $30,000 will be an average *weekly* order. We expect to place in excess of $100,000 each month."

Walter had hoped the shock wasn't showing on his face. Thacker was glad that it was, as that meant he had done his job impressing Walter Prince and ultimately, Walter's son Jeremy.

"There will be varying frequencies and dollar values, but the average will be approximately $100,000 per month. Mr. Prince, I want to ensure that you understand the level of confidentiality required in our transactions," Thacker again cautioned.

"I understand, and I am very glad that you chose Prince's for these purchases. I know you will be pleased with our service."

"I want to say this one more time, Mr. Prince. This conversation never happened. The growth in sales that you will soon experience is the result of your business acumen and not the U. S. government. You will never see me again. Do you understand?"

"Yes, Mr. Thacker, I understand."

With the final handshake, Victor's man had consummated the next step in recruiting Jeremy Prince. He wanted to make a clear and unmistakable gesture that Jeremy could not overlook.

"What do the latest polls show?"

"In Iowa you are polling in fourth place at 11%."

"That's up from 10% last week, right?"

"Yes, sir, that's right."

"You also have 57% name recognition, 42% positive, 45% negative with a plus or minus 6-point margin of error."

"57% name recognition. That's moving in the right direction as well."

"Yes sir, it is."

Senator Grant Wembley met every week with Madeline Chung, his chief of staff, who was moonlighting as Wembley's campaign manager for his yet-to-be-announced run for the Republican Party's nomination in the 2016 presidential election. Representing Wyoming for the past 17 years, Wembley was a stalwart in the Republican Party.

Working for years to carefully craft his political persona, Wembley prided himself on being adaptable. Over the course of his Senate career, he had changed his positions on key issues numerous times to align with polling data that he trusted as his guiding light.

He was once opposed to gay marriage; but as the cultural shift of the late 2000s took root, he was compelled to choose sides and became a strident supporter to curry favor with the mainstream media and Hollywood movers and shakers.

He had been opposed to nuclear energy; but as a large power company sought to build a nuclear power plant in his state, he conveniently changed his position to be pro-nuke.

He voted to support the Iraq war as well as the Patriot Act but had been an outspoken opponent both of active intervention in the Middle East and of the Patriot Act when the other party was occupying the White House.

He had no viable Republican opposition in solid red state Wyoming and had faced only token opposition in the Republican primary since his first election in 1998. For the past five months, he had been floating trial balloons about his prospective candidacy for president to collect data on how realistic a run could be. He trusted the data more than anyone or anything, and he spent hours poring over the latest analysis his staff prepared. So far, he liked what he was reading.

In recent weeks he had appeared on Sunday morning talk shows and had written op-eds—or had aides write them on his behalf—to increase his name recognition. The data indicated his efforts were paying off.

"How many mentions last week?" asked Grant.

"Two in *The New York Times*, four in *The Washington Post*, three on CNN, two on CBS and NBC, one on ABC, and six on Fox."

"Do we have the call set up with the donors on Friday?" continued Grant.

"Yes, 6 p.m.," Madeline replied.

"Are we still on track for a May announcement?"

Madeline pulled from her briefcase a 67-page schedule meticulously outlining all activities to be performed prior to the announcement.

"Yes, we are. I just reviewed the plan with the staff, and everything is on or ahead of schedule.

Grant Wembley's run for the presidency was among the worst-kept secrets in Washington D. C. Now he was only two months from making it official. As far as Victor Youngblood and Mouse Trap were concerned, Wembley's hat was already in the ring.

13

As Walter Prince was working to assemble a new socket-wrench display on the hardware store's counter, he heard the sound of the "ding" signaling a customer's entry. Without turning around, he instinctively responded, "Welcome to Prince's. How can we help you today?"

"Hi, Dad."

Walter's head quickly turned toward the door where his son, away from home for too many months, was now standing.

"Jeremy!" He quickly shuffled around the counter to shake his son's hand; but before he could get there, Rosita had somehow heard him coming and had sprinted to the front door to hug and kiss her only son.

"Jeremy! I'm so happy to see you!" exclaimed Rosita.

"I'm glad to see you too, Mom."

"How are you doing? Are you OK?! How long are you here for?"

"Slow down, Rosita; give the boy time to answer," Walter interjected.

"It's OK, Dad. I'm happy to see both of you, too."

Rosita grabbed her son's hand and would not let go. "You look so skinny. Are you eating? Is everything OK?"

Walter realized the reunion was drawing the attention of the handful of customers in the store and worked to direct Rosita and Jeremy away from the front door. "How about we go back to the office and catch up?"

Jeremy took a seat in Walter's office, and Rosita pulled up a chair right next to him and again grabbed his hand. "Jeremy, we have missed you so much!"

"Come on, Rosita, let the boy breathe."

"I haven't seen my son in three months; I can smother him if I want to."

"It's really OK, Dad."

They went through the usual catch-ups; How are things going? What have you been doing? The conversation brought joy to Rosita as she saw a return of the bright, outgoing, son that had seemed to be missing the past couple of years. She had feared that side of Jeremy was gone forever.

"So, what brings you home, Jeremy? Are you here to stay for a while?" It was a question that had to be raised but one that Rosita wasn't quite ready to ask.

"Come on, Walter, he just got here 15 minutes ago."

"I'm actually here for a few days, but I have some good news I wanted to tell you about."

"I'm always ready for good news." Rosita squeezed his arm even tighter.

"I got a job offer."

It was music to Walter's ear. "That's wonderful! Who with? Where is it?" Although he would never let Jeremy know, the struggles of keeping the store open were exacerbated by the need to continue supporting his college-graduate son. This was indeed good news.

"It's actually in the Washington D. C. area. It's with a company called Youngblood and Associates. Here's the offer letter."

Jeremy had wrestled with how much to share with his parents. He knew that they were disappointed in the transient lifestyle he had wandered into since graduation. He hoped the letter might provide tangible proof that his life was actually attaining some direction. A part of him also wanted to show off the $100,000 salary to buffer the impact of his moving to Washington D. C.

His parents' reaction was predictable.

"$100,000?! Jeremy, that's great!" His dad latched on to the generous starting salary.

"Washington D. C.! That's five hours away!" His mom lamented.

"I know, Mom, but I can come home more often than I have been. I'm really sorry I've been away for so long."

"So, it says you are going to be a project manager. What kinds of projects will you be managing?" Walter worked to rescue Jeremy from his mom's concerns.

"I just interviewed with them a couple of days ago, so I don't know all the details yet."

"Have you accepted the offer?" Walter asked.

"No, they asked me to wait a week, mull things over, and travel back to D. C. later this week. However, I don't really have much to think about. I'm going to accept."

"Jeremy, that's wonderful. I'm really proud of you." His dad's response made Jeremy happy.

"You're really moving five hours away?" His mom's response made him smile.

Although Mouse Trap was unlike anything else in the American business world, Victor knew a disciplined structure was necessary for effective management. Therefore, Victor had instituted a 20 X 20 organization. He had 20 project managers, with varying levels of responsibility, depending on the project size and complexity. Some project managers had a single large project for which they were responsible. Others had up to three small- to medium-size projects active at any time. In the Mouse Trap vernacular, a "project" had a wide-ranging definition and could include a person, such as a politician, movie star or sports star; a place, such as a city or park; an animal; a day; or almost anything that Victor assigned project managers to influence. In simple terms, he considered his project managers responsible for a "what."

The second half of the 20 X 20 Mouse Trap organization was 20 division managers who, in Victor's parlance, were responsible for the "how." Among the 20 divisions were Social Media, Network and Cable News, Movies and TV, Public Education, University Education, Executive Branch, Legislative Branch, Judicial Branch, Corporate Policy, Technology, and Music. Divisions were resources project managers used to accomplish their assigned tasks.

Both project managers and division managers typically started in a Youngblood & Associates function until they were recognized by Victor or one of his lieutenants, as having Mouse Trap potential. Mouse Trap was reserved for only the highest performers.

On this day the monthly project-status meeting was held with Victor serving as maestro at the head of the table. Each project manager was responsible for reporting on the status of his or her project. At any time, Mouse Trap could have close to 40 active projects, so each project manager was expected to give a succinct status. Even with the streamlined approach, project-status meetings often lasted more than three hours.

Two hours into today's meeting the team was barely through half of the agenda. It would be a long day.

"Next up is Project Citrus," continued Victor.

Each Mouse Trap project had a project name. In this case, Project Citrus was the code name for a project to extract pop music star Oscar Tangerine from a very difficult legal and public relations' nightmare.

"The guy's in big trouble. You've all seen the video," the project manager reported.

Oscar Tangerine had six consecutive number-one hits on the pop and R&B charts. His last four albums had gone multi-platinum. He had won Grammys in three of the last five years. At age 30 he was unquestionably at the top of the music world. Then everything came crashing down. Oscar was caught on video with two 15-year-old girls. Fortunately for Oscar, only a handful of law enforcement personnel and, of course, Mouse Trap's team members had seen the video. His bombshell arrest and obligatory perp walk were also on video and had been viewed 12 million times on YouTube in the first few days since it was uploaded.

"Where do things stand?" Victor asked.

"The DA is contemplating what charges to bring. Mr. Tangerine's record label's representatives have told his agent they are nearing a decision to release him from his contract. Three advertisers, a cell phone company, a soft drink company, and a fast food chain have already dropped him from their campaigns."

"The guy must be devastated." Victor sensed opportunity in Oscar's trials.

"Beyond devastated. He is on suicide watch," the project manager responded.

"Great! So, what options do we have?" Victor knew this opportunity was tailor made for Mouse Trap.

"We've made a lot of progress and we have a plan. First, we'll get control of all the videos of the encounter so there's no evidence. Next, we'll get the DA to drop the charges. We'll meet privately with the girls and their families and let them know how sorry we are about everything that has happened to them. We'll offer them money and scholarships to compensate for their pain.

"Next, we'll make a very public announcement that the charges have been dropped and that Oscar was falsely accused. His record label will stick with him and announce he'll be releasing a new album later this year. We have three new advertisers lined up and we have a news magazine that will publish a story about Oscar's work to improve the inner city. We'll get him an award at the next big industry gathering. Basically, we can remake the guy in a matter of a few months."

"And make sure he understands he'll be ours after that," Victor insisted.

"We will."

"Do it." Mouse Trap was working to perfection, as it almost always did.

"Next to report, Project Gator…"

"Your tamales are even better than I remembered, Mom."

"I bet they won't have tamales this good in D.C."

"Rosita, let it go! The boy has a great opportunity."

"I know. I'm just making sure he knows his momma is gonna miss him."

"I know, Mom. I'm going to miss you and Dad, too."

Jeremy was surprised at how happy he was to be back home in Abingdon and was still trying to come to grips with why he had chosen to stay away for the past six months.

"Hey, Walter, I was going through this morning's orders for the store and saw a really large one. It was for $30,000."

"Yes, I didn't want to steal Jeremy's thunder, but I had an interesting visit yesterday. I'm not really supposed to talk about it, but we have a great opportunity to get the store back on its feet."

"What do you mean you're not supposed to talk about it?" One hallmark of Rosita and Walter's years together was that they didn't keep secrets from one another.

"Well, this guy came by the store..." Walter described his visit and the large orders that would be coming to the store. He also mentioned that the orders could not be attributed to the government.

"It sounds kinda fishy. Do you think this is all legal?" Rosita was adamant that Prince's Hardware Store be run by the book.

"I know it's early, but the guy has followed through so far. I got a big order from Rosenberg Electric this morning. That's one of the companies he told me I would be receiving orders from."

Jeremy's trademark grin took involuntary control of his face. His first thought was that this Victor Youngblood guy is good. Using the Rosenberg name was genius, a perfect way to send him a signal. He wasn't sure if he should be impressed or creeped out. So far, the impressed response was winning.

"What are you smiling about, Jeremy?" Rosita asked.

"Oh, Mom, I'm just happy for you and Dad. I am glad you have this opportunity."

"This is crazy... While everyone's sharing their good news, I have some of my own." Rosita had intended to wait a few days before telling Walter about her secret but felt it was time to spill the beans. "I got a call this morning from a Savannah Richfield who represents a publishing company, whose representatives have been reading my columns and want me to be syndicated nationally. Starting next month, I'm going to be in over 200 newspapers throughout the country! Can you believe that?!"

"Rosita, that is great!" Walter exclaimed.

"Mom, I'm really happy for you." Jeremy was blown away. Victor was good—really, really good. Savannah Richfield? Why didn't he just slap Jeremy in the face? He wasn't exactly sure how Victor had pulled this off, but he was anxious to find out. He was even more anxious to be a part of an organization that had this kind of influence and reach. He would soon get his wish.

14

As Victor drove his black Range Rover down the tree-lined rural highway near Yellow Springs, Maryland, he passed the eastern boundary of Federick Municipal Forest. This landmark prompted the drone, hovering 100 feet above Victor's car, to signal back to Council Control Center that the road was clear and that he had not been followed. Victor glanced down at his phone to see that the Control Center had messaged him the go ahead to make the final turn off the paved road and onto the upcoming driveway.

Victor navigated the sharp 120-degree turn, his wheels crunching the jagged gravel. Two hundred yards down the driveway, he approached the first gate, which recognized the signal from Victor's vehicle and opened automatically. Another 100 yards and two guards brandishing M16's met him at the second gate.

"Good morning, sir. The Hex is clear and secured."

"Thank you. Anyone else here yet?" Victor asked.

"No, sir, you're first, as usual."

"Good."

"Let us know if you need anything."

"You know I will."

Victor rounded the final curve and glanced up at the rustic edifice called The Hex. The massive lodge was constructed of red cedar timbers with perfectly dovetailed joints at each corner. It was fashioned after National Park lodges of the Western U.S. Its rural setting suggested a casual atmosphere; however, The Hex was among the most highly secured and technologically advanced structures in the country. Its sole purpose was to host the six most powerful individuals in the world one day each month.

The Hex did not appear on any map nor in any satellite imagery. A search of the property in mapping applications or websites returned the images of a thickly wooded property with no sign of any structure.

Each month Victor Youngblood's security personnel swept the property to ensure no communication or listening devices were present. The Council's business entities owned the 800 acres surrounding The Hex and monitored the area via seven state-of-the-art drones that constantly buzzed the property. Privacy was non-negotiable for the structure that had hosted The Council for the past 62 years.

Victor pulled up the steep hill and turned onto the paved driveway circling The Hex. He drove around the back and entered the five-digit code, opening his personal garage door. Exiting his vehicle, he climbed the circular stairs from the garage to the main level and entered his personal room.

The Hex was comprised of seven large rooms. Six were elongated triangles, all the same size, forming a six-sided donut shape—or hexagon, which gave the facility its name. Each of the six rooms were accessible by the stairs leading up from the garage below. Each room had separate garage doors with compartmentalized garages.

Five of the six rooms were outfitted to meet the needs and desires of each of The Council's members, while the sixth was set aside for Victor Youngblood as a workspace to prepare for each Council gathering. Each of the six rooms had an interior door that led to the seventh room, a large six-sided space that formed the center of the donut, serving as The Council's meeting place.

As they did on the second Saturday of every month, The Council's five members gathered at The Hex. Victor always arrived before them to ensure meeting preparations were in order.

The Council's members went by the pseudonyms Able, Baker, Charlie, Dog, and Easy-- the first five letters in the U. S. Army phonetic alphabet, circa 1946 when The Council was formed. Their positions on The Council were known only to each other and to Victor Youngblood. Outside The Hex, council members lived relatively normal lives.

Council members abided by a strict code of absolute secrecy. Their charter stated that what The Council is and does is known only to the five Council members and Victor Youngblood. In reality, the complete story of the Council's reach was known only to one man, Victor Youngblood.

A few members of the Mouse Trap organization heard rumblings of some sort of clandestine group who somehow provided guidance and direction to the organization. However, a condition of joining Mouse Trap was a commitment not to discuss any rumors that might wander through the team—a commitment that was universally observed and strictly enforced.

Security personnel who work in the Council Control Center, as well as the heavily armed guards who protect The Hex and its surrounding property, were instructed whom to allow into The Hex and whom to exclude. Their access decisions were based on codes embedded on the windshields of Council members' vehicles coupled with Council fingerprint IDs. The security staff knew nothing about the Council members' identities nor their business at The Hex and understood that they were not at liberty to ask.

Early on this Saturday morning, Victor reviewed the agenda one last time as the Council members would be arriving shortly. It would be a full day because there were many pressing issues to decide. Within the next hour, The Hex would be ground zero for setting the world's trajectory for the next 30 days.

Jeremy decided to forgo Victor's offer of a ride back via private jet to D. C. and instead opted to drive his 2004 Toyota Camry on the 350-mile journey. He rationalized he was going to D.C. to stay and wanted to have his own transportation available. Besides, what was another 350 miles on an odometer that had passed the 200,000-mile mark?

The five-hour drive offered Jeremy a time of solitude and reflection. Was this really the right job for him? The answer consistently came back a resounding "yes." How much did he really know about Youngblood and Associates? He knew enough to be impressed; more importantly, he wanted to know more about how Victor so quickly and dramatically intervened in his and his parents' lives. In fact, he didn't just want to *know* about Victor's capabilities, he wanted to personally be part of them.

The only piece of the puzzle that Jeremy hadn't completely solved was the brief restroom encounter he had with Joseph, the Y&A employee who had whispered to him a cryptic message about the Hotel California. Shortly into his trip, he had put the classic Eagles' tune on replay and had listened to it a dozen times. So far he had experienced no epiphany about what relationship Hotel California might have with his future employer. He decided there was nothing to it and chose to let it go.

The direction of life was trending positive for Jeremy Prince. He would soon become the newest member of an intriguing enterprise known as Mouse Trap.

Diversified Communications and Technologies International, or Di-Com as it was known in Wall Street parlance, was founded in 1962. Through its first 30 years, it saw steady growth each year, even holding firm through the late 70s' economic downturn. By the mid-90s, Di-Com had become one of the largest communications companies in the U. S. Midwest. In the last 20 years, Di-Com's growth skyrocketed, primarily through timely acquisitions of companies that provide cellular phone towers, satellites, cable TV, internet servers, cloud storage, and high-speed Internet. Valued at $174 billion by 2015, Di-Com was the 11th largest company in the U. S. in terms of market capitalization.

For the last 14 years, Di-Com was led by President and CEO Lionel Ireland, who had a knack for finding undervalued companies with underutilized technologies and breathing new life into them. He was particularly adept at identifying companies that could complement other

Di-Com holdings to extract additional shareholder value through synergistic business relationships.

First making the Forbes 400 list in 2011, Ireland had steadily climbed in ranking each year since. He was a multi-billionaire; but in recent years, many of Ireland's closest friends and advisors detected his profound restlessness. Running the corporation didn't seem to bring the same level of challenge or satisfaction that it once had. Ascending to the role of CEO at age 42, he was now 56 and searching. In recent years he sought fulfilment in endeavors outside Di-Com. He climbed Mount Everest, started a cable news network, and bought a professional hockey team. None of those pursuits, however, satisfied the unquenched thirst that Ireland was experiencing.

In the last six months, rumors had grown more prominent that Ireland might be considering leaving the company, but no one knew exactly why. The information void was fertile soil for gossip to grow wild. Every crazy idea had been in the rumor mill, including that he had terminal cancer; that he had found God and was becoming a clergyman; and that he was going to spearhead a start-up, just to give him a new challenge. Many had hoped that today's Di-Com annual meeting would replace the wild rumors with facts. The carefully orchestrated meeting included talks from the CFO regaling the gathering on the company's financial strength; the Vice President for Investor Relations on the stock's strong outlook; and the Chief Technology Officer offering teasers on the whiz-bang products Di-Com would be unveiling in the upcoming months.

The speech that everyone had been awaiting was saved for last. The crowd grew restless, and the tension was palpable as Lionel strode confidently to the podium to the sound of exuberant applause.

"I don't know about you, but I'm impressed. No... more than impressed, I'm blown away! The financials are strong, the stock price is climbing, and we've got technology about to be released that will blow your mind. Di-Com is clearly on the right track." He skipped the ceremonial thank-yous and fluff that he disdained and instead brought his trademark blunt delivery that made him a pop culture icon.

"You know what's NOT on the right track? This country. This country is in the ditch." Lionel didn't like to dither, and his speeches were known for getting right to the point. This day was no exception.

"I know a lot of people are in denial and want to believe the best, but I'm not one of them. One of the absolutes that has kept Di-Com on the right path for so many years is that we don't allow spin or happy talk to influence any business decision. We try our best to create a culture in which all of our team members are expected to deal with the way things really are, not the way they want things to be."

"So let's talk about how things are in this country. Our finances are a disaster with 18 trillion dollars of debt. We have more people on the government dole than ever before. The unemployment rate is bogus; we have more people not working than in a generation. Our country is divided among every possible fissure you could imagine. You name it and we're divided. Around the world our influence is shrinking. I know some people think that's a good thing. I am not among them. America is a great country because America has always been strong—not perfect—but strong."

"I know many rumors have been out there about my future. I want to dispel one of them right now. No, I am not pregnant."

The perfectly timed joke was just what was needed to lighten the ever-tensing mood.

"But I do want to confirm one rumor that is very important to me. I am stepping down from my post at Di-Com. I love this company, and I have loved my time here; but a greater love is calling: my love for this country. I am announcing today my candidacy for president of the United States. I'm not doing this baloney about forming an exploratory committee or whatever politicians do. I'm running and I'm winning and we're going to fix this country!"

In unison the assembled rose to their feet in thunderous ovation. Lionel Ireland's name was added to the growing list of 2016 candidates for the presidency of the United States. Of course, the Mouse Trap had been long set for Lionel Ireland, and Victor was prepared.

The Council meeting had been going for two and a half hours with four of the nine agenda items completed, including the measles outbreak, the summer's oil prices, the U. S. budget for fiscal year 2016, and the construction of a high-speed rail project connecting New York City and Philadelphia.

"Next on the agenda is Oscar Tangerine."

"Remind us again, Victor, why we care about Mr. Tangerine." Baker's request was valid. The Council rarely delved into the affairs of individuals in the entertainment industry. Those engagements were important but typically set aside for the normal business of Youngblood and Associates' Public Relations and Marketing divisions. As usual, Victor had a plan.

"We can use Oscar Tangerine as a resource. He has 47 million followers on Twitter, 35 million on Facebook, and 40 million on Instagram. He recorded a song about a girl with a lizard tattoo; and in the next three months, over 20,000 girls got lizard tattoos. He holds great influence with the millennials who are important to many of our efforts."

"We don't use him now do we?" Dog already knew the answer.

Victor responded, "We don't, but we have the opportunity to do so. We've already got a plan in place to extricate him from his predicament; and in return, he will become an asset for Mouse Trap."

"I'm assuming you've outlined ways we can use this asset?" asked Easy.

"Our research indicates that Mr. Tangerine will have staying power in the industry for at least a decade, longer with our help. Having an asset with that kind of breadth and depth is definitely worth our investment."

Victor, who served as moderator for The Council's final decisions, sensed it was time to vote. "If the Council approves, I will call for a vote."

"Able, are you in favor?"

"Yes."

"Baker?"

"Yes"

"Charlie?"

"Yes."

"Dog?"

"Yes."

"Easy?"

"Yes."

"It's unanimous. We have the go-ahead for Mr. Tangerine."

"Victor, we look forward to hearing about your results," Charlie declared.

"Thank you. I look forward to reporting them."

"Next on the agenda is an update on the Climate Change Project…"

15

"Is Jeremy Prince still on track for this afternoon?"

"Yes, he is. He should be here at one o'clock."

"Great. My schedule is cleared for the afternoon, right?"

"Yes, all clear. Victor, I haven't seen you this interested in a new recruit in...well, maybe ever. What do you see in this kid?" Colin had spent the last seven years at Victor Youngblood's side. He had shepherded over 100 new recruits through the onboarding process, and he had never seen Victor take such a personal interest in a new hire.

"He's different. He's special. 2016 is coming fast, and I think we can use him in a big way," Victor opined.

"2016?! You're going to plug him into 2016? By the time he's through with the probationary period, the campaign will be in full swing and the window of influence will be closing."

"Yes it will be. That's why we're skipping the probationary period."

"No probation? Have we ever done that before?" Colin asked.

"I have a feeling about this kid. We've vetted him enough. We need him *now*," Victor declared.

"You're the boss. We'll have him here at one."

The 12,000-square-foot Beverly Hills mansion, known as the Tangerine Palace, had been home to Oscar Tangerine for the past four years. It boasted three swimming pools, ten bathrooms, and eight bedrooms, one of which served as Oscar's sanctuary over the last two weeks. Since news of his indiscretion hit the Internet, tabloids, and TV news, Oscar hadn't been seen in public. The rumor circulated by the paparazzi was that the pop star was on suicide watch. It was more than just a rumor.

"Is he any better?"

"I think maybe worse." Jorge Lopez was Oscar's closest confidant. His official title was executive assistant; but for the past two days, he was simply the doorkeeper honoring Oscar's wishes to have no visitors. Jorge knew Oscar's agent, Melissa, could be a voice to which Oscar might listen. He was willing to go against his boss's wishes and give Mellissa a chance.

"I need to talk with him." Melissa insisted.

"The only person he's been willing to let into the room was his mom and that was only after she nearly beat down his bedroom door," Jorge cautioned.

"At least I need to try."

"I hope you have some good news for him. He really needs it."

"I have news. It's up to Oscar if it is good news or not."

"Good luck." Jorge left Melissa to talk herself into the fortress.

Oscar's 12-year rise to stardom was a rags-to-riches story. For much of his childhood, Oscar lived on the streets of Bogota, Columbia. When Oscar was only twelve years old, his uncle recognized his talent and put him on a street corner to sing for pocket change from passersby. A Columbian record producer heard him one morning on the way to work and immediately was drawn to Oscar's voice. She took him under her wing, introducing him to voice coaches and record producers. His talent carried him out of Columbia and into the U.S. mainstream recording industry where he became an instant hit. His first album went multi-platinum. He had shown staying power with his first four albums hitting the charts at number one, each for over ten weeks.

The fear of returning to the life he once lived on the streets was driving Oscar away from the limelight and into the solitude of his bedroom. He hoped this horrible nightmare would somehow go away. In this same fear Victor saw an opportunity to gain an asset for Mouse Trap, an opportunity that brought Oscar's agent to be knocking on his door now.

"Oscar, open up; we need to talk," shouted Melissa.

"Go away. I don't want to talk to anyone."

"Oscar, its Melissa. I may have a way out of this."

"There is no way out of this. Go away!"

"Listen Oscar, there may be a way. Just hear me out."

After a three-minute silence, Melissa heard shuffling footsteps followed by a click. As she reached for the doorknob, she again heard footsteps, this time moving more rapidly. By the time she entered the room, Oscar had climbed back into bed and pulled the covers up over his nose. His eyes were barely peeping above the top of the blanket.

"Oscar, we need to talk."

"So talk," Oscar whimpered.

"Oscar, I need you to get out from under the covers so that we can have a serious conversation."

"I'm not turning myself in. I'm not going to jail. I'll do something drastic before that happens."

"That's why I'm here, Oscar. There may be a solution, but I want to talk with you face to face."

"But I don't…"

Finally, Melissa had had enough. If there was one thing she knew, it was how to make Oscar listen.

"OK, Oscar, that's enough acting like a little crybaby! Climb your ass out of that bed right now, or I'm going to pull you out by your ears!"

Slowly Oscar peeled the sheets away and scooted himself to the edge of the bed. He pulled his greasy hair out of his eyes and did his best to engage in conversation.

The movement caused a foul odor to waft in Melissa's direction causing her to wince. "Good lord, Oscar, how long has it been since you bathed?"

"I don't know. A week or so."

"When I leave here, job one is a shower. Got it?"

Oscar managed a subdued nod.

"OK, Oscar, back to the reason I'm here. Let's play 'What If' for a moment. What if there were a way that this whole thing could go away? What if the DA would drop the charges? What if the police no longer had the video? What if we could eventually get your endorsements back? What if we could say that this was all just a misunderstanding and that nothing really happened?"

At first Oscar was astonished at the prospect of this all being "fixed" but then convinced himself it was impossible.

"That will never happen. This is too big to go away," Oscar shook his head in disbelief.

"But what if it wasn't?" Melissa tempted.

"What does that even mean?" Oscar was starting to get frustrated because he knew the truth about what happened and making it all just go away seemed impossible.

"I don't know all of the details, but a man came by my office at the agency. He told me he can make it all go away—the charges, the video, the accusations, everything. He even said he could arrange for you to win a comeback award at the next big industry event."

"There's no way that's possible."

"But what if it were possible? Would you be interested?"

"Well, of course…but…what's the catch? What do I have to do?"

"I'm not exactly sure. At first the man said that he was just a fan and wanted to see you back on your feet. But then he noted that you may be asked to perform a favor from time to time."

Oscar cocked his head in confused suspicion. "What kind of favor?"

"He just said maybe record a song or make an appearance. It probably wouldn't be anything you aren't already doing."

Oscar shook his head emphatically. "No…this is crazy. It just sounds too weird."

"It sounds weird, but what if it's not?" asked Melissa.

Melissa's "what if" tactic seemed to be making inroads as Oscar walked over to the window and stared through a parting in the curtain for several minutes. He thought about his poor childhood in Columbia. He thought about being on stage in front of thousands of adoring fans. He thought about how much he loved the Tangerine Palace. He thought about how much he would HATE prison. After pondering his situation, he finally turned back quickly to Melissa.

"What do you think I should do?"

"I don't see any downside. To be honest with you, the alternative is prison, lost contracts; you'd probably lose this beautiful home."

Oscar peered around his palatial bedroom, bowed his head for a moment, released a heavy sigh, and then finally looked up at Melissa for the first time directly into her eyes.

"So, what do I have to do?"

"Just tell me you'll do it, and I'll pass the word along. I think it's worth a try to see if the guy will come through."

"OK. I'll do it."

And with those four simple words Oscar Tangerine became the latest addition to the substantial collection of assets held by Victor Youngblood's Mouse Trap.

"Jeremy! How was your week?!" Victor asked.

"It was an...interesting week. It was a good week and an interesting one."

Jeremy's interview was conducted in an ordinary Youngblood & Associates conference room. This time Victor had invited Jeremy into his public office, which was a large, comfortable space. Its contents included an imposing antique wooden desk, a small bar, two leather chairs, two leather couches, and a conference table that accommodated eight.

"Please have a seat, Jeremy. Let's talk." Victor saved the couches for his most personal conversations and this discussion with Jeremy certainly fit that category. "Jeremy, you said it had been 'an interesting week.' Tell me more."

Jeremy knew he was being tested and decided to play along with the charade. "I went back home to Abingdon, Virginia, to see my parents."

"That sounds wonderful, Jeremy. How were your folks?"

"They were actually doing well. Really, really well. You see, my dad owns a hardware store—just a local store, not a big chain. So, like many small business owners, he's been struggling. But as luck would have it, just this week he got a commitment for a large long-term order that is going to really put him back on good footing."

"That's terrific, Jeremy! I'm really happy for your dad."

"And it's not just my dad that had a good week. My mom writes a column for our local newspaper. She got a call from a syndicator this week who wants to start running her column in over 200 newspapers."

"Wow, Jeremy, you *did* have an interesting week!"

"Victor, I gotta say, you're good. I mean really, really good."

"I'm not sure I'm following you, Jeremy." Victor was a master at mind games and loved to pick and prod at new recruits to see what makes them tick.

"Rosenberg Electric. Savannah Richfield. I got the message; you guys have extensive capabilities. I am more than impressed. Thank you for helping my parents. They really needed it."

"I'm glad things seem to be looking up for them. Let's move on to why we're here. You've had a week to think about our offer, Jeremy. What's your decision?"

Jeremy cocked his head to the side and looked dubiously at Victor.

"Decision? What decision is there to make? When can I start?"

Victor broke into a huge smile, stood up from the couch, put his hand on the back of Jeremy's neck and pulled him close, now staring him in the face.

"You can start right now; let's go."

"Now? Uh...OK. Is there some HR stuff I need to sign or anything like that? I thought there would be..."

"We'll take care of all of that nonsense later. We've got a lot of work to do, and you're already behind."

Victor turned his back to Jeremy and walked to the rear of his office. He spun around, urging Jeremy to follow. "Come on; I said you're late."

A confused Jeremy took a few cautious steps toward Victor. "Where are we going?"

"We're going to my real office; come on." Victor pushed on a faux bookshelf, revealing a secret passageway.

Utterly confused, Jeremy was still not moving. "Your real office? What is this office?"

Victor disappeared behind the bookshelf, expecting Jeremy to follow.

"OK, I'm coming; hang on!"

His first view of Victor's office took his breath away. Whereas the warm, welcoming public office Jeremy had just left was dominated by dark wood paneling, a large maple desk, a floor-to-ceiling pecan bookshelf, and burgundy leather furniture, the room he was in now was filled with glass and polished stainless steel. The tranquility of the public office was replaced by the futuristic space that was nothing like Jeremy had ever seen.

"Welcome to my *real* office, Jeremy. Make yourself at home."

"This is uh…I've never…it's…"

His mouth still agape, Jeremy was unable to find the words to form a coherent sentence.

"I know it's a lot to take in, Jeremy. Let's start here at the desk. This is where everything is controlled. I call it my cockpit."

Still in stunned silence, Jeremy stood beside Victor, who had taken a seat in a streamlined white leather captain's chair behind the large glass-top desk.

"Let's start with the wall in front of me." Victor tapped once on the glass desk, which Jeremy learned was actually a control panel with two-dozen buttons and a keyboard. In less than a second the nine screens on the wall facing Victor had come to life, each with live feed from a news network broadcasting from somewhere around the world. Another tap on the desk selected the screen from which the audio feed was heard through speakers embedded in the office ceiling. Jeremy glanced down and saw that a large portion of Victor's glass desk had transformed into a video screen with the image synched to the audio feed.

"This is where I can view what's going on around the world. Every channel in existence is accessible here."

Victor clicked on the upper-left screen by tapping on his desk. He tapped again and the screen became a world map. He tapped on Europe, then Italy, then Rome, and a live news feed from Rome's Sky Italia network played live on Victor's wall and desk.

"That's amazing. I've never seen anything like this." Jeremy tried not to seem overwhelmed, but he was not succeeding. Victor would have been disappointed if Jeremy hadn't been blown away by the techno-wonders he was seeing.

"As you know, I'm hiring you to be a project manager. Over here I can get the status on every project." Victor motioned to the 25-by-12 foot glass wall on his right and again tapped on his glass desk.

JOHN FORD CLAYTON

The glass wall transformed into a grid of colored rectangles in red, yellow, and green. As Jeremy looked more closely, he saw that each rectangle had a project number and name with a collection of words, graphs, and photos. Jeremy's quick math estimated that there were over 30 projects represented.

"This is my project dashboard. I can get a status on every project with this wall. Green projects are going well, yellow projects are borderline, red projects are in trouble. I don't like red projects."

As with the TV screens, Victor could tap on his desk to pull up a particular project's status and the screen would appear on his desk.

"I'll show you how this works. Let's take this project titled Project Citrus. It concerns Oscar Tangerine."

"Oscar Tangerine? The pop star who was caught with the 15-year-old girls?'

"Allegedly caught, but yes, that's him."

"I don't understand. How is he a project?"

"I'm getting to that. Here's the video of Oscar's rendezvous with the teenagers, his text messages later that night, his e-mails to his agent, the status of Oscar's court date, a list of his product endorsements, the two that are about to drop him, the three new ones that will sign him a few months, the next number-one hit he's going to have, the public service campaign he's going to be the spokesman for, and his next girlfriend."

"I'm trying to keep up; but I gotta be honest, I'm totally lost. How do you have all of this information? *Why* do you have this information?"

"Perfect, if you said you weren't lost, I'd know you were lying."

Victor then turned off the project-status screen, restoring his wall to simple glass, and switched off the TV screens in front of him, returning peace and quiet to his office.

"OK, let's start from the beginning. Take a seat, Jeremy."

Jeremy walked around Victor's desk and sat cautiously in the curved stainless steel chair immediately in front of Victor. The chair was surprisingly comfortable, despite its odd futuristic shape.

"As we discussed in your interview, Youngblood and Associates is everything you've read that it is. It's among the world's largest and most influential marketing, public relations, lobbying, imaging, branding, and consulting firms. But you'll recall that I mentioned we had a more clandestine organization as well. That organization is called Mouse Trap."

Victor paused to let the name sink in to see Jeremy's reaction.

"Mouse Trap? So...like I'm guessing the reference is to catch someone or something by using some sort of bait...maybe?"

"Close. Let's walk over to the table."

Jeremy joined Victor at a glass and metal table a few feet away from Victor's desk. Victor pushed a button on the side of the table; and with a "whoosh," the top of the table flipped 180 degrees as Jeremy's confusion grew.

Jeremy wasn't sure the day could get any more bizarre—until it did.

"Are you serious?"

16

Jeremy stood in stunned silence trying to let his mind catch up with what his eyes were seeing. It was a reaction that Victor had seen dozens of times and yet one that still amused him.

"Not what you were expecting?" asked Victor.

"Not exactly; is that really a...?"

"Yes, it is."

Jeremy had been overwhelmed by how spectacular everything was at Youngblood and Associates. The lobby was adorned with glass and marble. The conference rooms and offices had leather chairs, wooden inlaid tables, and technology beyond anything he had ever seen. Victor's public office was the definition of class from floor to ceiling. His private office seemed to be set 20 years in the future.

The fact that he was now looking at cardboard and plastic in bright primary colors left Jeremy speechless.

"It's..."

Victor replied matter-of-factly, "it is the Mouse Trap board game by Hasbro. I'm guessing you probably played this as a kid?"

"Sure, everyone played Mouse Trap. But when you said I was going to work on a secret project called Mouse Trap, I didn't really expect...this."

Jeremy tried to muffle his obvious disappointment, but his eyes betrayed him. He never hid his emotions and this was no exception.

"That's OK Jeremy; that's the reaction I get from everyone the first time that they see it. It offers a nice contrast to everything else in this office doesn't it?"

Slightly nodding his head, Jeremy replied, "That it does."

Victor strode toward Jeremy and put his hand on Jeremy's shoulder in a fatherly gesture. "I understand your confusion, Jeremy; so let me explain. This game provides a perfect metaphor for everything the Mouse Trap program is about. I know it has probably been a while since you played this game but tell me what you remember about it."

Jeremy reached back into his memory to recall weekend game nights with his mom and dad. "I think the objective was to move your mouse from the start to the finish line while avoiding the mouse trap. Of course, building and operating the mouse trap is the fun part. That's what everyone wanted to do."

"Exactly, Jeremy! The mouse trap was the fun part! That's what we do here, the fun part! Let's walk through the board and I'll explain. We'll start with the mice." Victor picked up the red plastic mouse and held it in his open palm, right in front of Jeremy. "You were right; the objective of the game is for the mice to make it to the end of the board. The mice represent people trying to get from point A to point B."

"What kind of people?" Jeremy asked, still confused.

"All kinds of people; politicians, movie stars, athletes, business leaders, sometimes everyday average folks, depending on the situation."

"So, you want to catch them for what purpose?"

Victor held up a hand. "You're getting way ahead of me, Jeremy. We'll get to that in due time. Let's talk about the trap next, or as you called it, the fun part." Victor reached his hand into the small game board apparatus and placed his thumb and index finger on the crank. "As a reminder, here's how it works. I turn the crank, which engages this gear, which engages a second gear. That gear snaps the rubber band, which hits the swinging boot. The boot then kicks the bucket, which launches the marble zig-zagging down these stairs, ultimately leading to a chute that directs a marble to contact a vertical pole with a hand at the top. The contact with the marble causes the hand to nudge, knocking a second marble through a hole in the platform and down into a bathtub. The bathtub isn't level, causing the marble to roll to the other end and fall through another hole. Next, the marble lands on a lever, which launches a plastic diver into a bucket, which is on a pole with small notches supporting the cage. When the pole is contacted, the cage shimmies down the pole to capture the mouse waiting unsuspectingly below."

Victor glanced up to see Jeremy stroking his chin, clearly trying to understand the relevance of Victor's demonstration.

"Got it, Jeremy?"

Jeremy, clearly still not on board with the discussion, decided it wasn't the time to raise one of the hundreds of questions zipping through his mind. "Uh…yep, I…uh…got it."

Victor laughed heartily while slapping Jeremy on the back. "You gotta learn to lie better, Jeremy. We'll work on that. Here's the connection with the Mouse Trap. There is a single initiating event, the turning of the crank." Victor again turned the crank for effect. "After that, if the trap is properly constructed, you just sit back and watch it work until it ultimately captures the mouse. Our job here is to build the trap and to make sure that it is built in a way that we can turn the crank and watch. If we've constructed the trap correctly, we get the result we want without any connections back to our organization."

Victor struck a more serious, almost ominous tone. "Secrecy is one of our non-negotiable absolutes in Mouse Trap. When the mouse is caught, we don't want anyone seeing our fingerprints on the cage. We have a vast network of assets from which we can construct the Mouse Trap. We use it to manipulate the circumstances and people to meet our objectives. Your job will be to understand those assets and to deploy them so that all we have to do is turn the crank."

Jeremy sensed he was starting to get an inkling of Victor's analogy. "I'm getting closer to being on the same page with you or at least in the same book. Can you give me an example of how this might work in a real-world application?"

"Let's talk about your little Richfield College scheme. You constructed a Mouse Trap. Of course, you didn't know it was a Mouse Trap. You created the Facebook page and engaged Dr. Jefferson, who got students involved, leading to a larger outcry until the college president ultimately dropped the cage on Elijah Mustang, which was your primary objective. You turned the crank, but no one saw you turn it; and you got results. That's what we do on a much more significant scale."

Jeremy's eyes began to light up when his personal experience was introduced into the analogy.

"So you are going to pay me to do this every day? I mean, this will be my job?"

"It will indeed."

Jeremy flashed his trademark grin and exclaimed, "That's freakin' awesome! Tell me more!"

Victor pointed to the game board. "Take a look at the square that the cage is on. What does it say?"

"Cheese Wheel.'"

"You see, Jeremy, the mice love their cheese. They're so focused on getting the cheese that they don't see the dangers around them. One of the key facets of Mouse Trap is discovering what someone's cheese is and luring that person to the Cheese Wheel. Some people's cheese is obvious: money, power, fame, comfort; but other people have their own unique taste in cheese. It is our job to find out what that is."

Jeremy, now fully invested in the analogy, pointed to the board and counted to himself "There is one thing I see. There are 30 or so spaces on the board but only one where the cage actually falls. I'm guessing a part of the Mouse Trap program is trying to lead the mouse to that one square?"

Victor cocked his head in surprise and removed his glasses. "Brilliant question, Jeremy! Let's discuss the board. You are correct. There is only one square where the cage falls. But what if that's not the case? What if the board could change?"

Victor reached under the table and pushed a button. Jeremy quickly realized that this was not a normal plastic-and- cardboard board game. When he pushed the button, the Mouse Trap's components began to move. The stairs shifted a few inches to the left. The marble chute moved in unison, as did the foundation holding the cage so that the cage was suspended above a different square.

"You see, Jeremy, the trap can change..."

Victor again pushed a button, causing the game board's squares to morph. As Jeremy tried to comprehend what he was seeing, he realized the board wasn't made of cardboard but was actually a high-definition display rendered on the table.

A stunned Jeremy pointed to the table in disbelief. "You just...changed the board!"

"I did." Victor pointed to the board. "The square that used to say 'go back 4 spaces' is now the Cheese Wheel square. You see, there are more variables than just trying to lure the mouse to the cheese square. We can change the game."

Trying to reconnect with the analogy, Jeremy observed, "So, the mouse represents the people you are trying to influence. The Mouse Trap represents the different methods you have to do the manipulation. The board represents...I'm not sure what."

"Think about it, Jeremy. Where does the world happen? Where do actors, politicians, and CEOs function?"

Jeremy unconsciously scratched his head, stared off into space trying to find the words to respond to Victor but came up blank. "I don't know. I'm stuck on this one."

"In the culture, Jeremy. The game board represents the culture. A static game board represents a culture that we must accept. A game board that can shift represents a culture that can be influenced."

"Or...manipulated?" An enlightened Jeremy was beginning to understand Mouse Trap and could see its significant potential.

"Or manipulated," Victor repeated, raising an eyebrow, impressed with Jeremy's level of engagement and quick grasp of the Mouse Trap.

"But how? We discussed culture in civics, sociology, and a couple of other classes; and I know that the culture is always changing, but I never understood how."

"We have many tools to address culture, but it is complicated and will take a while to unpack. Don't worry, Jeremy, I have some of my most trusted staff ready to bring you up to speed. Based on how quickly you've grasped concepts today, I have a feeling it won't take long."

"Awesome. When can we start?"

"Before we go to the next step, Jeremy, we need to have one more critical conversation. Everything you're going to hear about Mouse Trap, and much of what I've already told you, is highly confidential."

Still looking at the board, Jeremy spoke almost under his breath, "I understand. I won't say a word."

Victor took a step closer to Jeremy, catching his attention. He peered into Jeremy's eyes with his most steely gaze and continued his warning.

"You really don't understand, Jeremy. That's why I'm trying to convey this information as clearly as I can. You cannot speak about anything you do here regarding Mouse Trap. You can't tell friends or family. Much of what we do here is a matter of life and death for everyone involved. Do you understand, Jeremy?"

Jeremy, now feeling the fear that Victor was hoping to instill, was more resolute in his reply.

"Yes, I do understand. However, people, like Mom and Dad, and my fraternity brothers will ask what I do here. What do I tell them?"

"We have that covered."

Victor handed Jeremy a folder labeled *Project Manager Job Description* containing a benign listing of duties such as marketing, lobbying and public relations.

"Everything you can say is in this folder. Anything beyond what's here is confidential. Jeremy, I need to make sure that you understand. This is the most important discussion we've had today."

Jeremy insisted, "Yes, I understand."

With Jeremy's third response, Victor became a less ominous and again slapped Jeremy on the back.

"Great! Now I have something to show you."

As Victor returned to his desk, immediately behind him was the large bookshelf that doubled as the secret passageway to his public office where the conversation began. To his right were the screens that provided a status of each project. Immediately in front of him was the bank of TV monitors with world news feeds. To his left was a large, innocuous frosted glass...until Victor pushed a button.

As the frosting dissolved from the glass, Jeremy's mouth opened in disbelief. He didn't think this day could get more jaw dropping, but he was wrong.

"What...is all of that?"

"That...is Mouse Trap."

The clear glass revealed a vast warehouse-like work area that was configured in pods. Victor's office was situated 20 feet above the floor overlooking the 500-foot by 400-foot work area.

"Technically, that's only part of Mouse Trap. We have offices in other locations, but this is the nucleus of Mouse Trap." Sensing Jeremy's understandable confusion, Victor explained, "You saw on the opposite wall the ongoing projects. What you see below us are the teams who are making those projects happen. The work area is organized in pods so that each team can freely collaborate. Each work area has a series of workspaces arranged in circles, with an open area in the middle for team meetings. The pods vary in size, based on the size of the team. There are 40 work areas, 20 project teams, and 20 divisions. That's where you'll be working."

Jeremy walked closer to the window, taking in the scene below. "So, I have one question—a thousand questions actually, but I have one main question right now: *Why?* Why do you have Mouse Trap? What is its larger purpose? Why would you want to influence politicians, actors, and whoever else is on that wall?"

"An excellent question Jeremy. That's going to take a while to fully explain, but here's the 40,000-foot answer."

Victor yet again executed a combination of taps on his desk and a four-foot diameter hologram of the earth was suddenly suspended in midair.

Looking underneath, as if there was some hidden magic, Jeremy asked, "Is there anything that desk won't do?"

"Of course there is; that's why we have people like you. But it will do a lot." Victor directed Jeremy's attention back to the globe. "This is a hologram of the earth rendered from over 10,000 images provided via satellite."

"It's very lifelike." Jeremy reached his hand to touch the hologram, but instead just passed directly through the image.

Victor then asked in his most contemplative tone, "Do you ever wish you could make it better, Jeremy? Do you ever wish you could make the earth a more just place, a fairer place, a more enjoyable place?"

"Yeah, I guess. To be honest, I don't think I've really thought about it at that depth."

"You will, Jeremy, because that's our vision with Mouse Trap, simply to make the world a better place."

Jeremy bought the altruistic explanation hook, line, and sinker. Of course, the key stipulation of such a grand vision is whose definition of "better place" wins out. Jeremy would find out soon enough.

"I'm not even sure what to say," Jeremy stuttered.

"That's OK, Jeremy, I've thrown a lot at you today. Let's move on to the next phase of your training. We have a lot of work to do and you're already behind!"

Victor returned to his desk and pushed a button, saying, "Zeke...Candi, he's ready."

And thus began Jeremy Prince's tutelage, which would be the start of a very wild ride.

"I supported the Republicans to take back the Senate thinking they would actually do something, not sit back and let the President continue to bully them into submission." Howard Finch exclaimed.

"You sound like you're surprised." Ted Beckett retorted.

"I *am* surprised. They said they would stand up to him and fix this screwed up country. I expected them to do what they said."

"You expected a dadgum politician to do what he said? Howard, that's a good 'un."

The LTJ Club to burst into raucous laughter.

"No offense intended, Elijah."

With a perfectly-timed deadpan voice, Elijah Mustang replied, "The only thing I'm offended by is that you still consider me to be a politician!"

And again, laughter filled the diner.

Every Wednesday morning at 7:00 a.m., the LTJ Club (Liars, Thieves, and Jokers) met for breakfast at the American Eagle Diner in Kingston, Tennessee. Comprised mostly of retirees, the LTJ gathering ranged from three attendees to 20, depending on doctor's appointments, honey-do lists, as well as arthritis and other various ailments— both real and imagined. On this April morning, attendance was on the high side at 16, including Elijah Mustang, who at 59 was among the youngest members of the club. Just back from his trip to Honduras, he was thirsty for some masculine adult conversation. As often as his schedule allowed he attended these breakfasts, a practice he started while running for Congress over 20 years ago. He used these get-togethers to gauge the local electorate's pulse. In the process, he made some of his closest friends.

"Say, Elijah, things sure have calmed down since the town was flooded with all of those news reporters."

"Yeah, that professor lady really raked you over the coals!"

"I'll take your word for it. To be honest, I barely knew anything about it. Just when everything was getting crazy, I was on a plane to Honduras; and I just got back two days ago. I didn't have TV, Internet, or cell phone coverage the whole time I was gone; so I didn't know anything about it until someone brought me a newspaper. It was kinda weird reading about myself and all of the terrible things I had done. I haven't had that many lies told about me since I was in Washington!"

The LTJ Club again burst into laughter.

"So, Elijah, was D. C. as screwed up then as it is now?"

"That's a good question. I thought it was broken when I was there, but it seems so much worse now. The parties are putting their thirst for power ahead of the country. If you have a 'D' after your name you hate everyone with an 'R' after their name, and vice versa. The thing that makes me the angriest is that some of our leaders are talking about how terrible America is, about how we're greedy and unfair. About how we aren't as good as other countries, about how we should be more like country X or country Y. I am absolutely convinced that America is the greatest country that has ever existed! You know what makes it that way? Y'all make do. Normal, everyday people—not politicians or CEOs or movie stars. America is great because of y'all."

A couple of "Amens" could be heard from the gathering.

"I spent the last three weeks in a tiny town in Honduras where people were really struggling just to survive. You know who was there to help? Americans! There was a doctor from Nebraska, a dentist from California, a team of a dozen from Georgia building a home, and three engineers from Delaware digging a well. All those folks were there volunteering their time and talents to help people they didn't even know. That's what America is really all about. Americans care!"

As Elijah spoke, he began to choke up because his words came from a belief in America that was deeply rooted in his soul.

"That's what makes America the greatest country that has ever existed!"

It was a rousing, spontaneous speech that brought not only the LTJ club to applause but also many of the other diners who had turned to listen to Elijah. The applause embarrassed Elijah as he didn't realize he was speaking so loudly and passionately and didn't want to bother those around him.

"I'm really sorry, folks. I sometimes get carried away. I didn't mean to disturb you."

His genuine apology only cemented his credibility with his audience, who again responded with both laughter and applause.

Sitting in a corner booth was "that professor lady," Dr. Molly Jefferson, sipping a cup of coffee and hoping no one would recognize her. Already embarrassed at how the protest she instigated had spiraled out of control, she wanted to crawl under the table after getting a glimpse at the real Elijah Mustang. Her earlier suspicions were confirmed. She had been wrong about Elijah—really, really wrong. She vowed that someday she would make efforts to apologize but just not today and not in such a public place.

17

Victor handed Jeremy over to the tutelage of two of his most trusted team members. One mentor was Zeke Gibson, who at age 76 was the only person with the organization longer than Victor. He served as second in command with the title of Chief Operations Officer. Zeke knew almost as much as Victor did about Mouse Trap's inner workings, but Victor knew even that was debatable.

The other mentor was Candi Gates, who developed much of the social media presence that Victor had implemented in the last five years to both harvest from and plant in the digital world. Social media was an enhancement that multiplied both the reach and speed of Mouse Trap many times over. Young, brilliant, and brash, Candi had become indispensable to Victor. She was among the few who could get away with questioning Victor's instructions, at least to a point.

Settling into one of the work pods Jeremy had viewed from the perch above in Victor's office, he couldn't help but gaze up and wonder if he was being watched. A deep tinting on the windows ensured his question would not be answered, just as Victor had designed it.

"Jeremy, I have been excited to meet you and am anxious to start your training. Victor told us all about how you singlehandedly disrupted the college graduation with a counterfeit Facebook account. That was very impressive."

Zeke's words were intended to bolster Jeremy's confidence and calm any nerves lingering within him. Zeke's role was to be the kind elder statesmen.

Jeremy lowered his head humbly and replied, "Thank you. It was really..."

"Yeah, it was a really big stinkin' deal. Whoopee, you made a fake Facebook account. We have 30,000 of 'em." Candi's self-appointed role was to keep Jeremy humble and her scolding was the first step in that process. She made sure Jeremy knew she was unimpressed.

"What? You have 30,000 Facebook accounts?" A confused Jeremy looked to Zeke for confirmation.

Zeke knew he had to get the tutelage back on track quickly. "OK, let's slow down a bit. We have a lot to cover."

Candi then spoke in a mockingly simplistic voice, "Yes...we...will...talk...really...slowly...so... that...you... will...understand."

Accustomed to Candi's antics, Zeke ignored the taunts and continued, "Let's start with the basics of how

Mouse Trap works. Everything begins with Victor. He identifies an objective that is to be accomplished. Let's say, for example, he wants to get a rock star out of a difficult legal situation. You have probably heard of Oscar Tangerine and the legal issues he's facing. Let's say Victor directs us to address Oscar's predicament. In the metaphor of the Mouse Trap board game, Oscar would be the mouse, as he is the target. In our team's terminology, Oscar would be the project. A member of the Mouse Trap organization would be given the responsibility of project manager for Oscar Tangerine. Every project has a code name. The Oscar Tangerine project is named..."

"Project Citrus" Jeremy interrupted. "Victor discussed that with me."

"OK, Jeremy, you are already ahead of me." Zeke said, surprised by Jeremy's recollection.

Candi just rolled her eyes.

"My job offer said I'd be a project manager, so I guess this is the kind of stuff I'll be doing."

"So listen closely, we don't want to have go to through this again." Candi didn't miss an opportunity to admonish the young apprentice.

Working to stay on task, Zeke continued, "The project manager must determine how to carry out Victor's direction, how to construct a plan to achieve the objective. This plan is represented by the Mouse Trap's many moving parts. In the Mouse Trap game, these parts are the crank, the wheel, the bathtub, the ball, and the other parts of the contraption that ultimately catch the mouse. The key is in disguising the Mouse Trap so that the Trap's constructor as well as the initiator who turns the crank are concealed. In other words, we don't want anyone to be able to associate anything we do with anyone in this organization. That is a prime objective of the design and construction of a Mouse Trap."

"OK, I think I'm starting to understand, but what could you do about a guy like Oscar Tangerine who got caught in bed with teenage girls? Is Mouse Trap just like a legal thing to get him out of trouble?"

Zeke looked askance at Jeremy, while Candi just chuckled.

"He has *so* much to learn," Candi remarked in a demeaning tone.

"And that's why we're here, to teach him," Zeke responded.

Recognizing he had apparently asked a dumb question, Jeremy assumed a deferential tone. "I'm sorry; I guess maybe I don't understand. I'll withdraw the question and try to listen better and learn more quickly."

"It's OK, Jeremy; we're just getting started. It takes everyone a while to fully grasp the breadth of Mouse Trap. So, back to your question, Mouse Trap is not like a 'legal thing.' We have very extensive capabilities. Just about anything you could imagine is at our disposal. Let's address Mr. Tangerine's situation. We have to start by getting him beyond the legal dimension of his predicament, but that's just the beginning of the process. His story has been on TV and radio, and throughout social media, so we'd need to restore his reputation. After that, the ultimate end game would be—*and this is really important for you to understand*— to make him an asset for Mouse Trap."

Zeke paused to let everything sink in.

"Candi, this is a good time to explain our social media resources since we have already broached that subject."

"OK. I promise I will talk very slowly so Super Boy will understand."

By now Jeremy was expecting Candi's cutting remarks; so he simply grinned, nodded and offered, "Super Boy thanks you."

Candi began, "Over the past five years, we've developed a very extensive social media footprint. As I mentioned earlier, we have 30,000 Facebook accounts, which have 500,000 unique friends. We estimate that friends of those friends reach over a hundred million people. We can use those accounts as outlets to publish videos, news stories, surveys, basically anything we want to push. Let's stick with the Oscar Tangerine example. Let's say, hypothetically speaking, that the district attorney announced that a mistake had been made, that Mr. Tangerine was a victim of mistaken identity, and that he's Innocent. We could push that story on the timeline of 30,000 people with one click of a mouse. Within minutes, users would start re-posting and liking the story; and within a few hours, it would be on over half the users' timelines in the U. S. Now that's a powerful tool."

"Wow, that's incredible." The wheels in Jeremy's head were whirling. "What you could do with that is... unlimited."

"And Facebook is just the start; we have 20,000 accounts on Twitter, 15,000 on Instagram, and 5,000 on Snap Chat. We have hundreds of others on emerging social media platforms. If we need a story to get hot, we can make that happen."

"That's amazing. I see why you thought my one little Facebook account was underwhelming."

"What Candi showed you is just the tip of the iceberg. Social media is just one of 20 divisions that makes up the Mouse Trap organization."

"And I thought Victor's office was amazing. This is unbelievable. What are the other 19 divisions?"

Over the last 70 years, Mouse Trap's organizational structure had morphed and evolved into the current 20 divisions. Each division served as a resource for project managers to use in constructing a Mouse Trap.

Zeke continued. "Until being overtaken in recent years by social media, the Network and Cable News Division provided the broadest and most timely avenue for us to deliver messages to the masses. It is still a critical resource for Mouse Trap and provides us the ability to directly influence news reporting through both network and cable platforms. We have cultivated relationships over the past 40 years that have yielded assets deeply entrenched throughout all levels of the news media hierarchy."

Candi showed Jeremy an example of how this resource was used. "We have an ongoing project named 'Project Blindfold.' Its purpose is to suppress reporting on the growing Middle Eastern movement known as ISIS. Just a few days ago, ISIS posted this video on a series of social media accounts they operate."

Candi pulled up a 10-minute video that showed 30 men dressed in black with black hoods covering their faces, each escorting a blindfolded man in an orange jumpsuit. The video showed a ceremony culminating with each black-clad man wielding a large knife, grabbing the hair of his escort and calmly sawing off his head.

"That is terrible!" Jeremy couldn't help but cringe and look away from the screen.

"It is terrible. And it happens at least once a month, sometimes more often," Zeke lamented.

Candi then changed the video to a series of short snippets. "These are the news reports from the following day for all of the news networks and over a dozen cable news outlets. Not a single one of them reported on this heinous act."

Jeremy was shocked. "What?! Why not?"

"Because they were told not to."

"Who told them not to show this atrocity? This is awful!" Jeremy was trying to get the images out of his mind, but some things just can't be unseen.

"A producer told them not to. An executive told the producer. Someone else told the executive. Someone told that person and so on. It's a fairly complicated communications chain with several moving parts," Zeke explained.

"Kind of like a Mouse Trap." Jeremy had the first of many ah-ha moments that would come on this day.

"Yes, Jeremy, kind of like a Mouse Trap."

"I can't help but ask *why*? Why wouldn't we want this reported?"

Zeke knew this question would come. It always did. His role up to now as the grandfatherly advisor provided the perfect contrast for the serious lesson he had to impart to his curious student. He pointed to Jeremy and mustered his most authoritative voice.

"That...is a question that can *never* be asked! We DO NOT EVER ask *why*. We each see only one small tile in the mosaic. Victor is constructing the complete picture and our job is to trust that he knows what he's doing. Do you understand?"

"Yes...I guess." Jeremy's response was less than convincing.

"We are going to spend a lot of time together, Jeremy; and we are going to discuss many topics. The most important message I am going to convey to you is to trust Victor and never ask *why*. With the limited perspective you will have, at times you will not understand some of the things you will be asked to do. You must not only accept but also embrace the assignments you are given. I am going to ask you again, *Do you understand, Jeremy?*"

"The honest answer is that I don't totally understand, but I'll accept it and strive to understand."

Zeke was pleased with Jeremy's honest answer. "That's fair enough. We're making progress. Let's move on to the next division, Movies and TV. Influencing popular culture and ultimately public perception and opinion by using movies and television is an essential capability for Mouse Trap. This division is responsible for inserting messages, both overt and subliminal, into entertainment channels. This division may also influence the casting in major productions to include or exclude certain actors to support Mouse Trap's initiatives. The Movies and TV Division's actions typically take longer to take root than social media or cable and network news, but the results are more enduring as they often enter the lexicon of pop culture and may be referenced for decades.

"Next is the Public Education Division. The public education system has been a valuable tool in influencing generations of Americans. Many opportunities are available including determining what curriculum to teach and what to omit; which initiatives are funded and which are starved; and what social messages, such as accepting and rejecting certain lifestyles, are advanced to students. The growing federal Department of Education is an effective resource for Mouse Trap as a highly centralized delivery avenue, providing a more streamlined way to reach young minds. The most recent initiative Mouse Trap is sponsoring is a national standardized curriculum, which when fully implemented will provide a vehicle to deliver tailored messages to millions of students.

"Next we have the University Education Division. In earlier Mouse Trap organizational structures, a single division was responsible for Education; but Victor created separate divisions for Public Education and University Education a decade ago. He recognized that both the ways these divisions are influenced, as well as the benefits Mouse Trap derives from them, are profoundly different. The University Education Division has proven immensely successful in reaching easily influenced young adults, who often have unfettered adulation for their college professors. University students also provide a significant army of foot soldiers who can be quickly mobilized to protest almost any issue with a modest nudge."

Jeremy knew his job was to listen but felt compelled to interject, "So, with the thing I did at Richfield College, I unwittingly used some of the same approaches you do with Mouse Trap?" Having just graduated from college himself, Jeremy had a deep understanding of how easily many college students could be manipulated.

"Yes, your work at Richfield was what first brought you to Victor's attention," Zeke affirmed.

"That's crazy!" Jeremy exclaimed,

Zeke continued his tutelage. "Next is the Executive Branch Division. Through decades of diligent efforts, Victor now has a means to influence every U. S. government agency, including the White House. This division provides Mouse Trap with capabilities that cascade throughout multiple divisions. The Executive Branch Division also provides a way to influence regulatory decisions affecting millions of individuals and billions of dollars.

"Next we have the Legislative Branch Division. It maintains a meticulous file on every U.S. senator and congressman with an assessment of our ability to influence each. Although this division requires significant effort, its capacity to affect the U.S. is far-reaching. Among the resources the Legislative Division uses as leverage are the addition or reduction of campaign funding and its near total control of the House and Senate's ethics investigatory powers. Mouse Trap also works to ensure that legislators who can be most influenced are those in the most important leadership roles in both the House and the Senate. Lastly, the Legislative Branch Division plays a key role in screening prospective political candidates, favoring those viewed the easiest to influence and suppressing the more independent thinkers.

"Next is the Judicial Branch Division. The nine Supreme Court Justices serve in the premier judicial branch and are the frequent targets of Mouse Trap initiatives; however, there are also 13 federal judicial courts ranging from 6 to 29 judges; 89 federal district courts, and thousands of state and local courts in which most decisions are made. The Judicial Division's responsibility is to influence court decisions to meet Mouse Trap's objectives. One of this division's most effective tools is prosecutorial discretion, whereby a single, well-positioned individual can make important judicial decisions."

"So, I'm guessing the Judicial Branch Division is working on Project Citrus?" Jeremy asked.

"You might be hearing breaking news in the next few days that Mr. Tangerine's fortunes have recently taken a turn for the better," Zeke said provocatively.

"We'll next discuss the Corporate Policy Division. Over the last decade, corporate legal and human resources avenues have been valuable tools in advancing Mouse Trap initiatives. Working in conjunction with the Judicial Division, targeted cases are decided, establishing legal precedent. Those cases are discussed in heavily attended corporate conferences and documented in business journals, resulting in revised corporate policies. Businesses are motivated by the prospect of avoiding lawsuits and potential multi-million dollar settlements. Initiatives such as diversity and social justice have achieved corporate inroads through these Mouse Trap actions, which impact tens of millions of Americans.

"One of our stealthier groups is the Technology Division. Many organizations (including IBM and the

U.S. military) and individuals (including Steve Jobs and Al Gore) have been credited for the technological advances seen over the past 40 years. However, a completely surreptitious entity that deserves as much credit is Mouse Trap. Mouse Trap had a major role in developing the Internet, which connected computers around the world, providing a valuable resource that serves Mouse Trap's data-collection needs. Mouse Trap's hands-on participation in advancing e-mail technology has allowed for including a back door to intercept any e-mail anywhere from anyone to anyone. Cloud computing is the most recent technological trend that Mouse Trap supports. With individuals and businesses adopting this emerging technology at breakneck speed, critical information that was formerly securely stored on individual personal computers or corporate servers is now readily accessible with the tools and capabilities that Mouse Trap employs. Other advancements in which Mouse Trap has played a major role include wireless technology, such as cell phones, smart phones, and Bluetooth, each with embedded covert technology designed by and for Mouse Trap."

"So, now I understand how you connected me to Richfield."

"With all due respect, Jeremy, you don't really understand how we did that; but you are correct to assume the Technology Division played a role," Zeke tried not to sound condescending.

Jeremy made a mental note to further research the Technology Division archives to understand how he was discovered.

"Next is the Health Care Division. The U.S. general population understandably sees health care as a means to treat injuries and illnesses; but to Mouse Trap this division has great utility in carrying out some of the more challenging assignments. Mouse Trap is involved in many cutting-edge medical advances, which can be used to both reward allies and punish enemies. Mouse Trap is also involved in macro-social engineering initiatives, such as directing Medicare decisions on which end-of-life treatments are offered to an aging populous. Mouse Trap also plays a major role in the abortion industry, not for the purposes of women's rights but more for population-control measures to weed out those deemed least likely to contribute positively to society. The recently passed Affordable Care Act provided ideal inroads for Mouse Trap's access to health care decisions as well as health care information. The Health Care Division worked with the Technology Division on designing the Affordable Care Act web portal to provide an easy means for Mouse Trap's information gathering."

Jeremy worked hard to suppress his instinct to ask *why*. For the time being, he succeeded.

"Next is the Science Division, which has waxed and waned over the past 40 years. It is currently enjoying a renaissance as Mouse Trap has successfully ushered in what Victor calls a new age of enlightenment. Much of the public, particularly those under 30, are convinced that anything attributed to science and/or said by scientists is by definition true. Mouse Trap capitalized on this phenomenon by advancing concepts such as man-caused climate change, alternative energy, and science-based arguments for the universe's origin. The Science Division works to promote the notion that these are topics of settled science and not open for debate.

"Much like the Movies and TV Division, the Sports Division delves into many facets of popular culture. Mouse Trap developed deep ties into the governing bodies of both college and professional sports, providing opportunities such as deciding which cities are awarded professional sports franchises and where league championships and all-star games are held. The Sports Division has also cultivated lasting relationships with those closest to many of the country's biggest sports stars and uses them as a resource for shifting public opinion.

"Whereas Mouse Trap divisions such as Sports, Music, and Movies and TV tend to have the most success influencing younger and more progressive individuals, the Talk Radio Division succeeds at reaching an older, more conservative following. Talk radio is more difficult to influence; but when it is the results are significant. Talk radio hosts hold great sway over their listeners, who typically believe what they hear to be true. Any success Mouse Trap has in reaching this audience often yields lasting benefits.

"The Financial Division deals with the U.S. banking and finance infrastructure, including Wall Street, the Federal Reserve, and the U. S. tax system. We'll save those details for a later discussion. Zeke was intentionally vague about the actions of this key division as it was actually the center of the Mouse Trap universe and the real reason for its existence. It was a reality that Zeke knew Jeremy was not ready to hear.

"When project managers need to reach beyond the boundaries of the U.S., they typically engage the International Issues Division. This division has been responsible for initiatives ranging from the mundane through regime change. It is a resource that has grown in responsibility over the past 20 years as economic globalization has taken hold.

"Akin to the Sports Division, the Music Division deals with music production companies as well as individual artists. Without their knowledge, many artists have been cultivated to be assets for Mouse Trap. Much like the Oscar Tangerine situation, musical artists disproportionally get themselves in sticky situations that require outside help. Mouse Trap is eager to offer help in exchange for future consideration. Over 50 such artists in all music genres are indebted to Mouse Trap and are considered assets.

"Next is the Religion Division. A general truth about Mouse Trap is that it thrives in situations involving a highly centralized command and control structure with a small number of individuals holding great power over many followers. This truth is most evident in the Religion Division. Mouse Trap has selected personnel for key leadership positions in the most centralized religions and denominations. In many, Mouse Trap assets now hold majority positions on boards, councils, and conferences. In these roles Mouse Trap can influence doctrine, the assignment of clergy, and the acceptance and rejection of various social beliefs.

"The Original Content Division is the most creative Mouse Trap organization. It is assigned a broad set of responsibilities. With facilities in three locations, it boasts a movie studio responsible for creating videos, including many loaded on social media platforms such as YouTube and Facebook. Original Content also employs songwriters who embed key messages in songs assigned to Mouse Trap's musical assets. This division is also responsible for creating the images seen on the thousands of bogus social media accounts Mouse Trap owns. This division has perfected the ability to create computer-generated images that look just like high-resolution photos. This advancement provides a means to create social media accounts without using photos of actual people.

"The Special Projects Division receives assignments that don't fit into any of the other 19 divisions. Its primary asset is its versatility as it may address broad topics such as influencing military decisions, the arts community, and state-level elections."

When Zeke had finished describing the Mouse Trap organization, Jeremy deeply sighed and slumped into his chair. "This is overwhelming. And the public has no idea they're being...*manipulated*?"

Zeke sensed a discomfort in Jeremy that he knew he needed to quickly suppress. "I'm not sure they'd want to know, Jeremy. I would argue that they are better off with Mouse Trap in place than if everything happened randomly and without purpose or direction. With Mouse Trap we can manage the country's affairs."

"We can make the world a better place," Jeremy mumbled.

"Exactly," Zeke responded, believing his student was learning.

"I wasn't stating that as a fact. I was repeating what Victor said. He pulled up his hologram of the world and said that Mouse Trap's purpose is to make the world a better place."

"It is indeed," Zeke reassured.

After a long pause while trying to absorb the volumes of information he'd been given, Jeremy decided it was time to move on.

"OK, what's next?"

"Do you realize that it is 10 o'clock? We've been doing this for over 12 hours. How about we call it a day and start fresh tomorrow?"

"Wow, I had no idea. I'm sorry to keep you two here so late."

Day one of the intense training of Jeremy Prince was complete. He'd been given information that rocked his world—information that was incredible, overwhelming, and more than a little bit dangerous. He was energized!

18

"For too long this country has been dominated by lily white, hetero-centric, Judeo-Christian, patriarchal one-percenters. Well, I've got news for you: America is much bigger and more diverse than those of you in the privileged majority."

The crowd erupted in applause as Mitchell McCoy, the junior senator from Connecticut gave the crowd the red meat—or more aptly for this assembled crowd, the green kale—it was longing to hear.

"I feel compelled to remind this majority that a large portion of this country is not Euro-Caucasian. America is and always has been multi-racial, multi-cultural, and multi-ethnic. We're white, black, brown, yellow and red;

and we're proud to be a melting pot society. That reality doesn't make us weak; it makes us strong!"

Another huge applause filled the Freeman Athletic Center on the campus of Wesleyan University, in Middletown, Connecticut. The 1,200-seat gymnasium was bursting at the seams, certainly well beyond the fire marshal's posted capacity. On this day, however, no one cared about such minutiae. On this day they were all gathered hoping to be among the first to hear a very important announcement. They would have to be patient.

At age 38, the brash and bold Mitch McCoy fashioned himself as the ultimate avant-garde politician, the new guy on the scene who would shake up Washington with fresh, contemporary ideas. His blonde-haired, blue-eyed boyish good looks supported the persona he hoped to portray. Reality was that even at such a young age, he was the ultimate D. C. insider.

The son of a four-term congressman and three-term senator, he attended the most exclusive Washington prep schools from pre-kindergarten through high school. He graduated—barely—from Georgetown University with a degree in political science. Upon graduation he worked for three years in the senatorial office of his father's best friend. Then he leveraged relationships to gain positions as a lobbyist and the CEO of three non-profits; ultimately, he was appointed to fill the vacancy of a Connecticut senator who was selected to serve as Secretary of Labor. He was elected to this senate seat in 2014, defeating his

Republican challenger by the slim margin of 50.2% to 49.8%.

In addition to his entrenched D. C. connections, McCoy was by all accounts a despicable human being. Although married to the same woman for 15 years, his philandering ways were among Washington's worst-kept secrets. His time in the non-profit arena was less than stellar. While CEO of the We Can Cure Cancer Foundation, he successfully increased the charity's donations by 15%; however, he also increased expenditures by 50% with extravagant parties; trips overseas; and a growing staff, consisting primarily of friends and colleagues with whom he wished to curry favor. Upon his exit as CEO, 98.7% of the Foundation's revenues went to expenses with only 1.3% devoted to actually finding a cure for cancer.

To round off his résumé, McCoy also had close financial ties with some of the world's most oppressive governments, including China, Saudi Arabia, and Venezuela—while railing against what he considered injustices in his own country. But none of that mattered to the crowd assembled for today's gathering. They were willing to set everything aside in exchange for the glorious words they were about to hear.

"To the majority that is heterosexual, please know that everyone isn't like you. The LGBT community is among the fastest- growing contingent in the country, and I'm happy to say among the most powerful!"

The third—of many more to come—standing ovation left the room euphoric.

"Who would have thought we could say that 20 or even 10 years ago! Just five years ago such a statement would have brought gasps of disapproval, not spirited applause. But the last time I checked, it wasn't five years ago it's today, and today, America is big enough, open enough, and welcoming enough for everyone!"

The remark brought equal parts applause and admiring laughter.

"A message to my friends in the South: America was founded on the solid bedrock of religious freedom and tolerance. That means we don't all have to believe in the same god or in any god at all if we choose not to do so! We can worship or not worship. We can attend the church of our choice or no church at all. For too long if our belief system didn't align with the majority, we were ostracized, proselytized, and vilified. Well, no more! We're sick and tired of being left outside the stained glass walls of this country, and today we're breaking down the door!"

At the conclusion of the latest standing ovation, a large majority of the crowd decided to remain standing, knowing more appealing words would soon come.

"To my fellow men who have enjoyed for so long a preferred spot in this country, a time of true equality is coming. Women are tired of earning 78 cents for every dollar we make. They are tired of continually banging into the glass ceiling over and over again. They are tired of being left out of the board room, the country club, and every other old boys' club that says, 'No women allowed.' We're here today to give a clarion warning that things are about to change!

"And finally let's talk about the injustice that is baked into our economy. We all know that for the first century of our country's existence the reality of slavery put millions in chains and bondage, while a privileged few lived in the master's mansion. In America's second century, the robber barons took advantage of the American workers' sweat and toil to make themselves millionaires. Even in our still-new third century, we have a modern economy that has led to the greatest economic gap in the history of mankind. It's not just the haves and have nots; it's the have-it-alls' and the have-nones."

Heads in the audience bounced up and down like bobble-head dolls on the dashboard of a Conestoga wagon navigating a cobblestone street. The sounds of agreement echoed throughout the auditorium with a chorus of "That's right!" and "Yes, it is!' For a few moments, three-syllable chants of "Mitch Mc-Coy" rang from the assemblage until the object of their adoration finally quieted them with raised arms. He had one more message to deliver, and the throng was eager to hear it.

"I have a magic number for you: $150 trillion. Let me repeat that $150 trillion. That's how much wealth has been accumulated and hoarded in this country, most of it out of reach of those who need it most. Much of it accumulated by those whose ancestors were slave owners, robber barons, and other members of the privileged elite.

"Let me put $150 trillion in perspective. We have around 300 million people in the U.S. If that wealth were divided equally, each person—every man woman and child—would have around $500,000. For a family of four, that's $2 million. Do you have your $2 million?" The crowd again compliantly replied with ear-splitting "nos!"

"We have an antiquated revenue system that focuses exclusively on income. Most of the millionaires and billionaires pay their accountants big money to avoid reporting any income and to avoid contributing to the greater good of society. Well, today I have a remedy for that problem. It's a remedy that will help those who need it most. Today I'm proposing to supplement our income tax system with a wealth tax. If you have over $1 million hoarded away, it will be subject to taxation. That wealth will be used to meet our country's greatest needs: the blight that so many of our inner cities have become in the care of our broken capitalistic society. The hunger and poverty that is so crippling to Appalachia. The mountain of debt that our country has accumulated. It could all be washed away by a simple change to the tax code, a simple change designed to achieve justice!"

Something about the word *justice* brought the crowd to a fevered pitch. The word had a ring to it that was music to the ears of the mostly 20-somethings gathered together.

"I can tell you from what I'm hearing here today and everywhere I've visited in the last three months, there's a passion and a hunger for REAL change. All this passion needs is a voice, a voice for the disadvantaged, a voice for the minority, a voice for the forgotten, a voice for the left behind."

A scream from the audience was heard: "You can be that voice!" followed by raucous applause and more chants of "Mitch Mc-Coy! Mitch Mc-Coy!"

Mitch put his hands up in mock surrender, laughed uproariously, and played along. "Me? You want me to be that voice?"

The applause and chants reached a crescendo, causing some of the more seasoned members of the gathering to cover their ears.

"*Me*? To be THAT voice?"

Applause and chants were non-stop.

Mitch raised his hand to briefly bring the noise down to a loud roar.

"Well, OK then, I guess there's just one more thing to say. Today, I'm announcing my candidacy for the president of the United States. I'll be your voice and I'll be your president!"

Even those outside the building could hear the roar, and some swore they saw the building quake. It was truly a historic day.

Just as Mitch was finishing his speech, Victor entered the Mouse Trap Command Center.

"I'm sorry I'm late. Did everything go as planned?"

"Yes sir," Colin replied.

"Did he follow the script?"

"Almost verbatim."

"Great. Thanks for the update."

"I really want to thank you for agreeing to meet with me."

"Where is the district attorney?"

"He was unable to make it today."

"But I don't understand; that's who requested this meeting. Who are you?"

"My name is John. I work with the district attorney on difficult situations such as yours."

"What do you mean by *difficult situations*?"

"That's what I'm here to discuss."

The meeting was held in a cabin at Gettysburg National Park. It was advertised as a private update from the district attorney with the two victims of the Oscar Tangerine attack: 15-year-old Brittany Powers, her best friend 15-year-old Maddie Simpson, and their parents. The fact that they were instead meeting with a stranger known only as John was more than slightly distressing.

"I don't like this, Momma."

"Sir, we're going to need some answers really quickly."

"That's why I'm here. I have a great deal of news to share with you, and I'm going to need you to stick with me to the end."

"Then you'd better start talking."

Maddie's dad, Ryan, had been the most vocal throughout the entire ordeal. When the incident first broke, he pushed the DA to allow him to make the rounds on the morning and entertainment news shows to skewer Oscar Tangerine at every opportunity. The DA finally convinced him that it would be best for everyone to lay low and let the legal process take its course. Ryan was also reminded that his going public would reveal his daughter's identity, an identity that had somehow been kept secret thus far.

"As I said, stick with me to the end. This first part is going to be the most difficult." John knew the news he had to deliver wouldn't be received well, so he struck his most compassionate tone to convey the seriousness of the matter. "I'm here to inform you that the DA has decided not to pursue criminal charges against Oscar Tangerine."

"*What?!* That's outrageous! He assured us that he would prosecute to the fullest extent of the law! This is crap!" Predictably, Ryan was the first to respond, pacing the room like a caged lion.

"Dad, I don't understand. What's going on?!

John continued, "Some of the key points of the case have changed. Somehow, the DA no longer has the video or the results of the rape kit. All of the empirical proof is gone."

"*What?!* How is that even possible?!" Ryan demanded to know.

"I still have the video on my phone. See, it's right here...Wait a minute, it's gone! Where did it go?" Maddie cried.

"I understand this is very difficult news to hear. I assure you the DA is devastated that this has happened. He doesn't have an explanation either. I can also assure you he exhausted all of his resources before coming to this difficult decision."

"I want to meet with him personally. I want to hear this from him, from his mouth," Ryan demanded.

"To be honest, he didn't think he could face you; that's why he sent me."

The full story of what happened to Brittany and Maddie was even more devastating than the partial account that was leaked to the media. Best friends and next door neighbors, they bought tickets to the Oscar Tangerine concert the minute they went on sale. The girls were excited to get tickets on the floor of the Wells Fargo Center in Philadelphia. After convincing their moms to drop them off at the concert four hours early, they stood in line to make sure they made it to the front row as soon as the doors opened.

The concert was even better than had they expected. Their exuberance caught the eye of a roadie who invited them backstage after the concert to personally meet Oscar Tangerine. At first he was friendly and polite, but then they heard the click of the dressing room door lock; and things got really bad, really fast. Oscar took his turn with Maddie first while stage hands forced Brittany to watch. Then Oscar turned his attention to Brittany as she cried, screamed, and pleaded to be let go.

After Oscar was done, some of the roadies took a turn as well before finally letting the girls go, threatening them to keep quiet and never tell anyone what happened.

The girls were strong and didn't heed the threats. Instead, they told their moms immediately. Their moms took them to the police, who took them for a rape test, which provided clinical proof of what had happened. After confronting Oscar Tangerine and his roadies, the police found that one of the guys had inexplicably filmed the entire incident on his smart phone. He had even sent the video to Maddie, apparently as a threat. It was a harrowing experience, especially for 15-year-old girls.

"I know you've all been through a lot; and I know this news is difficult to hear, but I want to help."

"*Help*?! How can you help?!" Maddie's mom was certain that nothing could help their deteriorating situation.

"The ordeal that you girls have endured has to be unbearable. I'm so sorry that you are going through this. I represent an organization that works to find injustices like you are experiencing and does what it can to make things right."

This characterization of John's organization couldn't be further from the truth, but experience had shown it was an effective means to put people at ease and, more importantly, for Mouse Trap to get what it wanted.

"*Make things right*?! How can you possibly make this right?!" Ryan demanded.

"I know we can't undo the horrible things that were done to you, but we want to try to make your situation more bearable."

"Exactly what did you have in mind?" Ryan asked suspiciously.

"You girls are freshmen in high school, correct?"

"That's right."

"Which means in a few short years you'll be looking at college?"

Both sets of parents instinctively lowered their heads. The blue-collar jobs didn't provide much margin for college savings, and the girls' post-high school plans were uncertain at best. It was a fact that Mouse Trap research had revealed about the families. Neither family had much in the way of finances and none of the parents went to college themselves.

"Maybe, but college is expensive. I'm not sure exactly what we'll do," Maddie lamented.

"What if college were taken care of, for both of you?"

"What do you mean?"

"What if we paid all of your college expenses? Tuition, room, food, books, everything."

"But why would you do that?" Ryan asked.

"Maddie and Brittany have been through more than any 15-year-old girls should ever have to endure. We can't do anything about prosecuting Mr. Tangerine, but we can make their circumstances a little better."

"Are you serious?" Ryan was still trying to grasp John's proposal.

"There's more. We know that your life is going to be difficult for a while. We'd like to help your parents out as well."

John handed each parent a money order for $100,000.

"What's this for?" Ryan asked.

"Expenses, pain, suffering. Your families have been through a lot."

Ryan sensed there had to be a catch. He got up from the table and walked over to the window, drumming his fingers on the cabin's roughhewn wall. "Pain and suffering? Is this like some sort of a legal settlement? Is this from Oscar Tangerine? If it is, we don't want any part of it!"

"Us neither! He can keep his filthy money," Brittany's mom, Faith, echoed.

"No, this is not coming from Oscar Tangerine. I know in this age of skepticism it is difficult to accept that an organization would have altruism as its core belief, but please know this is free and clear of Mr. Tangerine."

"What do we have to do to accept this?" Faith asked.

"Nothing, and I literally mean *nothing*. Over the next few days, the DA will be announcing that charges are no longer being pursued against Mr. Tangerine. To save face, the DA's office will not say that the evidence was lost, even though that's what really happened. At the same time, Mr. Tangerine will most likely proclaim his innocence and declare that these accusations were made up to make him look bad."

"So, he'll basically lie," Brittany said pointedly.

"Yes, he'll lie. The reality is there's nothing you can do about that. That's why we think it is best for your families to lay low for a few days. Since the girls are under age their names haven't been released to the public. There's no reason to put them through that now. Give it a couple of weeks to blow over and you can get on with your lives. Hopefully our contributions will help you all deal with this going forward."

John had brokered many similar deals and knew when he had made a breakthrough; he could see it in the eyes of the families. This time was no different. He spent another hour with the Simpson and Powers families, answering questions, ensuring them there was no fine print, and convincing them it was in their best interest to put this nightmare behind them and move on with their lives.

Another box in the Project Citrus to-do list was checked. The project was running smoothly, as most Mouse Trap projects did. Victor Youngblood wouldn't tolerate anything less.

19

Entering the American Eagle Diner, Ted Beckett shouted out his breakfast order as he passed by the counter: "OK Tracy, I'm feeling adventuresome today. I'll have biscuits and gravy, a side order of sausage—links not patties—and a large orange juice. High pulp, I like lots of pulp. I like to chew my orange juice."

Tracy shook her head and deadpanned, "Got it Ted, same thing you order every week."

The weekly meeting of the Liars, Thieves, and Jokers Club was in full swing by 7 a.m. with eight members already discussing the day's hot topics.

Ted Beckett plopped own in his usual seat on the back bench next to his pal Percy Glanville, who gave Ted a disapproving glare.

"Hey Ted, would you mind dialing back the manspreadin'? I feel threatened by your aggressive posture."

"What? What the heck's *manspreadin'*?" Ted asked curiously.

"C'mon Ted, you know what you're doing—manspreadin'; cut it out!" Percy demanded.

Ted looked at his comrades who had all eyes trained on him with serious expressions on their faces.

"*Manspreadin'*? Huh? You lost me Percy."

"Ted, I'm serious; I'm really startin' to feel real uncomfortable."

The other members of the LTJ Club maintained their serious demeanors, some shaking their heads at Ted in disapproval.

"Y'all are weird this morning." Ted decided to try changing the subject. "Hey, did y'all see the Vols got a commitment out of that running back from Georgia? He's supposed to be a five star."

"Ted, I'm sorry; but you leave me no choice. I am going to have to get the law involved." Percy walked across the diner to where Deputy Sheriff Yancey was eating with two of his fellow deputies. A brief conversation with a couple of knowing head nods led to the deputy sheriff putting on his hat and following Percy back to the LTJ Club's table.

Conjuring his most authoritative voice, Deputy Yancey approached the table and announced, "Ted, I'm afraid I'm going to have to ask you to cease and desist with the manspreading."

Percy shook his head in mock shame. "Ted, I really wish it didn't have to come to this; but I asked you myself very nicely and you ignored my request. We got a table full of witnesses that saw the whole thing." All heads nodded in agreement with Percy's account.

"I think Tracy spiked y'all's coffee this morning."

Deputy Yancey again interjected, "Ted, this is a serious issue; I need for you to comply with my request."

Starting to get a bit nervous, Ted finally showed some concern. "Now dang-it, guys, this ain't funny no more; come on, what're y'all talking about?"

Deputy Yancey then reached for his radio and pushed the button. "Headquarters, this is Deputy Yancey, I've got a 1764 dash 7 in progress. Yep, a manspreading. I'll be bringing in the suspect shortly; please get a cell ready."

Now fully concerned, Ted spoke in a high-pitched tone, "Suspect? Cell? What's going on?!"

"Ted, I'm going to have to ask you to stand and put your hands on the table."

His voice now cracking, "I ain't never been arrested for nothing, Deputy! I don't want to go to jail!" Now almost in tears, he pleaded, "Don't tell Alice, she'll be mad. Her mom warned her that I'd end up in jail; the last thing I want is for my mother-in-law to be right!"

Percy was the first member of the LTJ Club to crack as he let out an ear-piercing howl followed shortly by every other member of the club.

Ted still wasn't sure what was going on. "What are y'all laughing about? This ain't funny."

The deputy broke into a grin and turned to head back to his table. "Sorry Ted, the guys put me up to it." For the next three minutes, chuckles, snickers, tears, and snorts filled the diner as the latest LTJ Club prank was pulled off to perfection. As the raucousness finally started to die down, Ted was still confused. "OK, I got it; y'all played a joke on me, but what's *manspreadin'*?!"

This question led to another two minutes of laughter before Percy finally wiped his eyes and attempted an answer.

"We was talking about it before you got here, Ted. Manspreadin' is where a man sits down in a chair and spreads out his legs to take up more space than one chair."

"Huh? Well heck, that's just sittin'. Why is there a name for that?"

Percy continued, "Believe it or not, the New York police are giving subway riders citations and fines for sittin' too wide. Women have been complaining that men take up too much room and that they don't have anywhere to sit."

"Good Lord, this country is more screwed up than I thought," Ted cried.

"Elijah, have you ever heard of such nonsense? *Manspreadin'*!!"

The LTJ Club members always yearned to know what Elijah Mustang thought about every topic and had developed great skill in coaxing him to opine.

"I read about that last night, but there's way more to the story than what the article conveys." Elijah always had a way of connecting a smaller symptom with a larger national problem. "Number one, men should always give up their seats to ladies; so a core problem is that we men have lost our courtesy and dignity. Number two, people should handle these types of problems themselves and not get the police involved. Other men should set the manspreaders straight, or ladies should handle the situation themselves. Number three, I would think the New York Police Department has enough challenges that they don't need to expend resources on people taking up too much space on the subway."

The Club members nodded in agreement.

"Everyone is so hypersensitive that it's a wonder we ever get anything done in this country. We've become a bunch of victims waiting to whine about the latest transgression that someone did to us. We'd all be a lot better off if we just let stuff go, didn't get our feelings hurt so easily, and were willing to quickly forgive people if they do happen to make a mistake. We expend so much energy on these little offenses that really don't matter."

The rest of the club chimed in with the usual "Amens" in agreement with their de facto leader, Elijah Mustang.

Meanwhile, a couple of tables over the camera rolled, catching Elijah's every word. With some minor edits to add captions and context, the video would be ready to store with the others. In a few short days, they'd all be uploaded to YouTube, and Elijah would be in the national limelight for the second time this year. And this time, it would rock his world in ways he could never imagine.

The last three months had been a blur for Bobby Lincoln. It seemed like only last week he was blindsided by the gathering at the horse farm of his friend, Cam Calvin. At age 58 and in the final few months as governor of Kentucky, Bobby and his wife Christi were looking forward to leaving the political arena. He had planned to ease into retirement, maybe sit on a few non-profit boards, do some consulting, and give a few speeches. The last thing on his mind was starting a new campaign, especially one for president.

Bobby agreed to explore this option, but he made it clear to his supporters that his default position would be "no." He would only agree to run if he was convinced that no other candidate, or group of candidates, would carry the messages about which he felt most passionately.

Over the last 90 days, Bobby Lincoln had met with over 100 prospective donors. He heard pitches from over a dozen consultants who advised him on the viability of a Bobby Lincoln candidacy. He met with experts who gave him crash courses on the Middle East, nuclear power, the Chinese Yuan's projected direction, the emerging United Kingdom Independence Party, and countless other topics about which presidential candidates were expected to be experts.

Through this vetting process, he had also asked himself a series of candid questions. Did he think the country was going in the right direction? The answer was a resounding "no." Were there any prospective Republican candidates that he could enthusiastically support? He had to admit there were not. Could he be content if the country elected a candidate who would continue sending the country down what he considered to be a very dangerous path? Again, the answer was "no."

His name had been floated to the media months before, and he was already being included in polling data. Surprisingly, he was polling strong, usually second or third among potential Republican candidates.

As the days passed, his default "no" slowly turned to a mild "maybe." The last, and most important, voice he had been awaiting was his wife Christi. His friend since he was a Kentucky Wildcats' basketball player, and she was a Wildcats' cheerleader, Christi was his closest confidant. She knew him like no one else. As his candidacy became more promising, she saw a new excitement growing in him. His enthusiasm reached a new level when, late one night lying in bed, she gave her vote of approval by simply saying, "Bobby, I think you should do it." That was the last shoe he was waiting to drop. It was decided; he would run.

Now, standing at the edge of the stage, just outside the view of the standing-room-only crowd at the University of Kentucky's Memorial Coliseum, he was waiting for the long, flattering introduction to conclude so that he could stride across the stage and make his big announcement.

"...he' s a man of integrity, a man of honor, a man of courage, and a man who turned around this Commonwealth of Kentucky; ladies and gentlemen, please welcome to the stage the governor of our great Commonwealth, the Honorable, Bobby Lincoln!!"

The crowd rose to their feet and cheered for what seemed like ten solid minutes before Bobby finally urged them to return to their seats.

"Are we making any more progress on him?" Victor asked.

"A bit, but we're not close to comfortable yet. To be honest, I think he's going to be a problem."

Zeke knew that Mouse Trap should have had most of the top-tier candidates under control by now, but Bobby Lincoln was an exception. He had served quietly as governor and until three months ago was on no one's radar screen as a viable presidential candidate. Now, he seemed to be gaining significant momentum. Both Zeke and Victor were impressed by his announcement speech and saw that he would have broad appeal in both the primary and general elections. Bobby Lincoln was a force to be reckoned with.

"I have an idea how I'm going to deal with him." This pronouncement came as no surprise to Zeke. In all his years under Victor's leadership, he had never seen the man without a plan. This would be no exception.

"Great. I can't wait to hear it," Zeke replied.

"...we need to return this country to its strong, deep roots. Roots that were based on faith, family, and freedom, all of which are under attack by those who want to see this country unmoored from its 200-year foundation. And that's why I'm today announcing my candidacy for president of the United States."

20

"OK, Jeremy, so you've had three fun-filled 14-hour days of nothing but Mouse Trap. Everything clear? Got any questions?" Zeke asked.

Victor had already pinged Zeke in an early morning call to get a status on Jeremy's progress. Knowing his boss was in a hurry, Zeke felt pressured to quicken the pace of Jeremy's training.

"Crystal clear. No questions. Ready to move on to the next subject." Jeremy laughed to himself at the notion of everything being clear, but he knew his next level of enlightenment would only come through experience.

"Great, just what I wanted to hear. Let's continue. In Mouse Trap we work under a classic matrix organization. On the side of the matrix are the 20 divisions we've been discussing over the last few days. Today we're going to address the top of the matrix, which is staffed by 20 project managers. While the division managers do the *how*, the project managers do the *what*."

"So, 20 division managers and 20 project managers. Are they even by design?"

"Yes, Victor likes order. The 20-by-20 organization is his creation."

"I'm told I will be a project manager. If there are always 20 project managers, I assume I am taking the place of someone who left the organization."

"That's very perceptive Jeremy." Zeke lowered his head and mustered a slight shake. "But it's very tragic. Bryce Dunn was one of our most accomplished project managers. He was driving home from work a few weeks ago and apparently lost control of his vehicle and careened down a steep bank into the Potomac. He was killed instantly. He left behind a beautiful wife and two young daughters. Very, very sad."

"Wow, that's terrible." Jeremy wasn't sure what to say.

Suddenly, the door to the training room swung open, almost hitting Jeremy's outstretched leg. The mood in the room quickly turned with the ever-energetic Dakota Ethridge's entrance.

"Sorry I'm late. The morning meeting went a little longer than planned."

"Jeremy, I want you to meet Dakota Ethridge, one of our most experienced project managers. Dakota has been with us...remind me how long have you been on Mouse Trap, Dakota."

"Seventeen years, but it seems like 17 months. Time flies on Mouse Trap."

"Nice to meet you." Jeremy extended a hand. He already sensed more camaraderie in the first 60 seconds with Dakota than he had felt over an entire day with Candi.

"Great to meet you, Jeremy." Dakota, a six-foot-five, 250-pound hulk-of-a-man, thrust a hand to Jeremy. "Zeke and Victor have told me a lot about you. Glad to have you on the team. You're gonna love it here."

"Dakota, as you know, Jeremy is filling Bryce's position," Zeke reminded.

"Hell of a bad deal about Bryce. I still haven't gotten over what happened to him."

"Why don't you give Jeremy the basics of what a project is, how projects function, and what you do as a project manager?"

"How much time we got?" Dakota asked.

"As much as you need," Zeke replied.

"OK, hope you brought dinner."

"Just as a benchmark, we stayed here past 10 the night we talked about divisions; so Jeremy is accustomed to a long night of training."

"10?! We'd better get started," Dakota laughed.

"I'll listen as fast as I can," Jeremy assured.

"OK, let's go. With project management at Mouse Trap everything begins with Victor. The process starts when he asks for a meeting with you to discuss a new project. He'll tell you the name of the project; it will be something concise like Project Judas, Project Whiskey Mike Delta, or Project Citrus."

"That last one is for Oscar Tangerine." Jeremy noted.

Dakota pointed to Jeremy. "Smart kid, Zeke."

"Hand-picked by Victor, so you shouldn't be surprised," Zeke interjected.

Embarrassed by the compliments, Jeremy chimed in, "You guys know I'm sitting here, right?"

"Take the compliment and be happy. This job will humble you soon enough." Zeke had seen many young project managers overwhelmed by a Victor Youngblood assignment.

Working to get back on track, Dakota continued, "After you get the name of the project, Victor will tell you the project objectives, which are usually succinct and simple. Of course, simple doesn't mean easy to implement; simple means he makes it clear what he wants to accomplish. Then, your job is to put together a plan to meet those objectives. You usually will have between a week and a month to develop the plan, depending on the project's urgency and complexity. The plan must include what divisions you need to use, the amount of effort you expect from each, and the schedule you commit to meet."

"So, is this a written plan?" Jeremy asked.

Dakota looked disturbingly at Zeke, then struck an ominous tone in responding to Jeremy. "A written plan? Hell no, you have a one-on-one with Victor to describe the plan verbally. You are expected to be able to explain it without notes or PowerPoint slides. You just tell him what you're going to do."

The discussion made Zeke realize that he'd left out a fairly important tenet of Mouse Trap. "One thing I've failed to discuss, Jeremy, is our mandate that Mouse Trap is a paperless enterprise. When you walk through this entire floor, you won't find paper or even printers. Everything is done electronically and verbally."

"Wow, that will be quite an adjustment from college," Jeremy replied.

"There are a number of reasons for the policy but the primary one is security. We don't want someone accidently taking a work paper home that would expose a Mouse Trap initiative. I'm sure you can understand," Zeke cautioned.

Sensing another potential distracting segue, Dakota pressed on, "So, after you report your proposed plan to Victor, he'll give you one of three responses: a go ahead, a go ahead with a few tweaks, or a go back to the drawing board. Don't worry. Everyone's first few plans are always sent back for a re-do, so just be prepared."

"Thanks for the heads-up."

Dakota continued, "Let me use a contemporary project as an example. We have already mentioned Project

Citrus, so we'll use that. That's my project. Victor gave me the assignment about six weeks ago He explained that Oscar Tangerine had been caught raping two teen-age girls—all captured on cell phone video. It was only a matter of time before he would be indicted by a grand jury and it would be all over the news. Victor wanted to let that process play out; but before Oscar actually went to trial, he wanted us to intervene and get the indict-ment overturned. The objectives that Victor gave me for Project Citrus were to get the charges dropped, restore Oscar's status to better than the original, and secure him as an asset for future Mouse Trap deployment."

"Whoa, you mean he actually did it? He actually raped those girls, yet Victor wanted to cover for him?" Jeremy asked, astonished.

"He actually did it; and yes, that was my assignment from Victor."

Seeing the wheels turning in Jeremy's brain, Dakota allowed a few moments of silence to marinate in the room for Jeremy to process the information. After Jeremy stared down at the floor for a solid minute, his thoughts came quickly: "Why would Victor want to get this guy off if he really raped those girls?" Then he remembered that Zeke told him he couldn't ask *why*. Restraining from asking that question was going to be hard to deal with, but his desire to find out more about Mouse Trap and his project management future provided fuel for Jeremy to press on. Realizing he had zoned out for a few moments, he quickly raised his head conveying to Zeke and Dakota that he was again fully engaged in the tutelage. "OK, sorry about that; I'm with you. Let's keep going."

Dakota continued, "After I got the assignment from Victor, I had to develop a plan. The one that I pitched to Victor to meet Project Citrus's objectives involved 11 of the 20 divisions. With a few tweaks Victor agreed, and I was on the fast track to get everything implemented. Here's how we deployed the divisions. We had to start with the video evidence. For that we used the Technology Division, which can access email and Internet servers. We can also use wireless technology to delve into cell phone storage media. So, we had the Technology Division scour not only the police and DA servers but also the cell phones of the victims and their families, and deleted all instances of the video."

Jeremy was actually starting to understand the basics of Mouse Trap and was more than a little impressed. "That's amazing!"

"Next we deployed the Judicial Division, whose job was simply to get all charges dropped and Mr. Tangerine released. In fact, you should be hearing about it in the media very soon.

"Next we approached the victims to let them know that all charges against Oscar were being dropped. Remember, one truism about Mouse Trap is that nothing can lead back to us, so we had friends of friends of friends do the leg work for us. We used the Financial Division to incentivize the girls and their families to not pursue the matter any further. To sweeten the pot, we used the University Division to guarantee both girls scholarships when they graduated from high school. They were even given a list of colleges from which to pick.

"Next, we focused on reputation recovery. For that step, we will start with the Social Media Division pushing out stories about Oscar's being falsely accused. Every avenue, including Facebook, Twitter, Instagram, and SnapChat, will be used. The Original Content Division will create links to videos highlighting the injustice that was almost foisted upon Mr. Tangerine and emphasizing how he is the victim in this terrible misunderstanding. Within a day over 100 million people will have heard through social media outlets that Mr. Tangerine had been falsely accused.

"To supplement the social media campaign we'll deploy the Cable and Network News Division to create lead stories about Mr. Tangerine's innocence. Those stories will reach another several million homes. Within three days only the most isolated citizens will not have heard about Mr. Tangerine's false accusations."

Jeremy, recognizing that he had been one of the unsuspecting members of society for his whole life, began to question what was real and what was fabricated. "So, how many Mouse Trap projects have been completed in the last 22 years?"

"Hundreds. Why do you ask?"

"I'm just wondering how many times I've swallowed a Mouse Trap story and didn't have a clue."

Working to stay on task, Dakota ignored Jeremy's pondering and continued, "We'll then go for longer-term efforts by using the Corporate Division to focus on Mr. Tangerine's endorsements. Almost all of his clients dropped him after the accusations, but we'll fix that. We won't go back to anyone that dropped him, to show how their premature actions injured him. Instead, we have several companies connected to Mouse Trap—indirectly of course— lined up to have Mr. Tangerine as the centerpiece of their summer advertising campaigns.

"Next, we'll use the Music Division. We'll have Mr. Tangerine record duets with 10 of today's top female artists. Seven of them are already lined up with the other three close to agreeing.

"Lastly, we'll work with the Movies and TV Division to cast Mr. Tangerine in three episodes of *This is Home*. He'll play the older brother who comes home from the war in Iraq and is celebrated as a war hero."

After allowing Dakota to describe the project manager's role in detail, Zeke reengaged in the conversation. "And that Jeremy, is how a project is put together. Great job, Dakota. Any questions, Jeremy?"

Jeremy spoke with his hands unconsciously waving in the air as if drawing the scene on an invisible screen. "Let me see if I have everything straight. Oscar Tangerine really did rape those girls, but your job was to manipulate the situation to make it appear as if he didn't?"

"You got it," Dakota responded.

Jeremy shook his head in amazement. "And you can really do all the stuff you just explained?"

Dakota quickly responded, "Not only *can* we do all of this stuff; most of it is already done."

Supplementing Dakota's point, Zeke interjected, "And Project Citrus is actually a very simple, short-term project. It will be over in less than a year. We have some projects that use all 20 divisions and have been ongoing for years. A few Projects have been active for decades."

Zeke and Dakota spent the rest of the day with Jeremy going through another half-dozen projects, each highlighting a facet of Mouse Trap, and each bolstering Jeremy's excitement about his new career. He was pumped!

Inside a large cubicle farm at the National News Service, Tyler Edison was taking a break to see what was happening on his Facebook timeline when he came across a post that caught his attention.

"Have you seen these videos of Elijah Mustang?" He asked over the four-foot cubicle wall to the neighbor to his north.

His fellow cube-dweller responded, "No, but I think maybe someone on my timeline linked to one of them. I didn't click it, though."

Since initially assigned to cover the Richfield College protest story, Tyler had been intrigued by Elijah. After their impromptu airport encounter, Tyler felt he had the real inside story no one else had. He continued to be bothered that he never had the chance to share it. Now, unexpectedly, Elijah was back in the limelight. Someone with the screen name Mustangluvr1985 had recorded Elijah's short, inspirational speeches in the American Eagle Diner and had posted several of them on YouTube. In the last week, the most popular speeches had over 3 million views and counting. Elijah's heartfelt pro-American orations hit a chord with the online community, and the videos were going viral.

"Do you remember me telling you that I actually met this guy a couple of months ago? He was the dude who was supposed to give the commencement address at that college in Tennessee, but the students protested to get him disinvited. Courtney sent me to Tennessee to cover the story, and I actually ran into him in a restaurant in the airport. I thought he was a pretty good guy, but I never got to report on the story."

"That's nice." It was obvious his fellow cube dweller had reached the boundaries of his interest in Elijah Mustang.

Pointing to his screen, Tyler ignored that he was being ignored and continued, "You know, this is how I remembered him: just a genuine, good guy. With all of the hits his videos have, I'm obviously not the only one who thinks so."

"Yeah, that's nice."

"I'm going to talk with Courtney to see if I can do a follow-up story. I really think there's something here," Tyler continued.

After a long pause Tyler prompted his neighbor, "That's when you say 'That's nice.'"

"Oh sorry...that's nice."

"How is the training going?" It had become Victor's favorite question.

"Your instincts are still good; the kid is really bright."

Victor took off his glasses and glared down the point of his nose at Zeke with mock incredulity. "*Still?*"

Zeke was one of the few who could get away with a modest dig about Victor's age, which recently reached 74. Ignoring his boss's remark, Zeke continued, "He's ready to read. I was thinking Projects Grasshopper, Bullet Train, and Snowcap might be good places to start."

Victor shook his head. "No. Give him everything." The general approach to training new recruits followed a standard tried-and-true process that had served Mouse Trap well for over 20 years. A new team member would spend the first few days with a seasoned veteran. It was unusual for Zeke to be personally involved in the training, but Jeremy was proving to be no usual recruit.

After the introductory training, new team members were then given a work station with a computer and access to information about two or three successful projects. The intent was to slowly expose them to how Mouse Trap worked, while exploring the project files to understand what made them successful. Since no paper was allowed in Mouse Trap, every tidbit of information about every project was loaded into Omnia, the system created to serve all Mouse Trap's needs.

Omnia was designed with a hierarchical access protocol of Levels One through Seven, which each level providing more information to the user. Most new employees were given Level Two access while they were learning, with higher-level access commensurate with experience and performance. Level Seven was set aside for only Victor and Zeke.

"Do you mean give him *everything*?" Zeke asked.

"I mean exactly what I said. Give him *everything*. Level Six. Give him access to every project we've ever had, both good and bad. Especially active projects. I want him to see what's going on right now."

"You're the boss," Zeke responded.

"*Still?*"

"Yes, still."

Cracking the door to his boss's office, Tyler Edison peeked through the small opening and asked, "Hey Courtney, do you have a minute?"

"Sure, Tyler, come on in. What do you need?"

Entering the spacious office – at least compared to Tyler's six- by-six-foot cubicle, Tyler took a seat at the edge of a chair directly in front of the desk. "Do you remember a couple of months ago when we ran the story on that guy in Tennessee who was supposed to speak at the college graduation, but the students and faculty were protesting?"

"Elijah Mustang," Courtney responded matter-of-factly.

"Exactly, you do remember." Tyler said, excitedly.

Courtney continued, "I just got a link to a series of videos with him going on and on about how great America is."

"I got it too! That's exactly what I wanted to discuss. You may not remember, but I got to meet him in the airport. He seemed to be a really good guy and now these videos are going viral. I'd like to do a story on him."

"A story? What kind of a story?" Courtney asked suspiciously.

"I think the guy is really fascinating. He's a CEO and a former U. S. congressman. He's been the subject of a college protest. I've done a little research; he's donated several million dollars to build homes, hospitals, and churches in Central America."

"Those may be interesting facts, but what's the angle of the story?"

"I don't really have an angle yet, but I'm certain one will emerge. The bottom line is that these videos going viral shows there's renewed interest in the guy."

Shaking her head, Courtney got up from her desk and walked away from Tyler. With her back turned, she uttered a dismissive, "I just don't see it, Tyler."

"Would you trust me on this one? Give me a week to put something together. Let me travel to Tennessee, talk with the people who know him, and maybe even speak with him."

Turning to face Tyler again, Courtney conveyed a willingness to consider the proposal for the first time. "If you do it, the story can't be that we screwed up the first time reporting on the protest."

Knowing he was getting a "yes," Tyler ran with it. "Got it. I promise this is going to be a great story. I'll see you in a week!"

21

April 10, 2015
579 Days Until 2016 U. S. Presidential Election

The first few days on the job confirmed Jeremy's decision to join this—he wasn't even sure whether to call it a company; but whatever Mouse Trap was, the first few days put to rest any lingering doubts. This experience was proving to be beyond his wildest imagination.

He was greeted at the door by Zeke, who had been awaiting his arrival. "All right, Jeremy, we're ready to move on to the next phase of training. Walk with me." Before Jeremy could respond, Zeke had pivoted and was quickly disappearing. Jeremy was amazed at the rapid pace the 70-something Zeke was still able to maintain.

Zeke and Jeremy wound their way through the massive Mouse Trap facility until they finally reached a work pod at the southwest end of the building.

"This is your new home, Jeremy."

Jeremy walked into the open work space and did a quick once over. Like all Mouse Trap work pods, the largest workspace, located at the front of the pod, was set aside for the project manager. In this case that was Jeremy. Situated around the project manager space like numbers on the face of a clock were smaller workspaces for project team members. In Jeremy's workspace, the smaller areas were empty because Jeremy's team was not yet in place.

Wanting to exude confidence, the young project manager responded curtly, "Looks great. What's next?"

"A lot of reading, Jeremy. Come over here and take a seat."

Jeremy walked around the conference table at the center of the pod and plopped down at what would become his new home. He grasped the arms of the chair like an Indy car driver grasps the steering wheel of his steed. Although he tried, he couldn't suppress an involuntary smile.

"OK, Jeremy, now touch the screen."

Jeremy extended his arm and touched the center of the monitor, which immediately offered him a login and password prompt.

"OK, your login is your social security number."

Jeremy cocked his head to the side and glanced over his shoulder at Zeke. "I don't remember giving you guys my social."

"You didn't."

"Oh…"

Jeremy entered the nine-digit login.

"The password is your mom's maiden name, followed by the last four digits of your cell phone number."

"I didn't…*oh never mind.*"

Jeremy entered the password and another authentication screen popped up with a box in the center.

"Is that a…?"

"Fingerprint scanner? Yes, it is."

This time Jeremy swiveled in his chair to look at Zeke face to face.

"Now, I *know* I didn't give you my fingerprint."

"You didn't."

"But how…uh…I don't understand…"

"Jeremy, my counsel to you is to expect to be amazed by everything you see here at Mouse Trap. It is truly unlike anything that has ever been created anytime, anywhere, in the history of mankind. Now, close your mouth, and put your finger on the scanner."

"Which finger?"

"It doesn't matter; they're all in the system."

Jeremy just shook his head' resisted the urge to employ his middle finger; and opted for the standard right index finger, placing it in the center of the box. In just under a second, the screen came to life with a pleasant female voice saying, "Welcome to Omnia, Jeremy."

"Omnia? If I remember from English class...or was it history...either way, Omnia is Latin for...*everything*, right?"

"Yes it is."

Everything? He allowed that thought to sink in for a moment while watching the screen, which offered a series of icons.

"OK, Jeremy, let me walk you through a few features of Omnia." Zeke extended his bony finger to highlight one of the icons. "This one is the project app. You will be using it most frequently in your research. It contains information on all projects within Mouse Trap, both past and present. You should start there and read about as many projects as you possibly can."

"Got it. What about these other icons?" Jeremy asked.

"Remember, I told you to be amazed, right?"

"Right."

"OK, I will walk through some of them with you, but we don't have time to explore them all right now." Zeke put his hand on Jeremy's shoulder while reaching for the monitor.

"This app with the graduation cap connects you with any higher education website."

"OK, not exactly sure what that means," Jeremy remarked.

"We're not going to open every one of these because we need to focus on projects right now, but I'll indulge your curiosity on this one. Go ahead and tap that icon."

When Jeremy tapped the icon, a map of the United States appeared.

"What university are you interested in perusing?" Zeke asked.

"Let's go with my alma mater, Virginia Tech."

"OK, tap on the state of Virginia."

When Jeremy tapped, an outline of the state of Virginia appeared on the screen with every college and university highlighted on the map.

"OK, now tap on Virginia Tech."

When Jeremy did, the university's system administrator's screen came up. As he watched the screen, the administrator login and password were typed as if a ghost were in control of the keyboard. A moment later, Jeremy— or to be precise, Omnia—had administrative access to the entire Virginia Tech IT system.

Partially impressed, partially frightened that he was somewhere he didn't belong, Jeremy asked cautiously, "What *is* this?"

"Omnia is programmed to examine a computer system, determine who has the highest access rights, and replicate and retain the access information."

"So I, well…we…have access to…?"

"Everything."

"Really?! Everything?!"

"*Omnia*," Zeke reminded his trainee of the system's name.

Jeremy showed his IT aptitude by swiftly navigating through the Virginia Tech website finding grades, athletic tickets, campus security, and on-campus security-camera feeds.

Jeremy mumbled to himself, "This is…"

"Amazing?" Zeke answered.

"Yes, amazing. And Omnia has this access for every college and university in the United States?"

"Who said it was limited to the United States?"

Working to fully grasp his newfound gizmo, Jeremy allowed caution to take control for a moment. "So, Omnia knows this is me. Does Virginia Tech know it's me?"

"I'm not going to get into the programming details, but the short answer is *no*. Omnia enters a system using the administrator login; then upon leaving, it erases any evidence it was there."

"It's going to take me a while to comprehend all of this, isn't it?"

"More than a while. Enough playing around; let's get back to the home screen."

"But I just…"

"You'll have time later, but we need to move on. Now this app with the badge…and we're not going to play with it now…provides access to the criminal justice system, basically every police department in the world. This one with the capitol dome provides access to every government system. This one with the icon of the person opens any account on any social network. This one with the skyscraper provides access to any corporation's internal networks. This one with the envelope opens the e-mails of anyone, anywhere."

"E-mails? Are you serious?" Jeremy asked curiously.

"This one…," Zeke tried to continue.

"Hang on, can you please show me how the e-mail app works?"

"Jeremy, we need to stay focused."

"Just for a moment."

Zeke hung his head, knowing the shortest path to being able to move on would be to indulge his student in a brief demonstration.

"OK, but only once; and then we have to move on. Now, tap that app."

A small window opened requesting an e-mail address.

"Enter the e-mail address of someone you want to investigate."

"OK, I got it."

Jeremy entered the e-mail of a former girlfriend at Virginia Tech. The screen flashed for a couple of seconds and up popped an e-mail reader showing the last 50 e-mails received.

"So, these are like real time? She hasn't even read these yet?"

"It appears she hasn't."

"That's crazy."

"OK, enough demonstrations, let's move on," Zeke responded.

"But tell me how this works."

"Not now, Jeremy. We have to move on."

Zeke was happy about Jeremy's enthusiastic curiosity but knew he needed to get Jeremy back on task.

"I'm going to point out one more, and then we are going to dive into the project module."

"Deal."

"This app with the dollar sign is our path into the financial system."

"Which financial system?"

"Any financial system. Any bank, investment account, Wall Street trading company, all the way down to local community credit unions."

"I don't guess we could…"

"No, Jeremy, we couldn't. Let's dive into the project model. That's where you'll be spending your next few days."

Jeremy sat up straight in his chair and exclaimed, "Let's go!"

22

After finally deterring Jeremy from exploring more of Omnia's dimensions, Zeke directed his focus on the app that mattered the most to his development: the Project App, which Zeke left Jeremy to explore on his own.

Zeke had explained the basics. One tap on the App and Omnia Project opened. Many sort fields were presented to Jeremy. He could select by year; project manager; subject; project number; project status; or by a field that Zeke hadn't fully explained, impact.

Jeremy first tapped on *Subject*, selected *All* and then hit *Find*. He was curious how many projects were actually in Omnia Project. In less than a second, his query returned: 1,237. Mouse Trap had executed over a thousand projects. "That was crazy!" Jeremy thought.

He couldn't decide where to start, so he opted for randomly perusing the database. What he read blew his mind. "Could this really be true?" he wondered. Much of what he had read in the news, seen on TV, heard from his professors, and generally experienced in life was really part of a larger, perfectly orchestrated plan? It was the ultimate conspiracy theory, without the theory. He wasn't sure if he should feel afraid or honored to be part of this surreptitious undertaking.

As he dove into the research, he noted that projects were coded using one of five colors. Green projects were active and on track to meet their objectives. Yellow projects were active and in danger of missing their objectives. Red projects were active and had missed at least one objective. Gold projects were completed and met all objectives. Black projects were closed and did not meet their objectives. He decided to explore as many projects as possible, delving into the details of those that piqued his interest the most.

He read about Project 212, which was—or more correctly stated "is"—responsible for what was first touted as global warming and later rebranded as climate change. Named for the Fahrenheit temperature at which water boils, Project 212 developed stories, created videos, and inserted narratives in movies and TV shows promoting the concept of climate change. As Jeremy quickly tapped through the well-organized project file, he found that Project 212 influenced the highest levels of the U.S. government. It created new governmental organizations responsible for funneling billions of dollars to address the problem. It advanced the concept of a carbon tax, which diverted billions of dollars from the European economy to European governments and was developing similar schemes for other major economies. It invested in companies that offered solutions to climate change and ensured there were customers for those solutions. Project 212 was an ongoing, active project and was coded yellow because of lingering skepticism among some segments of the population. The impact field showed a three out of five, with a notation of the potential to grow to a four.

Jeremy decided to quickly tap through as many projects as possible without diving into the details of any one in particular. After Project 212 he opened Project Petrol, which was responsible for managing the supply, demand, and ultimately price for oil. It had been active since the 70s, shortly after Victor assumed his position in support of The Council. The project was among the longest running at Mouse Trap. As Jeremy read more about Project Petrol, he realized it was also among the simplest. It appeared to be exclusively about money, manipulating events that made the price of oil go up or down. Mouse Trap's interests would know about price fluctuation in advance, would buy or sell very large volumes of oil and in turn make a fortune—actually, many fortunes. Project Petrol had been responsible for enriching Mouse Trap's coffers to the tune of many, many billions of dollars in the last 40 years. This project was coded green.

Project Judas was intended to deemphasize Christianity in the U. S. Among its objectives were to decrease the public's reliance on the Christian faith; break down the nuclear family; and highlight failed Christian personalities, particularly those caught in sexual sins. Another objective of Project Judas was to turn the public away from a faith in a higher being and instead rely on government, science and logic. Jeremy didn't fully understand the utility of Project Judas and hoped to have an opportunity to discuss it more with Victor or Zeke. This project was coded yellow.

Project Jekyll was created to defend, protect, and insulate the Federal Reserve from external scrutiny, and in turn provide Mouse Trap's interests with an avenue of influence into Federal Reserve policy. Project Jekyll was coded green.

Project Caste was responsible for maintaining an urban underclass in the United States. A note in the project-status field included the following statement: "A signal of the success of Project Caste is that, despite spending over $20 trillion dollars in the last 40 years on solving the problem of poverty, the U.S.'s poverty rate has remained unchanged." Project Caste was coded green.

Jeremy decided to enter his name in the search field for project managers. The search returned no records. He was a project manager but had no projects associated with his name. Pausing in thought, he then entered *<none>* in the project-manager field, hoping to find a project that he might be assigned. Again, no records were found. "What was the name of the guy I am replacing?"

he wondered. "Bryan? No, that wasn't it. Bruce? Nope. Bryce? It was Bryce!"

Jeremy quickly entered the name *Bryce*; 16 projects were returned. He then filtered for the active projects; a single project remained: Project 2016. As he read about this project—probably his project, he learned that Project 2016 was established to select the next president of the United States. Although the election was still 18 months away he was surprised to find thousands of files already loaded into the Project 2016 folder.

He next searched for other election-related projects and found similar ones for every U. S. election going back to 1992, and each one was coded gold, meaning the project was complete and had met its objectives. Projects 1992, 1996, 2000 and 2004 all had impact scores of four out of five. Project 2008 and 2012 were categorized as five out of five.

Jeremy spent the rest of Friday and all weekend reading 500 Mouse Trap projects' reports, not leaving the office until after 9 each night. He walked out the door each evening with a range of emotions and dozens of questions. He understood the mandate that Zeke had made crystal clear. He was never to ask *why* and was supposed to trust Victor, but he couldn't help struggling with connecting many of the projects he was reading about with Victor's larger objective of making the world a better place. How would maintaining a consistent level of urban poverty make the world a better place? Or managing the oil supply? Or deemphasizing Christianity? He would comply with Zeke's directive to trust Victor, but the questions still lingered. For now, he'd keep them to himself.

23

O n May 7, 1945, General Alfred Jodl, representing
remnants of the Nazi regime, signed Germany's
unconditional surrender, formally marking an
end to the war in Europe. The months that followed were
desperate for much of the European continent but particularly for Germany. Millions of businesses and tens of millions of homes had been destroyed during the war, leaving
behind a large, homeless, starving populace.

Although many U. S. servicemen were relieved to return to their loved ones in the States, a significant occupying contingent remained to maintain peace and
order, as well as to provide humanitarian aid to the war-
ravaged region.

Among those staying in Europe were five officers—
three majors and two colonels—who had served to support the Allied victory. The five were responsible for over
10,000 soldiers who served as boots-on-the-ground forces

to restore order out of the chaos resulting from the war. These soldiers told story after story of the horrors they encountered while patrolling the continent. Accounts of concentration camps had become widely known, but beyond those nightmarish situations were millions of Europeans who were living in squalor throughout the continent. The soldiers' stories made their way up the chain of command to the five officers.

The stories had an impact on the officers, who in turn raised Washington D.C. decision makers' awareness of the humanitarian crisis. The information led to support from various governmental entities. In the two-and-a-half years between the end of the war and the end of 1947, the U. S. provided $15 billion in aid. The much-needed funds supplied food and medical supplies as well as construction materials and equipment used to begin rebuilding homes and businesses.

In their relief efforts, the five officers regularly interfaced with General George Catlett Marshall, the United States Army's Chief of Staff during World War II and later Secretary of State in the Truman administration. As a result of their interactions, General Marshall spearheaded the development of the European Recovery Program, more commonly known as the Marshall Plan.

The Marshall Plan, passed by Congress, was a four-year initiative, beginning in April 1948, which provided $17 billion to European countries to aid with economic recovery. Most historians credit the Marshall Plan with changing the entire European continent's economic fortunes.

In developing the Marshall Plan, General Marshall recognized money alone would not address Europe's financial crisis. The war had taken its toll on the working-age male population, and there was a shortage of experienced managers who could help with the logistics of efficiently spending $17 billion in aid. To help with this shortage, Marshall persuaded the five officers to take early retirement from their military careers and start their own private enterprises. Marshall convinced them that they could most effectively assist with reconstruction from the private sector.

Taking the General's advice, the five spent a weekend together in a cottage outside London discussing their options. They debated many arrangements including creating a single company, in which all five would assume leadership positions. Late on Sunday night of that fateful weekend, a breakthrough decision was finally made. The officers decided to create five separate companies, which would align with each officer's training and experience.

Major David Riley had a degree in civil engineering from the University of Georgia. In the Army his primary responsibility was coordinating the construction of roads, bridges, barracks, and other similar infrastructure projects. With this experience Riley started the Bulldog Construction Company, named for the University of Georgia mascot.

Colonel Wayne Packard's expertise was in logistics. His Army responsibilities included marshalling the shipment of tanks, heavy artillery, and other materiel from factories in the U. S. to the European battlefield. This experience led to his creating Packard Transportation.

Major Hubert Stahl, who hailed from Chicago, served in the Army as a finance manager. A natural to manage the group's financial affairs, he chartered The Chicago Group, a firm specializing in financial management services.

Colonel Boyd Tillman served in the Judge Advocate General Corps during the war after obtaining his law degree from the University of Louisville. He took responsibility for all legal and contractual matters through the Bluegrass Law Firm.

The final member of the group, Major Kelly Quinn, was the youngest but most charismatic member. Quinn was a natural leader to whom people were drawn. It was Quinn who first met General Marshall, convincing him that the European crisis was a matter of urgency. Marshall even brought Quinn along to meet with Congressional committees to provide a firsthand account of what was really happening in post-war Europe. Quinn had a knack for interfacing with the D. C. movers and shakers and parlayed that skill into Quinn Consulting, a lobbying firm. In fact, he was a trailblazer in the lobbying profession, long before it became the far-reaching enterprise it is today.

Late that Sunday evening in the London cottage, the officers formalized their plan. They would have a transportation company to get supplies to Europe, a construction company to facilitate the rebuilding effort, an accountant to make the financial arrangements, a lawyer to develop the contracts, and a D. C. liaison to remain connected to the funding source.

At least two of the officers had one final concern. If the companies were separate, how could the officers continue working together, while avoiding the appearance of collusion or impropriety? As usual, Kelly Quinn devised a creative plan to address the concern. They would form a covert organization through which they would meet to address matters beneficial to all. They named this organization The Council. Quinn advised that when The Council met the members should assume secret identities to avoid the possibility of Council activities being linked to their alliance.

They borrowed from their military experience and adopted pseudonyms from the phonetic alphabet that was in place during the war. Colonel Tillman would be known as Able, the first letter in the phonetic alphabet, for his role as The Council's attorney. Major Stahl would be known as Baker, one letter away from the word *banker*, in honor of his financial expertise. Major Riley would become Charlie for his role in construction. Colonel Packard would be knowns as Easy for his equipment transportation expertise. The remaining member of the newly formed Council, Major Quinn, proudly adopted the moniker Dog, the fourth letter of the alphabet. He loved the name as he doggedly pursued every possible connection he could in the nation's capital.

During the four years of the Marshall Plan (1948-1952), millions of homes; thousands of businesses; and dozens of hospitals, and police and fire stations were constructed. Many hundreds of thousands of equipment items were shipped from the states including tractors, bulldozers, generators, automobiles, and trucks. The Marshall Plan was a win for the Europeans; a win for the U.S. economy; and a win for The Council members, each of whom became a millionaire several times over.

The Council met on the first Saturday of every month to ensure their apparatus was functioning as smoothly as possible. Quinn ensured funds were flowing from Washington. Tillman worked to funnel as many contracts as possible through The Council members' businesses. Packard developed relationships with hundreds of U.S. suppliers and became the go-to business for transporting equipment across the ocean. Riley employed over 30,000 Europeans to rebuild the continent's infrastructure. Stahl orchestrated the financial details for all Council entities to ensure all members had what they considered their fair share.

By the end of 1952, the Marshall Plan was being phased out and U. S. Government funding was going away. The European economy was beginning the long recovery process. Those circumstances left The Council with the difficult decision of whether to stay in Europe and work to build their businesses through European channels or to return to the States and start from scratch. On a Saturday in late 1952, in their usual cottage meeting locale, The Council members debated the merits of both options. The pull of family was too great and a return to the U. S. won out.

In the 50s and 60s, The Council successfully replicated its business model in the U. S. The five members continued meeting the first Saturday of every month and addressing each other by their phonetic names during Council meetings. In 1953 with all their businesses booming, they acquired a 1,200 tract of land in rural Maryland and constructed a large six-sided structure known as The Hex in which they held monthly Council meetings.

Each year The Council's influence continued growing in tandem with The Council members' bank account. However, The Council encountered a significant barrier in 1973. Quinn had used his personal and management skills to climb the Washington D. C. hierarchy and by 1971 had secured a position in the Nixon Administration as chief political strategist. In this role Quinn found himself embroiled in a white-hot scandal called Watergate.

Quinn called an emergency meeting of The Council and shared the predicament that he was in and how a deep-dive investigation might implicate other Council members and reveal The Council's existence. He suggested securing the services of an up-and-coming Washington D. C. superstar named Victor Youngblood.

Still in his 20's, Victor had already established a reputation for getting clients out of difficult situations.

Quinn opined that the predicament was serious enough that they had to bring Victor into the fold, fully explaining the Council's functions to earn his trust.

Victor and The Council turned out to be the perfect partnership. Working his magic, Victor ensured that none of the Council members, including Quinn, would be implicated in Watergate's widely cast net.

For his end of the bargain, Victor saw in The Council's design great untapped potential - potential reinforced by the Watergate scandal unfolding on TV with a new facet of the story reported every day. Victor was fascinated that so much damage could be done by the digging of two reporters, Woodward and Bernstein, and pondered what influence he could have if those reporters worked at his behest. What if he had dozens—or even more—working under his direction and for his interests?

To answer this question, Victor proposed an undocumented merger, whereby his growing Youngblood and Associates firm would focus its efforts on fully exploiting The Council's potential. The merger would provide great growth opportunities for both parties.

After a long meeting and much debate, The Council agreed to forge a strategic alliance with Victor, so long as it was clear that Victor was subordinate to The Council, working at the pleasure of Council members. Victor agreed.

One of the first issues Victor brought to The Council was succession planning. In 1973, The Council members ranged in age from 59 to 65. Victor encouraged each member to assist him in identifying an apprentice who could step into their role on The Council when they retired.

Through the 1970's, Victor continued to refine his vision of how to grow The Council. In 1978, he first proposed the Mouse Trap concept to Council members, who enthusiastically endorsed it. In 1980, he introduced the 20-by-20 organizational structure still used today.

Thirty-five years later, many of The Council's key elements remain the same; Council meetings are still held the first Saturday of every month in The Hex; and Council members still go by the names Able, Baker, Charlie, Dog, and Easy.

However, The Council of 2015 is much different than The Council of 1973. All five original members have passed away, and a new Council is in place. There has even been turnover in some of the second-generation Councilmen. Compared to the early years, The Council's breadth and reach are breathtaking and the technological capabilities have become more sophisticated than even the U.S. government. While The Council managed hundreds of millions of dollars in the 70s, they are now responsible for hundreds of billions of dollars. One of the subtlest, yet potentially ominous changes is Victor Youngblood's growing role. Careful to maintain a servile demeanor while in The Council's presence, Victor is quietly accumulating power and wealth. It would only be a matter of time until Victor decided he no longer needed The Council, but that time had not yet come. However, it was most certainly coming.

24

As they did every Sunday, the Everman family was gathered at the Dayton, Ohio home of Bronson and Edith, patriarch and matriarch of the Everman clan. As usual, the conversation was as spirited as Bronson's hot wings; and as always, sons Brad and Jake didn't miss an opportunity for a debate of the day's hot topics.

"Hey Jake, what was it you were saying a couple of weeks ago about my man Oscar Tangerine?" As a high school teacher, 46-year-old Brad was more in tune with pop culture than his older brother Jake and had insisted that Oscar Tangerine was innocent. Brad was certain the accusation was a mistake, and recent entertainment news seemed to confirm his assertion.

Jake responded, "It just confirms what I tell you every Sunday: *Don't believe anything you hear in the news.*" When the shocking allegations of Oscar Tangerine's transgressions first hit the news, 50- year-old Jake saw it as an opportunity to opine about the current generation of celebrities' moral shortcomings.

"I would like to hear you actually say the words *I was wrong.*" Brad didn't get many opportunities to best his big brother and wanted to fully enjoy it when he could.

"I'm not…"

"Come on, you can say it: three simple words *I was wrong*; I know you can do it."

"Who is Oscar Tangerine?" Intervening to stop the argument, Edith Everman was both mother and peacemaker.

"Only the most awesome singer. He's got like a hundred hits, tons of awards; and best of all, he's a really good guy." Sixteen-year-old Jasmine volunteered to provide the first answer to her grandmother's query.

Jake decided to fill in the details. "There was a report a couple of weeks ago that he had molested two teenage girls. Supposedly there was video evidence. Oscar went into hiding, which only made him look guiltier."

Brad was happy to play the role of Oscar Tangerine's defender. "Then, it was announced a couple of days ago that it was all bogus. The DA decided not to press charges, there actually wasn't any video, and the guy is totally innocent."

Always seeking justice, Jake contributed to the conversation. "What should really happen is that they should find the girls who made the false accusations and put them on trial."

And so the conversation continued in the Everman household, as well as in millions of households around the world: Oscar Tangerine was a good guy, falsely accused. Once again a Mouse Trap project had worked to perfection.

25

April 13, 2015
568 Days Until 2016 U. S. Presidential Election

As Tyler Edison walked into the American Eagle Diner, he couldn't avoid a feeling of *deja vu*. Had he been here before? He was sure he hadn't, but everything seemed so familiar. He decided that watching YouTube videos dozens of times of Elijah Mustang's holding court with his pals had fostered a keen sense of familiarity. Soon, the smell of bacon frying, biscuits baking, and coffee brewing commanded his attention.

Surveying the diner, his focus quickly turned to a large table in the back. Tyler was sure he had found Elijah Mustang sitting among his usual friends, most of whom he recognized as background players in the YouTube videos. He took a deep breath and approached the table, which was already in full revelry by 7 a.m.

"Umm...Mr. Mustang?"

Tyler's formality amused the members of the Liars, Thieves, and Jokers Club.

"Mr. Mustang?! Dang, Elijah, you teachin' a class this morning?" an amused Roger Caldwell howled.

"Uh, we actually call him Dr. Mustang because of the wisdom he possesses," cried Bubba Driscoll.

"Ignore them; they're already drunk on red-eye gravy." Elijah extended a hand to Tyler. "Good morning, I assume you are Tyler?"

"Yes, Tyler Edison; it is great to meet you."

"Who's the young buck, Elijah?" asked Howard Finch.

Ignoring his LTJ Club members, Elijah addressed Tyler, "Glad you could make it. How about we grab a table ALL THE WAY on the other side of the restaurant?"

"Sounds good to me," a relieved Tyler replied.

"Have a good breakfast, Mister Mustang, oh... make that *Doctor* Mustang?!" Again, laughter filled the restaurant.

"Is this seat OK?" Elijah asked.

"Yes sir, it is fine," Tyler responded.

"OK, first thing, let's drop the *sirs* and *Mr. Mustangs*. I'm just Elijah, OK?"

As Tyler took a seat in the booth, he replied, "Sure thing, Elijah, no problem."

"You said you were with the National News Service and wanted to interview me. What exactly are you wanting to discuss?" Elijah decided to understand the ground rules before starting any substantive discussion. Interviews had always been minefields but even more so now that so many journalists were looking for their next *gotcha* victim to bury.

Tyler started with a conciliatory tone. "First, I really want to thank you for meeting me. I know you are a very busy man."

"It's no problem. I'm not that busy, but I'm just concerned you traveled all the way to Tennessee for nothing. I can't imagine why a national news organization like yours would want to talk to a small-town guy like me." Elijah maintained his natural humility.

"You do understand that you've become an internet sensation don't you?"

"I've heard something about some videos with me babbling on, but I don't know that I'd call that a sensation."

Tyler retrieved his pad of paper from his backpack and began reading from his scribbled research notes. "There are nine videos posted to YouTube, each with over three million views and one with over seven million."

Not totally grasping the import of Tyler's statistics, Elijah simply replied, "OK...I guess."

Tyler chuckled. "That's much more than just *OK*. Companies pay millions of dollars for a few-thousand views. These videos were posted by an unidentified individual with the screen name Mustangluvr1985. Do you have any idea who that is?"

"I have no clue. So, this is what you want to interview me about, these videos?"

"Sort of but not exactly. I want to interview you partly because of the videos, but I really want to understand the man behind the videos. Who *is* Elijah Mustang?"

Not really sure what to say, Elijah replied, "OK, I guess we can start—unless we already have—in which case, please continue."

Sensing he had assuaged the concerns Elijah was likely to have about agreeing to this interview, he decided to venture into the sensitive topic of Richfield College. "Great. Thank you! I'd actually like to start on a topic other than the videos. The first thing that catapulted you into the national headlines was the protest at your alma mater, Richfield College. I am sure you won't remember, but we actually met during the protest's early stages?"

Caught off guard, Elijah peered into Tyler's eyes, trying to recall. After an awkward silence, Elijah's sharp mind started spinning. "Ruby Tuesday, McGhee Tyson Airport in Knoxville."

Tyler was excited. "I can't believe you remembered that. Yes, we chatted for a few minutes there. NNS had sent me to cover the protest, but everything escalated quickly and then ended the next day before I was able to do any reporting. So, what are your thoughts on that whole protest ordeal?"

Elijah shook his head, "To be honest, I don't really know much about the protest. As you are aware, I was in the Knoxville airport waiting to catch a flight to Central America just before it apparently got out of hand. I was already in Honduras by the time it got really crazy. Not sure if you are very familiar with rural Honduras, but there's not a lot of news that makes it out that far. The Hondurans are more concerned with providing the basics for their family, things like food, shelter, and clean water."

Not ready to give up, Tyler pressed on. "But you must have heard about it from friends, family, and co-workers?"

"I've heard a few versions of it from the knuckleheads at the other end of the diner, but you can't believe much of what they say."

"Here's a quick summary of what happened. There was a protest spearheaded by Dr. Molly Jefferson, who said you were racist and intolerant and should not be given the mantle of speaking at graduation. She got several students to agree with her, leading to the local Knoxville newspaper writing a story about it, which led to a larger protest, which led to national attention with national news outlets descending on Bard's Ridge to cover the protest. The very next day the Richfield College president announced that the administration was seeking a different graduation speaker, then the protest quickly dissolved."

"OK. Not sure what you want me to say about that," Elijah responded.

"See, here's why I am interviewing you. The videos that we talked about earlier contain no hint of racism or intolerance, so I did some research. For the life of me, I can't find a single thing that is controversial. I even called Dr. Jefferson, who said that she was misled about you and that she regretted the protest."

"OK. I'm not trying to be difficult; I just don't know what I'm supposed to say. *I* know I'm not a racist, or whatever they said about me. I just don't feel the need to prove that to anyone."

Tyler again chuckled at Elijah's simple, yet powerful confidence. "I guess I don't know what I expect you to say either. That's why I want to find out more about you. Can we talk for a moment about your friends at the other table?"

"Sure, what do you want to know?"

"I've heard them referred to in a couple of videos as the Liars, Thieves, and Jokers Club. Is that correct?" Tyler readied his notepad to capture Elijah's response.

"Yes, that's the name they have informally given themselves. Mostly they are a bunch of harmless curmudgeons, who like to have fun."

Pursuing further, Tyler asked, "What's their connection? Do they all work with you?"

"No, no, not at all. The connection is that they enjoy each other's company as well as biscuits and gravy. They're quite an eclectic collection of goofballs. There's a retired policeman, a retired doctor, a retired plumber, a retired hardware store owner. Are you starting to sense a common theme?"

"Retired?"

"Exactly. That guy who gave you a hard time about calling me Mr. Mustang—you won't believe this, but he has a PhD in Nuclear Engineering from MIT. He was the Physics Division Manager a few ridges over at the Oak Ridge National Laboratory before he..."

Tyler interrupted, "Let me guess, *retired?*"

"Yep. A brilliant guy, probably the smartest guy I know."

"So, you are obviously not retired. What's your connection to the club?"

"Well, that all started back in what I call my 'stupid years,' the ones when I foolishly dove into politics. I figured the American Eagle Diner would be a great place to test the waters and see if I could connect with the voters in my district. I've been coming here ever since, and the guys in the club allow me to be an honorary member."

"Let's talk about your years in Washington." Tyler again consulted his notepad. "With no political experience, you were elected to the United States' House of Representatives with 65% of the votes. You were reelected two years later with 75% of the votes. Then you chose not to pursue a third term. Why not?"

"This is going to be a very short discussion; as I said, those were the stupid years of my life. Washington is a steaming cesspool of liars, cheaters, and corrupt pompous asses, and those are the good guys. I couldn't wait to get out of there. End of subject."

Although he had more questions about Elijah's time in Congress, this was obviously not a comfortable subject for Elijah; so Tyler chose not to poke the angry bear and moved on to the next topic. The discussion continued, covering Elijah's early life and his family's financial struggles; his time at Richfield College; his starting and growing Promise Transportation and his family life—from the joy that his three daughters brought him to the heartbreak of losing his wife Becky, much too early.

It was clear to Tyler that Elijah Mustang lived life with passion. It was also clear that this man was no racist or anything else the protesters at Richfield College had accused him of being. Tyler Edison arrived at the same conclusion that everyone who knew Elijah Mustang had reached; he was a good man. Any lingering doubt was wiped away when they moved to the last topic on Tyler's list.

"So, tell me about Promise Ministries. What is it all about?"

The passion in Elijah rose even greater as he began to answer. "It is about giving hope to people who don't have much to be hopeful about. People who most of the world has forgotten."

"That's admirable. So, where does Promise Ministries operate?"

"We're in five Central American countries, as well as in a number of rural Appalachian communities. We have nine Promise Homes, which provide food, shelter, and education for children who wouldn't otherwise have these necessities. We have a dozen medical clinics that are staffed by both doctors from the home countries as well as U. S. doctors and nurses who donate their time on mission trips. We have lost track of how many homes we have built but it is over a thousand. We offer business classes so that enterprising people can provide for their families and grow the local economies.

"Our newest initiative is Promise Connection. This is where we pair up needy children who have no family with American couples who want to provide a loving home. I can't begin to tell you how rewarding it is to see the smiles of both the children and parents when they come together.

"Throughout Appalachia our focus is on food exchanges, where we equip local residents to grow foods that can be shared with others. These exchanges are different from the normal food pantry concept by focusing on building sustainable communities that can thrive on their own. The communities learn farming, economics, and basic business principles. We sponsor over 40 food exchanges in Georgia, Kentucky, North Carolina, South Carolina, West Virginia, and Tennessee. Seeing families go from dependency to self-sufficiency is very rewarding. Their whole countenance just beams when they no longer have to ask for assistance to survive. We are very proud of this ministry."

Tyler was struck by the use of the personal pronoun *we*. He was also moved by how deeply Elijah cared about serving others. "I assume from reading about you that you are a Christian, is that correct?"

"Yes, that is correct."

"So, I guess a big part of what you do is work to convert these people to Christianity."

"I would say that is sometimes the result of what we do, and we are intentional about it, but first we work to meet their needs. I have heard it described using the terms *hands, heart, and head.* For many years Christians worked to evangelize populations from other countries by arguing them to heaven; they started with the head. First we work with our hands to meet their physical needs. We see that as a way to *show* them Jesus' love. Through that approach, we hope to win their hearts and ultimately share the gospel of Jesus with them."

"*Hands, head, heart.* That's interesting." Tyler knew it would take a while for that concept to settle into his consciousness. As a religion major, he had studied many of the world's religions; but Elijah had moved his understanding of religion from the theoretical to the practical. He glanced at his watch and realized they had been talking for three hours. Knowing he had to wrap things up, he changed subjects.

"I know we have covered a lot of ground, but I'd like to conclude by coming back to the YouTube videos. With millions of views, they have obviously struck a chord with the public. Do you know why?"

"I guess you would have to ask the public that question. I was just speaking from my heart with my buddies, and I didn't even know I was being recorded. My comments were not intended to be heard by millions of people. I was just being me."

Just being me. Tyler knew that was the perfect ending to the interview. He had traveled all the way to Tennessee to discover who Elijah Mustang really was, and he had been given a fulsome and rich answer. His next job was to introduce the real Elijah Mustang to the world. Although excited to complete this task, he feared he wouldn't do Elijah justice.

Tyler and Elijah shook hands and parted ways. The interview was over. Tyler knew the easy part would be writing a story about the intriguing Elijah Mustang. The difficult part would be convincing his editor to actually run the story but that was a battle he was willing to fight. He knew this story needed to be told, and he'd fall on his sword to see that it was.

26

Jeremy had spent all of nine days in training for Mouse Trap. He had somehow crammed over 130 hours of work into those nine days; nevertheless, it was only nine days, nine *really long* days.

"How was your first week, Jeremy?" Victor asked.

Jeremy cocked his head and scratched his scalp, searching for an accurate and complete answer. "*Overwhelming, exhilarating, intimidating, confusing, enlightening.* How many words am I allowed?"

Victor and Jeremy were back in Victor's office where just over a week before he had introduced his new protégé to the universe of Mouse Trap. After four days with Zeke and five days digesting as much of Omnia as he could, Jeremy was about to be thrust head first into the fire.

"I understand all those descriptors and would be surprised if you weren't feeling each one. That said, are you ready to go?"

Jeremy's face scrunched as he asked hesitantly. "Ready to go *where?*"

"Ready to go to work. We have a lot to do."

"Well...yeah, I mean I guess so; but I understood from Zeke that I'd be in training for a while...like maybe for several months."

Victor smiled while putting his hand on Jeremy's shoulder. "You don't need any more training do you, Jeremy?"

"Well, I..."

"Here's the bottom line; I brought you into Mouse Trap because you are an extremely bright and talented young man. You are correct; new recruits usually go through a few months of training, followed by an apprentice period working with an experienced project manager. I don't plan to do that with you. We have an immediate opening in our project-management ranks, and we have a project that needs a manager. So congratulations, you are now a Mouse Trap project manager."

"Thanks...I think."

"OK, let's get started."

Victor rose from the chair and walked behind his command center. He tapped his desk a couple of times, and the screens on the wall in front of him synched to form one large screen with this date prominently displayed:

November 8, 2016

"Know what that date is, Jeremy?"

"Let's see; it's 2016 and November; I'm guessing the next presidential election?"

"Always ahead of the curve; you got it, the next presidential election. At Mouse Trap we have significant interest in whom the American people choose as their next leader. In fact, we have such an interest that we'd like to apply our resources to influence the outcome." Victor paused to let Jeremy absorb what he had been told. "If we have an interest in whom the American people choose, we also have an interest in whom they do not choose."

"That makes sense. Where do I fit into the equation?"

Victor tapped the desk again, and the election date was replaced by the image of a middle-aged man. "Recognize this guy?"

"He looks familiar, but I'm not sure."

"This gentleman's name is Bobby Lincoln, the governor of the Commonwealth of Kentucky. He made the headlines this past week by announcing that he's running for president."

"Ah, see, that's why I didn't know him. This past week my life has been Mouse Trap, Mouse Trap, a tiny bit of sleep, and then more Mouse Trap."

Ignoring Jeremy's whining, Victor continued, "He's a sharp guy, a successful governor, a religious man; he doesn't drink, doesn't smoke, and has been married to one woman his whole life. He was a basketball star at the University of Kentucky and got his law degree from Columbia. Just an all-around top-notch guy, he's also articulate, good looking, and funny."

Finishing Victor's thoughts, Jeremy interjected, "In other words, he's the perfect presidential candidate."

"Exactly. He would be ideal." Victor allowed his response to sink in just long enough. "And we want to make sure he doesn't win."

As with many things Jeremy had heard over the past seven days, he paused as his mind quickly sifted through a flood of thoughts. His first instinct was to ask why Victor didn't want Bobby Lincoln to be president but then recalled Zeke being adamant that he never ask *why* in Mouse Trap. Instead, he simply uttered, "OK."

Jeremy's measured response caught Victor off guard. "*OK?* That's it? Just *OK?* You don't have any questions?"

"Of course I have questions, but I suspect you'll answer most of them in explaining what the project will be; so I'll just focus my energy on listening."

"Zeke told you that you couldn't ask *why*, didn't he?"

Not knowing if it was a trick question, Jeremy cautiously responded with the truth, "Well, yeah, sort of."

"At least Zeke is consistent. OK, let's forge ahead. Your first assignment will be to lead Project Wildcat. There is one overarching objective and that is ensuring that Bobby Lincoln does not secure the Republican nomination for president. Ideally, we'd like for that to happen sooner rather than later. The Iowa Caucus is on February 1, 2016, about nine months away. We need Mr.

Lincoln out of the race by October 1, 2015, so that we can focus all of our energy and resources on our chosen candidate."

Jeremy knew he shouldn't ask and knew he wouldn't get an answer, but the urge was too great to resist. "And your candidate of choice *is*?"

"That's another project and another project manager. You have enough on your plate to focus on Bobby Lincoln. You have a one-on-one meeting scheduled with me on May 27th. In that meeting I expect to hear your plan for how you'll meet the objective. Any questions?"

"Over the next few weeks, I'm sure I'll have a thousand questions; but for now, I'm good."

"Zeke will make sure you have everything you need." Victor put both hands on Jeremy's shoulders and stooped to look him straight in the eyes. "You're going to do great things here at Mouse Trap. I can't wait to watch them unfold."

"You got a minute?"

"Yeah, but not much more than that. I'm working a priority task for headquarters."

"OK, I just wanted to give you a quick download from my interview with Elijah Mustang."

It was a discussion that Tyler Edison was both looking forward to and dreading. He was dreading it because he knew his boss didn't want to hear that the entire media apparatus had completely blown the story about the Richfield College protest and the mischaracterization of Elijah. He was looking forward to the discussion because he was energized by meeting with Elijah and felt an obligation—no, a passion— to try to set the record straight about Elijah's character. As a journalist Tyler was trained to ingest rhetoric from public figures with a generous helping of skepticism. He was often disappointed by the public figures he met, but Elijah was definitely an exception to that rule. Elijah was genuine, honest, and decent.

Tyler could almost hear the squishing sound of Courtney's eyeballs as they rolled upon hearing Elijah Mustang's name. "Remember, I didn't make any promises about publishing a story about Mr. Mustang. I just said you could interview him."

"I understand; that's why I want to talk with you. The bottom line is every one of us had this guy completely wrong." As he spoke, Tyler moved from the threshold of Courtney's office door to a few steps inside.

"This better be good. The story is months old. I don't see any upside to digging this guy up again," Courtney warned.

"That's exactly the point; the guy is back in the spotlight again. He's the latest YouTube sensation. The videos of his impromptu speeches are getting millions of hits; and they are growing, not slowing down. The interesting thing is I don't think many people have made the connection between the kerfuffle at the college and the videos."

"So, I'm guessing you are going to tell me that it is our job to make that connection?" Courtney's tone conveyed surrender as she knew this discussion was going to last much longer than a minute.

"OK, hear me out." Tyler had now taken a position right in front of Courtney's desk. "Before I ever met with the guy for the interview, I went back to read about the protest to see what the complaints were about him. They were mostly nonspecific, not much that could really be proven or disproven. So, I read over a dozen articles about him and his company, and absolutely nothing was controversial. I checked social media—again, nothing but positive. I even created a social media account and fabricated a critical statement about the guy; and in the shark-infested waters of the comments section, almost everyone defended him."

"OK, I got it; he's a good guy. We're a newspaper; we don't usually sell many papers writing about good guys."

Finally showing a bit of frustration, Tyler tried to recover the conversation. "It's more than him being a good guy. He has an intriguing charity called Promise Ministries, which builds hospitals and orphanages throughout Central America. He even has an adoption program that connects orphans with loving parents. Get this: he gives away close to 90% of his salary to the charity, and he travels several weeks a year to personally involve himself in the work of the charity."

"Like I said, sounds like a good guy...snooze."

Now fully frustrated Tyler responded, "*No!* You don't get it! He's not just a good guy! There's a reason his videos are getting so many hits. There's just something real and genuine about him that is missing from our public figures today. You know that quote attributed to Maya Angelou that says, "At the end of the day people won't remember what you said or did; they will remember how you made them feel." I know this sounds corny, but after the interview I felt like I'd been in the presence of someone significant. I've never had that feeling before."

Courtney sighed deeply, knowing the only way she was going to get the rest of her day back was to concede something to Tyler. "OK, what is the ask? What do you want me to do?"

"I want to write an article about the guy. I want to connect the videos to the protest, and I want us to say we blew it."

"For what purpose?"

Tyler quickly cycled a series of prospective responses through his mind before finally verbalizing the one he knew would give him the green light. "Because it will sell a crap load of papers. Like I said, this guy is hot now. Millions and millions of hits on social media, and people want to know more about him. I'm the only one who has taken the time to research and interview him, so we have a leg up on the competition if we act quickly."

Knowing she'd been had by her own logic, Courtney finally gave in. "OK, write the first draft and send it to me for review. Play up the part about his good deeds, and play down the part about us blowing the college protest story."

"Thank you! I promise you won't regret this." Securing what he came for, Tyler quickly exited the office before Courtney changed her mind. He plopped down in his cubicle to finish the story that was already 80% complete. He had no way of predicting the far-reaching impact his article would have in the coming months. Tyler Edison was about to tip over a domino with many more lined up behind it ready to fall.

27

May 2, 2015
549 Days Until 2016 U. S. Presidential Election

"I am pleased to see that you all made it here safely. As I stated in my e-mail to each of you, this is a critically important meeting. If you're agreeable, we are going to forego the usual agenda and focus most of our time on the U.S. presidential election coming up in just 18 months. Is everyone OK with that being the primary topic this month?"

Victor struck his usual deferential tone when addressing The Council. He wanted each of them to think of him as servile to The Council's initiatives or, more importantly, to The Council members themselves. With the new Council members he had assembled over the last 10 years, Victor commanded every aspect of The Council's activities. Victor was clever enough in his dealings that

The Council members never knew they had become simply figureheads.

"I am OK with that." Able was the first to respond. Baker, Charlie, Dog, and Easy all agreed.

"I truly appreciate your forbearance as I walk us through this topic. I would like to start by summarizing the field of candidates at this early point in the race."

Victor pointed his phone at the center of The Hex, and five 70-inch screens descended from the ceiling offering each Council member a clear view of what Victor was about to discuss.

"This is where things stand as of now." Victor tapped his phone, and each screen displayed the images of six individuals. "Six candidates are confirmed for the Democrat Party." Victor tapped again. "And nine candidates for the Republican Party." Victor summarized each candidate's background and standing in the way-too-early polling.

"What is your assessment of the candidate who would most benefit our interests?" Dog could always be counted on to encourage Victor to cut to the chase. Victor was keenly aware of this attribute. In fact, Victor designed his presentation around each Council member's tendencies, tendencies that he knew as well as he knew his own.

"I'm glad you asked." Victor tapped and then highlighted a face on the Democrat screen. "This is Mitchell McCoy. He's from the state of Connecticut. He has some non-conventional ideas, such as a wealth tax to extract money from the millionaires and billionaires whom he says are hoarding resources. He wants to raise the minimum wage to $15 per hour. He wants to tax corporations at 75% on any profits above 5%. He wants single-payer healthcare. He wants the U.S. military to come under the United Nations' direction."

"OK, I've heard enough; he's obviously not our guy," Dog interrupted Victor again.

"I believe his is exactly our guy, at least on the Democrat side of the race," Victor responded.

"So, you're suggesting we get behind a guy that has no chance of winning the general election. I'm guessing that means our *real* guy is on the Republican side this time?" Baker was the best of The Council members at following where Victor was leading.

"Very astute, Baker. That's exactly the plan. This guy...," with a tap of his phone Victor scrolled to the Republican screen and highlighted the gentleman on the left side of the second row, "...is Grant Wembley, senior senator from Wyoming. Mr. Wembley has been in the Senate for 18 years. Before that he served in the House for 12 years. He has four grown kids and seven grandkids. He's an avid outdoorsman. He supports his local Little League baseball team. In other words, he's an all-American guy."

"Those are all great attributes, but what's in it for us?" Charlie was the member most interested in seeing The Council continue to thrive and grow. His questions always had a Council bent to them.

"Take a look at this graphic." Again, Victor clicked the remote, and the image on all screens showed a series of tables. "Each of these entries is a donation to Mr. Wembley's campaign or to a charitable cause dear to his heart. To the right is legislation that Mr. Wembley sponsored or supported."

"So, the guy's for sale?" As usual, Dog cut quickly to the heart of the matter.

Victor nodded. "And he's a bit strapped for cash, so our timing is good."

In the last seven U. S. presidential elections, The Council had been increasingly influential. The Council's members understood that many languages were spoken in Washington D. C.; but the most prominent one was the language of money, a language The Council spoke fluently. The Council's first foray into presidential elections was in 1992 when it invested over $10 million in the winner. This investment paid over tenfold in the succeeding four years in terms of influence, inside information, and access to the world's most powerful politicians.

The Council built on its 1992 success by growing its investment in each election cycle to a monumental $200 million in 2008 and $300 million in 2012. All "'invest-ments" filtered through the vast resources under The Council's control, including 20,000 Council-created identities—each fully outfitted with a social security number, a driver's license, and a faux occupation. There were also hundreds of corporations, scores of unions and trade groups, and dozens of non-profits—all without any trace of illegality.

"So, what's the play? How much is our initial investment?" Easy offered his first salvo into the fray.

"I am meeting with Senator Wembley in a couple of weeks representing Youngblood and Associates. I will tell him I can guarantee a cash influx of $20 million immediately, with lots of headroom to go well above that as the campaign unfolds. I expect that will get his attention." Victor had a way of speaking that inspired The Council's confidence. Council members assumed this would be the "normal" process that had been deployed in each of the last six presidential campaigns: Invest a large sum of money in the eventual winner and in return have access to all branches of government and to have direct input into executive orders and, more importantly, into agency directives that impacted literally billions of dollars of commerce.

"I don't know much about Mr. Wembley. How is he going to rise from relative obscurity to the highest office in the land?" Easy was typically the last to speak but once his flywheel started spinning, he was difficult to quiet.

"That's a great question. Mr. Wembley is currently polling in fifth place among the nine Republican hopefuls. That's actually a great spot to be in at this time. We don't want him to peak too early." Victor clicked to the next image on the screen. "This guy is Bobby Lincoln, the governor of Kentucky. He's had a very successful eight years in office. He's bright, articulate, funny, handsome, sincere, and actually quite humble—all traits that endear him to the American people."

"So, what are we going to do about Mr. Lincoln?" Dog quizzed.

"Just like the last 20 years, if there's someone in the way of our guy, we have to bring him down," Victor replied bluntly.

"What's your plan?" Dog continued.

"I have a new Mouse Trap recruit who's perfect for the job. I will update you on that in the near future."

Victor and The Council continued to review the list of announced and probable candidates, discussing their strengths and weaknesses. He knew exactly what buttons to push on each member so that The Council would unanimously conclude that Grant Wembley was their guy. Had they known what fate would be awaiting them, they would have most certainly chosen a different path. Unfortunately, they were in the dark, just as Victor Youngblood had planned.

The first Monday of the month was a day that Elijah almost always dreaded. It was the standing date for the monthly meeting of the Promise Ministries Board of Directors.

When Elijah started Promise Ministries almost 30 years prior, it consisted of him and a few friends and family members who had a heart to serve Central America's hurting and needy. As the ministry grew, Elijah saw the need for more formality and more wisdom that could result from establishing a board of directors. Since the beginning, Elijah had hand-picked the directors, focusing on those who shared his passion for service. The fact that they were some of his closest friends provided a bit of a buffer to Elijah's dread of these meetings but only a small one.

Intellectually, Elijah understood that the meetings were necessary, but he would often say that the board somehow managed to cram 15 minutes of real work into three hours of meeting time. This night would be an exception.

"We have been given an amazing opportunity that I want to share with you. A representative from USAN has contacted us to assess our interest in expanding into South America." Barbara Driscoll had been serving as chairman of the board for almost two years. She was regarded as being among the most capable to serve in the role. She shared Elijah's love for the ministry, if not his zeal for meeting efficiency.

"I'm sorry, what's USAN?" a board member asked, speaking for most who were unfamiliar with the acronym.

"Union of South American Nations, more commonly known in that region as UNASUR, based on the Spanish translation *Union de Naciones Suramericanas*. It is an intergovernmental organization comprised of 12 South American countries." As Elijah spoke the depth of his intellect continued to amaze even his closest friends. Some people know a little about a lot; others know a lot about a little. Elijah was the rare exception that seemed to know a lot about almost everything.

"Exactly," Barbara responded. "In the last year USAN has been searching for ways to reach out to the poorest citizens of their countries. Looking for success stories in other regions, they say our name kept coming up for what we've done in Central America. They'd like for us to consider expansion."

"So the obvious question is..."

"Money." Barbara headed off the question before it was asked. "USAN has taken an interesting tack regarding funding. With countries like Brazil, Chile, Argentina, and Columbia, they could—and have thrown tens of millions of dollars at the problem of poverty. They've found that the more money they provide, the more...," Barbara paused, trying to find the right words, "unscrupulous characters get involved. They have foundations spending 90+% of the proceeds on administrative costs to solve the problem. They have celebrities who come in for a couple of days, bring camera crews, make a big splash, and then leave. They have opportunistic businessmen who create charities out of the ether, just to get a share of the cash."

"So let me guess. We are welcome to help; we just gotta raise the funding." a skeptical board member interjected.

"Sort of, but it's a bit more complicated than that. I was impressed with how much my USAN contacts knew about us. They knew our administrative costs were low.

They knew all of the countries where we have a presence. They even knew about the vision for Promise Ministries. The bottom line is that they believe the most effective aid organizations are those that have skin in the game, not those that are given big bags of money to come in and help. So, for every dollar we raise, they will match dollar for dollar up to three million. After three million, we get three dollars for every dollar we raise up to ten million. After ten million we'll reassess the relationship. They'll also provide us land in their countries to build Promise Homes, Promise Schools and even churches. They'll also guarantee us police support in the areas where we build to ensure everyone's safety. Lastly, they'll give us direct access to the highest levels of their governments to raise issues, discuss success stories, and offer advice on other ways to help the poor in their countries. This is a golden opportunity for Promise Ministries. What do you think?"

The board understood that this could be a game changer for Promise Ministries. Each of the seven board members turned to Elijah, seeking his perspective before speaking.

Feeling the gaze of each set of eyes squarely upon him, Elijah sensed the responsibility to weigh-in. "On my first trip to Central America, God very clearly gave me a vision for reaching the suffering people of that region. Since that day He has kept the flame of that vision burning and has been faithful to provide the means to satisfy it. He has blessed us beyond anything that we could have ever imagined." Elijah paused, shaking his head and being stirred to tears. "The fact that we have this opportunity to reach the people of South America is incredible."

Brought onto the board for his business acumen and his feet-on-the-ground counsel, Kyle Fortner tried to interject some reality to the discussion. "So, we have to provide half of the funding for this new opportunity? You guys do recall that our budget has increased only modestly over the past five years. Where do we think we'll get millions of dollars more?"

"God will provide." Elijah knew that this was a subject that could not be resolved by hours of debate and that a rational plan could not be developed to quickly raise millions of dollars. He did have the experience of the past 30 years that assured him that, where God provided an opportunity, He would also provide the resources to see that opportunity come to fruition. "I don't know how, and I can't lay out a 20-step plan right now; but I know He will provide. Let's set aside the money issue and spend time on what this might look like. Let's dream a little."

For the next four hours, the board discussed the logistics of expanding to South America. They considered which countries provided the best opportunity to start and looked at specific areas within those countries that the USAN suggested as needing the most assistance. It was the most satisfying board meeting that Elijah could remember. He just had to wait to see how God would provide. He wouldn't have to wait long.

28

Jeremy rubbed his hands together until they were raw. He licked his lips but couldn't muster enough moisture to provide any relief. He even got up from his chair and paced the floor of the office trying to calm his anxieties. Jeremy was certain he had never been this nervous in his 22 years of life. He had good reason to be nervous. This was his first real test in this new, crazy, amazing, unbelievable, surreal job in which he found himself. That would be enough of a challenge, but it was compounded by this being a one-on-one with Victor. Jeremy found something terribly intimidating about his new boss. Something? How about everything? His deep baritone voice; his tall stature; his deep-blue eyes that seem to peer deep into your soul. Yes, Jeremy knew he had a good reason for his nerves. Just as he finally began to calm himself, the door opened.

"Jeremy! How is my newest star protégé doing?"

"I am doing well, Victor."

"Omnia tells me you are."

Jeremy was taken aback. "Omnia? Omnia told you I was doing well?"

"Yes, Omnia has several levels of artificial intelligence built into it. It learns how knowledgeable a person is by the number and types of queries that person runs. I get reports from Omnia each evening. She...I call her a she...is impressed by how quickly you have learned to navigate her. You seem to have a knack for this."

"Thanks...I think. I've never been complimented by a computer before."

Victor burst out laughing. "And a sense of humor as well. Yes, Jeremy, I think you have found a home here at Mouse Trap! Now, down to the business at hand. I asked you six weeks ago to develop a plan to derail Governor Bobby Lincoln's campaign. Let's hear what you've come up with."

Jeremy's heart began to race again; he took a deep breath and began, "OK...I've been doing a lot of research..."

"Yes, Omnia told me."

Jeremy chuckled awkwardly and appreciated Victor lightening the mood a bit. "Yes, I'm sure it did."

"*She.*" Victor corrected.

"Oh yes, *she*...anyway, I went back to Governor Lincoln's college days. He was a fairly good student with a 3.5 GPA, which is impressive considering he was also playing basketball for the University of Kentucky, a very time-consuming pursuit. I've looked at his court records; he has a few speeding tickets but nothing beyond that. He has a number of investment accounts and a net worth of around five million dollars but nothing unusual. I've accessed the video feed from the security firm that monitors his house, and again, nothing exciting. He and his wife seem to have a good relationship and an active sex life. I've reviewed all of his personal and state e-mails, and a couple of things have emerged. His biggest benefactor is a guy named Cam Calvin, a third-generation coal mining magnate, who has a net worth of over $300 million. More importantly, he's well connected to many deep-pocket investors, businessmen, actors, and athletes. He actually seems to idolize Governor Lincoln and has already hosted three fundraisers for him. Get this: almost 80% of Governor Lincoln's presidential fund came from investors tied to Cam Calvin. If we can somehow get to Cam Calvin, we can dry up the Governor Lincoln's primary source of funding."

It took a lot to impress Victor Youngblood. As the mastermind of both Mouse Trap and Omnia, the guy was brilliant. But he knew that Jeremy Prince was a prodigy, and he liked the confirmation that his instincts for finding talent were still sharp well into his 70s.

"Very good, Jeremy. This is well done."

"There's one more guy, Gary Carlisle, who serves as both the Governor's chief of staff as well as his campaign manager. From their e-mail exchanges, the Governor's actions, as well as his speeches, Mr. Carlisle is obviously the behind-the-scenes brains, while the Governor is a bit of a figurehead. Don't get me wrong, Bobby Lincoln is a bright guy; but when you hear him talk about the gross domestic product, the difference between Sunni and Shia Muslims, and the need to regulate trade with Mexico, the Governor's lips may be moving, but you know Gary Carlisle is his primary source of information. If we can get Mr. Carlisle a better gig somewhere else, the Governor's security blanket would be removed."

"So, what do you propose as a next step, Mr. Prince."

"I think we should focus Project Lincoln on Cam Calvin and Gary Carlisle. For Cam Calvin, we should try to throw a wrench into the relationship. Show something that Governor Lincoln has done that would erode Cam Calvin's trust. With Omnia, I'm sure we can find some viable options. For Gary Carlisle, the guy is brilliant and he works in state government making 130 grand a year. He could easily be a corporate VP making at least triple that. I think we should arrange a new business opportunity—a promotion for Mr. Carlisle."

"Good work, Jeremy. This is fantastic. Both initiatives are approved to go forward. I'm impressed."

Not quite expecting such praise and quick decision-making, Jeremy simply said, "Thank you," then rode the tide of his accomplishments to move ahead. "OK, I think we should…"

Victor raised a hand. "Slow down, young Prince. Do you know what else Omnia has been telling me, Jeremy?"

"No, I don't. What has it…uh…she, been telling you?"

"That you have been working 14 to 16 hour days, including weekends. Take some extra time off. Head up to see your folks. I'm sure they miss you. In fact take a week off and come back to work refreshed and renewed next Wednesday, ready to implement your plan."

"Thank you, Victor. I really appreciate that. I do miss my mom's strawberry pie. Tell Omnia I'll see her next week."

"I'll tell her, Jeremy. I know she'll miss you. Enjoy your time away."

Jeremy could not possibly comprehend the series of events that he had just set in motion—events that would eventually make him question everything he thought he knew about both his new job and, more importantly, his new boss.

Three long strides were followed by a majestic leap toward the heavens. Just as the ball had reached its apex, it was snatched from the sky. The next sound heard was a loud splash as the surface of Watts Bar Lake was pierced.

As he capped off most days when home in Tennessee, Elijah sat on his dock playing fetch with his beloved dog Clyde, a Blue Merle Aussiedoodle. Clyde swam to the shore, climbed out of the lake, dropped the ball at Elijah's feet, shook the water off his gray- and-tan coat, and then readied himself for the next throw.

Since his daughters moved out of the house, Clyde provided the only companionship Elijah had most nights. Although he'd admit to moments of melancholy loneliness, he enjoyed these peaceful evenings with his canine best buddy.

The peace on this night would end, however, when Elijah's cell phone rang. Against his better judgement, he answered, "This is Elijah."

"Elijah, this is Sammy Southern from Newstalk 101.7. How are you this evening?"

"I was fine until I stupidly answered the phone."

A burst of laughter was heard through the phone, followed by "Elijah, that's funny man, very funny!"

Sammy Southern was Knoxville's number-one rated talk-radio personality. He hosted a talk show from six to ten in the morning with an emphasis on East Tennessee issues and personalities.

"I'm glad I could brighten your mood, Sammy."

Sammy and Elijah were acquaintances who had met through a number of East Tennessee civic outings benefiting local charities, such as United Way and Knoxville Area Rescue Ministries. Sammy had encouraged Elijah to come on his show many times but hadn't found the right carrot to entice Elijah. He thought the time was ripe to try again.

"Elijah, I've been reading about Promise Connection where you place orphaned Central American kids with homes in the U. S. That's some strong stuff, man."

"Thanks, Sammy, but I know you didn't just call to compliment me."

"I'm going to be blunt, my friend; I want you to come on my show. Would you at least consider it this time?"

"Come on, Sammy, you know that's not my thing."

"But we can talk about whatever *is* your thing: Promise Connection, Promise Transportation, your kids, whatever you want to talk about."

"Maybe even some YouTube videos, huh?" Elijah asked knowingly.

Realizing that Elijah had somehow figured out his real motive, Sammy tried to pay dumb. "YouTube videos? What are you talking about?"

"Come on, Sammy, don't insult what little intelligence I have left."

Deciding to come clean, Sammy changed course. "OK, the YouTube videos are becoming a really big deal; and yes, we may discuss those. But seriously you can talk about anything you want. I have slots open next week. Can I count you in?"

"I don't think so, Sammy; it's just not..."

"I'll have you on for a full hour, and I guarantee we'll discuss Promise Ministries at least half the time. You can give out the website. I guarantee the listeners will respond. Think of all the money you can raise, Elijah."

Elijah paused for what seemed like an eternity, recalling his last Promise Ministries' board meeting and the opportunity to expand to South America, an opportunity that could only be pursued with a hefty influx of cash.

"You still there, Sammy?"

"Still here, Elijah, just waiting to hear a yes."

"And at least half of the time we'd talk about the ministry?"

"Guaranteed. I promise you won't regret this, Elijah. I'll talk to you tomorrow to settle on the exact date. We are going to have a good time, my friend, a really good time."

Elijah hung up and stared into the sun setting over Watts Bar Lake. "What have I gotten myself into, Clyde?"

It was just another step toward a year that Elijah could never have imagined.

29

"Your first meeting this morning is with Victor Youngblood."

"Victor Youngblood? That name is familiar. Do I know him?"

"He's a PR guy."

"We already have a PR guy. Why am I meeting with him?"

"Ted Miller, Randy Martinez, and Olivia Brumbaugh all strongly encouraged you to meet with him."

Those three names, being at the top of Grant Wembley's donor list, caused his ears to perk up. "Oh, OK, I'll make time then."

''That's good because he's already here."

Each morning Senator Wembley met with his chief of staff, Madeline Chung, to review the day's calendar. Most of the recent meetings involved his prospective transition from Wyoming's senior senator to the highest office in the land, the president of the United States. Many meetings presented *quid pro quo* opportunities in which power and/or access would be exchanged for a donation to the Wembley for President Campaign Fund. The meeting with Victor Youngblood would be similar in purpose but much, much different in scale—a fact that Grant Wembley would come to learn all too well over the course of the next year and a half.

Looking at his watch, Grant asked, "Wow, is he early?"

"He really didn't have an appointment. I was just told that he'd be here first thing this morning and that we needed to make sure we cleared your schedule for him."

"OK, I guess the schedule is cleared," Grant replied.

"I'll show him in. Oh, I almost forgot, great news on the fundraising front. Last night we got over $10 million in contributions."

"Ten million?! Last night?! From whom?"

"That's the weird part; it was small-to-medium contributions from hundreds of donors. You didn't go on any talk shows and give out the campaign website did you?"

"Of course not, you'd know if I did."

"Well, congratulations, things seem to be looking up for you. I'll get Mr. Youngblood."

A cash influx of $10 million more than doubled Senator Wembley's coffers. Although the campaign was in its early stages, this was definitely an encouraging sign that things were trending in the right direction. He'd soon discover why.

"Come on in, Mr. Youngblood; this is…"

With a huge smile and an arms-wide-open greeting, Victor immediately demonstrated how he got his start in public relations.

"Grant Wembley in the flesh! I've seen you so many times on Fox News I feel like we're already friends." Victor extended his right hand. "I'm Victor Youngblood. I can't tell you what a pleasure it is to finally meet you."

There was something imposing about Victor Youngblood beyond his six-foot-four stature. He commanded respect, even from a U.S. senator. "It's nice to meet you as well, Mr. Youngblood."

Sensing his boss was starting the conversation from a position of weakness, Madeline tried to take control of the situation. "Victor, why don't you take a seat; and we'll get down to business."

Victor looked Madeline in the eye, then looked at Grant. "Senator, I hope you don't find this too forward; but I would really appreciate it if we could have a one-on-one conversation."

Madeline interjected, "That's OK, anything you can say in front of the Senator, you can say in front of me."

In a move akin to a Jedi mind trick, Victor simply looked at Senator Wembley and offered a smile, to which

Grant responded, "It's OK, Madeline; I'll meet with Mr. Youngblood alone."

"But..."

"It's OK, Madeline; I'll be fine."

Shooting daggers at Victor, Madeline responded, "Fine!" and walked briskly out of the room.

Grant gestured in the direction of a set of couches situated in the front of his spacious Russell Senate Office Building suite. "Let's take a seat, Mr. Youngblood."

Looking around the room as he sat, Victor complimented his host on the decor. "You must be quite a sportsman, Senator."

Grant's office walls were adorned with over 20 taxidermy specimens, including bison, elk, moose, antelope, bighorn sheep, deer, northern pike, rainbow trout, and walleye.

"Well, I am from Wyoming, where the Great Plains meet the Rocky Mountains."

It was a response that Grant had regurgitated hundreds of times to comments about his office. It was his way of perpetuating the notion that he was an actual outdoorsman without having to tell the truth, a refined skill of most politicians. The reality was that he had not bagged a single animal mounted on his office walls. In fact, he'd never killed anything bigger than a squirrel and that was by accident when the scared critter dashed in front of his car. Grant worked hard to portray himself as a rugged outdoorsman, but he was exactly the opposite. His office was a perfect metaphor for his entire life:

a carefully orchestrated, synthetic persona that in no way represented the actual man.

Gazing around the room, Victor shook his head in awe and commented, "Wow, I bet you have some amazing stories about how you took down these beasts."

In reality Victor already knew everything there was to know about Senator Grant Wembley. He knew he was no hunter. He knew he was no fisherman. He knew he was a malleable ball of clay that he could form into anything he wanted—exactly the reason he was chosen.

"Yes, yes, lots of stories, but you didn't come to hear my hunting stories. I understand we have some mutual friends."

"We do indeed, Senator; and they all speak very highly of you."

By "highly" Victor of course meant that Grant was available for hire to the highest bidder, and the bidders came no higher than Victor Youngblood.

"You are too kind, Mr. Youngblood."

Victor decided it was time to end the niceties and get down to business.

"Senator, you have announced your candidacy to be the Republican nominee for the president of the United States."

Taken aback a bit by Victor's abrupt change of topics, Grant responded, "Yes, I...uh...have."

"Senator, I am going to cut to the chase. I represent a large number of very influential people. We have a significant interest in the election's outcome and would like to find the right person to support. I'm here today to determine if you are that person."

"I appreciate that and would welcome your support. I think I have a lot to offer the American people. I've been a U.S. senator for 18 years, I've been on the Senate Armed Services Committee, I..."

"We're familiar with your résumé, Senator; that's not really the question."

"OK, well..."

"Senator, how badly do you want to be president?" Victor asked pointedly.

"Well, I think I could serve this country..."

Victor shook his head. "Cut the crap, Senator. How badly do you want to be president?"

"I'd like to lower taxes, reduce regulations..."

"*Senator*, how badly do you want to be president?" Victor asked a third time.

Grant let out a huge sigh, looked down at the floor, and then finally up to Victor. "I've never wanted anything more."

"That's good. We can provide significant assistance in achieving this objective. By now you've probably been told that your campaign had a substantial influx of donations in the last day or so, something on the order of $10 million."

His mouth gaping, Grant was momentarily unable to speak.

Victor filled the silence, "We wanted to demonstrate that we are serious about supporting a campaign and that we have the resources to be of significant assistance."

Finally able to muster a response, Grant replied, "But I understood the large influx was actually from hundreds of small donations."

"It was. We have many options available to us when it comes to expending our resources."

Grant took a moment to let that statement settle. "OK, you have my attention. What do you want in return for this very generous donation?"

"You need to understand two things before we go any further. Number one, this recent donation is a drop in the bucket compared to what we can provide going forward. Number two, we are vetting a number of candidates to find the one who best aligns with our objectives."

Number two was a total fabrication. In reality, Victor had a Mouse Trap Project active for months to identify the candidate who could most easily be manipulated to meet the ultimate plan Victor had hatched. Grant was clearly their guy, but he didn't need to know that yet.

Grant offered a nervous reply, "Other candidates? Well...I really think you don't need to consider other candidates. I really think I'm your guy," forgetting that Victor had left the "what do you want in return" question unanswered.

"That's encouraging to hear. I'm sure you have some questions about exactly what we want in return."

"Well, uh...certainly, yes; but I'm sure we can work something out."

"The most important thing we're looking for in a candidate is flexibility. We need to find someone who is open to a variety of suggestions and ideas that we may have—nothing illegal, of course."

"As I said, I feel certain that we can work something out," Grant stammered.

"Senator Wembley, I'm very encouraged by our meeting today and want to ensure you that you will be given every consideration as we seek to finalize the candidate we choose to support."

"What do we need to do today to make this happen—to not consider other candidates?" The deal-making politician in Grant had finally come to the surface.

Victor allowed an awkward silence to fill the room before finally responding. "If you're serious about going forward, we do have somewhat of a litmus test."

"I'm listening."

''The Army is requesting a new armored personnel carrier, but the request is hung up in the Subcommittee on Airland. If you could break that free, you would not only do the army a great service, it would also be a gesture that would show that you are serious about working with us. When the request is approved, you could expect the next installment to the Grant Wembley for President Fund, on a similar scale to the last one. You should have recently received information about the armored carrier via e-mail."

"OK, I'll..."

Before Grant could respond, Victor got up from the couch and extended a hand to him. "Senator, I'm afraid that's all the time I have. I sincerely appreciate you meeting with me, and I look forward to expanding and growing our relationship."

"Mr. Youngblood, this was most certainly an unexpected visit; but I am confident that we can make this work," Grant declared.

"I hope that we can, Senator. Good day."

Victor quickly left Grant Wembley's office. Before the door shut, Madeline entered to check on her boss. "What was that all about?"

"Madeline, we gotta talk."

"How much longer before we are able to move into this space?"

"Still looks like another four weeks."

Walter Prince was a patient man, but his patience was beginning to run out. "Four weeks?! You were supposed to be done by now."

"The job turned out to be more complicated than we had thought, and don't forget you added the extra loading bay. That impacted the project by at least two weeks."

The project was an expansion of Prince's Hardware, the first in over 20 years. Just a few months earlier,

Walter and Rosita Prince were entertaining the thoughts of closing the business because of declining revenues. However, with the additional commerce the government contracts generated, business was booming and more space was needed. Walter had recently purchased a shuttered pharmacy next door and was in the process of converting that space into a warehouse with three loading bays. He was now dealing with his construction contractor who did not have the same sense of urgency as Walter. He finally concluded that yelling wasn't going to accelerate the schedule, so he tried a bit of diplomacy.

"I appreciate everything you've done. It looks great so far. I'm OK with the four weeks, but I really can't accommodate any more delays. We already have product clogging our aisles."

"I understand; we'll do our best."

"Thank you, I really appreciate it." As Walter extended a hand to the contractor, he heard a scream from inside the store and ran in that direction. Upon turning the corner to head down the plumbing aisle, he saw the source of the scream. His wife Rosita was engaged in a full-on mama-bear hug with Jeremy, whom she hadn't seen in almost two months. Her back was to Walter as Jeremy peered over his diminutive mom's shoulder, his face red from the grip of her embrace. He displayed a huge grin, which elicited its own contagious smile from Walter.

Walter took a step toward his son. "It's wonderful to see you, Jeremy. How have you been?"

Before Jeremy could respond, his mom momentarily released her grip to ask, "How long are you home for?"

"I am actually here for a few days. I don't have to leave until Tuesday afternoon."

The answer tightened Rosita's grip on her son.

"For heaven's sake, Rosita, let the boy breath."

"It's OK, Dad, I've missed you guys too." Jeremy looked around the store noticing the shelves and aisles full of product, a sight he hadn't seen since he was a young boy. "Wow, Dad, looks like business is going great!"

"Things are definitely looking up. I'm not complaining, but rapid growth brings its own set of challenges. I'm trying to hire additional staff, which has proven to be difficult. I've also leased the empty building next door to convert into a warehouse to clear these aisles, but it is running behind."

Although Walter's words spoke of tests and trials, Jeremy heard in his dad's voice something that hadn't been there in years: excitement, passion, and pride. He took a brief moment to reflect on yet another dividend from his time at Mouse Trap. It was further confirmation that Jeremy had made the right decision to join this unconventional organization.

"How about a nice big piece of strawberry pie?"

"Mom, I thought you'd never ask."

"Do you ever wonder if it's worth it, Gary?"

"If *what's* worth *what*?"

"If these long nights are really worth the time away from our families. If the years of our lives that are being consumed will ever bear fruit. Do you really think we have a chance to win? If we do actually win, do you think we will be able to make a difference?"

"I like the quote attributed to Henry Ford: 'Whether you think you can, or you think you can't—you're right.' And Bobby, I think you *can* turn this country around the same way you turned Kentucky around," Gary reassured.

As they wound down yet another long day, Bobby Lincoln and his chief of staff, Gary Carlisle, were having their weekly discussions about the future. Governor Lincoln was ever the introspective man, always needing confirmation that he was doing the right thing. Gary Carlisle was perfect in his role as trusted sidekick, content to be the Robin to Bobby's Batman—always the encourager and quick to support his rhetoric with facts.

"Bobby, your policies moved the Commonwealth of Kentucky from near the bottom of the pile to the top third in education, employment, and economic development; plus, teen pregnancies dropped. Your common sense conservatism worked for Kentucky, and it will work for the country."

It was a variation of a pep talk that Gary had given Bobby dozens of times in the past ten years. On this particular night, Bobby just needed to hear it again.

"I believe that Gary; I really do." Bobby was continually working to convince himself he was as good a leader as Gary thought he was. Bobby's effort was not lost on Gary. He was comfortable working in the background, fashioning many of the policies for which Bobby Lincoln would receive credit. This arrangement brought Gary Carlisle a full measure of contentment.

Gary was among the most genuine men anyone would ever encounter. Exceedingly smart, he had an elephant-like memory and a penchant for details. Most importantly, he was the conscience of his boss, with a character grounded in equal parts faith, hard work, and small-town wisdom. He was truly a good man, making the events that were about to befall him particularly tragic.

"Let's call it a night, Gary. Crystal will be up waiting for you."

"She probably will." Closing the screen on his laptop, Gary grabbed his car keys and started to head for the door. "Good night, Governor."

"Good night, Gary. Drive safely."

30

It was a pastime that Cam Calvin didn't get to enjoy as often as he'd like. If he were fully in control of his schedule, he'd start every morning in the stables of Golden Poplar Farms, saddling his favorite filly, Bonnie Lou. Instead, he could only set aside one day a week, Saturday; but he maintained that routine religiously.

He would arise at 6:00 a.m., read the newspaper, eat a bowl of cereal, brush his teeth, and walk down to the stable by 6:45. He'd visit with each horse before prepping Bonnie Lou for the morning ride. Their journey would lead them to the western border of the property, around the lake, past the guest house, and ultimately back to the stable. One circuit would take a leisurely 30 minutes, and Cam always made the route twice. His favorite hour of the week, it provided peace, solitude, and a time to ponder life's biggest questions.

On this particular Saturday morning, Cam was right on schedule. He had just placed the saddle on Bonnie Lou when he heard a nearby rustling and thought he saw movement out of the corner of his eye.

"Is someone there?"

It unfolded like so many protests before. Person A doesn't like something that Person B said and/or did. Person A explains his or her grievances to a few friends who are convinced that Person B has done wrong. Soon enough, Person A has accumulated enough like-minded people that they publicize their concerns to cause Person B embarrassment and shame, and ultimately deprive them of some opportunity they had previously been afforded. This scenario has become so formulaic and predictable that we can all unconsciously repeat it like the tune to an ad jingle playing involuntarily in our heads.

Such was the case six months ago in tiny Bard's Ridge, Tennessee, on the campus of Richfield College. A professor had concluded that a gentleman named Elijah Mustang had committed atrocious acts that should disqualify him from speaking at the college's graduation ceremony. The professor found a series of sympathetic ears in students who joined her protest, chanting slogans, and carrying signs. Before long the rabble had grown to dozens and then hundreds of students demanding the administration send Mr. Mustang packing and find a more suitable speaker.

We all started reporting on the protest, first the local newspapers and then—BAM! We all showed up. Media trucks with satellite dishes lined the streets of Richfield College. National news reporters filled every hotel within a 30-mile radius. Then somehow—exactly how nobody knows— the protest swelled and became more serious. Rocks were thrown, cars overturned, trash cans were set on fire. The pressure mounted, and Richfield College's administrators finally did the only thing they could to quell the unrest. They announced that they would disinvite Mr. Mustang and find an alternate graduation speaker. The protestors cheered. They had accomplished their objective in starting the protest. Life returned to normal on the quiet little campus in Tennessee. We in the media packed our trucks, pens, and laptops, and then headed down the road to the next train wreck, just like we do every...single...time.

The problem is, nobody bothered to ask one important question: Was Elijah Mustang guilty of the transgressions for which he was accused? The question has become relevant as Mr. Mustang is back in the limelight starring in a series of surreptitiously recorded videos that have caught the fancy of millions of viewers on social media.

So, back to the question: Was Elijah Mustang guilty of the transgressions for which he was accused? This reporter took the time, albeit six months too late, to find out. I spoke with many people close to Mr. Mustang and even interviewed Mr. Mustang himself. I researched his company Promise Transportation. I investigated his charity, Promise Ministries. I looked closely at his Congressional record. Yes, Elijah Mustang served in the U. S. House of Representatives for four years. After spending weeks reviewing the factual record of Elijah Mustang, I have come to the painful conclusion that we blew it. Every...single...one of us blew it. We accepted the narrative that if enough people cry foul, then there must be a foul. We didn't just do a disservice to Mr. Mustang but to our profession as journalists who presumably only report the facts. Boy, did we screw this one up!

Courtney slowly removed her glasses; looked up from the draft with an expression as if someone had taken her reserved parking spot; raised both arms, palms up; and asked, "What the hell is *this*?"

Tyler cocked his head slightly and replied, "I gotta admit, that's a more reserved response than I was expecting."

"I'm serious. What the hell *is* this?"

"You didn't even finish reading the article."

"I didn't need to!" Then Courtney read aloud, "Boy, did we screw this one up!" Shaking her head. "I think this is EXACTLY what I told you NOT to write!"

"But we did. We screwed it up, not just NNS but every media outlet. I wonder how many other protest stories we've gotten wrong. It's like when someone on death row is proven innocent, the obvious question we all ask is 'How many others are innocent?'"

Still shaking her head, Courtney was fully animated. "What exactly do you expect me to do with this?"

"I expect you to publish it," Tyler said, matter-of-factly.

Now chuckling, Courtney replied, "Publish it?! Are you serious?"

"Very serious."

"What possible motivation would I have for publishing this?"

"Let's see. The truth. Journalistic integrity. Setting the record straight. Clearing the name of a good man."

"Let me make this as clear as I can: no, no, no *and no*."

"I understand your hesitancy but..."

"How many times do I have to say NO for you to get the message?"

"Hear me out; the guy is back in the public consciousness. Sooner or later some publication is going to figure out that we all screwed up and is going to correct the record. Wouldn't you rather NNS be the one doing the correcting rather than being corrected?"

After an awkward silence, Courtney again put on her glasses and scanned Tyler's draft. For the first time conceding that Tyler could have a point, Courtney asked, "How many hits do his videos have?"

"The most viral is up to over ten million."

After a huge sigh Courtney finally offered, "I'll take this up the chain. Sit on it until I get back with you. I'm making no promises!"

"Courtney, I'm telling you, he's a good guy. I really think this is the right thing to do."

"We'll see."

31

May 31, 2015
527 Days Until 2016 U. S. Presidential Election

Although his goal was to get away from work for a few days, Jeremy Prince couldn't resist the urge to turn on the morning news to start his day. Since his exposure to Mouse Trap, Jeremy had found watching the news amusing to see what world events his organization had orchestrated. On this morning, there was the usual unrest in the Middle East, concerns about the fragile economy, and a story about a big trade in Major League Baseball. Then this report hit the airwaves:

> *"...and now in politics, Kentucky Governor Bobby Lincoln, who has announced his candidacy for the presidency, confirmed today that*

> *his chief of staff, Gary Carlisle, who was tran-*
> *sitioning to become his presidential campaign*
> *manager, was killed in a one-car accident on a*
> *remote highway in central Kentucky. He leaves*
> *behind a wife of 27 years, a daughter age 19,*
> *and a son age 23. In other news..."*

Jeremy turned off the TV. He wondered how Carlisle's death would impact his project. He knew Bobby Lincoln would select a replacement soon enough but would he or she have the same impact that Gary Carlisle had? Jeremy decided to do a quick web search on his tablet for "Bobby Lincoln Campaign Manager Gary Carlisle." He found several stories about Mr. Carlisle's death and decided to click the link to a story in the *Lexington Herald Leader.* The story covered the facts of Mr. Carlisle's death, his role as chief of staff with Bobby Lincoln, his pending transition to campaign manager, and some of his background information. Then Jeremy noticed this sentence:

> *This news was particularly difficult for*
> *Governor Lincoln, as one of his most influen-*
> *tial supporters, Cam Calvin, was also found*
> *dead this morning from a horse riding accident.*

Initially thinking, "That's odd," Jeremy clicked on a link to the story about Cam Calvin. The article stated that Mr. Calvin had apparently had been thrown from a horse at his farm as he was found lying across a fence with a broken back and neck, his horse saddled and walking nearby. He thought, "Wow, what are the odds of both guys I was supposed to be researching dying on the same day?" Then it hit him. All of the blood rushed from his face; his heart began to pound; his palms moistened. His thoughts came so quickly he couldn't process them all. The odds were astronomical!

"Crap!" he involuntarily exclaimed. "Crap! Crap! Crap! Surely not! Crap!" Jeremy jumped from the couch and began to pace frantically as his mom entered the room.

"Good morning, Sweetie. How are you?" Rosita said.

"Crap! This can't be!"

"What can't be? What's wrong, Jeremy?"

"I...I... just need to think, Mom." He ran out of the house into the back yard facing a greenbelt and ventured into the edge of the woods, almost as if to hide.

"It was just four days ago," he thought. "Is it possible that someone...that Victor...could have pulled this off in just four days?" These events were all dizzying to Jeremy. He didn't know what to do, where to turn, whom to talk with. It would be three days until he returned to Mouse Trap. He couldn't possibly wait that long to talk about this. That's it! He'd go back to Mouse Trap and confront Victor. In fact, he'd go right now! He felt in the pocket of his shorts (the one's he'd slept in) and found his keys. Without a word to his parents, he made a beeline for his car and started on the journey back to Bethesda. Jeremy knew he'd make what was usually a six-hour trip in record time. In the blink of an eye, he was on Interstate 81 headed north.

Mitch McCoy knew it would be difficult. He considered that when he decided to run. He expected this to be an uphill battle all the way to election day; however, he'd have to admit the campaign was proving even more challenging than he had envisioned.

One of his primary platforms was establishing a wealth tax on millionaires and billionaires to transfer a portion of the accumulated gains from the hands of individuals into the coffers of the country. He felt this tax was not only necessary to get the country back on a sound financial footing but also a form of social justice to right the many wrongs capitalism had exacted over the last 200 years.

This position presented a daunting conundrum for the McCoy for President Campaign. It had been estimated that fund raising in excess of a billion dollars would be needed to wage a successful run for the Oval Office in 2016. Any candidate would need support from the same millionaires and billionaires upon whom Mitch McCoy planned to impose this new levy. This inherent conflict made the news he had just received particularly satisfying.

"$10 million in just one day?!" Mitch wanted to make sure he'd heard his campaign manager correctly.

"Yes, $10 million. And it's not from fat-cat Wall Street bankers. It's from several hundred individual donors," his idealistic campaign manager declared.

Mitch snickered, "I don't care who it's from as long as it has dead presidents on it."

The donations proved to be fuel for Mitch's exuberant confidence, which many simply labeled arrogance.

Mitch continued, "I knew my message was resonating. I knew people would come around. Maybe I'll get some media attention now! Maybe they'll figure out I am the real deal."

He tried to calm his racing heart to no avail. He even employed breathing exercises he'd learned from the college yoga class he took ostensibly to meet hot girls. He'd never hyperventilated in his 22 years on Earth, but he reckoned this was as close as he'd ever come. He'd made the journey from Abingdon to Bethesda in record time, even with the unplanned stops for three speeding tickets, tickets that would be "handled" by Omnia.

Along the way, he tried to keep his mind away from the chaos by listening to classic rock on the radio. The Eagles' hit "Hotel California" was in the rotation. After the song was over, Jeremy couldn't seem to get out of his head these lyrics: "You can check out any time you like, but you can never leave."

Jeremy finally reached the front door of Youngblood and Associates and headed to the secure entry into Mouse Trap. Although it was a Sunday, he expected Victor to be at work. Jeremy had never known him to be anywhere but at the Mouse Trap offices or traveling on a Mouse Trap project. Many had jokingly assumed that Victor must have had a clandestine apartment tucked away somewhere in the massive complex because he was literally always at work. Today was no exception.

Bursting through Victor's office door, he started, "What in the hell did you do, Victor?" Jeremy had rehearsed his opening line for the last four hours; but he still wasn't sure it had conveyed the right mix of exasperation, anger and shock.

"Je-re-my!" Victor replied in a singsong tone, emphasizing every syllable. "Aren't you supposed to be taking a few days off?" Omnia had been tracking Jeremy's travel since he left Abingdon, so Victor suspected he was on his way to pay him a visit. He had received notification when Jeremy pulled into the parking garage, so he was prepared for what he expected to be an interesting conversation.

"Victor, you killed them! Why did you have to kill them?!"

"Jeremy, I'm afraid you are going to have to slow down and explain what you are talking about."

"Don't give me that crap, Victor; you know exactly what I'm talking about." No one...ever...ever talked to

Victor Youngblood in this manner. Jeremy was both too young and too new to know better, an attribute that Victor found both refreshing and challenging. Jeremy continued, "It can't be a coincidence that both Gary Carlisle and Cam Calvin died on the same day in mysterious accidents."

"*Mysterious?*" Now finally striking an offended tone as the work of his Mouse Trap field agents was being called into question. "What's mysterious about them? Mr. Carlisle died in a tragic automobile accident. Unfortunately, that type of accident occurs every day. Mr. Calvin was in a small enclosure with a 1000-pound beast where anything can happen."

"So you know." Jeremy waved his arms wildly in the air; his worst fears seemed to be confirmed. "I knew that you knew. Now my only question is *What level of involvement did you have?*"

Victor calmly responded, "Jeremy, is your real question *What level of involvement did YOU have?*"

Jeremy ran his hands through his hair and shook his head involuntarily. "This can't be happening."

"Jeremy, let's back up, slow down, and tell me what you think you know."

"Victor, one of the reasons you said you hired me was because I was a smart guy. Would you really want to hire someone that couldn't put the pieces together of what happened last night?"

"I am going to ask this one more time, Jeremy. Tell me what you *think* you know."

Jeremy sighed, conceding he'd have to go down the rabbit hole where Victor was coaxing him to go. "OK, Victor, I'll play along." He reset his tone from exasperation to recitation. "You determined that you, for some reason, didn't want Governor Bobby Lincoln to be the next president of the United States. You employed me to do opposition research and find some vulnerabilities that could be exploited. I spent a few weeks with Omnia and determined that there were two main guys who made Bobby Lincoln tick: the money man, Cam Calvin, and the brains behind the governor, Gary Carlisle. I briefed you on my findings, you seemed to like what you heard, and then you generously gave me a few days off to spend with my family. I woke up this morning and turned on the news to hear of the untimely passing of Mr. Carlisle. I didn't think of anything nefarious at first but assumed his death would affect Project Lincoln. I decided to do some quick research to see who might be a likely candidate to replace him, only to find that Mr. Calvin had also just met his demise."

The pace of Jeremy's speech accelerated while he worked hard to maintain a neutral tone. "Then the pieces of the puzzle started coming together; I mentally calculated this would be an impossible probability that these two events were unrelated. Next, I made the connection that I may be indirectly responsible for the death of two innocent men. Then I almost crapped my pants, wondered what the hell kind of organization I was a part of, got into my car, and drove to Bethesda in the clothes I slept in last night. Yep, that about summarizes the situation. Any questions?"

Victor calmly rose from his chair, walked past Jeremy who was still standing immediately in front of the desk, and took a seat at the small table at the other end of his office. He pressed a button revealing the fully assembled Mouse Trap board. He studied the board, leaving an awkward silence hanging in the room for what seemed like an eternity. He then motioned for Jeremy to join him. "Come on over."

Jeremy reluctantly took a seat at the table. "I am going to take you back to your first day at Mouse Trap. Do you remember our discussion? In a perfectly constructed Mouse Trap, you just turn the lever and all of the succeeding mechanisms engage, ultimately catching the mouse."

"I remember, but what..."

"It's my job to construct the Trap using all of the resources of our organization. You only have one piece of the Trap. All I ask is that you complete the projects I have assigned to you. I'll orchestrate many projects working together to build the overall Mouse Trap."

Jeremy stared at the board trying to fully comprehend what Victor was telling him. He wasn't sure he was having much success. "So... are you telling me there are other shmucks like me who are also responsible for the death of these two men?"

"No, Jeremy, that's not what I'm telling you. You are one part of a large, very complex apparatus. It is impossible for you to make a linear connection between the projects that I assign to you and outcomes you might observe in the media."

"So, you're basically telling me I'm a peon and to focus on my job and shut up?"

"Jeremy, in the early 40s the United States embarked on an ambitious endeavor called the Manhattan Project, which employed over 130,000 people. That critically important project ultimately won the war in the Pacific. Of those 130,000 people, it is estimated that fewer than 100 actually knew the full scope of the project and its ultimate purpose. Project leaders compartmentalized the tasks such that each individual focused solely on their jobs without knowing how they fit into the larger project. Even Vice President Harry Truman didn't know about the Manhattan Project until he stepped into the president's job upon FDR's death."

Again, Jeremy paused to study the board, drinking in Victor's message. He knew he had reached an important turning point in his brief time at Mouse Trap. He had a life-changing decision to make. On the one hand, maybe he could walk away. This gig was obviously much more complicated than he'd ever imagined. He'd never dreamed that he'd have a part, however small or insignificant, in the death of another human being. On the other hand, he was fascinated by everything to which he had been exposed. He was stunned to find that much of what he'd consumed as random news throughout his life could actually be a carefully orchestrated plan. The part of his psyche that led him to instigate the Richfield College protest was captivated by the prospect of discovering just how deep this thing called Mouse Trap actually went. Yes, it was a life-changing decision that he was about to make.

Jeremy looked up from the table and gazed into Victor's steely eyes with his own determined countenance. "I want to be one of the hundred."

"Come again, Jeremy."

"You said that fewer than 100 people knew about the Manhattan Project's purpose. I want to be one of those few in Mouse Trap."

Taken aback by Jeremy's boldness, Victor had to employ his own pregnant pause, ultimately culminating in an approving smile. "Are you sure you know what you're getting into, Jeremy?"

"I'm certain that I *don't* know what I'm getting into, and that's what excites me. I just jumped Victor. My feet have left the ledge. I have no idea where I'll land, but I'm ready to find out."

Victor had hoped that Jeremy might be the one that he'd been waiting for—the one who could step into a leadership role at Mouse Trap once the ultimate plan was fully executed. He'd never dreamed that Jeremy would be this anxious, this early; but he wasn't complaining. He knew that he still had to temper his student a bit, but he was ready for the next big reveal.

"Jeremy, I'm excited to hear your enthusiasm. I'm going to stoke the flame just a bit more. Walk over to my desk with me."

Jeremy and Victor walked behind Victor's desk.

"Now, take a seat."

"In your chair?" Jeremy asked cautiously.

"In my chair."

"Uh...OK."

"Now, log in to Omnia," Victor directed.

Jeremy executed the log-in protocol.

"Click on your profile. Now scroll down and you'll find a new section in green."

"Yes, I've never seen this before. What is that?"

"Click on the dollar sign."

Jeremy clicked on the dollar sign and a new screen opened.

"What is Merchants and Wall Street Bank?"

"That is one of the financial institutions that we... control."

"What a minute, what is this? This has to be a mistake. This account has my name on it, and there's a balance of $250,000." His voice carried a growing concern. "I don't owe $250,000 to anyone."

"No, you don't Jeremy. That's not a debt; that's a deposit."

"It's what?"

"I'm very proud of the work you did on Project Lincoln. You worked long hours and produced great results. Here at Mouse Trap I reward results, so congratulations on your first bonus."

"A $250,000 bonus? You gotta be kidding me!"

"It's all yours Jeremy. And I think you'll find in time that's a fairly modest investment. We hire the best people and reward them accordingly."

Any nagging feeling that he'd made the wrong decision by committing to Mouse Trap was quelled with this new revelation that not only was he signing up for the ride of his life, he was about to become a rich young man.

"Victor, I'm all in. I want to learn everything there is to know about Mouse Trap. *Everything.*"

"In due time, Jeremy, in due time."

"Hey Courtney, you wanted to see me?" Entering Courtney's office, Tyler hoped his hunch for why he was summoned was right.

"So, I spoke with the team upstairs about your Mustang article. Remind me again why you wanted to publish this so desperately."

"If you've already talked with the team upstairs, then you already have an answer and we don't have to do this dance again," Tyler crowed.

Starting to get agitated, Courtney fired back, "You know, I'm still the boss."

"If you're still the boss then why did you have to go upstairs to get permission to publish the article?"

Now fuming, Courtney was taking the insubordination personally. "Why do you have to be such a jerk?"

"It's a gift, I'm told."

Courtney just shook her head, knowing this conversation was heading in a direction she had neither the time nor interest in going.

"OK, you can publish the article. The only stipulation is that the focus has to be on Elias Mustang."

"*Elijah* Mustang," Tyler corrected.

"Whatever. The focus has to be on Mustang, and not that we screwed up. Got it?"

Tyler had heard all he needed to hear; his initial hunch was proven to be spot on. He replied, "Got it and thank you." Then he turned to leave before poking his head back into Courtney's office one last time. "Did I ever mention that you are one of the best bosses I've ever had?"

"Jerk!" Courtney responded.

32

"Goooooood morning, East Tennessee, you have found the Sammy Southern Show on the radio. We crank it early on this show and we don't hold back. We're the butter on your biscuit, the syrup on your pancake; we're the captain in your crunch and the pop in your tart. We're so glad you decided to join us this morning 'cause we've got a good one for you. I am joined this morning for an entire hour by our own East Tennessee YouTube sensation, the one and only, Elijah Mustang."

"For those of you who may have been stranded on a deserted island, imprisoned in a North Korean gulag, or on a sojourn to the Northern region of Siberia, I will recap Mr. Mustang's exploits. You see, Mr. Mustang was secretly videoed at a local restaurant extolling the virtues of this great country and lambasting some of the idiocy that threatens its greatness. Those videos were uploaded to YouTube for the world to see; and boy, has the world seen them! There are a dozen videos uploaded, each with millions of views. There's just something about Mr. Mustang's passion for this country that has struck a chord with people. I don't think we fully understand *why*. We're going to spend some time this morning examining just that question.

"But first, I have a confession. I've known Elijah for several years. We've been to a number of local fundraisers and have even played a few rounds of golf together. I considered Elijah Mustang my friend long before he became such an Internet sensation. I've known him as CEO of Promise Transportation. I've known him as head of Promise Ministries. Most importantly, I've known him as a really good guy who at his core is all about people. That's why I'm excited he has joined us in the studio this morning. Elijah, welcome to the show, my friend."

Staring at Sammy, Elijah just shook his head at the effusive compliments. "Thank you for having me, Sammy, and for those kind introductory words. I can't live up to that buildup, but I thank you anyway."

"Oh...and I forgot, humble. For all of his accomplishments in life, Elijah Mustang is one of the most humble guys you'll ever meet."

Elijah continued to shake his head at Sammy, uncomfortable with the shower of compliments being poured on him.

"So, let's get started. You've had quite an interesting year, haven't you, Elijah?" Sammy asked.

"I guess it would seem so; but to be honest, all of this silly attention has been external to my real life. It's almost like it has happened to someone else. I've just been eating breakfast with my pals and chatting about current events like we always do. Someone just decided, for some reason, to video our conversations and put them on the Internet. Apparently they have attracted a bit of an audience. Still not exactly sure why"

Sammy continued, "OK, let's probe that, Elijah. Believe it or not, there have been a few articles written about the phenomenon that you have become. The general consensus seems to be that you have tapped into an appetite for rekindling American greatness—a greatness that has been missing from our leaders in recent years. The interest in your videos seems to have been magnified by the authenticity of it all being captured via secret recordings. It is clear that you aren't performing for the camera. Instead, you are sharing a heartfelt love for this country that appears to be at your core. Does that ring true? Do you truly love this country?"

Elijah was starting to feel more comfortable with discussing a topic other than himself. "Sammy, I truly love this country. I love everything it stands for. I love what it has done to liberate people. I love what it has done to cure disease and raise millions out of poverty. I love the compassion that we have for the hurting people of the world. I love its founding; and I love how it has evolved to become an even greater nation, despite what the folks in Washington say and do. I love the United States of America. It is the greatest country in the history of the world."

"What would you say to America's critics? That it was founded on the backs of slavery? That it is fueled by capitalistic greed? That we have unfair income inequality? That social injustice is a real problem?"

A few awkward moments of radio silence ensued until Elijah finally chimed in, "Sorry, Sammy, I was just waiting for you to finish your list."

Sammy chuckled and urged, "OK, that's the list for now. Please let me know where those critics would be wrong."

Elijah continued. "Don't think I said they're wrong, Sammy. America, like every country that has ever existed, is made up of imperfect people. Imperfection leads to ills such as slavery, greed and injustice. What's beautiful about America is that we have a way to deal with those ills. We could spend the next four hours and barely scratch the surface of the questions you have raised, but here's a quick synopsis. Slavery is now illegal in our county. In fact, the bloodiest war in our nation's history was fought to abolish slavery. Regarding greed, we have laws to determine when greed becomes a crime and a system to channel greed when it is legal. If you think it is greedy for a man to own a 100-foot yacht, the wonderful thing about our systems is that someone has to build that yacht, which creates jobs, which lifts people up the economic ladder."

Elijah was just hitting his stride. "You mentioned injustice. What *is* injustice? Some would say the fact that only certain people are born white isn't just. Some would say if a person makes over a certain amount of money it isn't just. I could go on and on, but the beauty of America is that we have free speech and can debate and decide as a country what justice is and how to achieve it. Our system is messy and it's frustrating, but it's the best system the world has ever devised. If someone finds a better one, I'm all ears."

Sammy broke into a wide smile halfway through Elijah's discourse. He felt compelled to share one important point with his listeners. "Some of you may be wondering; so I'll let you know that was Elijah Mustang off the cuff with no notes. His contagious love for this country comes across as clearly over the airwaves of this radio station as it does on a YouTube video."

Sammy and Elijah spent the next half hour discussing Promise Transportation's history from Elijah's one truck to the thousands it has today. True to his word, Sammy also allowed Elijah to share the work that Promise Ministries was doing throughout Central America. He also shared the exciting new expansion opportunity that the ministry had been given and information about how listeners might give to the cause. After a commercial break, Sammy was anxious to pivot to another topic.

"Elijah, before you became a YouTube sensation, you caught the nation's attention for a very different reason earlier this year. You were the subject of a protest at Richfield College. What can you tell our listeners about this?"

"To be honest, not very much. The ruckus started when I was preparing to go to Honduras for several days, so I didn't even know about it. It hit a crescendo when I was deep in the rural region of the country with no Internet or cell-phone coverage. By the time I got home, everything was over and the media had moved on to whatever they decided was the next crisis they needed to cover."

Sammy chuckled and shook his head in disbelief. "So, let me get this straight: The whole Richfield campus was in chaos, every national media outlet was in town, all because of you. And you didn't even know about it?"

"Didn't know a thing."

Sammy burst into a full belly laugh. "Elijah, that is awesome. I guess you read about everything after you returned to the States?"

"Actually, no I didn't. I know people don't really understand this, but I honestly don't care about the protest. I am not even sure what they were protesting. I am at peace with my life, the decisions I've made, and where God has me. I didn't see anything good coming out of reading about that situation, so I just moved on."

"Speaking of moving on, let's change topics. The National News Service published an article this morning about you. How's that for great timing for this interview? It was written by a columnist named Tyler Edison. I think you may be familiar with Mr. Edison."

"For some reason he felt compelled to come to Tennessee and interview me a few weeks ago. He reminded me that we met at the Knoxville Airport back during all of the protest brouhaha. He was coming to town to cover it, and I was headed out of the country."

"I'm guessing you haven't read the article?" Sammy queried Elijah.

"I have not."

Sammy squirmed in his chair with excitement at having the privilege of being the first to share the story with Elijah. "Elijah, I thought I'd never see this day, but the article is actually titled 'We Were Wrong.' It is all about the Richfield protest; the media descending upon quiet little Richfield College; and believe it or not, how the media got the story all wrong, about how they got you all wrong. The article discusses Promise Transportation's successes, the things you have been able to do with Promise Ministries, and the circle of friends you have in the community. It says there was absolutely zero substance to the protest, yet the national media skewered you for several days. The article is a total vindication of you and a total condemnation of the national media's herd mentality."

Sammy paused to give Elijah time to respond. After understanding it was his turn to speak, Elijah simply replied, "OK."

"*OK*? That's all you've got to say?"

Without a hint of frustration, Elijah simply replied, "I'm not sure how I'm expected to react. I wasn't upset when they decided I was a bad guy, and I'm not relieved now that they've maybe decided I'm an OK guy. I'm not defined by people who don't know me. I'm defined first by who I am in Christ, next by my family, and third by my close friends. I really don't mean this disrespectfully, but I simply don't care what someone who doesn't know me thinks about me."

"Elijah, this is a good time to take a commercial break. When we come back, we'll go to the phones; and the audience will have the opportunity to interact directly with Mr. Mustang. Thank you for tuning in to the Sammy Southern Show."

Sammy removed his headphones to address Elijah directly. "Elijah, I really appreciate your taking the time to come on the show. Hope I didn't blindside you with that National News Service article, but it was published shortly before we went on the air."

"It's OK, I just..."

As Elijah was speaking, the producer tapped on the studio window to get Sammy's attention.

"What is it?" Sammy asked, a bit agitated that his guest was interrupted.

''The phone lines are crazy. Every single one instantly lit up and our system shows dozens of people trying to call in. I'll do a quick screen to get the best calls but expect to be slammed."

Sammy turned to Elijah, "Well, sounds like this is about to get interesting."

Elijah shook his head, not certain what was about to happen. "OK...I guess."

"Here we go in 3...2...1."

"Good morning, East Tennessee, and welcome back to the Sammy Southern Show. If you're just joining us, this morning we have live in the studio Mr. Elijah Mustang, CEO of Promise Transportation; head of Promise Ministries; a YouTube star; and just confirmed by the National News Service, an all-around good guy. We have several callers in line to speak with Elijah, so let's start with Duane on Line 1. You're live on the air; welcome to the Sammy Southern Show, Duane."

"Yeah, this is Duane. I'm out here on I-40 traveling through Knoxville and I caught your show on the radio and I wanted to call in. I'm a truck driver for Promise Transportation, and I just wanted to thank Mr. Mustang for everything he does for us truckers. Most drivers want to work for Promise. The pay is good, the routes are flexible, and Mr. Mustang really cares about his people."

Elijah, momentarily forgetting he was live on the air interjected, "How's your wife doing, Duane?"

Sammy looked in amazement as he pushed the mute button on his mic. "You know this guy?"

"Thank you for asking, Mr. Mustang; she's doing much better. That's another thing; Promise treats us like human beings. My wife had some health issues back in the spring, and Promise let me take some time off the road to take care of her. I really appreciated that. Anyway, gotta get back on the road. Just wanted to call in to the show. Thanks for taking my call."

Still stunned by the conversation, Sammy had to ask, "So, you must have a few thousand drivers; you can't know all of them personally."

"Of course not, but I know Duane. He's based here in Knoxville, and his family had some real challenges earlier this year. I am just glad they seem to be doing better."

Over the next 45 minutes, Sammy fielded many similar calls. One from a man who had been to Nicaragua with Elijah and described first-hand how Promise Ministries was touching the lives of so many people in Central America. Another caller described how Elijah funded an entire Boy Scout troop's trip to Colorado. His friend Mac from Richfield College called to tell the story of Elijah's personally funding the campus payroll when the college was struggling. The stories were different, but they all carried the same message: Elijah Mustang was the real deal.

After the second such call, Elijah was clearly embarrassed and began to make a slashing motion with his hand to encourage Sammy to stop taking calls. Sammy didn't oblige.

The last call was a harbinger of things to come.

"Hi, Sammy, thank you for taking my call. After watching Elijah on YouTube, reading the article about him that was published this morning, and listening to him on the radio, I have four simple words: *Elijah Mustang for president!*"

Sammy cheered, the handful of onlookers in the studio applauded, while all Elijah could do was hang his head, shaking it in embarrassed disbelief.

After a few more calls and some parting words, Sammy thanked Elijah for coming on the show. Once they were off the air, they exchanged pleasantries; and as Elijah was shaking hands to leave, one of Sammy's assistants brought him a note.

"Ummm, Elijah, I think you ought to read this."

It was a message that would change everything.

33

March 1, 2016 – Super Tuesday
252 Days Until 2016 U. S. Presidential Election

Ten months later...

"**I** truly believe that tonight will prove to be a historic turning point in this election. It is a night that the people spoke and spoke clearly. They rejected the politics of division. They said that money can't buy the presidency. They said they were sick and tired of being told that they don't matter. Yes tonight, America, you took back your country!" And the crowd erupted.

On this Super Tuesday election night, Mitch McCoy had all but secured the Democratic nomination for president. He had won 11 out of 13 states, losing only Alabama and Arkansas. He was leading in the polls for the upcoming primaries. All the political pundits now considered Mitch to be the presumptive nominee.

On the Republican side, Grant Wembley was speaking from The Jefferson Hotel in downtown Richmond, Virginia. He was buoyed by Super Tuesday wins in Massachusetts, Vermont and Virginia, and exit polls suggesting likely victories in Minnesota, Oklahoma and Alaska. Of course, he was truly buoyed by the financial largesse from Victor Youngblood's network of real, and not-so-real, donors totaling over $85 million, representing over 70 % of his total fundraising.

A Republican primary that had peaked with 14 candidates was now down to two. Former Di-Com CEO Lionel Ireland, Grant Wembley's only remaining competition, was giving a similar speech in Dallas. Ireland boasted of a Southern bloc of victories in Alabama, Arkansas, Georgia, Texas and Tennessee.

After this Super Tuesday's results were tallied, Wembley and Ireland were separated by only a handful of delegates. Political prognosticators were divided as to whether the Washington insider Wembley, or the political newcomer Ireland would ultimately leave the Republican Convention in Cleveland as the party's nominee. Both were committed to fighting to the bitter end.

No one knew that the decision would soon be made, not in the upcoming primary states but instead in an office building in the heart of Bethesda, Maryland.

"Tell me what you think."

"I'm pleased that we did so well in the South, but it's frustrating that we can't seem to shake Wembley. It doesn't make any sense; everything about this election seems to be trending toward outsiders. Grant Wembley is the ultimate Washington insider, a firmly entrenched senator, who is the personification of the D. C. establishment. Yet somehow he's neck and neck with Lionel Ireland."

It was 1 a.m. EST, just a few hours after the polls had closed in Alaska, the final Super Tuesday GOP caucus. Victor Youngblood was meeting in his office with Angie McDonald, his handpicked manager of Project Shamrock. McDonald had the task of securing the GOP nomination for Lionel Ireland, the billionaire businessman but political neophyte. She had successfully navigated through the early stages of the primary season, ensuring Ireland was one of the two remaining GOP candidates still fighting to garner the 1,237 delegates required to win the nomination. True to Mouse Trap's tenets, Ireland had no clue that Angie was orchestrating many of the circumstances that had brought him this deep into the GOP primary.

Angie used many of the resources available to Mouse Trap's project managers, including pushing favorable articles about Ireland and unfavorable articles about his rivals in various media outlets as well as orchestrating large supportive crowds at Ireland for President rallies. She also was responsible for most of Ireland's campaign staff, including his campaign manager. In American politics no candidate can make significant progress without large sums of cash. Victor's influx of $55 million ensured Ireland had the traction he needed to make it this far.

Victor stroked his salt-and-pepper goatee; managed an understanding nod; and prepared Angie for what would certainly be a shocking revelation, even for a Mouse Trap project.

"You've done good work here, Angie. I am very proud of you."

Knowing that such overt compliments didn't come very often from Victor Youngblood, she relished the kudo. "Thank you, sir; we just have to put away Senator Wembley, and we'll be home free."

"I think I can help you with that."

Confused, Angie responded, "How's that, sir?"

Victor turned his head toward the office door and spoke in an amplified tone, "Come on in, Jeremy!"

Still befuddled, Angie looked pensively at the opening door when she saw an unfamiliar face appear inside.

"Angie, I'd like for you to meet Jeremy Prince."

Although corporate gossip was strongly discouraged at Mouse Trap, human nature demanded the occasional coffee-pot discussion about the latest scuttlebutt within the organization. For months the name *Jeremy Prince* had been a hot topic of conversation, as many had heard he was Victor's latest protégé. She had assumed that this new disciple must be at least in his thirties. The fresh, just-out-of-college face was not what she was expecting.

"It's nice to meet you, Jeremy." She extended a hand in greeting.

"Nice to meet you too."

Victor allowed the awkwardness to linger in the room for a few moments before he finally spoke. "Angie, you may have heard Jeremy is one of our up-and-coming project managers."

"Well…I've heard…"

Victor interrupted before she could finish, "He is the PM for Project Cheyenne, named for the capital of Wyoming, home to Senator Grant Wembley. Angie, Jeremy has been leading the Mouse Trap efforts for Senator Wembley's presidential campaign. He's been your primary competition."

Equal parts confused and angry, Angie muttered, "I don't understand, why would you want to…"

"I'll explain," interrupted Victor.

The last nine months had been eventful for Jeremy. After coming to terms with the unfortunate events surrounding Bobby Lincoln's campaign manager, as well as his chief fundraiser, Jeremy resumed his role as Project Lincoln PM. In this position he led the surreptitious efforts resulting in Governor Lincoln being the third GOP candidate to drop out of the race, even before the Iowa caucus and New Hampshire primary. Lincoln was never able to muster any passion for the campaign after the loss of Cam Calvin and Gary Carlisle, and this lack of passion showed in his campaigning.

Impressed by Jeremy's efforts on Project Lincoln, Victor gave him the helm of Project Cheyenne. For most of the GOP primary, Victor kept Project Shamrock's existence from Jeremy, in the same way he had kept Project Cheyenne from Angie. However, he knew it was time to begin bringing his greater plan to the forefront.

"I understand that you are confused, Angie. I want to tell you a story. *There was once a king who reigned over a vast country. The king had a daughter whom he loved more than anything in the world. His daughter was beautiful, but her beauty confined on the inside. On the outside…not so much. Being a loving father, the king never wanted his daughter to be thought of as anything but beautiful; so he orchestrated a kingdom-wide beauty pageant. His only stipulation was that his daughter must ultimately be the winner. To ensure his desired outcome, the king hand-picked the other young ladies who would compete against his daughter. He went to great lengths to select the homeliest maidens in his kingdom to participate in the pageant. When the votes were cast, lo and behold, his daughter was crowned the winner. She was ecstatic, which meant the king was happy, which meant the kingdom was happy.*

"You see, our involvement in this election is similar to the king's predicament. There's a candidate who would be most beneficial to our interests; however, that candidate might not be the most appealing to voters. So, we have to help him along by ensuring his primary competition is weak. That's the role the two of you have been playing for the past several months. Now, we have circumstances exactly like we want them."

Angie, one of the more outspoken Mouse Trap project managers, took Victor's story to the next level. "But couldn't the king have just declared his daughter the winner of the pageant without going to all that trouble? After all, he was the king."

Thankful to be able to continue his allegory, Victor responded, "Ah yes, Angie, he could have; but it wouldn't have been the same. His daughter had the satisfaction of knowing the kingdom selected her as the most beautiful, not that she was just handed the prize."

"Even though she wasn't," Jeremy interjected.

"Even though she wasn't *what*?" asked Victor.

"Even though she wasn't the most beautiful, the kingdom voted that she was. She thought she was. The king may have even convinced himself that she was. In reality, others were more beautiful than she was."

Ready to move on to his primary reason for bringing Angie and Jeremy together, Victor wrapped things up. "That's not what the record shows and that's all that matters. But enough about the king. I want to talk about your projects. We've landed exactly where I had hoped we'd land—with the final two viable Republican candidates being Senator Wembley and Mr. Ireland. That's a tribute to the two of you. Well done. You will both be duly recognized for your efforts."

Both Angie and Jeremy knew what Victor meant by "duly recognized." Their account balances were about to swell by another six figures—maybe more.

Victor again pivoted the conversation. "But now it's time to focus our efforts on a single candidate. Based on all factors considered, we're going to roll with Lionel

Ireland for the balance of the primary. He will be of greatest benefit to Mouse Trap's interests."

Angie's pride swelled as she, like all Mouse Trap employees, loved receiving praise from Victor Youngblood.

"Angie, you'll remain as project manager for Project Shamrock, shepherding Lionel Ireland's campaign. Jeremy, the job you did to get an impotent wimp like Grant Wembley this deep into the primary was stunning. I'm appointing you as head of Project 2016, which will lead the overall election efforts through the November election."

Angie looked confused. "I don't understand. What efforts are there beyond Lionel Ireland?"

Victor walked slowly to the door of his office, looked back at Angie and Jeremy, and then opened it.

"This is Phillip Sweet. Like you, he has been a project manager devoted to this campaign season. He's been the PM for Project Marx, which has been responsible for Mitch McCoy's Democratic campaign."

Victor spent the next hour bringing Phillip up to speed with Mouse Trap's management of the Republican and the Democrat primaries, describing his vision for Jeremy's new Project 2016 role, and discussing how they would all work together to shape the election landscape for the next eight months. They concluded their discussion; and Angie and Phillip left Victor's office, while Jeremy stayed behind.

"OK, Victor, I asked this several months ago; and you weren't ready to talk about it. I know Zeke cautioned me not to ask, but I really want to understand *why*. Why are you going to all this effort, spending what has to be hundreds of millions of dollars? What are you hoping to accomplish?"

Victor knew the question would come again. He'd finally decided he'd let Jeremy into the tent a few more feet. He was ready to talk…almost.

"OK, Jeremy, I'd be disappointed if you didn't ask again. I don't have time or energy to get into the details tonight." He glanced down at his watch. "Actually, I guess it's technically morning. I promise this is a discussion we'll have very soon."

"I'm gonna hold you to that."

"I know you will, Jeremy. I wouldn't expect anything less."

34

" I don't care how you describe it; nationalism is racism. Thinking that one group of people is somehow better than another is the height of ignorance and intolerance. Songs like "God Bless America" only serve to perpetuate this ridiculous viewpoint that America is somehow superior to other countries. We are calling on Major League Baseball to cease playing this song during the seventh-inning stretch. We will be protesting at all spring training games this weekend and if we don't get a response from Major League Baseball we'll continue into the regular season by protesting in front of every Major League Baseball stadium in the country. We don't plan to leave until this song is silenced forever."

"Joining us today in studio is frequent Fox News contributor Elijah Mustang. Mr. Mustang, I understand that you have an alternative viewpoint?"

"Thank you again for having me. I, of course, do not share this opinion. America is the greatest nation in the history of the world. It..."

"That is an incredibly ignorant statement, which you can't possibly believe or defend!"

"I do believe it with every fiber of my being," responded Elijah.

"And that's exactly the kind of racist bloviating that we are working so hard to eradicate."

A few moments of awkward silence filled the airwaves as the host stared at Elijah.

"Mr. Mustang, do you have more comments to share?"

"I was just waiting for the young lady to finish her interruptions. When she's done, I'll be glad to continue."

"Please go on."

"'God Bless America' is a beautiful song that inspires and invigorates thousands of people throughout the country every time it is played. They..."

"And it offends millions of people who don't even believe there is a God and millions more who, if they do believe, don't think that God favors one country over another."

In the ten months since the Sammy Southern interview, Elijah's life had changed dramatically. Immediately following the interview, Sammy's office had been contacted by a Fox News producer, who had listened online to the interview and suspected that Elijah would be a hit with Fox News' viewers. After several weeks of cajoling and a few trips to Tennessee, Elijah was finally convinced to appear on one of Fox's evening shows. The producer's hunch was correct; Elijah was at home in front of the camera. His downhome folksy wisdom and love for his country resonated with viewers. He was quickly in high demand as a contributor on several of the network's shows.

What began as a single appearance grew to once every few weeks, then to almost every week, and finally weekly appearances on three different shows. Elijah referred to his budding accidental television career with the frog-in-the-pot analogy. The frog doesn't realize the temperature is rising a degree at a time until he's in 212 degree boiling water. Likewise, if Elijah had been told from the beginning that he'd be traveling from East Tennessee to New York City every week, he would never have signed up for the deal. He had threatened to discontinue his appearances several times, but the pot had been sweetened so much that he was willing to continue. He wondered how close the pot was getting to 212 degrees.

Among the concessions he was able to secure was a small studio in his home so that he could sometimes be on live T.V. without traveling to New York. For appearances requiring an in-studio visit, Fox agreed to a charter service, enabling Elijah to fly into New York, make his appearance, and fly back to Tennessee on the same day. The final piece that sealed the deal was Fox's agreeing to broadcast a story about Promise Ministries and to provide contact information for fundraising purposes. The story earned the ministry over $2 million, which left Elijah beholden to the network to continue his appearances.

Elijah's popularity also fostered a demand for speaking engagements. He was so bombarded for bookings that he had to hire an assistant just to sort through all the requests. At first he tried to accommodate every cause he deemed worthy; but it became overwhelming. For every engagement he accepted, he turned down ten.

One casualty of Elijah's growing popularity was his CEO position with Promise Transportation. While he continued in the role publicly, he was only a figurehead, turning over the day-to-day management to his COO, Beth Hope. He had been contemplating that move for a couple of years; but he had envisioned devoting his full time and energy to Promise Ministries, not to being on television and traveling throughout the country speaking.

Promise Ministries had been the primary beneficiary of Elijah's popularity as donations to the organization had quadrupled over the past ten months. That financial growth had allowed the ministry to take advantage of the opportunity to expand to South America. Promise Ministries had just opened its first medical clinics in rural Ecuador and Bolivia and its first Promise Home in Argentina. Plans were in place to expand into four other countries in the next six months. The realization that his TV appearances had real tangible results provided the fuel for him to stay on the air, despite his deep discomfort with the contentious on-air exchange he had just experienced.

As the lights came down, he turned to the host and exclaimed, "I honestly don't know how you do this every night. That was awful."

"That's not what our ratings say, Elijah; they are through the roof!"

As Elijah rose from his chair, shaking his head, he was met by his on-air nemesis, who quipped, "I thought that went well, didn't you? Would you want to grab a cup of coffee?"

Elijah just sighed and mumbled incoherently. Moments before she had been berating him on national TV, and now she was chipper and perky and wanted to get a cup of coffee. Elijah never understood how people could be performers for TV and someone completely different in their everyday lives. Everything he said he felt in his core. Everything she said was playing a role.

Elijah's TV appearances had blossomed beyond mere popularity to a devoted following who thirsted for Elijah to consider a larger—much larger—role in national affairs. Echoing the final caller in the seminal Sammy Southern interview, bumper stickers with the phrase "Elijah Mustang for President" were appearing all over the country. It wasn't just a campy gesture, but an actual movement to draft Elijah to run for president as the candidates emerging from the two parties were less than satisfying to a plurality of Americans. At every speaking engagement, Elijah saw signs in the audience urging him to consider running.

Much to Elijah's chagrin, the crowds seemed to be growing. The thought of running for president stirred within Elijah many strong emotions, none of them good. His first thought was that this was just a joke, but he later found that some were indeed serious about his candidacy.

He knew these misguided individuals meant well; but after his miserable experience as a congressman, he saw this encouragement to re-enter politics as unconscionable.

One such individual was in the Fox studios waiting to greet Elijah upon his exit. "Great show Elijah. You got a minute to chat?"

❧

"Drop out?! You gotta be kidding me! I just won six states. Lionel Ireland and I are in a dead heat! I don't want to drop out!" Grant Wembley's voice began to quiver as it often did when conflict invaded his world.

"You can wait a couple of weeks if you'd like but not any longer."

Denver Cochran was Grant Wembley's campaign manager, so to the outside world Cochran worked for Wembley. To the world that really mattered, Wembley danced at the end of Cochran's puppet strings. Handpicked by Victor Youngblood, Cochran was responsible for every detail of the Wembley for President Campaign. He decided on every interview, approved every speech, vetted every campaign ad, and hired every member of Wembley's campaign staff, staff, now numbering over 250 paid positions and thousands more volunteers.

"A couple of weeks?! We have Kentucky, Kansas, Louisiana, and Maine coming up this weekend. Let's wait and see how we do before we..."

"It's over, Senator. The money has dried up. We have your concession speeches ready for both the press and your campaign staff."

"This is coming from Youngblood, isn't it? I want to speak with him personally."

"I'm sorry, sir; I don't know anyone named Youngblood."

"Oh yes you do. Don't tell me..."

Falling back on his 20-year career as a Navy Seal, Denver Cochran chose the direct route, looking Grant Wembley straight in the eye. "Let me make this as clear as I can. I don't know anyone named Youngblood and neither do you. The Grant Wembley for President Campaign is over. You have no more money. You will announce your campaign suspension within two weeks. Your staff will be released. After sufficient time to ponder your next move, you will announce your full support for Lionel Ireland. Do you have any questions?"

Sinking low into his seat, a despondent Grant Wembley responded meekly, "No, no questions."

🎻

"So, Jethro, what brings you to Manhattan?"

"Oh, just here on business. Thought I'd stop by and say hey."

"Well...hey," a suspicious Elijah Mustang deadpanned.

After a few awkward moments, Jethro Poindexter interjected, "You're really a natural at this TV thing."

"Not sure if that's a compliment or an insult."

The half-hearted joke sent Jethro into a full belly laugh; and for the 320-pound man, that was a Richter scale event.

Jethro Poindexter was founder and CEO of the ever-expanding fast food chain known as Jethro's Chicken House. What Jethro started as a single restaurant in suburban Nashville, Tennessee, in 1979, had grown to over 650 restaurants in 37 states. In lending his name to the chain, his ubiquitous presence in television ads, and the large pictures of his smiling face in every Jethro's restaurant in the country, he was among the most recognizable faces in the fast food industry.

Jethro was a fixture in the Nashville area, owning a minor league baseball team and frequently hosting social gatherings on his 700-acre ranch. His get-togethers were known for their eclectic list of attendees, including country music's biggest stars, professional athletes, and Jethro's Chicken House fry cooks. With his jolly personality, Jethro was always the star of the show. Friends often debated which was more impressive, his encyclopedic catalog of jokes or his gift for their perfectly timed delivery.

"Exactly what kind of business are you in town for, Jethro?"

"What?" a confused Jethro replied.

"You said you were in town for business. I was just wondering what kind of business."

"Oh...yeah...you know, just meeting with investors... and stuff," Jethro stammered.

"That's interesting. Investors. Right here in Manhattan...in the News Corp Building...at the Fox Studios... in the same studio where I am...at the same time I'm here."

Realizing that his ever-astute friend knew something was up, Jethro feebly tried continuing the charade. "What are the odds?"

"Astronomical. What's going on, Jethro? Why are you here?" persisted Elijah.

"Is there a place we can talk privately?"

"I don't like the sound of this."

"It won't take long."

"I've heard that before," Elijah lamented, knowing he was settling in for a long conversation.

Elijah and Jethro had been friends for 20 years. Promise Transportation was the exclusive freight carrier for Jethro's Chicken House. Jethro was a generous donor to Promise Ministries. Elijah even coaxed Jethro to accompany him on a mission trip in 2007; however, the 100-degree plus Nicaraguan heat was incompatible with Jethro's rotund stature. Jethro promised to increase his giving in return for Elijah's promising never to ask him to go on another trip.

Jethro and Elijah shared a deep love for their country. For most of Jethro's 69 years, he considered himself to be politically neutral, staying above the fray when partisan rancor was interjected into a conversation. That neutrality began to change in the early 2000s, buoyed by the 9/11 catastrophe. He observed that while he was building his chicken empire, the country he loved was slipping away. As a result, he went all in during the 2008 election, throwing his enthusiastic support behind the eventual loser. That loss still haunted Jethro, who was determined to do everything within his power to make 2016 turn out differently. In fact, it was the real reason for his "business trip" to Manhattan.

Elijah and Jethro navigated the Fox Studios finding an empty conference room where they could continue their conversation in private.

"OK, Jethro, what's really going on? Why are you here?"

"Have you been following the election?" asked Jethro.

"You know I have. I don't really want to, but I have to for these crazy shows."

"What do you think?"

Elijah just shook his head. "I think what everyone thinks: *Is this the best we can come up with?*"

Jethro nodded his head vigorously, his jowls following a half-beat behind. "Exactly. I don't know hardly anyone that would give a nickel for either one of 'em. McCoy is essentially a socialist who would tax this country to death, and that Ireland guy is just scary. Who knows what in the Sam Hill he'd do."

"OK, so we agree on that. Back to my original question: *Why are you here?*" Elijah pressed.

Jethro's smile started with his sparkling blue eyes, continued with a wrinkled nose, and was capped off by a full open-mouth grin. "I'm here for you, good buddy."

A thoroughly confused Elijah raised both arms to his side and asked; "For me? Why for me?"

Sticking a finger playfully in Elijah's chest, Jethro continued, "Because you can fix all of this and you have the platform to do it."

"I'm sorry, Jethro, my brain is apparently moving too slowly this morning; I can fix *what?*"

"This country, Elijah! You can fix this country!" Jethro reached in his jacket pocket, pulled out an *Elijah Mustang for President* bumper sticker, and held it up for Elijah to see. "These are selling faster than the printer can make them. America is calling you, Elijah. You gotta run."

After a blank stare for a few moments, Elijah responded, "You are on crack. Not that watered down street junk, you are on high-grade 100% pure crack."

After another chuckle, Jethro continued the sales pitch. "I'm serious, Elijah. You can do it. You are the smartest guy I know. You have the business experience. You've already served in Congress, so you know how screwed up that is. You're genuine. You're humble. Most importantly, you love this county."

"You came all the way to Manhattan to tell me this? I'm afraid I'm going to have to disappoint you, Jethro, I... "

Jethro raised a hand to stop Elijah. "And it's not just me." He again reached in his jacket pocket to pull out several sheets of paper. "I've got a whole list. It includes half our Tennessee congressional delegation, one of our senators, the lieutenant governor, artists, ball players, engineers, regular Joes. They all signed this list. It's got Democrats and Republicans, black, white, Latino, and everything in between. Elijah, people are crying out for you to run. You can't just ignore them."

"Jethro, I'm flattered; I really am, but I'm trying to get out of this political mess, not deeper into it."

Ignoring Elijah's protest, Jethro continued, "And here's the good news. This isn't just a list; this is an application to get on the ballot in Tennessee. It only takes 275 signatures, and we have over a thousand. All you gotta do is sign. The work is already done for you."

"Jethro, running for president is not something that you and your buddies go out and just decide to do on the weekend. You gotta have money...big time money. You gotta have an organization with hundreds of people. You gotta have lots of time. McCoy and Ireland have been planning this for years. The election is in just eight months. Why am I even talking about this? It is crazy."

"You're talking about a conventional campaign. We don't need another one of those; we need something different. I agree that you'll need some money. That's why the people on that list didn't just sign their names. They have pledged over $8 million to get things going. You just gotta say you'll give it a try."

Elijah let out a huge sigh. "Like I said, Jethro, this is crazy. Where would you even start?"

Sensing a small breakthrough, Jethro pounced. "You'd start right here! Sign this application and I'll take it from here. If you're right and it's crazy, no harm done; it will just fade away. If I'm right, this will start a national wave."

The back and forth continued for several more minutes. For every argument Elijah offered, Jethro had a counter until Elijah finally gave in.

"You're not gonna quit, are you?" asked Elijah.

"Not until you sign." Jethro smiled.

"I've done some really, really, dumb things in my life; but I think this could be the dumbest."

Elijah grabbed the application, scribbled his John Hancock, and thrust it back at Jethro.

Jethro embraced his longtime pal, then looked him in the eye. "Buddy, I think you just made history."

35

"Gentlemen, we have an interesting opportunity before us. The Republican primary is down to two candidates, Senator Grant Wembley and former Di-Com CEO Lionel Ireland. As you know our focus has been on Senator Wembley for the past several months, but I'd like to present you with information that could potentially change the direction you'd like for me to take."

Victor Youngblood was playing his role as faithful servant of The Council—a role Council members believed he had been performing for the past 30 years. In reality, for the past 20 years Victor had been subtly and surreptitiously accumulating power from The Council. The Republican primary provided the perfect milieu to demonstrate Victor's strength and The Council's growing atrophy.

Victor stood in the center of The Hex and addressed The Council. "I think we need to further explore Lionel Ireland's unexpected rise."

The reality was that Victor had been cultivating Lionel Ireland for years, long before he began to invest Mouse Trap resources in Grant Wembley. It's also inaccurate to say that Lionel Ireland's rise had been "unexpected," at least to Victor. In fact, Victor's plan for the primary had worked to perfection. He used Grant Wembley to clear out less desirable candidates, one at a time, while Lionel maintained a consistent level of voter support.

"We have recently reached out to Mr. Ireland and believe that he would be supportive of The Council's objectives. At the same time, I'm also concerned about Grant Wembley. He is the consummate politician. While we may have his attention during the election, he could easily get flipped if the political winds blow in a different direction. Alternatively, Lionel Ireland is a businessman. He understands deals. He understands money. He understands the importance of maintaining relationships. I think we need to consider throwing our support behind him."

"Wembley has always been a politician. Why are we just now determining he may not be our guy?" Baker was the first to speak.

Victor responded, "When the campaign started, everyone whom we thought had a chance at winning was a politician. We selected Wembley because he was the best of the lot. Now that Ireland has shown staying power, I think he might be someone we should seriously consider."

"The election is only eight months away, isn't it late in the game to change horses?" Dog asked.

"I am very comfortable that Mr. Ireland will be someone we can reach. As I mentioned, we've already been in contact indirectly, and all interactions have been very positive."

"McCoy's the guy on the Democrat side. How does Ireland do against him?" Easy chimed in.

"Early polling shows McCoy with a modest lead but within the margin of error; so it's basically a dead heat. And that's before we apply Mouse Trap's resources to Ireland's campaign."

The reality was that Mouse Trap had been in control of all three campaigns for over a year, a fact Victor decided The Council didn't need to know.

"We could wait it out another month or two and see which one emerges with the nomination. I'd hate to change over to Ireland only to find Wembley secured the win," Charlie observed.

Knowing Charlie's question was just a trial balloon and not a true proposal, Victor decided on a soft response. "We could absolutely do that. As always, I'll defer to the wisdom of The Council."

"Victor, I think it is time to make the change. I think Ireland's our guy. I've actually done business with him in the world outside this room, and I've found him to be solid." It was Able's first volley into the conversation. After more discussion others followed with their agreement, acquiescing to Able's firsthand experience with Ireland. The Council formalized their decision, voting unanimously.

"Victor, you are authorized to go forward with our support for Ireland. Wembley's out."

Victor knew the days of his Astroturf deference to The Council were soon coming to an end; but until his plan had reached its climax, he had to maintain the charade.

"OK. I appreciate your time and direction. If that's what pleases The Council, I'll get the ball rolling this evening."

"Look, everyone he's here!"

"Every eye in the restaurant turned to the entrance, followed by perfectly synchronized gasps, and finally the clicks of camera phones."

"What's going on?"

With his hectic schedule, Elijah hadn't been to the American Eagle Diner in almost three months. In that short span of time, circumstances had changed dramatically. A large sign outside the restaurant read *American Eagle Diner: Home of Elijah Mustang As Seen on T.V.* Inside was a life-size cutout of Elijah, beside which patrons could take photos. The most peculiar of all, the other members of the Liars, Thieves and Jokers Club who had become minor celebrities themselves were actually signing autographs.

Finally, after the initial shock had passed, a couple of diners started to clap, leading to everyone in the restaurant joining in to give Elijah a standing ovation.

He wasn't sure how to react; so he just nodded in recognition, gave a courteous smile, and hurried to the back of the establishment where his dining companion awaited him.

"What in the world was that all about?" Elijah asked.

"Apparently it was all about you."

"I don't get it."

"And that makes you even more appealing. Your authenticity is evident to everyone."

Realizing he'd not even said *good morning*, Elijah quickly changed the subject. "I'm sorry, Pastor; I didn't even ask, how are you doing this morning?"

"I'm doing well, Elijah. Probably not as well as you."

"This is crazy."

Stephen Roberts was friend, pastor, and confidant to Elijah. Pastoring the New Hope Church for the past 15 years, Pastor Roberts had come to know Elijah as well as anyone. They shared the joy of watching his daughters grow up with Pastor Roberts baptizing each one. Unfortunately, they also shared the heart-wrenching experience of the passing of Elijah's wife; Pastor Roberts officiated the funeral. Their friendship was forged in the fires of both joy and pain. Elijah knew he could turn to Pastor Roberts when he needed wise counsel. This was just such a day.

"So, I think I did something really dumb," Elijah admitted.

"Oh? What's that?"

"I think I signed something I shouldn't have signed."

"I'm listening."

"You remember my friend Jethro Poindexter?

"The chicken guy?"

"That's him. He visited me in Manhattan a couple of weeks ago while I was on one of the news talk shows...he can be very persuasive. There's this nonsense that's going around about me running for office again..."

"Not just running for office but for president," Pastor Roberts interjected.

"So, you've heard?"

"Elijah, everyone has heard. It's not a very well-kept secret."

"Well...Jethro took it to the next level. He actually had an application for me to get on the ballot in Tennessee... and...well...he coerced me into signing it."

Pastor Roberts' voice went up a few octaves. "That's great news! When do you plan to..."

Elijah waved his hands in objection. "No! It's *not* great news! In fact, it's not news at all. I'm NOT running for president; that's ridiculous! I'm just worried about what Jethro's going to do."

"Why aren't you at least thinking about running?"

"Come on, Pastor, you too? You know me. I'm just a regular guy. This has gotten way out of control, and I have to put a stop to it."

"Maybe that's what we need,"

A confused Elijah responded, "*What's* what we need?"

"A regular guy. Maybe we just need a regular guy, who's not a lifelong politician or a billionaire. I can't think of a better *regular* guy than the one sitting in front of me."

"Pastor, I was counting on you to be the sensible one. Look, I'm not qualified for this. There's nothing unique or special about me. I'm a trucker from a small town in Tennessee."

"Have you ever considered that God may have put you in this position?"

"*What?*"

"Look around this room. So many eyes have been watching us the whole time you've been here. You got a standing ovation for just walking in the room! You are on national TV every week. Jethro even got you to sign an application to run! Something is going on, Elijah; and you can't just dismiss it out of hand."

Elijah let out a big sigh, not sure what more he could say to discourage what he considered to be a silly conversation.

"You remember the story of Queen Esther?" Pastor Roberts continued. "The times were desperate. All of Esther's fellow Jews were going to be killed, but she was in a position to intervene and save them. Her first answer was that there was nothing she could do but then her adoptive father Mordecai spoke the famous words that she may have come to her royal position 'for such a time as this.'" Elijah, we are living in desperate times. Perhaps God has put His favor on you—a regular guy—for such a time as this."

Shaking his head, Elijah cautioned, "Pastor, I don't know..."

Meanwhile a few tables away, a camera phone, pointed in the direction of Elijah's table, was recording every word that was spoken. Like so many times before, the phone's owner would review the footage and decide if anything was worthy of uploading to YouTube. Known to Elijah's fan base as Mustangluvr1985, Dr. Molly Jefferson continued her covert efforts to show the world the real Elijah Mustang, the person for whom she still carried a great burden resulting from her ill-conceived protest that shamed and defamed an innocent and good man. A protest for which she felt she must continue to pay penance.

"At least pray about it," Pastor Roberts urged.

"Can I pray that this will all stop?"

"You can pray whatever you want...but I'd advise the always-useful 'thy will be done' prayer."

Elijah let out what had to be his tenth sigh of the conversation, then simply muttered, "This is crazy."

36

"Remember, everyone, Tuesday night is the Ohio primary. Make sure to go and vote." Patriarch Bronson Everman always taught his children that voting was their most important civic duty.

"I'll probably skip it. Our guy is already picked, though I'm not sure how." Brad Everman, the Democrat of the family, was lamenting the foregone conclusion that Mitch McCoy would be his party's nominee. "I just don't understand how it could be narrowed down to one person this early in the process. It's like I don't even have a voice."

"At least we have two choices in the Republican primary, although neither is my guy," Jake Everman, Bronson's eldest son, responded. "I'm starting to hear some weird things about Wembley, so I guess I'm going with Ireland. As a CEO, I know that it takes a lot of skill to do the job he's done; however, I gotta admit, he makes me sorta nervous."

"It figures you'd go for the billionaire." Brad would never let an opportunity to dig at his big brother pass him by.

"You know, just because someone has money doesn't mean they're a bad guy," Jake shot back.

"I think it pretty much does."

"Well, you…"

"How about some pecan pie?" Mom Edith interrupted, always knowing how to diffuse a family political argument. She'd had over 40 years' practice.

For all of Bronson's lectures about the importance of being a good citizen, the message stuck more with some of his kids than others.

"So, remind me what is a primary again?" Maggie, at age 46, was still the baby of the clan and not as well-versed in politics as her older brothers.

Cameron, Jake's college-age son, volunteered to answer. "Aunt Maggie, it's when the two parties decide who is going to represent them in the presidential election. States vote on different days. Ohio votes this coming Tuesday."

Cameron's sister Amy was beginning to develop a cynical side. "I think it's all rigged."

"Come on, Amy, I'm not all that crazy about McCoy; but there's no way it's rigged," Brad responded.

"Yeah, honey, this has been the process we've followed for over 200 years. It's not perfect, but it's still the best process in the world," Jake lectured his daughter.

"How does it possibly make sense that there are people winning who no one will admit to liking or supporting? The only explanation is that it's all part of some big conspiracy," Amy continued.

"Dad, I've been meaning to tell you that Amy's been hanging out with some weird people at college," Cameron joked.

"Yeah, it sounds like it. Honey, one thing I can promise you, there's no big conspiracy," Jake assured.

※

"What's the status on Wembley?" Victor asked.

"As we expected, the major media outlets circulated the stories about Wembley's suspected drug use and his out-of-wedlock children. Almost verbatim what we sent out through our channels," Jeremy responded.

"Great. Jeremy, after Sunday you should be able to devote full time to Project 2016."

"You feeling good about Project Shamrock, Angie?"

"Yes, everything is good to go."

"OK, we're all set for Tuesday. The Ohio primary should push Ireland over the top. The next day Wembley will drop out, and then we're smooth sailing for McCoy vs. Ireland. Well done, guys, very well done." Victor's plan was on schedule.

37

"I'm sorry, Senator. Things aren't looking good. You've lost Florida, North Carolina, Illinois, and Missouri." Campaign Manager Denver Cochran was delivering the bad news.

"But…what about Ohio? Am…I…uh…winning Ohio?"

"With 85% of the precincts reporting, Ireland is leading 58 to 42. More than double the margin the pollsters expected. It's the end of the line, Senator. I'm sorry."

A dejected Wembley turned his back and began to quiver.

"You'll need to do the concession speech shortly," Cochran continued.

"I'll do it in few minutes. I just need to…to…to compose myself," Wembley blubbered, while wiping away tears.

"Are you crying?" a disgusted Cochran asked.

"Just give me a couple of minutes."

"You make me sick."

Wembley couldn't muster a response but simply buried his face in his hands.

"Ohio's a wrap. That's all five states. Everything is on track for both McCoy and Ireland. Both campaign managers are within our sphere of influence, and both are on board with the path forward," Jeremy stated proudly.

"Nice job, Jeremy. I appreciate your efforts. Make sure and pass along my gratitude to your team."

As Victor turned to leave, Jeremy quickly interjected, "Uh...Victor, I would like to follow up on our earlier conversation, if I could."

"Which earlier conversation?"

"The one from a few days ago. The one about *why*."

"The one about *why*..." Victor repeated matter-of-factly. He knew the question was coming again. Jeremy's curiosity wouldn't allow it to remain unanswered. That curiosity was one of the traits that endeared Jeremy to Victor.

"I think it would help me to do a better job if I understood the bigger picture, if I understood where this was all leading."

"OK, Jeremy. I agree that it's time we had this conversation. But I want you to understand that no one person knows what I'm about to tell you. Different members of my leadership team know their compartmentalized parts, but no one knows the whole. You should not take lightly the fact that I am willing to share this with you. It is a testament to how far you've come in such a short time."

"I understand and I definitely appreciate it," Jeremy replied, neither fully understanding nor appreciating the conversation he was about to have.

Victor had been looking for a protégé like Jeremy for years. He thought he had found such a person on three separate occasions but was disappointed each time. In hindsight the signs of failure were there in all three cases; Victor had determined he was just too anxious to see the signs. In the short year he had spent with Jeremy, Victor had mentally inventoried these same cautionary signs; and each time Jeremy passed with flying colors. Victor felt it was time to fully commit to young Jeremy Prince.

"Jeremy, what kind of shape would you say the world is in right now?"

Jeremy could sense it was an important question and didn't want to provide a flippant or vacuous answer. "That's a complicated question on this side of Mouse Trap. I probably have a different answer now than I would have had a year ago."

Impressed by Jeremy's answer, Victor rephrased, "OK, fair enough. What kind of shape would you say most people would say the world is in? Those outside of Mouse Trap."

"Most people would say it is in pretty rough shape. There are wars, economic uncertainty, poverty, famine, climate issues, inequality, injustice...I could go on and on. The bottom line is that most people are probably pretty pessimistic."

"Why do *you* think that is, Jeremy?"

Knowing the more quickly he responded, the more quickly he would get Victor's answer.

"I'm not sure, Victor. That's an intriguing question."

"It is because man has yet to find the perfect model by which to govern himself."

Jeremy was underwhelmed by the mundane and wonkish answer. "OK...I guess."

"You see....that..." Victor pointed directly at Jeremy. "That's why this is such an incredibly important concern. Most people don't get it. The way man governs himself has a direct effect on how he lives his life. How safe he is. How prosperous he is. How happy he is. How successful he is. Right now the way man governs himself is the source of all of the strife in the world. Man is governing himself by flawed models."

"You are going to have to unpack this some more for me, Victor. I'm not totally following," Jeremy responded, wondering if he'd been too honest.

"It's OK, Jeremy. Since this has been my own private master plan for so long, it's good to give me a chance to explain it to someone. Let's discuss the major forms of governance. We'll start with socialism, the system that's become the most prominent; and by the way, that's no accident. There's so much good about socialism. Its focus is fairness and equity. Who could argue with that? The biggest problem with socialism is that man doesn't see the connection between his talents and efforts, and his results. There's something in the human spirit that needs to achieve. Socialism fails to meet that need."

"Socialism was certainly pushed in college, but most of the really engaged students knew it didn't work." Jeremy tried to make the connection with Victor. "The next logical step from socialism is communism, I guess?"

"And there's much good about communism. The concept behind central planning is good; but the larger the country, the more complicated it becomes. And, it still fails to recognize the need for individual accomplishment that man craves."

Jeremy was staying engaged in the conversation. "Some countries are still governed by monarchies."

"They are Jeremy, and they can be great countries if the people love their king and the king loves his people. Unfortunately, that's not always the case. Monarchies are not a sustainable model in the 21st century. The same fatal flaw is found in dictatorship. The system can't rise and fall on the talents and capabilities of a single man."

"So, that leaves us here in the good ole USA with our capitalistic democracy. What about that? Isn't it the best system ever devised?" asked Jeremy.

"It definitely has its strong points, Jeremy. People feel in control of their destiny. They associate their level of skill and effort with their outcome. Unfortunately, many people are left behind because some are more skilled and willing to put forth more effort than others, leading to inequity between the achievers and the underachievers. That's not a sustainable model either."

"So, I'm guessing you've figured out that perfect system that you mentioned?" Jeremy asked.

"I believe there is a structure whereby you can take the best of all models and fix the ills of the world. The perfect system exists. People need to believe they are free. They need to believe the choices they make are their own. They need to see a correlation between their skills and efforts, and their results. But at the same time, they need to be managed to ensure efficiency and equity. And for some critical decisions people don't need to have a say. Those critical decisions need to be made for them."

"So, how do you convince people of that? Is that what this election is all about? Are Ireland and McCoy on board with your system? Are they going to deploy this new approach?" Jeremy's voice began to raise, excited to finally hear Victor's grand plan.

"I'm not going to deploy this system. The people are going to demand it. People must be unhappy enough to demand something different. For the past eight years, we've succeeded in making people ask for change. Rather than true change, they got more of the same, only worse, which makes them want even more change."

Now pacing the floor, Victor continued, "In this election, we are offering them two candidates who are at their core very unappealing; thus that thirst for something different only grows greater. I am going to offer a cool drink to quench that thirst. For the past 20 years, we have been accumulating wealth, developing Omnia, recruiting tens of thousands of Mouse Trap agents. We are poised to make our move in a few months when people have finally said, 'Enough.'"

Clearly deep in thought, Jeremy then replied, "I do have a question that has been nagging me. In the first few of days of training with Candi and Zeke, they showed me a gruesome video of ISIS beheadings. They said beheadings happen regularly in regions controlled by ISIS. Then they showed news headlines from the following day highlighting that the beheadings were not reported in the media. I was shocked and asked why they wouldn't be reported. They said that we told them not to. I asked why we would not want the media to report on them and got a stern lecture from Zeke about not asking *why*. Now that I understand the bigger picture about Mouse Trap and what you're hoping to accomplish, I still don't understand why we wouldn't want the media to report on these atrocities. You can't be OK with this kind of violence."

Victor nodded, understanding Jeremy's confusion. "The key is *focus*, Jeremy. We have to maintain laser-like focus on our ultimate objective. An important facet of implementing my vision for the country is to ensure there is friction and division. We want to foment discontent. We want the people to be so frustrated that they demand something different."

Jeremy shook his head, still not on board. "I am sorry to be slow, but I'm still not following."

Victor continued, "Our greatest threat to Mouse Trap was on September 11, 2001. In the days following the attack on the Pentagon and the World Trade Center, Americans came together in a way that hadn't happened since World War II. There was one America, and everyone was singularly focused. That's the exact opposite of the environment we now have. We need to stimulate discord. Showing these beheadings runs the risk of again uniting the country behind a common enemy. I want the enemy to be from within, not without. I want Republicans to see the enemy as Democrats and vice versa. I want the rich to be at odds with the poor, blacks with whites, and so on. That has to be the focus!"

"Abe Lincoln," Jeremy stated.

"What's that?" a confused Victor asked.

"In Mr. Grigsby's high school American history class, I had to memorize an Abraham Lincoln speech. For some reason I still remember it:

> *Shall we expect some transatlantic military giant to step the ocean and crush us at a blow? Never! All the armies of Europe, Asia, and Africa combined, with all the treasure of the earth in their military chest, with a Bonaparte for a commander, could not by force take a drink from the Ohio or make a track on the Blue Ridge in a trial of*

*a thousand years. At what point then is the ap-
proach of danger to be expected? I answer. If it
ever reach us, it must spring up amongst us; it
cannot come from abroad. If destruction be our
lot, we must ourselves be its author and finisher.
As a nation of freemen we must live through all
time or die by suicide.*

Victor thought for a moment and then interjected, "I agree that change must come from within, but I don't characterize it as danger or death. Remember, Jeremy, I'm going to make things better. Don't ever forget that."

Jeremy continued, "So you mentioned that your new system will have the best of capitalism and socialism. You didn't mention anything about the best of a dictatorship."

Victor involuntarily smiled his most devilish smile. "Yes, Jeremy, my boy, that will be necessary as well. And you, young Prince, are going to be right by my side to enjoy the ride."

A huge knot filled every cavity of Jeremy's being, a phenomenon he hoped his face didn't betray. Fortunately, Victor was too wrapped up in his utopian dream to notice.

Victor continued, "I just have a few more moves to get into position. It won't be much longer, and everything will be in place."

Jeremy thought to himself, "That's funny. I just had the same thought."

38

" . . . I understand that many of you are un-happy with the choices you're left with; but I must urge you to avoid cynicism, disengagement, and frustration. Instead, channel your passion into making yourself better, which will make your family better, which will make your neighborhood better, which will make your town better, which will make your state better, which will ultimately make our great country even better than it already is.

"Despite all of our current challenges and struggles, I truly believe we still live in the greatest country the world has ever known. It is a country of freedom, liberty, and prosperity. A place where a poor boy from the sticks of Tennessee, with no mom or dad, can grow up to be blessed to lead one of the largest trucking companies in the country. It is a country where our opportunities are limited only by the degree to which we are willing to work hard and dream big. It is a country of great generosity that sees hurting souls and offers them a helping hand.

"Yes, I truly and wholeheartedly believe our best days are ahead of us in this beautiful, blessed land that we call America. Thank you for having me here today. May God bless you and your families."

Elijah's address to the Nashville Area Chamber Commerce brought the crowd to their feet in boisterous applause. After what seemed like several minutes of cheering, the gathering was momentarily quieted as the Chamber's president stepped to the microphone.

"Ladies and gentlemen, I have some exciting and stunning news to share with you. I hold in my hand an interesting sheet of paper." The Chamber's president smiled at Elijah, who looked curiously back. "This…this is a petition to be on the ballot in the state of Tennessee as an independent candidate for the president of the United States. And…it's signed by Elijah Mustang!!"

Once again the crowd rose, roaring their approval, with some approaching the stage to shake Elijah's hand.

His first inclination was to ask how in the world the Chamber got his petition; then his question was answered as he saw a grinning Jethro Poindexter, sitting on the front row. All Elijah could do was shake his head in disbelief.

Jeremy typed *Cam Calvin and Gary Carlisle* and hit the Omnia search button. The search returned thousands of hits, mostly related to Governor Bobby Lincoln. Jeremy then customized his search to exclude anything related to Governor Lincoln. Still hundreds of hits returned. He again filtered his search for *May 30, 2015*, the date both men had died. That search was limited to a few dozen stories, mostly about their untimely deaths. One search result caught Jeremy's eye. It was an area of Omnia that he'd never seen titled *Trapped*. When he clicked on the search button, Omnia responded, *I'm sorry, but the information you are requesting is above your access level.*

"Above my access level?" Jeremy thought he had the highest access level possible. He then reasoned that if a search for Cam Calvin and Gary Carlisle resulted in finding whatever *Trapped* was, there must be other names associated with this curious result. He typed common names, such as *Jones Trapped*, which returned three results. *Smith Trapped* returned two results. He wrote down the names of the Joneses and Smiths, and started the next search when his solitude was interrupted.

"Jeremy, my young apprentice! How are you? Working on another Saturday I see."

"Oh…uh…yes…working."

"What are you working on?" Victor asked. He began to walk behind Jeremy's desk as Jeremy tried to hide the scribbled names.

"Oh, just still trying to learn about Omnia. It is such a powerful tool; I don't think I could ever perfect it." He hoped Victor was buying what he was selling.

"Yes, Omnia is quite powerful." Walking from behind Jeremy's desk, Victor paced in the center of the office and then turned abruptly to face Jeremy. "Jeremy, have you ever asked yourself what our most powerful asset is here at Mouse Trap?"

"I'm guessing it's maybe Omnia?"

"Omnia does provide us with information beyond anyone's wildest imagination. But it's not our greatest asset. Want to take another guess?"

Jeremy could sense that this was one of those situations in which Victor wanted to pontificate, so he followed the script in his answers.

"We have hundreds, maybe thousands of outstanding professionals in Mouse Trap; so I'd say our greatest asset is our people."

"Great answer, Jeremy. We do have outstanding people, but they are not our greatest asset."

"How about the tens of thousands of synthetic identities that we've created?"

"Yet another great answer, Jeremy. Through those identities we can flow great sums of money, flood social media outlets, and elicit a public outcry. But no, that's not our greatest asset."

Jeremy decided to give the answer one more go. "OK, how about the relationships that we've cultivated throughout American culture? There's not an area of this country that we can't influence."

Victor paced the floor with a quickened step, then spun around and pointed his finger in the air. "That's close, Jeremy, very close. But it is not exactly what I'm looking for. Jeremy, our greatest asset...the one that's beyond our people and even beyond Omnia, is trust. In Mouse Trap we ultimately try to influence the decisions people make every day. If I can garner their trust, I can make them do anything."

The answer surprised Jeremy and caused him to pause and think, "*Trust?*" Then his stomach turned somersaults, wondering if Victor was trying to send him a not-so-subtle message.

Victor continued, "We've become very proficient in the game of trust. We have found the things that people trust the most and have invested significant resources in those particular carrots. Our first target was the national media: network news and national magazines and newspapers. For many people, if they hear a story from a news outlet, they trust it; they don't question its veracity. We now control every major headline and lead story throughout the media.

"Young people trust the superstars they worship. As you know we have a large stable of celebrities: actors, singers, athletes, through whom we can send messaging. We also have appropriated labor unions, major religious denominations and organizations, political parties, government agencies, major corporations, and minority groups. We think we have secured over 75% of the entities that people trust. The wonderful things about trust are that it has such power, and people give it away so freely. If I find what you trust, I can send a message through that avenue and tell you that the sky is going to be green polka dots tomorrow, and you'll believe it. Yes, Jeremy, our greatest asset is trust; and it is critical that we exploit that asset to the fullest extent in order to meet our ultimate objective, a new governmental order."

Jeremy was still trying to fully process Victor's rhetoric. "Trust...to be honest, I never really thought about it."

"Most people don't, Jeremy." Victor continued, "Trust is a critical currency here at Mouse Trap. One that we should never take for granted. With it, we are going to change the world."

39

"OK, what are the latest polls showing?" Jeremy was meeting with his project managers, Phillip Sweet for Project Marx, and Angie McDonald for Project Shamrock. Victor Youngblood was observing the meeting from the conference room door.

"Ireland is opening a decent lead, just outside the margin of error. There's definitely some separation occurring," Angie reported.

Victor stepped into the room to observe Jeremy's response.

Jeremy didn't hesitate. "OK, get with the network and print news teams. Tell them to step up the negative reporting on Ireland. Go with 80% favorable stories for

416

McCoy for the next four days; then we'll re-run the polls and see the results. Either of you have questions?" Neither did. "Great, I'll see you both later this afternoon."

Both Angie and Phillip exited, leaving Jeremy and Victor alone.

"Good move, Jeremy. Remember, we want the polling to stay close throughout this election. We want the public to stay engaged, to remain frustrated, to be discontented. We want them ready to accept real, consequential change."

"Yes, Victor."

"I'm feeling good about this, Jeremy. I think we have all of our bases covered. I believe everything we've been planning all these years is finally going to pay off. Nothing can go wrong."

"It is great to see you again, Elijah. Thanks for taking time to meet me."

"No problem, Jethro. Any excuse to go to Calhoun's. Please tell me you're not going to trick me into signing anything this time."

"Trick you!?" Jethro feigned being insulted. "How could you say such a thing?"

"Just drive," commanded Elijah.

Old friends, Jethro Poindexter and Elijah Mustang were driving through downtown Knoxville on their way to dinner to catch up on life. At least that's what Jethro had told Elijah.

"Hey, old buddy, I gotta make one quick stop by the convention center. I've got an event here in a couple of months, and I just need to make sure everything's lined up."

"Really? The great Jethro Poindexter makes his own conference arrangements?" Elijah asked.

"I was going to be in Knoxville, and I told the gals in the office I'd stop by for them. Come on, you're as much of a hands-on guy as I am; this shouldn't surprise you."

Jethro pulled his Ford Raptor into the parking garage, griping about the $10 fee. He pulled into a spot and got out of the truck.

"I'll just stay here if it's OK, Jethro."

"Naw, come on with me, Elijah. I don't like the idea of you being in this dark parking garage by yourself."

"OK, but this is a quick stop, right? I've had Calhoun's ribs on my mind all day."

"Quick stop. Got it."

Jethro and Elijah exited the parking garage, crossed Clinch Avenue, and entered the Knoxville Convention Center's north entrance, where street level was the third floor. They navigated down the escalator to the second floor, and Jethro approached the door of Exhibit Hall A.

"I think this is where the guy I'm looking for is supposed to be." Jethro gestured toward Elijah. "Here, you go first."

"What? Why?" a confused Elijah asked

"Just go first!"

"Why do you want…"

"Dang it, Elijah, why do you have to make everything so hard?" Using his large paw and all of his 300-plus-pound frame, Jethro shoved Elijah through the door. As Elijah stumbled into the room, an assembled crowd erupted in applause. Instinctively pushing back against Jethro's hand, Elijah tried to exit and muttered, "I think we're at the wrong place."

"Nope, Elijah, this is exactly the RIGHT place!"

The cheering grew even louder as a disoriented Elijah began to see familiar faces. To his left was his entire leadership team from Promise Transportation. They were surrounded by a large number of what appeared to be truck drivers, some of whom Elijah recognized. Next to them were the members of Promise Ministries Board of Directors as well as the entire Promise Ministries' staff. In the other direction were Ted Beckett, Bubba Driscoll, and the rest of the Liars, Thieves, and Jokers Club. His old Pal Mac from Richfield College was there along with a smattering of other Richfield staff and alumni.

His undoing was seeing his daughters--Rachel, Shelly, and Kathi— all wiping tears from their eyes as they approached their dad with a collective embrace.

Elijah turned and saw a beaming Jethro.

"Well? What do you think?" asked Jethro.

"What is *this*?"

"This is your campaign kickoff."

In addition to the familiar faces were around 200 acquaintances and fans who received an invitation to this secret gathering. Jethro wanted a large enough crowd to be impactful but small enough that word wouldn't get out. Each attendee was sworn to secrecy in exchange for an invitation.

"My *what?*" Elijah asked.

"Your campaign kickoff. I know you have some lingering doubts about this whole thing, so we all wanted to offer you our support and encouragement to launch this campaign in the right direction."

"I don't..."

"Don't say a word, Elijah. Girls, escort him to the chair."

"The chair?! That sounds ominous!"

His daughters ushered him to a chair in the center of the room. As they walked, the crowd began to chant "E - Li - Jah, E - Li - Jah!"

Handed a microphone, Jethro began to hold court. "OK everybody. First, I want to thank you all for being here and especially for keeping this little soirée a secret. I think we really surprised our old buddy."

The crowd cheered.

Jethro continued, clearly loving the spotlight, as always. "Word has gotten out about your application to be on the presidential ballot in Tennessee and...well, buddy, this thing has spread like wildfire. In the first week, the Mustang for President Fund..."

Elijah mouthed to Jethro "The *what?*"

Jethro continued, ignoring his friend's question. "... has raised over $10 million. On top of that, we have a

campaign leadership team in place, comprised solely
of volunteers. We have two former congressmen…don't
worry they are the two you liked." The joke brought
hearty laughs from the assembled crowd. "We've got two
of your competitor CEOs from the trucking industry.
I've recruited three CEOs from the fast food industry.
We have a former secretary of agriculture and a retired
federal judge. And remember, we're just getting started.
What do y'all think about that?!"

The crowd resumed their chants of "E - Li - Jah, E -
Li – Jah."

After a few moments Jethro again quieted the crowd
to resume his role as master of ceremonies. "And now for
the best part." He gestured in the direction of the back
of the large exhibit hall. "Fire 'em up, boys!"

Large screens in front of the hall came to life with
a series of simulcasts. Jethro continued, "If we're going to do this thing right, we gotta do more than just
Tennessee. Whaddya say, Kentucky!"

On screen the Kentucky delegation cheered and
held up a paper while a designated spokesman declared,
"Elijah Mustang is on the ballot in Kentucky!"

The assembly hall cheered. Jethro repeated the process 17 more times. Elijah was officially on the ballot in
19 states. The last state reporting—the Lone Star State
of Texas—was the most difficult. The filing deadline for
Texas was the earliest in the country and only three days
away. To complicate matters, it required 1% of the total
votes cast for all candidates in the previous presidential

election, which equated to 80,000 signatures. The Texas delegation secured over 100,000 signatures in the two months since Jethro got the ball rolling.

Jethro continued, "And the great news is, we're well on our way to getting on the ballot in the other 31 states. This is really happening!"

"E - Li - Jah, E - Li – Jah."

Walking toward a stunned Elijah, Jethro continued, "Hey, I know y'all have heard all of ole Jethro you want to hear. How about hearing from our guest of honor, the next president of the United States!" Jethro gave the mic to Elijah, who at first acted as if he was being handed a rattlesnake before reluctantly taking it into his grasp.

"E - Li - Jah, E - Li – Jah."

Elijah took one more look around the room, trying to find something coherent to say. "You know, this was supposed to be an evening where my old friend Jethro and I were going to Calhoun's to enjoy a big plate of ribs."

Jethro hurried back to Jethro's chair, grabbed the mic and declared, "Oh, I almost forgot; Calhoun's is catering this event. They've got all the ribs you can eat, buddy!" Jethro then thrust the mic back into Elijah's hand.

"Well…OK then. Wow…I don't even know where to start. I'm humbled. I'm surprised. I'm overwhelmed. I'm scared to death. You really did all of this for me?"

The crowd cheered.

"I don't have a speech prepared, so I'm going to just keep this short and sweet. I feel the least qualified person on earth for this job. I honestly don't know what you see that would compel you to put on this kind of a show. I will say that I love this country with everything I have, and my heart is breaking to see it struggle so mightily. The two traditional party candidates do not instill any confidence that they can make it any better. So…I reluctantly and cautiously join with you…I can't believe I'm saying this…join with you on this crazy journey to see where this campaign leads. Let's get to work."

"E - Li - Jah, E - Li – Jah!"

Elijah began to shake many familiar hands, one of them belonging to Pastor Roberts, who pulled himself close enough to Elijah to whisper into his ear, "For such a time as this."

As the crowd reached a fever pitch, the local press arrived on cue, just as Jethro had planned. By tomorrow morning Elijah's official announcement would be national news and would shake the foundations of the 2016 presidential campaign as well as Victor Youngblood's well-laid plans. Things were about to get interesting.

40

May 7, 2016
185 Days Until 2016 U. S. Presidential Election

"We have some breaking news to bring to you. In a shocking development that could have far-reaching implications for the 2016 presidential election, popular YouTube sensation Elijah Mustang is reportedly joining the race as an independent candidate. Here to discuss the impact of Mustang's decision is our political correspondent, Chase Farrington. Chase, who will this hurt more, Mitch McCoy or Lionel Ireland?"

"Well, I think it could actually help Elijah Mustang the most."

"You don't think he actually has a chance to win do you?"

"Admittedly, it's a long shot; but you said *YouTube sensation*, which significantly underrepresents who Elijah Mustang is. He's a former congressman; he's the CEO of one of the largest trucking companies in the country; he's started a charity that has had significant positive impacts in Central America and that recently expanded into South America. On top of that, the country isn't very excited about either McCoy or Ireland; so the time is ripe for this type of run."

Victor Youngblood turned off the TV in his office and slammed the remote, shattering it into pieces. He started pacing as Jeremy came to the door.

"Good morning, Victor, I…"

"Have you seen the news this morning?!" an uncharacteristically frustrated Victor asked.

"Uh…you mean about Elijah Mustang?" Jeremy responded, taken aback by Victor's tone.

"Yes! We can't let this hamper our efforts. We have to get this under control immediately. How did we not see this coming?" he asked rhetorically.

"Well, I'm not…"

Victor didn't let Jeremy answer. "We are initiating Project Cobra. You're in charge. You are already familiar with Mustang from your stunt at that college where we found you. I want to know everything there is to know about the guy. I want to know what he drives, where he lives, what toothpaste he uses, how many email accounts he has. Everything."

"OK, we'll get started right now."

"Good. You're already late."

᷃

"Did you know that the last time we were all together was Christmas? That's way too long."

After the unexpected family reunion in downtown Knoxville the night before, Elijah was enjoying the company of his daughter Rachel; daughter Shelly and her husband Christopher, visiting from Florida; and daughter Kathi and her husband Vince, visiting from South Carolina.

"Yes, it is!" Rachel had the blessing of living close to her father, so she could visit him each week; but she missed her sisters terribly. "Here's your omelet, Dad," Rachel offered.

"Still bacon, provolone cheese, and jalapeno peppers?" Shelly asked.

"Of course. Why mess with perfection?" Elijah mumbled while chewing his first bite.

"Dad, I know last night was a lot for you to take in," Kathi noted. "Jethro ensured us that you would want us all to be there."

"Last night was…unexpected; but yes, it was wonderful to see all of you. It was very exciting."

"Dad, are you ready for some more excitement?" Kathi asked.

Elijah asked matter-of-factly, "What kind of excitement?"

Kathi looked at Vince, who smiled and nodded. "Dad...I'm pregnant!"

Elijah looked up from his plate and put down his fork— something he rarely did, his mouth agape. "You're...pregnant? I'm gonna be a granddaddy?"

"Yep, a granddaddy!"

Elijah leaped from his chair; hugged Kathi; at first shook Vince's hand, then decided a hug would be better; and then hugged Rachel, Shelly and Christopher before once again hugging Kathi. "That is wonderful news! I'm gonna be a granddaddy!" he said to himself.

Not an eye was dry in the house, especially Elijah's. He was known to be an old softy who cried easily at family gatherings.

"What do you know? When is it due? Is it a boy or a girl? Do you have names picked out yet?" Elijah asked in rapid-fire succession.

"It is due in December. We don't know the gender yet, and we are only starting to think about names," Vince responded, finally getting a word in the conversation.

"December? That's great. All this election nonsense will be over by then, and I can focus on being a granddaddy," Elijah chimed in, smiling.

All three daughters sternly glared at Elijah.

"What? What are you looking at? What did I say?"

Shelly, being the oldest, decided to start. "What do you mean, *this nonsense* will be over? You will have won the election and will be preparing for Inauguration Day."

"Oh, come on. You all know this is a Jethro stunt. I don't even know why…"

Rachel decided it was her turn. "Oh no you don't. We spent our entire childhood hearing lectures about giving our all no matter what. We were taught to do everything to the best of our abilities."

Trying to backpedal, Elijah interjected, "I didn't say I wasn't going to try…"

Kathi jumped into the fray. "Do you remember that time when I was playing soccer and we were having a terrible season? I was like seven or eight. I wasn't trying very hard, and you chewed me out. I told you that we hadn't won a game all year, and I asked why it mattered. Then you REALLY chewed me out. You said it mattered because my job wasn't to win; it was to leave the game knowing that I gave everything I had. Do you remember that?"

Now embarrassed, Elijah was lowering his voice. "Yes, I think I might remember that."

Kathi continued, "Dad, you taught us that whatever we choose to do, do it with everything in our hearts. Now you're not doing that!"

Elijah let out a huge sigh.

Shelly rejoined the conversation. "Dad, this country really needs you. You can do this. All those people are counting on you. They think you're going to fix this country. You owe it to them to give them everything you have!"

Elijah paused, obviously in deep thought. He then looked at Kathi. "Do you know what I remember about soccer?"

"What dad?" Kathi asked expectantly.

"You weren't a very good soccer player."

"Gee thanks, Dad."

"But…there's a *but* coming…*but*…after my little motivational speech, you played like a Tasmanian devil. You ran and chased the ball and dove and slid. You didn't accomplish much individually, but you inspired the rest of your team to play harder. Your team didn't win the championship, but you did go on to win some games and were competitive in the ones you lost. All it took was for one person to lead the way to show everyone else what they were capable of achieving."

"Maybe that's what I'm supposed to do," Elijah continued. "I know I'm not anything great. I know I don't have what it takes to be the president of the United States; but maybe I can somehow inspire people who are frustrated, disenfranchised, and just plain angry. Maybe I can be their voice."

Kathi responded, "Dad, I *know* you can."

41

May 14, 2016
178 Days Until 2016 U. S. Presidential Election

" In the first real polling since upstart-candidate Elijah Mustang announced his candidacy, the results confirm what many suspected; there's a genuine appetite for an alternative to what the mainstream parties are offering this election cycle. Mustang, whose candidacy is barely a week old, is polling at 12%, a level unheard of since billionaire Ross Perot's run in 1992. Billionaire Perot had significantly more resources than Mustang, making the Tennessean's polling performance that much more remarkable."

Watching in his office, Victor again broke his remote control. The sixth such casualty in the last week. "Jeremy!" he shouted. There was no reply. "Jeremy! Oh, forget it; I'll do it myself," he muttered. Picking up the phone, he dialed George Owens, his Mouse Trap Division Manager for Network and Cable News.

"George! Get everyone on the phone and tell them to quit pumping up Mustang! This thing is getting out of hand! Yes, right now! Use your resources and organize a call. Tell them to quit reporting on Mustang. They are creating a monster! Do it now!"

For the second time in 16 months, the national media had assembled in East Tennessee to report on Elijah Mustang's exploits. The first time, they all hurried into tiny Bard's Ridge to capture the campus protest. This time was totally different. This time they were here to cover the burgeoning presidential candidate's initial campaign speech.

Staged in the World's Fair Park in downtown Knoxville, the event created a palpable buzz. Several thousand people had devoted their Saturday to this auspicious occasion. Cars, many adorned with "Elijah Mustang for President" bumper stickers, filled downtown parking lots and garages. Satellite trucks lined both Henley Street and Clinch Avenue. Remnants from the 1982 World Fair, for which the park was named, included a festival lawn; a performance lawn; and an amphitheater, where the podium was situated.

Several luminaries spoke, including Jethro Poindexter; a couple of country music stars; a former Tennessee Volunteer quarterback; and a few elected officials, who were courageous enough to break ranks with their party to show their support for Elijah. After all the preliminaries, Elijah Mustang stepped up to the podium. Then, after many boisterous cheers and more than a few chants of "E – Li – Jah," Elijah began his much anticipated speech.

"Good afternoon. I want to thank all of my East Tennessee neighbors for coming out to see us today. And for those of you visiting us from out of town, welcome to the most beautiful place in the world. We hope you've found our hospitality as warm as our midday sunshine.

"I've got to be honest with you; this situation is very surreal to me. Never in a thousand years did I think I'd ever find myself here, actually running for president of the United States; but...here I am."

Again the crowd interrupted with cheers and chants until Elijah stopped them long enough to resume.

"I know very few of you actually really know me, so I'm going to spend the next few minutes on introductions. For the first introduction, I want to tell you who I am. I am a flawed, imperfect man who makes mistakes every day of his life; who will continue making mistakes throughout this campaign; and should a miracle happen and you choose me to be your next president, will make mistakes then too.

"I am a Christian. Being a Christian means I know that I've failed and that I need Jesus as my savior to lead and guide me every day.

"I'm a father of three beautiful daughters and two wonderful sons-in- law. I was a husband to Becky, the love of my life, whom I lost to awful, terrible, merciless breast cancer five years ago.

"I am the CEO of Promise Transportation, a trucking company I started with me and a truck 34 years ago. Now we have over 2,000 trucks on the road. I say that not to boast but to let you know that building Promise Transportation required working hard, being surrounded by brilliant people, and having a large dose of God's grace. I intend to use all three generously in both my campaign and, should you choose me, in serving as your president.

"Most people who run for office have some sort of scandal...some skeleton in their closet that they hope you never find. I'm here today to confess my scandal to the world. I'm embarrassed by it. I'm ashamed of it. It's clearly a dark blot on my life. For four years I was... a United States congressman. Please don't hold that against me."

The crowd laughed and smiled and cheered.

Elijah continued, "I have discussed with you who I *am*. Now, I'd like to let you know who I'm *not*. I'm not someone who is going to have all of the answers. I'm not a savior who is going to fix all of the country's problems. I'm certainly not as articulate as either Mr. McCoy or Mr. Ireland. I can't tell you the name of Latvia's president. I don't know the GDP of Norway. I'm going to disappoint you throughout this process with things I don't know. If you're looking for the candidate who knows how do to everything, please know that I'm not that guy.

"Now, enough about me. Let's talk about what's really important. Let's talk about *you*. Let's talk about what you are. You are frustrated. I hear every day how frustrated people are with the way the country is being run and how helpless people feel to do anything about it. I want to tell you that you have more power than you realize. You are much stronger than you understand. Let me explain."

Elijah reached below the podium and then held above his head a three-foot section of a thick rope. He continued, "This rope is used to secure a 200,000-ton cruise ship to its moorings. That's 400-million pounds held by this rope. And it is a rope I can hold in my hands. How is that possible? This rope is comprised of thousands of individual fibers, all tightly woven together. But if I begin to unravel this rope and ultimately get down to an individual strand...," Elijah help up a strand of rope, "I can easily break it with just the force of my own strength. And just to be clear, I'm not all that strong.

"This individual strand is where we stand as a country. We've allowed ourselves to be unraveled and separated. We're black, white, Hispanic, Christian, atheist, Jew, Muslim, gay, straight, transgender, Republican, Democrat, Southern, Northern, Western, pro-gun, anti-gun, young, old, and somewhere in between. Individually we feel like we're trying to move 400-million pounds, and it is just overwhelming. In fact, individually, it can't be done.

"The answer lies in this rope. We have to come together like the fibers of this rope. We have to say that before anything else, we're Americans. We have to take back control of our government from those who wish to unravel us. In the coming weeks, I'm definitely going to tell you where I stand on various issues; but the overarching message I hope to convey is that we have to come together as a nation, even when we disagree. And we'll always have disagreements; we just can't continue letting them divide us, or we'll be as weak as these individual strands. Together, ladies and gentlemen, you are strong. You are America!"

After more cheers, Elijah continued, "I've told you who I am, who I'm not, and what you are. Now, I want to tell you what you're not. You are not followers. You are not minions. You are not tools to be manipulated by politicians and billionaires. You are not helpless, and you are not hopeless. I'm making it one of my primary objectives during this campaign to remind you of that and to treat you with the respect that you deserve, whether you chose to vote for me or not and whether you agree with me on everything or nothing.

"In closing, I want to make a few promises to you. I know…and I apologize…I'm already sounding like a politician but here goes. I promise that I will always be honest with you. I know everyone that runs for office makes that promise; all I can say is that I will. I know I have to earn your trust, but I will do my best to do so. I promise I will give this campaign my all. This isn't a stunt or a trick. I am in this campaign to become your president. I promise that this will be an unconventional campaign. I don't even know exactly how yet, but it must be. The candidates from the two parties will spend about a billion dollars each. My campaign budget will have several fewer zeroes than that, so being unconventional is a necessity. Lastly, I promise that I will always remember I'm doing this for you. I'm doing this to give you an alternative to the two candidates currently running.

"Thank you for this great turnout. Thank you for your support. Thank you for joining me in returning this country – a country that's been adrift at sea for so long – to its foundation of being *of the people, by the people, and for the people*." Lifting the rope one more time Elijah declared, "You will be the rope that ensures our country stays securely fastened to its moorings. God bless you, and God bless this beautiful country!"

The crowd cheered for what seemed like minutes. Elijah walked into the throng, shaking as many hands as he could, although the thousands gathered made that impossible. It was a momentous occasion filled with energy and passion to almost all gathered.

Sitting at the back of the lawn with a laptop was a reporter who was dispatched from the National News Service to cover the event. Having actually written his report long before Elijah spoke, he just waited for the formality of Elijah finishing before hitting *send*.

Knoxville, TN – Earlier today Elijah Mustang, a small-town Tennessee businessman, announced his improbable run for president of the United States. What was supposed to be a large turnout consisted primarily of a handful of friends and family. Addressing the small crowd, Mustang offered no policy positions, no plans, and no apparent vision for his candidacy.

Media outlets throughout the country picked up this short report. Clearly, Elijah would be fighting an uphill battle.

42

In many facets Mouse Trap was unlike any other organization in existence; however, in some mundane day-to-day aspects, it functioned like any other large business. The Youngblood and Associates cafeteria was just such an area. Victor reasoned that it would be good for Mouse Trap personnel to mingle with regular Y&A employees to give them a mid-day break from their clandestine responsibilities. The only rule he instituted was a strict *no work talk* policy outside the doors of Mouse Trap. It was a policy Jeremy would bend...just slightly.

"Are the burgers any good?" Jeremy asked.

"Huh?"

"Are the burgers here any good? I haven't tried them."

"Uh...yeah...they're...fine."

"Great, I'll try one. You're Leonard Applebaum, aren't you?" Jeremy asked excitedly.

Adjusting his glasses, Leonard turned to look at his inquisitor for the first time in the conversation. "Uh... yes...that's my name. Do I know you?" Then he turned back to the food line.

"I've heard a lot about you, but I don't think we've actually met. I'm Jeremy Prince." Jeremy extended a hand in greeting.

Leonard's heart rate quickened. Although the rumor mill was strongly discouraged at Mouse Trap, Jeremy Prince's ascension to be Victor Youngblood's right-hand man was well known throughout the organization. This fact was especially appreciated by Leonard Applebaum, Omnia system administrator, responsible for establishing access rights. He knew that Jeremy was one of only a handful with Level 7 access to Omnia. With Jeremy now standing next to him, the palms of the stereotypically introverted IT genius began to sweat.

"It's...uh...nice to meet you too," Leonard stammered.

"It's funny that we'd run into each other here. I actually had a couple of questions about Om...," Jeremy caught himself, forgetting he had passed beyond the boundaries of the secure area, "...questions about my IT system."

"*Wwwweee* can't talk about that here," Leonard babbled in a hushed but frantic tone.

"Mind if I join you for lunch? Then we can maybe chat in your office afterwards."

"Well...I...uh...usually eat in my office."

"That's great; I'll join you!"

"Well...I don't really..."

"It's OK, my office is messy too. I don't mind," Jeremy declared before Leonard could come up with an excuse.

"OK...I guess."

Jeremy and Leonard completed their lunch selections, paid the cashier, and navigated through the maze back to Mouse Trap's entrance.

They showed their IDs to the guards, swiped their badges, and placed their fingers on the fingerprint scanner. Then they made their way down to Leonard's large, surprisingly spotless and well-organized office.

"Wow, this is great Leonard! Wish my office was this neat."

Leonard didn't answer.

"So...anyway...I have a question about my Omnia access. I understood from Victor that I have Level 7 access. Is that correct?"

"Yes, that's correct," Leonard responded.

"You just *know* that? You don't have to look it up?"

"There aren't many with Level 7 access. I know everyone who has it."

"OK, great. So, my understanding is that Level 7 is the highest level of access. Is that right?"

Briefly hesitating, Leonard then responded, "Uh yes, that's right."

"OK, well there's a file that I can't seem to open. I was wondering if maybe I was doing something wrong."

"Can you show me the file?" Leonard gestured to his terminal for Jeremy to log in.

After executing the log on protocol and searching for *Gary Carlisle* and *Cam Calvin*, Jeremy found the file *Trapped*. He then motioned for Leonard to watch.

"Look. When I click on this file, it says that I don't have access."

His face turning ashen, Leonard struggled to speak before finally muttering, "How did you find that file?"

"I was working on a project involving two gentlemen who unfortunately passed. I searched their names, and I was led to this file." He didn't reveal that he'd searched dozens of common names that also led to *Trapped*.

''That's...that's...a mistake. You shouldn't have been able to...I don't understand how..."

"I do have Level 7 access, *right?*"

"Yes."

"That is the highest access, *right?*"

There was no answer.

Jeremy continued, "A few moments ago you said I had the highest access. Is that correct, Leonard?"

"You shouldn't be here."

At age 23, Jeremy still struggled with asserting the authority he'd been given; but he thought now would be a good time to take it for a test drive. In his sternest voice he commanded, "Leonard, I'm going to ask you this again...do I have the highest access rights to Omnia?"

Leonard got up from his chair and hit what seemed like a random sequence of buttons and switches scattered throughout his office. He then approached Jeremy with a serious expression and whispered into his ear, "We need to talk."

♇

Over the past two weeks, Elijah had been on a whirlwind tour, traveling around the country speaking to Americans. His venues ranged from picnics with a few dozen in attendance, to high school football stadiums with a few thousand. In the evenings he had been working to form a leadership team to advise him for the balance of the campaign. Elijah settled on a team of ten, comprised of six men and four women. The team included experts in a variety of fields, including economics; foreign policy; domestic affairs; national and international business; politics; popular culture; national defense; and of course, fried chicken. The common thread for all was that they reached out to Elijah and asked to serve on the team. They were fed up with business as usual in Washington.

The inaugural team meeting was a few minutes underway with introductions just completed. Elijah got the ball rolling. "I want to thank each of you for serving on this team. I know this is a very unconventional way to run a presidential campaign, but I sense that's what our fellow citizens are craving. I'd like to start by going around the room and asking each person to state what you think should be our primary focus areas for the next few weeks. We have folks in all corners of the room ready to capture your thoughts on flip charts. Let's just get everything down on paper without trying to filter what's good and what's bad. We'll do that next. Let's start to my left."

"I think we ought to find the weaknesses in McCoy and Ireland and have talking points for Elijah to exploit them," the first respondent said.

"The Republicans and Democrats are having conventions next month. I think we should plan to have a convention-like event where speakers show their public support for the campaign with Elijah delivering the keynote address."

"I think we need to contact the major news outlets and get a slot on the Sunday morning talk shows."

"We really need to work on our PR campaign. The *Mustang for President* bumper stickers were a hot item long before Elijah ever declared his candidacy. We need to build on that with yard signs, posters, newspaper and TV ads."

"We have some nationally recognized personalities in this room. Using Facebook, Twitter, and other social media we should make it clear that we support Elijah."

"We should record Elijah at some of these big speaking events and create a campaign video to inspire excitement."

Jethro Poindexter noticed that with each response Elijah was becoming more fidgety and his body language was darkening. He knew his friend well and detected that something wasn't right. He decided to intervene. "Can we hit the pause button for a second? I know we said we weren't going to critique these ideas along the way, but I can't help noticing that Elijah seems a bit disturbed. What do you think, Elijah? This is your baby."

Elijah's first response was brought with a bit of hesitancy but then he took control. "I appreciate all of your thoughts; I really do, but you're simply reciting strategies that conventional campaigns have used for the past 50 years. We're not going to succeed by doing the same thing everyone else is doing. We have to do something different. We have to mount an unorthodox campaign. We have to get creative. We can't compete with the two big parties by following their playbook. For one thing, we are not going to raise a billion dollars. We don't even want to raise that kind of money. Also, we want this campaign to be about the voters, not about me. This is about giving them an alternative to the two parties. That must be our focus. Can we start again with that as a guiding principle?"

Elijah's words inspired new thoughts from his assembled team. The first team member to speak after Elijah's reboot was Vice Admiral (Ret) Jackson Adair, who had been Commander, Naval Sea Systems Command, commonly known in the service as NAVSEA. In this capacity Admiral Adair led a force of 60,000, who were responsible for design, construction and support for the Navy's ships and combat systems. Adair had served under both Democrat and Republican administrations and knew firsthand the dire condition the nation was truly in. He didn't know Elijah well, but he knew a drastic change in direction was needed. He volunteered his service in part to see if Elijah represented that change.

Admiral Adair began; "Citizens I meet despise the back-and- forth bickering that goes on during election years. What if throughout your entire campaign, you never allude to or mention your opponents by name. Simply focus on your platform and the voters. You could have a policy that the names *Ireland* and *McCoy* are never spoken."

Elijah looked to the ceiling in reflection. "I like it. Now that's something we can build upon. Who's next?"

43

"Let's go through today's agenda; we have a full one. With so much on the docket, I hadn't planned to spend much time on the election because Ireland is in good shape and everything is right where we need it to be." Victor didn't even look up to see The Council's reaction. "I had planned to spend some time on the situation in Syria, opportunities I see for The Council in the Olympics, and what we want to do about oil prices. We should start…"

Dog interrupted, "Hang on just a second, about the election… What do you think about this Mustang guy? He seems intriguing."

"Just a flash in the pan," Victor responded dismissively. "Nothing we should spend any time on. So…"

"Just a minute." It was Charlie's turn to interject. "I saw polling data indicating he was already in double digits after just a few weeks. I think he's worth a second look. It could be a great opportunity for us if we can influence him early on."

"It is my advice to The Council that we stay the course with Ireland. We've invested significant time and resources with him and…"

"Victor, we just changed horses from Wembley to Ireland three months ago. We haven't invested *that* much time," Charlie continued.

Briefly rattled that he had been caught in a lie, Victor tried to recover. "Yes, of course we've only been with Mr. Ireland for three months; but we've invested significant resources, both personnel and finances. I wouldn't recommend backpedaling now."

"What do we know about Mustang? I have watched some of his speeches on YouTube, and he seems to have captured the imagination of lots of Americans. I think we need to understand more," Baker chimed in.

Victor tried to hide his exasperation. "Ireland was the CEO of Di-Com, a global tech enterprise with a market cap of over $250 billion. Mustang owns a small trucking company in Tennessee. I don't think there's much of a comparison."

Easy joined the conversation. "The negatives are huge on Ireland. The guy may have accomplished a lot, but the people don't seem to be embracing him. Do we really want to put all of our resources in someone that so many Americans don't like?"

What Victor was trying desperately to restrain finally came bursting forth. "Why do you insist on talking about Mustang?! He is *not* our guy! How many times do I have to tell you we've decided on Ireland? It's not open for debate!" The words had barely left his mouth when Victor realized he'd entered new territory in his relationship with The Council.

At first there was awkward silence and five peering stares all in Victor's direction before Dog decided to speak first. "It *is* open for debate if we say it's open for debate," he snarled.

Charlie spoke next in a demeaning tone. "I think you have forgotten your position in this assembly. You serve at the pleasure of The Council in a support function. Do you understand?"

Able decided to play the role of peacemaker. "Gentlemen, I believe Victor has earned a degree of latitude, by serving The Council faithfully. Victor, while we understand the burden you carry, we cannot allow The Council to be addressed in this manner. Do you understand?"

Victor's mind quickly sorted through his options. He could accelerate the ultimate solution but that would significantly complicate other parts of his plan. He could tell The Council that they had been living a charade for the past decade and that he could damn well do whatever he wanted. However, he knew that response would only serve to temporarily soothe his bruised ego. He decided on the only alternative that would keep the focus on the greater plan.

"I must plead with The Council for your forbearance. As Mr. Able correctly pointed out, we do have many concurrent priorities. I allowed them to color my temperament, and I am truly regretful for my disrespectful exchange with The Council. I assure you that will not happen again."

The Council seemed to bite on Victor's deference and resumed their interest in Elijah Mustang.

"Thank you, Victor. I expect it will not happen again. I would like to make The Council's direction clear. In the next meeting, we'd like a full report on Elijah Mustang. Is he a candidate The Council should support? If not, why not. We want to know everything there is to know about him. Understood?"

"Yes sir, understood", responded Victor.

44

There was much debate in news rooms and editors' offices around the country. The announcement was clearly going to be important. Elijah Mustang was now on the ballot in all 50 states. He was a legitimate candidate. Beyond that, he was polling at 17%, eroding the support from McCoy and Ireland almost equally. He was still gaining recognition. For poll respondents who said they knew "some" or "a lot" about Elijah, he had the support of a substantial 29%, almost even with the mainstream candidates. Clearly, something was effervescing in the country's fascination with Elijah. This fascination pressured the media to broadcast the announcement live on TV.

On the other side of the debate, the major national news outlets received strict warnings to dampen coverage of Elijah. The warnings were coming from places they knew they couldn't ignore. They were conflicted. Nevertheless, more than half decided to take the courageous route and air the announcement live. Most of the national print media decided to deploy representatives as well. They knew they'd feel the consequence of their decision, but they sensed something historic was happening in the campaign.

The podium was situated on the north end of the floor at the Wesley Brown Field House on the campus of the United States Naval Academy. The location was selected specifically for the man for whom this event was scheduled. The request to use the facility came only 48 hours prior to the scheduled start time, with news reaching the Pentagon with fewer than 24 hours' notice. Washington bureaucrats sent frantic missives to the Academy brass ordering the event to be relocated; but out of respect for the honoree, the orders were temporarily "lost."

As the time came for the proceedings to start, Elijah Mustang stepped up to the podium for the introduction.

"I want to thank you for coming to this important event. I am especially pleased to see so many members of the media in attendance. Thank you for being here. I would also like to extend my heartfelt gratitude to the Academy for hosting this gathering. It is truly an honor to be at this historic institution.

"Since announcing my candidacy for president six short weeks ago, I've been overwhelmed by the support from so many people around the country. This experience has left me both humbled and encouraged. But today I come to you with a different kind of encouragement. Today I have news that will propel this movement to the next level. Today I'm excited to announce my running mate. He's a true American hero and one of the best men I've ever known. He's a 1974 graduate of these hallowed grounds. Ladies and gentlemen, I want to introduce to you the next vice president of the United States, Admiral Jackson Adair."

There had been much discussion among Elijah's leadership team about both this decision and this event. An argument was made to keep the announcement low key. Some said making a fuss would be too much like the mainstream campaigns. In the end, the argument that won the day was that this announcement would bolster the campaign and increase its legitimacy. The timing was also intentional, designed to precede either mainstream candidate's vice presidential selection. It would be a sign that the Mustang for President Campaign was well organized and coalescing. Based on the day's excitement, the team had clearly made the correct decision. Admiral Adair stepped to the podium to enthusiastic applause from midshipmen, Academy officers, and dozens of alumni who responded to the short-notice invitation.

"I want to thank you all for being here and the Academy for being such gracious hosts." The Admiral turned to face Elijah, who was standing behind him. "And Elijah, I want to thank you for the great honor and privilege of serving as your running mate."

Turning back to the assembly, he continued, "One of the most refreshing qualities of Elijah Mustang is his unabashed honesty. I am going to borrow some of that honesty today and tell you the Elijah Mustang movement first intrigued me, not for who Elijah is but for who he isn't. Like many of you, I was unsatisfied with the traditional parties' offerings, and I knew there had to be someone better. I was hopeful Elijah would be that someone. Now, after spending six weeks working shoulder to shoulder with this man, I'm on board exactly because of who he is.

"I have had the pleasure of working for three presidents, and I can tell you Elijah has everything they had and more. He is smart and hardworking. He has good judgment, and he loves this country. I have been with him speaking in front of thousands, and I've seen him one on one with the cleanup crew after these events. I can tell you that he treats everyone with equal respect and dignity. He is a man of high character. After seeing the mettle of this man, I can tell you he's the real deal. I wouldn't be standing here if he wasn't."

Leonard told Jeremy to be patient. He promised to help, but he had to wait for just the right time. He advised Jeremy to have no more direct contact and to try opening *Trapped* each day. For the last 23 days, Jeremy tried unsuccessfully.

On day 24 Jeremy again clicked on the name; something different was obviously happening. Rather than the instantaneous *I'm sorry, but the information you are requesting is above your access level,* the cursor hesitated. Jeremy moved to the edge of his chair and stared intently at the screen. Briefly the screen displayed *This is for Bryce*, then disappeared. Then the screen displayed an entirely different section of Omnia that he hadn't seen before. It was some sort of database. Jeremy was given the option of selecting Project Name, Division, Project Manager, or Mouse. Intrigued, he clicked on Mouse. He was then given the option of selecting Name, Project, or Date. He selected Name. In the center of the screen a series of alphabetized names appeared, last name first. On the right side of the screen was the alphabet vertically displayed. He randomly selected the letter *M* and names beginning with the letter *M* appeared. Having a hunch what the list was, he then selected *C*. Among the names listed was Calvin, Cam. He clicked and the screen displayed an image of Cam Calvin, a short biography, and links to several other stories and reports. What caught his eye most were the words *Trapped 30 May 2015* in large red letters and numbers. He found those red letters were also hyperlinked, so he again clicked. To his shock he found gruesome photos of Cam Calvin's equestrian "accident" and he had to look away from the screen.

Jeremy quickly returned to the list, occasionally finding familiar names, including politicians, company CEOs, celebrities, and even a few athletes. Most names he did not recognize. He noticed a search window and typed the name Bryce. Surprisingly, there were three hits. He had luck on the first try, Bryce Dunn. As he scanned the file, he found that Bryce had worked in Mouse Trap's IT department with Leonard in Omnia Access Control before becoming a project manager. The last note in Bryce's file indicated that he submitted his resignation. When he clicked on the red letters, a photo appeared of a badly damaged BMW upside down next to an icy river. The next photo was a close-up of what must have been Bryce Dunn with a devastating neck injury.

Jeremy glanced down at the lower left of the screen and noticed that the *Trapped* application provided a total number of database entries: 3,482. Jeremy had to let that number sink in: 3,482?! How is that even possible?! Just as he was in deep contemplation, trying to process this unbelievable information, his thoughts were abruptly interrupted.

"Jeremy, what are you doing?!" It was Victor but not the usual cool, calm, and collected Victor. It was a Victor he had not yet seen. Jeremy's heart raced as he quickly searched for the prompt to close out Trapped.

"Have you been watching?!" Victor demanded.

"Uh…watching what?" Jeremy replied, hoping Victor wasn't talking about Trapped.

"The TV! Mustang is all over TV!"

Jeremy first breathed a sigh of relief. Maybe he somehow hadn't been caught. Then he realized something else had changed his boss's demeanor. He needed to find out what it was.

"No, I'm sorry; I wasn't watching. *What…*"

"I'll tell you *what…*," Victor screamed. "He picked a running mate, an admiral! And the announcement was on TV! And it was at the Naval Academy! How could any of this be happening!? We were supposed to have directed through all channels that Mustang was to be marginalized. This kind of coverage will just make his legend grow!"

Jeremy was dealing with a flood of emotions. His first was relief, as it appeared he hadn't been caught. His second was fear. His boss was screaming at him. A boss responsible for 3,482 *Traps*. He certainly didn't want to be number 3,483; so he decided to engage.

"Project Cobra is working at full strength. I do not know why the media covered this event, but we'll work to address that. Research has identified some vulnerabilities. First, he earns over a million dollars a year. That makes him a one percenter. Mouse Trap had turned the public against high achievers a few years ago."

Showing signs of being willing to listen, Victor insisted, "Keep going."

Jeremy continued in a calm tone, trying to placate his anxious boss. "Despite making over $1.3 million last year, he paid very little in taxes. Four percent to be exact. So…he's a millionaire who doesn't pay his taxes. As we say back home in Virginia, that's easy pickins."

Victor seemed impressed by Jeremy's work and was willing at least to listen. "OK, what more do you have?"

"He was the CEO of Promise Transportation, but he was out of the office for 57 days. He was collecting a paycheck, but he was an absentee CEO. We can say that he'll be an absentee president as well."

Victor responded, "Yes, we can probably use that."

Jeremy pointed to his screen. "We have several more like that in the Project Cobra file. I can go through them with you if you want…"

"No, I'll read them later. Just make sure you contact the media divisions and have them change the message about Mustang."

Before Jeremy could say "will do," Victor was out of his office.

Jeremy breathed a huge sigh of relief that he hadn't been caught. Now he needed to decide what to do next. He knew his time was running short.

A similar conversation was occurring 2,500 miles away from Jeremy's office at the Ireland for President Campaign's downtown Los Angeles headquarters. This time, Lionel Ireland was the interrogator.

"Does someone want to explain these polls to me?!" Lionel Ireland was wildly waving a handful of papers. "Anyone?! Anyone have an explanation?! We've dropped in the polls each of the last five weeks!"

A meek voice from the back of the room mumbled, "You are still in the lead."

Lionel took three big steps in the voice's direction. "Who said that?!"

No one spoke up.

"I said, who said that?"

After several awkward moments, Lionel's campaign manager, handpicked by Victor, decided to fill the silence. "It's Mustang. He's taking ground from both you and McCoy. Our latest polls show you with 37%, McCoy with 34%, and Mustang with 29%."

Lionel turned back to the center of the room, arms waving wildly. "Who is this Mustang guy? How did we not know about him?!"

Lionel Ireland had a well-deserved reputation as a complete and total jerk. He ran his companies with an iron fist. He mandated a staff pruning each year, requiring the bottom 10% to be fired, even if they were long-term employees. He often berated and belittled executives, calling them sophomoric names like *stupid*; *idiot*; and his favorite *moron*.

He brought this "endearing" personality to the campaign, regularly chewing out staff for the most minor misunderstandings. It was easy to see why his approval rating was a dismal 31% among registered voters. Staffers would joke all that meant was that 31% of the voters hadn't met the real Lionel Ireland.

"Mustang's rise has been a surprise to everyone, but we're working on a plan of attack. We expect to have something to you soon," Lionel's campaign manager assured.

"You'd better, or I'll be looking for a new staff!"

The Mouse Trap-appointed campaign manager knew Ireland had no such power but allowed him the room to vent, at least for now.

45

" **I**n this city 240 years ago today at this historic venue, 56 men mutually pledged to each other their lives, their fortunes and their sacred honor to declare independence from a tyrannical government." Elijah was speaking in front of Independence Hall in downtown Philadelphia. Over 10,000 people had gathered on the birthday of their country to hear the growing cult figure address the crowd.

"Among the historic words that our founders put to pen were…" Elijah put on his glasses to read.

> *'We hold these truths to be self-evident, that all*
> *men are created equal, that they are endowed by*
> *their Creator with certain unalienable Rights,*

that among these are Life, Liberty and the pursuit of Happiness. That to secure these rights, Governments are instituted among Men, deriving their just powers from the consent of the governed, --That whenever any Form of Government becomes destructive of these ends, it is the Right of the People to alter or to abolish it, and to institute new Government, laying its foundation on such principles and organizing its powers in such form, as to them shall seem most likely to effect their Safety and Happiness.'

Elijah took off his glasses and continued speaking. "I believe these words are as relevant today as they were the day they were written. Our government is designed to derive its powers from us, the governed. I believe we have a government and governed that are doing exactly the opposite. Today we have both a government and a two-party system acting as if they possess the power to decide what we can and cannot do, as if they are the sole arbiters for how we live our lives. It's not supposed to be that way. Our forefathers worked too hard and shed too much blood for us to be in this situation.

"The beautiful thing about the Declaration of Independence is that it provides us with a roadmap." Elijah again read from his papers. "Whenever any government becomes destructive to the principles of freedom, it is our right to alter, abolish and institute new Government." He looked up again to address the crowd

461

eye to eye. "If you are fed up with what the two parties are doing to our country, you have the right to make a change. We are here to help you exercise that right. We're here to give you a choice."

Elijah recited a series of grievances against a bloated government, a political class who does not listen to the people, and two parties more worried about accumulating power than representing the electorate.

As with every speech since announcing his candidacy, Elijah's words were just what a disenfranchised and frustrated nation needed to hear. Yet, everyone wondered, "Will it really matter on Election Day?"

46

July 18, 2016
113 Days Until 2016 U. S. Presidential Election

"Chirp chirp chirp chirp chirp..."

Cedar Lassiter grunted, rolled over in his sleeping bag and opened one eye to look at the clock. When he saw the time, he muttered to himself, "Who is calling so early? It's barely noon."

After partially recovering his senses, he determined that the sound was actually an alert tone. He felt the bottom of his sleeping bag with his toes and slowly edged his cell phone up to where his hand could grab it. He pried open his second eye to see the message:

> *ACTIVATE: Republican National Convention, Quicken Loans Arena, Cleveland, Ohio. ASAP, forward to Level 3.*

As a Level 2 disciple in CivDis, the Civil Disobedience Network, Cedar had three jobs upon receiving the text. Job one was to forward the text to his Level 3 disciples, now numbering over 200. Job two was to round up his flock and ready for travel. Job three was to arrive at the appointed destination as soon as possible. As a Level 2 disciple, Cedar received $150 per day as long as the activation notice was in effect. For the unemployed, it was easy money.

He stumbled through the rented house, rousing his team. Within 30 minutes, they were on the road to Cleveland for the five-hour drive. One of the benefits of being an anarchist-for-hire was no shower required.

On this first day of the Republican Convention, the greatest need for the party, as well as the presumptive nominee Lionel Ireland, was enthusiasm.

Early in his candidacy, Lionel enjoyed a distinct level of excitement about his outsider status. A collective national frustration with the status quo provided a sense of optimism that Ireland could be the guy to fix this mess. However, as the primary plodded along, that optimism led to disappointment as Lionel Ireland's true nature was revealed. There was no debate that he was an achiever, but he was also rude, boorish, and absent any moral compass.

The Republicans hoped today's announcement of Ireland's running mate would provide a boost to the lethargic campaign. Unfortunately, the selection was the senior senator from Wyoming, Grant Wembley, runner-up to Ireland in the Republican primary. The words *Wembley* and *excitement* were rarely used in the same sentence. Wembley was not the lift the Republicans were hoping for.

After his loss in the Ohio primary, Wembley begged anyone who would listen to let him be the running mate. When the plea reached Victor, he saw that selecting Wembley would be a great fit for his ultimate plan and gave Wembley's selection the OK. Had Wembley known what was to come, he would have chosen a different path. Unfortunately, he had no such insight.

"OK, let's do a quick check to make sure everyone is on the line." Rebecca Montague, Mitch McCoy's campaign manager, was holding a conference call with 16 major media outlets from around the country. The call included all the major networks, most cable news outlets, and five of the top newspapers. A quick roll call confirmed all the invitees had signed in to the call.

"OK, I want to go over this week's convention coverage. For TV, we want to make sure cameras are outside the arena to capture the spontaneous protests. Make sure the angle is such that the crowd looks very large. For the commentators, make sure you use the words *scary*, *dark*, *pessimistic*, and *disaster* when talking about the convention. For the print media outlets, pick up on those same themes. You also need to discuss the disorganization, discontent, and anger among the delegates."

Rebecca continued, "We've already written a dozen stories about the next three days. They should be in your inbox by the time this call is over. As always, customize them for your use but make sure the original intent remains intact. Are there any questions? Hearing none, that's it for today's call."

47

" ... **W**hen I announced my candidacy 15 months ago, I told you I'm running and I'm going to win and we're going to fix this country! I'm here tonight to let you know that on November 8th we will finish the job! God bless you, and God bless the United States of America."

Lionel Ireland's speech capped off the 2016 Republican Convention. The crowd cheered; confetti and balloons fell from the rafters and Ireland's family joined him on stage, along with his running mate, Grant Wembley, and his family. They all smiled and waved to the crowd as upbeat music from the 70s filled the arena.

Everything about the Republican Convention went according to plan—at least according to Victor Young-blood's plan. Protesters lined the streets outside. Commentators said what a disaster the convention was. Newspapers dutifully reported that the event was scary, dark, and full of anger and discontent.

Victor couldn't be more pleased.

48

"Welcome back to the Moonlight Show. I'm your host, Kyle Flanagan. We have a great show for you tonight. Our first guest is a talented musician; a respected author; and oh, by the way, he could be the next president of the United States. Please give a big Moonlight Show welcome to Mitch McCoy!"

The band played, Mitch smiled and waved, and the crowd cheered as he took a seat on the interview couch.

"Well, Mitch...can I call you Mitch?"

"Please do."

"Mitch, you've had quite a year."

"Yes, it has been pretty crazy; but it has been a good kinda crazy."

"The Democrat Convention starts tonight in Philly."

Mitch nodded, "Yes, I'm leaving the studio and heading straight for the airport. We are looking forward to a great week."

Reading the questions he'd been provided, Kyle continued. "So, tell me what the primary was like. Did things go as you had planned?"

Mitch worked hard to make the rehearsed answer sound extemporaneous. "There are always obstacles to overcome, but I'd say we were very pleased. We had some outstanding candidates this year in the Democrat Party; so it is truly an honor that the voters responded to our positive, optimistic message."

Kyle started to grin. "Speaking of a positive, optimistic message, the Republicans held their convention last week."

Prompted by the off-camera audience coaches, the crowd booed heartily. Mitch also smiled and then replied, "Yes, but I didn't hear anything positive or optimistic. Instead, I heard fear and worry and pessimism. I don't think that's the kind of America I want to live in."

The crowd cheered with a few whistles and yells thrown in.

Kyle continued, "Now this campaign season is a bit weird as there's a third candidate that is making some waves. What do you know about this guy from Tennessee, Elijah Mustang?"

"Mustang...he seems, on the surface, like a decent enough guy. He's certainly playing the down-home populist card. I know he's trying to convince Americans he's one of them, but did you know he made $1.3 million last year? The reality is that he's one of the one percenters. I've also heard that he only paid 3% in taxes. Now that's not like many normal everyday Americans I know. Lastly, he has a cushy job as a CEO. Word is he took two months of vacation last year. So, unless everyday people are millionaires who pay 3% in taxes and take off two months for vacation, I'm thinking he's maybe not everything he's selling himself to be. I don't know. What does your audience think?"

Expecting a huge cheer, he got mostly silence with a few awkward claps. Kyle quickly tried to change the subject. "So, I understand you brought along a special guest."

Trying to recover from the whiff, Mitch was happy to change subjects. "Yes I did, Kyle. As you mentioned, our convention is starting tonight; and we are introducing a new convention theme song. Many conventions look back to a classic song to carry their message, but everything about our campaign is progressive and fresh; so we thought we needed our music to reflect that same tone."

Working hard to maintain his enthusiasm, Kyle continued, "Are you going to keep us in suspense? Who have you brought with you today?"

"Let's walk over to the stage and find out."

They both walked to the center of the studio where a full band was in place, absent its leader.

"Kyle, I want to welcome to the stage, a four-time Grammy winner who has three consecutive double-platinum albums and the current number-one download on iTunes. Folks...it's Oscar Tangerine!"

The crowd went nuts as Oscar walked on stage. After a standing ovation, Kyle regained control. "Oscar, welcome back."

"Thank you, Kyle," Oscar responded, wearing his trademark tangerine-colored skinny jeans.

"So, I understand we're going to hear a new, never-before-performed song tonight. What can you tell me about it, Oscar?"

"I'm such a huge fan of Mitch and everything he stands for. I wanted to write something that young people could get excited about. In this time of turmoil and craziness, I think we need someone who is strong and true. I named the song "Strong and True" because I think that's what Mitch brings to the table."

In reality, the Creative Division of Mouse Trap wrote the song. When it was first supplied to Oscar Tangerine, he refused to get involved. Then he was reminded that his debt of freedom was still outstanding, so he changed his position accordingly.

"That's exciting, Oscar. I believe we may have one more surprise; is that right?" asked Kyle.

"Well...you see...my bass player came down with a stomach bug just a couple of hours ago," Oscar declared playfully, "so we reached out to find a replacement, and... well...we found one."

Mitch reached into his back pocket, pulled out a rolled-up military-style baseball cap with a small red star on the front, and placed it on his head. He then pulled out a pair of $800 sunglasses and, slowly and dramatically put them on. Lastly, he grabbed the bass guitar, strapped it on, and raised both hands into the air victoriously. The crowd went wild.

Kyle smiled and laughed. "Ladies and gentlemen, put your hands together for Oscar Tangerine...featuring on bass...Mitch McCoy...debuting his new single, 'Strong and True.'""

49

"I think we need to reconsider our non-engagement strategy. The other candidates are beating up Elijah and we aren't fighting back."

Elijah was meeting with his leadership team, who had grown from 10 to 15. Tension was in the room because both Ireland and McCoy had stepped up their attacks on Elijah and everyone was feeling the heat.

"And everything they are saying are lies. We can't just do nothing."

The volleys went around the room for a couple of minutes before Admiral Adair stood to speak.

"In the military we have a saying, 'If you're catching heavy flak, you're over the target.'" These attacks on our campaign are a tremendously positive sign. We're gaining traction. If they weren't worried about us, they wouldn't be talking about us. Now is not the time to change strategies. Stick to the plan. It's gotten us this far."

The team agreed, with one exception. Elijah had not released his tax returns; normal politicians typically did. However, Elijah was trying to be anything but a normal politician. Because the meme of Elijah paying a small percentage tax rate had received a lot of airtime, refuting it was considered important. The message was simple. In 2015, Elijah had made $1.3 million—a hefty salary. However, he had given over $1.1 million to charity, such that his effective tax rate was only a few percentage points.

The team thought that once Elijah's returns were released, the accusation that he didn't pay taxes would be easily explainable to the media and clarified by fact checkers. Unfortunately, most media outlets reported that he made $1.3 million without mentioning his charitable giving.

Elijah's uphill battle continued.

50

E lijah was maintaining an unsustainable pace. He was speaking in a different city every day, most days at two or three events. He and his leadership team felt that compensating for the lack of media coverage of his campaign was necessary. He had just finished speaking at a rally in Baltimore, Maryland, when he was approached by a distinguished looking man whom he did not recognize and who seemed out of place.

"Very impressive speech, Mr. Mustang."

"Thank you. I really appreciate that," Elijah replied.

The man extended a hand. "My name is Tony Young." Victor used this pseudonym when he wanted to personally handle a situation but did not want to be publicly identified. "I have been following your campaign for the past few weeks, and I'm really intrigued by what you represent."

"Thank you." Elijah wasn't exactly sure if the comment was a compliment, but he chose to take it as such.

"Would you have a few moments to chat privately?" the man asked.

"OK." Elijah looked around the area. "I'm not sure where we could meet that's private."

"I actually think I saw a park bench just around the corner." Victor's staff ensured that the area would be vacated and that no one would be within earshot.

Elijah and Victor made the short walk to the bench, exchanging small talk along the way.

"Ah yes, here it is." Victor gestured for Elijah to take a seat.

"What did you want to discuss?" Elijah asked.

"As I mentioned, I am very intrigued...actually *impressed* is a better word...impressed by the amount of momentum your campaign has been able to achieve. The American people are really getting on board with you."

"Yes, we have been very blessed by the support we have received, but we understand this campaign is still very much an uphill battle. It's still David vs. Goliath," Elijah replied.

"I don't fashion myself to be an expert on the holy books, but I believe David may have won that battle, didn't he?"

"Indeed he did," Elijah responded with a smile.

"Let me get to the business at hand. You mentioned this is still an uphill battle. I'd like to help you level the playing field," Victor said, provocatively.

"And how would you propose to do that?" Elijah asked, somewhat suspiciously.

"To run a successful presidential campaign, you need resources—significant resources. You need people, media access, transportation, and money—especially money. I represent a group of individuals who would like to see you succeed. Individuals who could provide all of those resources."

"Why would these…individuals like for me to succeed?" Elijah asked, his suspicions growing.

"They just like what you stand for. They like your message. You should know that we could provide significant…"

"What part of my message do they like?" Elijah's tone had begun to turn skeptical.

"I want to make this clear; we can provide an entire campaign staff with experience in successful presidential campaigns. We can provide you with daily access to national media outlets. Most importantly, we can provide you with funding well into eight figures." Victor sensed the conversation slipping and wanted to get Elijah's attention. It worked but not the way he had hoped.

"You didn't answer my question. What part of my message do they like?" Elijah was now clearly agitated.

"Don't get the wrong idea. There's nothing nefarious going on; we just want to help." Victor tried to diffuse the escalating tension.

"I appreciate your offer, Mr. Young; but we're happy with the path we're on." Elijah got up to leave without shaking Victor's hand.

As he was walking away, Victor continued, "You know there's no way you are going to be able to win this election, don't you?"

Elijah kept walking.

"You're wasting your time, your staff's time, and the time of thousands of people who think you actually have a chance!" Victor shouted.

Elijah kept walking.

"You know you're just tilting at windmills! You are just another Don Quixote!"

Elijah was gone.

Victor grabbed the seat of the bench and flipped it onto its back. He glanced over and saw a couple of his associates, who had been standing guard, watching him. Realizing he was breaking character from his normally calm demeanor, he collected himself and headed back to the car that was waiting around the corner. It was time for him to begin implementing his plan, which had been decades in the making. Step one would begin with a drive to rural Maryland.

"I would like for us to focus this Council meeting on some opportunities that we've discovered in transportation. I believe there are near-term prospects that The Council will find very interesting."

The Council members all looked at one another knowingly. After the last Council debacle, they held an executive session independent of Victor. They were in unanimous agreement that if Victor didn't follow through on their direction to investigate Elijah Mustang and report back to The Council, there would be repercussions.

Dog was designated to speak for The Council. "Victor, The Council gave you direction in our last session. Do you recall that direction?"

Victor looked perplexed and then responded, "I'm afraid that you're going to have to refresh my memory."

Dog answered in a frustrated tone. "We asked you to look into Elijah Mustang and determine if The Council should consider supporting his candidacy!"

"Oh yes, I do remember."

"Then what is the status of your action?" Dog asked pointedly.

"Well, I haven't done anything," Victor responded bluntly.

The Council's ire was apparent as each member fidgeted in his seat nervously. Dog continued, "You ignored a direct order from The Council?"

"Yes, it appears that I did," Victor answered bluntly without emotion.

Dog was now furious. "Victor, you have left us no choice but..."

"But *what*?" Victor interrupted. "What are you going to do?"

"Victor, you are dismissed from this meeting. The Council will decide if we ..."

"Oh shut up, you blathering old fool."

The entire Council was now on their feet berating Victor. He held up a hand and spoke authoritatively, "No more! Sit down!"

To Victor's surprise, The Council all complied but remained agitated.

"What is this?!" Dog demanded.

Victor spoke condescendingly. "How could you be this blind? How could you be this stupid? You thought you were in control? You thought you were making the decisions? What a bunch of fools. For 20 years I have been preparing for this night. How could you not have seen this coming?"

The doors to The Hex burst open as ten men dressed in black entered the room. They paired off with each tandem approaching a Council member. Terrified, Dog asked helplessly, "What is this?"

''This is the end of The Council," Victor stated calmly.

"This is outrageous!" Screamed Able.

Two of Victor's henchmen grabbed Charlie's arms, prompting his protest, "Take your hands off me!" They didn't comply.

"But we trusted you!" Dog screamed, while being led away.

"Yes you did." Those were the last words The Council would hear. Each member was placed in hand cuffs with a dark hood placed over his head. The men were then led out the door to five awaiting SUVs.

As the first-generation Council members advanced in age, Victor convinced them to implement a succession plan whereby future Council members would have no familial ties, including no spouses and no children. The plan was designed to ensure the secrecy of Council activities as pillow talk was considered to be a significant risk. Accordingly, the current Council, all second or third generation, were all single men, thus making the execution of Victor's plan less complicated with fewer loose ends.

The SUVs completed the journey down The Hex's gravel driveway and turned onto the highway, each heading to a different destination. Four large trucks carrying two dozers and two backhoes passed them on the driveway. The large equipment went right to work on The Hex. Within two hours, nothing was left of the structure but a pile of rubble. The backhoes dug a large pit, and the dozers pushed the remnants into the hole until the debris was completely covered. They drove over the pile several times ensuring it was compacted. On the way back to the highway, the equipment buried the gravel road and removed the remaining fence. By just before daybreak, all that was left of The Hex was dirt and mud. The Hex and The Council no longer existed, and there was no evidence they ever did. Victor was just getting started.

51

Mildred Coyle was always the first to arrive at the firm. Her job was to brew the morning coffee, straighten up the conference rooms, and print the day's calendar for all three partners. As she gazed down the west hallway, she noticed that Craig Perkins appeared to have left his office light on overnight. As she walked in to flip off the switch, she saw the scene and let out a blood-curdling scream.

The police report showed that Perkins, age 72, a partner in the most prominent law firm in St. Louis, died of a self-inflicted gunshot. He left a note stating that the pressures of keeping the firm afloat were too great and that he could no longer bear the responsibility. Perkins, known to his fellow Council members as Dog, left behind no next-of-kin.

Four other death scenes were discovered throughout the country. A Manhattan banker found in his apartment had apparently choked to death on a piece of steak. A Hollywood movie producer's car was found upside down on the rocks at the edge of the Pacific Ocean, thirty feet below Highway 1. The owner of one of the largest construction firms in the Midwest was found floating in his backyard pool after a night of hard drinking. The deputy secretary of the Department of Energy had fallen down a flight of stairs, hitting his head on the marble floor at the bottom.

Each day in the United States, 7,000 people breathe their last breath. On August 7, 2016 the count included Able, Baker, Charlie, Dog, and Easy. For years they had spent every first Saturday of the month together in a luxury cabin in rural Maryland. Unfortunately, their connection was lost in the dustbin of history.

52

"Things are going to be changing soon. I will be moving into a new role...a more public role. Mouse Trap activities will be growing but must necessarily remain secret. I will still provide the ultimate guidance for Mouse Trap, but my day-to-day involvement will diminish. You will understand why soon enough."

Victor had assembled his project managers, division managers, and other key managers in a large conference room. Approximately 60 people were present. The last time the team remembered such a gathering was over five years ago. Something was clearly brewing.

"I will be handing over the day-to-day operations of Mouse Trap to Jeremy Prince."

Everyone in the room was shocked, none more than Jeremy himself.

"I understand that this will be a surprise to many of you. I understand Jeremy's youth, and I understand his tenure with Mouse Trap is barely over a year; but I also understand his unlimited potential. In this brief time, I have asked him to tackle some difficult assignments. He has exceeded my expectations with each one and you all know how high my expectations are. Most importantly, I have come to trust his judgment. While his youth brings with it energy and enthusiasm, only more time will bring a full measure of wisdom. That's why my longtime colleague, Zeke, will serve as Jeremy's deputy.

"I understand this announcement is unexpected, but it should be seen as a sign of optimism and long-term viability for Mouse Trap. If you think we've had successes in the past, hold on to your hat—things are about to accelerate exponentially. I want you all to be prepared for when that time comes. That's all I have."

Victor didn't provide a forum for asking questions and everyone returned to their work. Everyone except Jeremy.

Jeremy approached Victor as the two were left alone in the conference room. "You think maybe that's something we could have discussed in advance?" a confused Jeremy asked.

"Would have been a waste of time. This isn't a democracy. I'm not asking for your approval."

"What's this mysterious change that's about to happen that will take you away from Mouse Trap?"

''You'll find out soon enough." Victor walked away without looking back.

Jeremy wondered what could be so secret that it couldn't be discussed within the fortress of Mouse Trap, one of the most secure locations on the planet. He would have to wait, just like everyone else.

53

"We have been dropping in the polls. Our crowds have been smaller. We're not getting the positive press we need. That's not the kind of performance I would accept from Di-Com, and it's not the kind of performance I will accept from my campaign. It's time to make a change."

Lionel Ireland was having an all-hands meeting with his campaign staff. In addition to those gathered at the campaign headquarters in Los Angeles, satellite teams were dialed in via video conference from 20 locations.

"We're having a shakeup in campaign staff. We're starting at the top with a new campaign manager. I've done my due diligence in finding just the right person to lead us to the White House. I wanted someone with experience. I wanted someone with wisdom. I wanted someone with good character and judgment. I think I have found all of those qualifications and more in the person I have selected. Team, I want to introduce you to your new leader, Victor Youngblood."

Newspaper reports of the announcement were glowing. They should have been; Mouse Trap had written them. They noted what a community champion Victor was. Reports were that Youngblood and Associates sponsored Little League baseball teams and Pop Warner football leagues, funded entire hospital wings, and built an art museum in a disadvantaged neighborhood in Washington, D. C.

The reports also indicated that Victor was apolitical, never aligning himself with any particular party. It was noted that this fact should give Ireland a big boost with independent voters. Ireland's selection of Victor was widely heralded as an optimistic sign for the campaign's future. Another box checked in Victor's master plan.

In the Mouse Trap building's southwest corner was a large open area with 120 cubicles. Each cubicle was outfitted with only a computer and a chair. This area was known as the Comment Room. On this day all 120

cubes were occupied; and the sound of *click, click, click* could be heard throughout the room. The cube's occupants were paid to participate in the comment sections of hundreds of major, mid, and minor websites. Each day the participants were given a focus area. On this day their sole responsibility was to comment on every positive story about Victor and relate a personal story about how Victor touched their lives, changed their lives, or in some other way had a positive impact on their lives. Victor Youngblood was one hell of a great guy.

Click, click, click.

54

A s Jeremy started each day, he logged in to Omnia and checked his Omnia mail. Because it was a messaging application strictly limited to internal Mouse Trap communications, all messages were actually work-related, with an occasional admin message conveying a system-maintenance issue. He had received one such message today from the Omnia system administrator stating that security settings had been updated and that some action was required from Jeremy. He was hopeful this was the message he had been awaiting.

He opened the message, whose body simply stated,

> *Your security settings have been updated. Please click on this link to update your log-in.*

Before clicking, Jeremy got up from his chair and peered around his work area to ensure no one was approaching. The coast was clear. He returned and clicked on the link. A screen he had never seen opened. The greeting *Welcome to Level X* appeared; then a screen popped up with the following message:

> *Jeremy, this is Leonard. I have created Level X. Only you and I have access. This access provides us a means to communicate with no one else seeing. I have also partitioned an area of the master drive that is only accessible through Level X. It is named X drive. You will be allowed to copy files from any other area in Omnia into the X drive. You should first copy them from Omnia to your personal J drive, then from your J drive to the X drive. I do not know how long I can maintain this protocol, so don't be surprised if it goes away. This setup should allow us to communicate privately so that we won't have to be seen together. Lastly, here's a link with instructions of how to access Level X from outside of Mouse Trap. This will allow you to copy files from Mouse Trap to a drive that is outside the firewall.*
>
> *I know you understand what we're doing is extremely dangerous (and kind of fun), so please proceed with caution. You have my support. Leonard*

Copy files? Jeremy hadn't considered that as a viable option. His imagination was moving faster than his ability to organize his thoughts. Yes, this could be a game changer. He'd just have to formulate a plan for how this would all come together. Now he knew what he would be doing for the rest of the day and night.

> *Thanks Leonard. This is great. Yes, this is dangerous (and fun). I couldn't do it without you. Jeremy*

55

"Welcome to the team, Victor! It seems the press approves of your selection. There's been nothing but glowing reviews. We're even starting to see a bounce in the polls. I should have made this change weeks ago," Lionel Ireland announced.

Victor was meeting with Lionel Ireland and his running mate Grant Wembley as a kickoff to the new campaign direction.

"Thank you. I appreciate your confidence in me."

"Yes we..." Grant Wembley tried to interject but was cut off by Lionel.

"Victor, what are your thoughts about what our next steps should be?"

"Looking at some of the data behind our polling, it seems that voters would like to see you out of your suit and outside the boardroom. They want to know that you're a normal guy."

"OK. I can understand that. I am usually in public wearing a suit."

"We also aren't as strong as we could be with the National Rifle Association. The NRA is a major supporter of Republican candidates and they'd like to know you are solid on the Second Amendment."

"I wouldn't say gun rights are at the top of my platform, but I absolutely do support the Second Amendment. Do you have a suggestion for how to address that issue?" Lionel asked.

"I actually have a suggestion to address both the normal guy and Second Amendment issues in a single event," Victor replied.

"I'm all ears."

"I've done a little research and it seems Senator Wembley must be quite an accomplished sportsman. I understand his office is full of trophies that he bagged in his native Wyoming."

Lionel looked at Grant, surprised. "You didn't tell me you were a hunter."

A somewhat embarrassed Grant wasn't sure what to say. "Well...I don't like to talk about it a lot."

"Don't be modest, Senator; rumor has it the walls of your office are lined with elk, antelope, deer, moose, bighorn sheep, and bison."

"Well...yes, they are, but..."

"Great!" Victor continued. "My idea is that we make a road trip to Wyoming. Lionel, you'll be decked out in your hunting gear. The Senator can be our host and could invite some of his local hunting buddies. We'd obviously invite the press to document the whole event. It would be a great way to show yourself as a normal guy, strengthen your standing with the NRA, and give the Senator a chance to show off his beautiful home state."

"I love it! Wonderful idea, Victor! When do we go?" Lionel bellowed.

"1...I'm not sure this is such a great idea, we...," Grant protested.

"Nonsense, Grant, this is perfect. Victor, you work out the details. Let's make this happen as soon as we can."

"Will do, Lionel. I'll have a plan by the end of the day."

56

August 20, 2016
80 Days Until 2016 U. S. Presidential Election

"I sincerely want to thank you for inviting me to speak. It is truly an honor to be here. I suspect some people were opposed to my appearance, which meant others stood up for my privilege to be with you today…and I do consider it a privilege."

Elijah was correct; a small but passionate plea had been made to exclude him from the dais. Some questioned his participation; however, the overwhelming majority were in support of hearing his unique voice. The National Organization for the People of Color, also known as NOPOC, Voter Forum was being held at the Georgia World Congress Center in downtown Atlanta. Both Mitch McCoy and Lionel Ireland were also invited to speak. McCoy gladly accepted what would likely be an audience friendly to his message. He was on the docket to speak tomorrow. Ireland cited "schedule conflicts" and sent his regards. The forum's theme was *Our Vote Matters.*

"It is my intent to be very direct with you. I know your communities are hurting and frankly, not very many people are doing anything about it. I want you to know that your life matters. I want to make that as clear as I possibly can. Your...life...matters...The life you live every single day—that matters."

The pensive crowd offered a courteous applause. Elijah took a deep breath as he knew the import of his words and wanted to get both the delivery and tone just right.

"We're going to come back to that theme shortly, but I must take a few moments to clear up some misconceptions about me. I don't talk about my race very much, and I know that is disappointing to some of you. Let's just get this out on the table; some say that I'm not authentic. Some even call me an Uncle Tom. It's OK, that doesn't bother me; it just makes me really sad because that attitude is one of the many forces that keeps people of color from rising out of the terrible conditions that many have to endure.

"I want to make sure you know that I am proud to be a black man. I'm also proud to be a CEO. I'm proud to be from a small town in Tennessee, and I'm proud to be an American. It is true that I am blessed to have the job that I have, to have a nice home on the lake, and to have three beautiful daughters. But my life hasn't always been this way. Things haven't always been easy, if that's what you consider my life to be.

"I was born in inner-city Knoxville, Tennessee. I have no idea who my father was. My mother was addicted to drugs and overdosed when I was six. However, I was blessed to have grandparents who loved me. They rescued me from that situation and brought me to their home in a small town called Harriman, Tennessee.

"We didn't have much in the way of worldly possessions, but my grandparents taught me five central values. These values were so important to my grandmother that she stitched them on an old sheet and hung them on the wall in a frame made of barn wood. My grandparents taught me that the five keys to life are love, hard work, forgiveness, laughter, and the grace of God. I heard those values every day of my life. They've gotten me through a lot of tough situations. I share this to tell you that my story may be different from yours, but I do have a story." The applause was becoming a bit more generous as the crowd warmed to Elijah's message.

"Now, I want to get real for a few minutes. The circumstances so many people of color must face every day are absolutely heartbreaking. The poverty, substandard education, crime, lack of opportunities, drugs...it's beyond awful." Elijah briefly paused, knowing his impending words would sting. "But what's also awful is that not enough people care about it to do anything. We've had both Democrats and Republicans in charge, and nothing changes. Our cities have had black mayors. We've had black senators and black congressmen, and nothing changes." Elijah scanned the crowd of over 4,000 and saw a combination of crossed arms and interested faces.

He continued, "One of the greatest obstacles to digging out is coming to the realization that we are being lied to, manipulated, and used. What the people in power want from you is your vote, your money, and your passion. You see...we're a passionate people; and if we get energized about something, we're going to bring the fight. There are shysters who know that about us and know how to use *our* fight for *their* gain. In fact some of those shysters are in this building...in this audience today." Elijah heard a smattering of boos; and a handful of attendees got up and left the room, one shouting obscenities at Elijah.

"See...that's exactly what I mean. You don't even know what I have to say. Just listen! I know you are sick and tired of losing friends and loved ones to drugs and violence. You are sick and tired of the living conditions that so many of you endure. You are sick and tired of being pulled over by the police because of the color of your skin. You want the world to know that blacks in America face a special kind of struggle that needs to be fixed. And you are 100% correct!

"But that's not what some who claim to represent you are about. Many who say they represent your interests are actually revolutionary anarchists who want to overthrow the government. Listen to their demands. They want to disband police forces. Can you imagine your cities without the police? The anarchists walk through the streets chanting that they want dead cops. I know that's not something anyone in this room supports.

"These people don't care about your communities. They don't care if your grandmother needs diabetes medicine but can't afford it. They don't care if you don't have money to buy diapers for your baby. They don't care if your front door is riddled with bullet holes. They just want you to march with them in the streets waving signs and chanting. They want your passion.

"I understand that there have been some incidents with the police and that there are some bad cops who need to be prosecuted. But just last year 5,000 blacks were killed by other blacks! That's awful. Does anyone care about them? Where are the protests? Their lives are just as important. Their lives *matter*! Here's a really, really sad statistic: over 200,000 African American babies were killed in abortion clinics last year. That was 200,000 babies who could have grown to be doctors, lawyers, teachers, even presidents of the United States. 200,000! Do you care? Does anyone care? Where's the protest for them? Where's the march for them? You're being lied to, and you're being manipulated.

"I know this message is difficult to hear, and I know that many of you don't agree with me; but it's time someone was honest with you.

"I see my time is almost up. I want to end with the word *freedom*. That word has a special meaning in our community. For most of us, our ancestors were brought to this country as slaves. With the courage of steadfast men and women and with the bloodshed of millions, we gained our freedom over a 150 years ago. Too many of us won't embrace that freedom. It's there, but we won't take it. Break free from those who want to use you for their gain. Break free from those who want to channel your passion to ends that do nothing to change your communities. *Break free* from those who have blinded you from finding a better way.

"A better way starts with love, hard work, forgiveness, laughter, and the grace of God."

57

The Killpecker Sand Dunes, located north of Rock Springs, Wyoming, cover over 100,000 acres. The dunes, among the largest in all of North America, attract off-road enthusiasts who enjoy over 10,000 acres set aside for dune buggies, ATVs, and dirt bikes.

The dunes are also home to a herd of rare desert elk, which can be found nowhere else in North America. This elk was the reason for the group's gathering at the southern boundary of the dunes. Lionel Ireland, Grant Wembley, Victor Youngblood, and a handful of locals were preparing for the hunt. Approximately 20 media representatives had also made the trip to remote Sweetwater County to cover the event.

The plan, orchestrated by Victor, was simple. All would meet at this central location. Lionel would make some remarks for the press. There would be photo opportunities for Lionel and Grant. Then the hunting party would head deep into the dunes in search of the elk. The short hunting season for the rare creature runs from early October to late November, but Victor pulled some strings and got special dispensation for this one-time hunt. Many in the Wyoming Game & Fish Department were unhappy about the exception made for a group of politicians, but an anonymous donation of $1 million to the Friends of the Killpecker Sand Dunes Association cleared the final hurdles.

After preening for the media, the hunting party headed out in search of one of the few big-game animals that didn't adorn the walls of Senator Wembley's office. The group had rented two-seater dune buggies, requiring the group to split into pairs. Arranging for the most accomplished guide to accompany Lionel, Victor volunteered to travel with Grant. The plan was for each pair to head off in a different direction to scout and then rendezvous at a point in an hour.

After exploring their designated area, Victor stopped their dune buggy in a low spot in the dunes, removed his helmet, and climbed out of the vehicle.

"Beautiful country you have here, Senator," Victor observed.

"Yes, it is, very beautiful," Grant replied.

"I guess you've been to the dunes many times." Victor knew he hadn't.

"Well...uh...a few times, yes." Grant hoped Victor wouldn't press the question further.

"So, tell me the truth, Senator. How many of those creatures on your wall did you actually kill?"

"Excuse me?" Grant asked nervously, taken aback by the abrupt change in subject and tone.

"Senator, I know you're not a hunter," Victor announced bluntly.

The sound of an approaching ATV got louder and louder until it was obvious the vehicle was headed toward their location. Grant was relieved, hoping it would rescue him from what was becoming an awkward conversation. It did not.

The ATV pulled up immediately adjacent to Grant and Victor, and two men dressed in black hopped out. The men were from a division of Mouse Trap called Blackforce.

When Victor designed the Mouse Trap security apparatus over 30 years earlier, a single force was responsible for all Mouse Trap security-related activities and was manned almost exclusively by former U. S. military personnel. Victor learned early that U.S. military retirees were often reticent to execute the more violent Mouse Trap orders; so he split the force into two units: Greenforce and Blackforce. Greenforce was responsible for facility security and access, perimeter control, and escort and bodyguard services. U. S. military retirees were retained to man Greenforce.

Headquartered in what the outside world thought was an auto-parts manufacturing facility on the outskirts of Pittsburgh, Blackforce was responsible for executing certain Mouse Trap missions, particularly those ending up in the *Trapped* file. Blackforce was manned almost exclusively by former Soviet and Russian military personnel, whom Victor came to understand had lower standards than their American counterparts.

In the early 1990s Victor recruited Andrei Ovchenko to lead Blackforce. Ovchenko was a general who breezed through the military ranks of the Soviet Union in the 1980s because of his brutal enforcement of KGB orders. Ovchenko's inside politburo perspective offered him a front-row seat to seeing his nation's collapse. He was excited that Victor gave him the opportunity to continue practicing his brutal craft, even if he had to move to the country he spent his entire life trying to defeat.

Ovchenko was a short, stocky man whose most prominent feature was a large scar around his right eye that was accentuated by a black patch. Ovchenko's greatest contribution to Mouse Trap was selecting only the most ruthless countrymen to join Blackforce, whose ranks had grown to 58.

"What is this?" Grant asked fearfully.

"I'm afraid this is the end of the line, Senator," Victor responded matter-of-factly.

"What?"

"It's not personal, Senator. It's just necessary." Victor gestured to the men, one of whom bashed Grant in the head with a large rock, sending him sprawling onto the dune.

Without saying a word, Victor got back into the dune buggy and left the scene. Overhead, a Mouse Trap drone captured the proceedings on video for the *Trapped* archives. The morbid database would soon be adding another entry.

Victor topped the dune and headed back to join the group assembling at the rendezvous point. Getting out of the dune buggy, the party was curious why Victor was alone.

"Where's Grant?" Lionel asked.

"We found the herd just over that dune!" Victor exclaimed. "Grant has taken a position on the eastern point. He suggested we fan out and prepare for the hunt."

The excited party complied, readying their rifles for the kill. As predicted, the herd topped the hill, encouraged by four Mouse Trap ATVs that had worked to funnel the beasts in the direction of the waiting hunters. Victor knew this was the riskiest part of his plan and was excited to see the majestic elk come into sight.

The sound of rifles could be heard throughout the desert as each marksman hoped to bag a trophy. When the herd retreated and the dust settled, three elk were on the ground. The team celebrated the successful hunt. Intermingled with the sound of the hunters' rifles was a single gunshot from a Blackforce member concealed behind a large dune. Grant Wembley, who was still out of the party's view, received a direct hit to his temple.

"I am certain one of these is mine," Lionel bragged, as the group reached the downed elk.

"Yes, I am certain that it is too," Victor agreed.

Finally, one of the locals asked, "Has anyone seen Senator Wembley?"

All of the party agreed they had not. They split up to find the missing senator. In the chaos, a member of Blackforce slipped the weapon that felled Wembley into one of the dune buggies. Victor had directed this contingency in case someone wanted to run ballistics to find the deadly weapon.

It didn't take long for one of the group to find Wembley. It was not a pretty sight.

"Oh no! Everyone, over here! Come quickly!"

The official record would show that Senator Grant Wembley was killed in a tragic hunting accident—just as Victor Youngblood had planned.

"This is ridiculous. How is this happening?"

"It's OK. We knew this wouldn't be without challenges."

"I don't mind challenges, but this is just wrong."

Elijah had been scheduled to speak at a series of high-profile venues in the next two weeks, including four university forums. After complaints that his speech at the NOPOC voter forum was considered "controversial", each of the universities contacted the campaign officials to cancel Elijah's appearances.

Jethro Poindexter summed up everyone's sentiment as only he could. "I think there was a nationwide contest that traveled from town to town. They called it the Wizard of Oz contest. They were looking for the person in each town with no brain, no courage, and no heart. The prize for the winner was the high honor of being that town's college president. What a bunch of noodle-spine wimps!"

Elijah took the setback in stride. "Let's not focus on the cancellations; let's just see it as an opportunity to speak elsewhere. I don't want to be anywhere they don't want me to speak."

"On the positive front, our polling data shows you're continuing to rise. You are in a statistical tie with McCoy and only a few points behind Ireland," one of the team members noted.

"That's not what the news outlets are reporting. They say we've plateaued and some are reporting we're declining," Jethro responded.

"I don't have an explanation for the news outlets; but I can tell you we've invested in reputable, experienced pollsters, who insist things are looking up."

"Let's not allow polls, up or down, to dictate what we do. Let's focus on the task at hand, stick to our plan, and press on," Elijah encouraged. And press on they did.

58

"**B**reaking news overnight: Republican vice presidential candidate Grant Wembley was killed in a hunting accident in his native Wyoming. He and presidential candidate Lionel Ireland were in the Killpecker Sand Dunes area of Southern Wyoming when a stray bullet from one of the hunters in the group tragically took the Senator's life. Condolences are pouring in from around..."

Jeremy clicked the remote. His ability to stomach more Mouse Trap carnage was waning. For over a year he had to get up each morning, look at himself in the mirror and accept where he was going to work. Since the deaths of Cam Calvin and Gary Carlisle, he knew he had stumbled into the most dangerous organization in the world. Over time he came to realize just how dangerous it was. Like many in the Mouse Trap organization, he came to that realization too late to do anything about it. He knew that he had no other choice but to stay unless and until he could find a way out. He knew that no one simply walked away from Mouse Trap. You were either in or assumed room temperature.

Upon reflection, no single event had flipped the switch within Jeremy but was instead a cumulative revulsion with what his organization— *no, that was too impersonal*—what HE was responsible for. What pushed him over the edge was the discovery of the *Trapped* application and the staggering number: 3,482, which had recently grown by one.

Leonard had written a code that would send a message to Jeremy through Level X informing him when an addition had been made to *Trapped*. Jeremy was reviewing drone footage of Victor and Grant Wembley in the Killpecker Dunes. His heart racing, Jeremy knew this footage could be a critical piece of the puzzle he was working to construct. Victor broke his own most important Mouse Trap rule: don't be near the mouse. Whether it was carelessness, arrogance, or an air of invincibility, Jeremy didn't care. He was just glad to have a potential opening.

For the past year, Jeremy's every waking moment was spent trying to craft an exit strategy. He knew there was no such strategy that involved his leaving alive and everything else remaining unchanged. If there was one lesson he had learned from Victor Youngblood, it was that his exit would have to be cunning, momentous, and perfectly executed. He hoped that he had learned this lesson well. His life depended on it.

59

September 5, 2016
64 Days Until 2016 U. S. Presidential Election

The venue was intentional. The Thomas Jefferson Memorial was situated on the southern boundary of the National Mall in Washington D. C. The neoclassical structure included a portico, imposing columns, a domed roof, and marble steps leading from the ground level up to the primary structure. The podium was situated at the top of these steps. Lionel Ireland stepped to the microphone carrying a heavy heart; at least that's what Victor Youngblood told him to carry.

"I would like to thank you for coming today. As you know, we have had a difficult couple of weeks. The tragic accident that took the life of American patriot Grant Wembley leaves us all struggling to accept that he is really gone. Our thoughts and prayers continue to be with

Grant's family: his beautiful wife Sage and his children Matthew, Chastity, and Belinda. It is actually because of them that we are here. I want to acknowledge them here today on the front row."

The overflow crowd offered heartfelt applause for the grieving family.

"After the accident we didn't want to think about a presidential campaign. To be honest, I didn't know if I wanted to continue. However, a pep talk from Sage changed everything. She told me that Grant wouldn't have wanted us to miss a beat, that he would have urged us to redouble our efforts. She insisted that we needed to get on with the business of winning. I must confess, Mrs. Wembley can be very persuasive.

"Mostly she pleaded with me to select a replacement for Senator Wembley as soon as possible and to pick someone he would have approved of. I've done research, asked friends whose opinions I value, and prayed hard about this decision. Those efforts pointed in one direction. Today, I want to announce my running mate, Victor Youngblood."

Victor walked out of the memorial structure and joined Lionel next to the podium to the crowd's applause, again subdued because of the circumstances surrounding Victor's being selected.

Victor took the podium. "Thank you for your kind reception. I want to echo Mr. Ireland's words regarding Senator Wembley. He was both a great man and a great American. And yes, it has been a difficult two weeks. I didn't know Senator Wembley very long but for a man of his stature and character, it didn't take long to develop a fondness for his intelligence, wit, and integrity. He will truly be missed. Like Lionel, at first I didn't want to continue with the campaign, but I too, was inspired by Mrs. Wembley to carry on; so carry on we must.

"To that end, I want to thank Lionel Ireland for this opportunity. This is something I never dreamed possible. I am not a politician and never aspired to be. I am a businessman, and my travels have led me to every state in this great country. I am continually amazed by the people I meet. They are fiercely independent and fiercely loyal to their country; traits I admire beyond my ability to fully communicate. It is interesting that we selected this venue for this announcement. Inside this memorial's dome in large letters is a quote from President Jefferson. I wrote it down while I was waiting to come out to speak." Victor reached into his pocket to retrieve the quote he had memorized 30 years prior.

"It says, 'I have sworn upon the altar of god eternal hostility against every form of tyranny over the mind of man.' This is a truism that is central to the kind of campaign Lionel Ireland is running. He's not a career politician trying to trick, coerce, or manipulate you into voting for him. He's going to be honest and forthright with you and ask for your support. That's something that I can get on board with, and I believe the American people will too."

Victor's plan was coming together, but the best was yet to come.

60

"OK, are you ready for this?" Victor asked pointedly.

"Yes...I'm ready," Lionel Ireland replied, not totally convincingly.

"OK, one last time, let's go over the three topics. Repeat them back to me."

"President Poroshenko, fifth-generation fighters, and fission energy."

"No! That's not right! Sixth-generation fighters and fusion energy! Come on Lionel, I'm handing you this on a silver platter. All you have to do is perform," Victor demanded.

Victor not only had arranged for Lionel to know the debate questions in advance but also had inserted three relatively obscure questions so that Lionel could show a command of even the minutest details.

"I understand. I'll get it."

"You *understand*? Do you understand that the debate starts in two hours?"

"I just had a brief lapse. When the moderator asks the question, it will prompt me and I'll do fine," Lionel stammered.

The last three weeks had been interesting in the Ireland for President Campaign. Victor had inserted *and* asserted himself even before being named campaign manager; however, his ascension to vice presidential nominee put extra wind in his sails. The deal was simple. Victor would get Lionel elected. Lionel would serve as the figurehead and would be recorded in the annals of history as the 45th president of the United States. All Lionel had to do was get out of Victor's way and let him run the country. Both agreed to the arrangement. Lionel clearly understood he didn't have a choice.

"Good evening, ladies and gentlemen. We want to welcome you to campus of Hofstra University in Hempstead, New York, for the first of three presidential debates…"

The debate rules were explained; the requisite thanks yous were exchanged; and for the first 45 minutes, the routine questions were asked as each candidate staked out the typical partisan positions. McCoy called for taxing the rich; Ireland retorted that Americans are already taxed too much. McCoy demanded a cut to defense spending; Ireland wanted to rebuild the military. McCoy claimed the greatest threat to mankind is climate change; Ireland countered it's all a hoax. McCoy said black lives matter; Ireland corrected *all* lives matter. Then came the first question for which Lionel had prepared.

"Candidates, what is your position on continued U. S. funding for ITER? I'll start with Senator McCoy."

Mitch stared for an awkward moment and then tried, "Would you mind repeating the question?"

Lionel chuckled and mocked, "You know, this isn't *Who Wants to be a Millionaire?*"

The crowd laughed and McCoy, clearly irked, tried to muster a smile.

"What is your position on continued U. S. funding for ITER?"

Mitch finally found a few words, though he might have been better off to have passed. "We have had a lot of discussion about the size of government, and we want to be judicious with our tax dollars; so funding for ITER would have to compete with the many other needs we have in this country such as our crumbling infrastructure, our decaying inner cities, and our poorest citizens."

"You have another minute and a half, Senator," the moderator reminded.

"I'll yield my time to Mr. Ireland. I'm sure he has some important insights into ITER."

"Thank you for the question; it is an important one. Of course the investment in ITER is significant with the current price tag close to $20 billion. This is a case where I think it's good that we're teaming with 35 other countries so that our share is just under $4 billion. I do support the project, not for its carbon- footprint reduction but simply for the economics. Fusion energy could be a game changer, and the tokamak is the most promising technology to harness the energy of fusion. I only wish it were being built in the U. S. rather than in France, but I do support the project."

Similar exchanges occurred on questions related to the development of the sixth-generation fighter program and to the candidates' support of Ukraine's President Poroshenko. McCoy fumbled with generalities, while Lionel provided detailed, cogent answers, demonstrating his command of the facts.

The only issue McCoy and Ireland agreed on was whether a third person should have been on stage.

"Candidates, there has been much discussion about Independent candidate Elijah Mustang. Some polls show him neck and neck with the two of you. Should he have been included in this debate tonight?"

"Mustang joined the party too late. While Mr. Ireland and I have been putting together policy positions and campaign staffs, and speaking to Americans around the country for the past two years, Mustang has been running a small trucking company in Tennessee. He has not earned the right to be on this stage," McCoy proclaimed.

Ireland declared, "Mustang seems like a nice enough guy, but is being a nice guy sufficient qualification to be the president of the United States? Would you want a nice guy to pilot your plane? Would you allow a nice guy to operate on your injured child? Would you let a nice guy manage your retirement account? I'm guessing the answer is *no*. Then why would you ask just a nice guy to run this country? You wouldn't, would you? You'd want a qualified, experienced, professional."

61

"Jeremy, I must confess that I miss coming to Mouse Trap to work every day. I did it for 30 years taking no vacations and working most weekends. It is all I knew. Being on the road campaigning has been more of an adjustment than I expected."

Jeremy's first thought, "Now you're going to try to have a normal human conversation?" But he kept that thought to himself.

"I imagine it has been an adjustment."

Victor was conversing via a secure encrypted cell phone while in the back of an SUV, somewhere between Cleveland and Columbus. Jeremy was in his Mouse Trap office using his secure terminal equipment, also known as STE.

"Anything I need to know?" Victor asked.

"I don't think so. Things are going smoothly in all major projects. Zeke is being Zeke—which, of course, is awesome."

Victor put Jeremy in charge of Mouse Trap because of his grasp of technology and his potential to lead the organization for years to come. Both Jeremy and Victor knew that Zeke would play a crucial role in the transition. He had irreplaceable experience and wisdom; however, at age 77, he was not a viable option to lead the organization years into the future.

"Is everything ready for tomorrow night?" Victor asked.

The vice presidential debate would be held the following night. It would be Victor's big coming-out party. The nation was normally lukewarm about vice presidential debates, but the tragedy surrounding the death of Grant Wembley, coupled with the glowing media attention Victor was getting, made interest in the event unusually high.

As with the first presidential debate, Victor was able to insert his own three obscure questions, about which McCoy's running mate would likely know very little.

"Yes, everything should be ready. It is going to be a great night," Jeremy maintained.

"Thank you, Jeremy. I'm really proud of the work you are doing. Keep it up."

At the end of the call, Jeremy opened the file with the debate questions and made a few edits. He named the file *VP-DBT-QS-Rev1* and included the following brief message:

Things have changed. See revised questions attached. Please discard previous version.

He then hit the send button, putting into motion a series of events no one expected, including Jeremy.

62

"**G**ood evening, ladies and gentlemen. We want to welcome you to the campus of Longwood University in Farmville, Virginia, for the only 2016 vice presidential debate. Tonight's debate participants are Sally Naughton, the Democratic vice presidential candidate, and Victor Youngblood, the Republican vice presidential candidate. I am Jill Hernandez from NNS, and I will be moderating tonight's debate. I wrote the questions, which have not been discussed or reviewed with either candidate.

"The candidates will have two minutes for opening statements. I will then ask the first question, and each candidate will have two minutes to respond. A coin flip determined that Mr. Youngblood will deliver the first opening statement."

"Thank you, Jill, and thank you to Longwood University for hosting this event. Your generosity and hospitality have been tremendous."

Victor then turned to look directly into the camera and spoke with great reverence. "As many of you know, I'm not supposed to be here. I wish that circumstances were different and that I was not here. Within the Ireland for President Campaign, we still feel the sting of losing such a great man as Grant Wembley. It is for his honor and in his memory that we know we must press on, so press on we will.

"We believe this country needs a fresh beginning. Too many Americans are still without jobs. Our standing in the world has plummeted. Our economy is anemic. Terrorism continues to rage around the globe. We are too dependent on the Middle East for energy resources. We believe the Republican Party offer clear solutions for each of these problems. I look forward to a vigorous debate with Ms. Naughton to demonstrate that we do."

Naughton's opening statement followed the script. Raise taxes on the rich; invest in addressing climate change; fix poverty; and McCoy's cornerstone program, a wealth tax on the top one percent.

With each question, Victor displayed an uncanny grasp of the details, such as in the following exchange.

"Candidates, what is your opinion of Great Britain's recent vote to leave the European Union?"

It was Naughton's turn to answer first.

"It was a terrible decision that the people of Great Britain will come to regret. So much of the pro-Brexit propaganda was simply fear-mongering. There were very few fact-based arguments in favor of leaving. Frankly, there was a racist undercurrent in the claim that increasing Muslim immigrants was going to somehow destroy the country. I think the nations of the world need to work to find ways to come together, not tear themselves apart."

"Mr. Youngblood, your response?"

"Few fact-based arguments?" he questioned incredulously. "Great Britain sent £350 million to the EU every week that they will now be able to invest in British priorities. The EU has no major trade deals in place with the two largest emerging markets in the world, China and India. Leaving the EU allows Great Britain to negotiate its own deals. Concerns about immigration are not racist. In the past three years, close to 300,000 immigrants have flooded into Great Britain because of the EU's policy on free movement of labor. It was a decision that was up to the people of Great Britain, and we need to respect that decision."

Similar exchanges continued with Victor offering facts and figures for each argument he made. And then things got interesting.

"Mr. Youngblood, reports have surfaced that Senator Wembley's death may not have been an accident. You were in the hunting party with the senator. What did you see that morning?"

The unflappable Victor Youngblood worked hard not to flap. His first energy was focused on not allowing his body language to betray him. Then he dug deeply within himself to find just the right tone before answering.

"I am not going to dignify your question with an answer. This is a debate, not a show on TMZ, Ms. Hernandez."

The moderator persisted, "Mr. Youngblood, the reports have actually implicated you in Senator Wembley's death. It is said that you were the last person to see him alive and that no one saw him get shot. Is that true?"

"This is outrageous that you would even suggest…"

"The reports even say there's video evidence of your involvement. Are you aware of any such video?"

Victor decided to take his argument to the American people as he turned away from the moderator and again looked directly into the camera. "Never in the history of televised debates has such tragedy as Senator Wembley's death been used as a political stunt. After this debate is over, the truth will quickly emerge. Senator Wembley's death was an accident. I had no involvement, and there is certainly no video to the contrary. Afterwards, I expect a formal apology from both Ms. Hernandez and her network. This is truly outrageous."

The debate continued for another hour, but it could have ended after the questions about Senator Wembley because that's all anyone remembered from the evening.

Jeremy had been looking for an opening for over a year. Each avenue he tried led to a dead end. He came to understand why Victor and Mouse Trap were able to survive and thrive for decades. Victor had instituted a multi-layer defense system to insulate Mouse Trap from any vulnerabilities. The no-paper rule ensured all data would be contained inside Omnia. Multiple firewalls ensured no data ever left the system. Physical security, manned by a large armed force, guarded the perimeter of the facility. Positive reinforcement in the form of generous bonuses, often in the millions, ensured employees were motivated to keep their work secure and not discussed outside the walls of the facility. Negative reinforcement came in the form of co-workers who were no longer on the team, their fate the worst-kept secret in all of Mouse Trap. That is, of course, the way Victor wanted it.

Even Mouse Trap's overarching philosophy, which kept the organization's activities at least three degrees of separation from any malevolent actions, ensured that nothing could be traced to Victor. It was an almost flawlessly designed system until Jeremy began to detect a few cracks.

Through his relationship with Leonard, the creation of Level X offered the first glimmer of hope. Victor provided the biggest breakthrough by breaching his own rule and becoming personally involved in Senator Wembley's death. Jeremy also saw opportunity in Victor's stepping out of the shadows into the public eye. The icing on the cake was Victor's obsession with documenting, via video, each time a mouse was "trapped," even when he was personally involved.

Jeremy put all of these pieces together to devise the best opportunity for action thus far. He knew the plan was far from perfect; but he also knew that the more power Victor accumulated—and it was difficult to imagine his having more than he already had—the less likely Jeremy would ever be able to stop him. His plan involved five sequential steps.

Step one was to accumulate as much information as possible about Senator Wembley's death and get it outside the walls of Omnia. That step was complete. Step two was to take the public shine away from Victor by raising the specter of his involvement during the nationally televised debate. That step was accomplished. Step three was to send the information, including the video, to law enforcement via an e-mail account that could not be traced to him. He opted for both federal prosecutors and the FBI. He hit the send button at the debate's conclusion. Step four was to send the same information to a variety of media outlets. He knew most were already under Mouse Trap's control, but he hoped at least one would see the opportunity for a historic story. Step four was executed immediately after step three.

Step five, his final step, was frustratingly out of his control. This step was the fallout from the first four steps. By Jeremy's estimation, the minimum fallout would be public embarrassment for Victor that would at least derail his vice presidential aspirations. The maximum estimated fallout was Victor's arrest and prosecution, which would send the entire Mouse Trap enterprise crumbling to the ground. Jeremy was willing to accept anything in between. Now all he could do was wait.

63

J eremy was surprised at the degree of normalcy when he arrived at the Mouse Trap offices. He drove to work but didn't really expect to enter the building. His imagination had conjured up a variety of scenarios that included satellite news trucks parked around the building; federal agents bursting through the door to confiscate everything; and key Mouse Trap leaders being led out the door, complete with hands-over-their-faces perp walks.

What he found was business as usual. Per his normal routine, he was among the first wave to arrive. He followed his standard protocol, passing through security to get into the Mouse Trap work area. He went to his office, flipped on the light, and logged in to Omnia. He quickly checked

Level X and had nothing from Leonard. Although things seemed normal, he had a strange sense of foreboding. He didn't have to wait long to find out why.

"Good morning, Jeremy." The voice sent his stomach rumbling and his heart racing. He looked up and his worst fears were realized. He tried his best to remain calm.

"Good morning, Victor. I am surprised to see you. I thought you'd be on the campaign trail." Jeremy wondered if his voice conveyed the same anxiety he was feeling.

"I had some things to take care of in the office."

Jeremy wasn't sure what to say, so he didn't say anything for what seemed like an eternity. Then Victor broke the silence.

"Why did you do it, Jeremy?"

Jeremy instinctively protested, "Do *what*?" He wasn't even convincing to himself.

"Don't insult me, Jeremy. At least be man enough to take responsibility. Did you want more money? I could have given you more money. It couldn't have been more authority; I put you in charge of everything."

Jeremy thought he'd try one more time. "Victor, I don't..."

"I got all of your e-mails, Jeremy. The FBI, prosecutors, the media, all of them."

"How did you..."

"Let's make a quick phone call."

Victor walked behind Jeremy's desk, nestled in uncomfortably close, and pushed the speakerphone button, dialing a number from memory.

"FBI, Director Thompson's office."

"Hi, Angie, this is Victor. Would you put Gavin on the line?"

"Sure, Victor, just a second."

Jeremy's eyes were the size of dinner plates.

"Hi, Victor. Glad you called. I was just talking about you."

"Yes, Gavin. After the commotion at the debate last night, a couple of members of my leadership team were understandably worried about what was happening. I was hoping you could clear things up."

"Sure. I understand the concern. Those were some serious accusations. Since they involved a vice presidential candidate, we wanted to do a quick check right away; so we had a team working overnight. I have already told Victor; the good news is that the video is a total fabrication. We have more believable Sasquatch videos. There was also nothing of value in the information that was sent. I want to assure your team that we are not pursuing this matter any further. We'll be making a public statement to that effect this morning so as to minimize any impact this may have on the election."

Jeremy's mouth was wide open, and his skin began to turn an ivory white.

"That's great, Gavin. I can see the relief on our team members' faces."

"And rest assured, we've notified the media that they shouldn't be reporting on such an obviously fabricated story. They are all on board," Gavin continued.

"Any idea of the source of the e-mail?" Victor asked.

"Not yet, Victor, but we're on that. Please know that we're going to look hard at the motive behind the video as well as the sender's identity. This person could face some serious federal charges. I gotta run to a meeting, Victor. We'll talk again later."

"Great. I really appreciate your quick attention to this matter, Gavin."

The two old friends hung up the phone as Jeremy sat stunned in his chair.

"Do you think you are the first person to try something like this? I've been doing this longer than you've been alive, Jeremy."

Jeremy was dazed. He asked, almost rhetorically, "You killed a United States' senator, and nobody is going to do anything about it?"

"Yes, Jeremy, I killed a United States' senator; and nobody is going to do anything about it," Victor said smugly. "Jeremy, this is not a game."

Jeremy had no response.

"I have to get back to the campaign. Unfortunately, you leave me with only one option. Security is waiting outside the door. I'm really disappointed, Jeremy. I had big plans for you."

Victor knocked on the inside of Jeremy's open door and commanded, "OK, come on in." There was no reply. He knocked again, louder. No reply. He opened the office door to look into the hallway. As he reached for the doorknob, Jeremy heard a beep and glanced down at a popup window on his screen. He had left Level X open. The message on the screen simply said, *RUN!!!*

As part of the security protocol, each office was outfitted with a video camera that sent a signal back to the Omnia hub, which was adjacent to Leonard's office. After seeing Victor enter the building on the security camera, Leonard pulled up on his monitor the feed from Jeremy's office. When it was obvious things weren't going according to plan, the best Leonard could do was send the security force to respond to a Level 1 disturbance on the other side of the building. This diversion would at least give Jeremy a chance.

Seeing Leonard's message, Jeremy leapt from his chair and pushed past Victor, who fell sprawling onto the floor. He ran down the hallway, past the single guard who remained. Before more security arrived, Jeremy descended two flights of stairs and ran out the maintenance exit, away from the main building's entrance. He was on the run of his life.

"Where were you?!" Victor asked frantically.

"We got a call to go to the first floor, northwest corner," the security guard replied.

"Did you get him?"

"Not yet, but we have men fanning out through the area. We'll find him."

"No. Call them back. I'm going to get some outside help on this one."

Victor made the short walk to his office and dialed the phone. "Gavin, this is Victor again. I know who was behind the video. It was one of my employees. I just confronted him, and he attacked me and ran out the back exit. I'll send you all of the information. Please know that he's dangerous and could be armed. Thanks, Gavin."

Knowing this was a high-risk play, Jeremy had a getaway plan in case something like this happened. He sprinted out of sight, then ducked between buildings and cars until reaching a parking garage a mile and a half from the Mouse Trap offices. He walked up four flights of stairs and pushed the key fob until hearing a chirp. It was a nondescript 2012 Honda Accord, among the most common vehicles on the road. It was registered to one of Mouse Trap's synthetic identities. Inside the car was $10,000 in cash, a driver's license with Jeremy's photo, and a false ID. There was also a laptop, burner cell phones, and a suitcase full of clothes, mostly with Georgetown University's logo so that Jeremy could easily blend in as a student. He put the key in the ignition, and the car started on the first try. Twenty minutes after shoving Victor out of his way, Jeremy was on I-70 North on the first leg of a 1900-mile, 26-hour journey. Time for Plan B.

64

"We are supposed to be getting a truck-load of generators this afternoon. Do we have a place to put them?" Walter Prince started each day meeting with his warehouse manager. With so much material now flowing through Prince's Hardware, managing logistics was a full-time job.

"We should be able to move around the plumbing equipment to make room for them."

"Walter, come here! Jeremy is on the phone!" Rosita was yelling from the office into the warehouse. Walter and Rosita hadn't heard from their son in a several days, and they were anxious to get an update.

As he walked into the office, an excited Rosita exclaimed, "I'm putting him on the speaker phone! OK, Jeremy, your dad is here."

"Hi, Jeremy. It is great to hear from you."

"Mom, Dad, I need for you to listen. You know I told you my boss was going to be taking a leave of absence from the company, and I was taking on more responsibility?"

"Yes, we are so proud! Everyone at the store is excited!" Rosita exclaimed.

"Well…things have changed…a lot," Jeremy cautioned.

"What do you mean?" Walter asked.

"It turns out my boss is not what I thought he was. He actually has done some very bad things. I'm not there anymore."

"What? Where are you?" Rosita asked.

"I'm in a car. I can't exactly say where."

"Why not?! What's going on Jeremy?!" Rosita queried with growing concern.

"I don't know exactly what's going to happen, but I may get blamed for some things that I didn't do."

"Jeremy, you aren't making any sense," Walter interjected.

As Walter was speaking, he heard a loud commotion coming from the front of the store. Within seconds he heard a cacophony of voices, screaming what sounded like commands. Then the door to the office burst open.

"Federal agents! Put your hands where I can see them!"

"What's going on?!" Rosita asked hysterically.

The command was repeated. "Put your hands where I can see them!"

"What's happening?!" Jeremy asked.

"Walter and Rosita Prince, you are under arrest for defrauding the Federal Government."

"What!? What's going on Walter?!" Rosita screamed.

"I don't know."

Walter and Rosita were thrown to the ground, face down and handcuffed.

"Mom?! Dad?!" Jeremy cried frantically.

As Walter and Rosita were escorted out the front door, at least a dozen police cars with lights flashing were lined up in front of the store. Members of the local and state media had been called in to document the scene as Rosita and Walter Prince were shoved into the back of separate police cars and hauled away.

Jeremy brought along three burner cell phones just for this type of situation. He quickly dialed one of them.

"This is Victor."

"What did you do Victor?!"

"Well, hello, Jeremy. How are things going?" Victor asked happily.

"You son of a bitch. My mom and dad have nothing to do with this."

"Sure they do. They profited from our relationship as much as anyone."

"Let them go, Victor!"

"*Let them go?*" he repeated, incredulously. "I don't have your parents, Jeremy. It is my understanding they are in the U. S. Marshal's custody. Sounds like a pretty serious situation."

Jeremy abruptly ended the call. All he wanted was confirmation that Victor was involved. He was now even more resolute. Another 12 hours to his ultimate destination.

65

"**A**ny word from young Mr. Prince?" Victor called to check with Zeke every few hours. Zeke assured him he'd let Victor know the second Jeremy was located.

"Excuse me, Victor, but I have a quick question," Lionel Ireland said timidly. Lionel was becoming even more deferential around Victor.

Victor simply held up a hand and turned his back to Lionel.

"OK, Zeke, I want to know the minute he sticks his nose back on the grid. Got it? Find him!" Victor hung up the phone and turned back to face Lionel. He asked impatiently, "What?"

"The debate starts in ten minutes, and I just wanted to clarify one thing about the Indonesia question."

A frustrated Victor replied, "We've been over this a dozen times! They are going to ask you…"

"Good evening, ladies and gentlemen. We want to welcome you to the campus of Washington University in St. Louis, Missouri, for the second of three presidential debates. Tonight's debate participants are Mitch McCoy, the Democratic Party's candidate, and Lionel Ireland, the Republican Party's candidate. I am Gerald Maloney from American Cable News. I will be moderating tonight's debate.

"This debate will be unique. It will be a town hall format. The candidates will interact directly with the audience who will be asking questions that are on their hearts and minds. The town hall meeting's participants are uncommitted voters selected by the Gallup Organization.

"Let's get tonight's debate started with the first question from Chad Burroughs from Cape Girardeau, Missouri."

Although Victor used all of Mouse Trap's capabilities to properly "manage" the debate, the town hall format led to unavoidable vulnerabilities, as evidenced by the first question.

"Good evening, candidates. I hope you will excuse me. I am somewhat nervous. As you heard, we are all undecided voters. The biggest reason that I am undecided is that I don't really like either of you. I am actually interested in knowing more about the independent candidate, Elijah Mustang; but neither of you will agree to debate him. Tell me why I should vote for one of you instead of Mr. Mustang."

Peppered in with questions about the economy, racial tension, Indonesia, the Trans Pacific Partnership, and fighting ISIS were three separate questions about Elijah Mustang. He was clearly gaining traction with the voters and was going to be difficult to ignore any longer.

Finally, the moderator took control. "OK, candidates, you've heard from the voters several times tonight. I'm going to put you on the spot. The third and final debate is ten days from today. Will you accept the challenge from these voters and include Elijah Mustang on stage with you?"

Lionel was the first to respond—sort of. "Well, these debates have been planned for months. There would be significant logistical…"

The voters began to boo, shout, and point fingers.

"OK, hang on just a second." Gerald tried to regain control. "The Commission on Presidential Debates will handle the logistics. All you need to do is show up. Are you in?"

Lionel realized there was only one acceptable answer. "Sure, bring him on. We'd love to have him join us."

"Absolutely. I don't know why he hasn't been at the first two," Mitch McCoy responded enthusiastically.

"Sounds like we have a date."

The crowd applauded. The debate continued unremarkably for the next 90 minutes. Backstage, Victor Youngblood pounded on the table, sending three cups of coffee tumbling to the floor.

66

"**D**oes anyone else have mixed feelings about being invited to join the debate?" one of Elijah's leadership team members asked the group.

"Mixed feelings? What's the downside?" asked Jethro.

"We're rising in the polls. We have intentionally not interacted directly with Ireland and McCoy. We're running an outsider campaign. It seems like joining the debate is exactly the opposite of what we need to do. No upside, all downside."

Some on the leadership team agreed that the debate was a risky proposition.

Elijah disagreed, saying, "You are thinking like politicians. You are thinking about how this might affect the campaign. Our candidacy has always been about the voters, and this is a big win for them. To be candid, many people say they support us just because they can't stand the other two. I don't want that to be the reason people vote for us. I want the electorate to be informed about us. We definitely hope they like what they hear; but if they don't, at least they know where we stand."

"I'd like to remind everyone of one thing," Admiral Adair interjected. "Remember when I told you we only got flak when we were over the target? Well, we're dead center at low altitude, so expect them to come at us hot and heavy over the next week. It's going to be a bumpy ride."

Leonard – just wanted you to know that I'm in position. I still have a lot of work to do; but if you are receiving this message, you know I was able to access Level X from my location. Stick with the plan. Jeremy

67

October 19, 2016
20 Days Until 2016 U. S. Presidential Election

"Remember, tonight is all about Mustang. Our polling shows he is now taking more votes from you than from McCoy, so every person you turn away from him has a better chance of coming over to our side."

Victor was giving his usual pre-debate pep talk to Lionel.

"Our deal with McCoy is that he'll deliver the low blows; you focus on the head shots. Got it?"

"Got it."

As Lionel was responding, Elijah emerged from the hallway, startling both men.

"Well, hello, Mr. Youngblood!" Elijah taunted, brushing by Victor and Lionel backstage. "Been to Baltimore lately?"

"Baltimore? What are you talking about?" a confused Lionel asked.

Elijah simply chuckled as he continued walking.

Admiral Adair's prediction proved to be correct. Both candidates spent the last week firing all barrels at Elijah in TV ads, speeches, and talk-show appearances. Elijah stayed the course and stuck to his voter-focused campaign. The debate offered that strategy its greatest challenge to date.

"Good evening, ladies and gentlemen. Welcome to the campus of Murray State University in Murray, Kentucky, for the third and final 2016 presidential debate. Tonight's debate participants are Mitch McCoy, the Democratic Party's candidate, and Lionel Ireland, the Republican Party's candidate. And we welcome to the dais for the first time, Independent candidate Elijah Mustang.

"I am Tina Jackson from C-SPAN. I will be your moderator. The forum for tonight's debate was originally scheduled to mirror the first debate with pre-arranged topics of 15 minutes each. However, the candidates agreed to change tonight's format to be more interactive and to allow questions to be asked among the candidates to better integrate Mr. Mustang into the discussion."

Elijah thought, "Which candidates agreed to that?"

"We will start this evening's debate with the topic of the economy. Our first question is for Senator McCoy. Senator

McCoy, our nation is experiencing its greatest budget deficit in its 240-year history. Many economists say this level of deficit is unsustainable, so something obviously has to change. What is your plan for reducing the deficit? Is it tax policy, reduced spending, or a combination of both?"

"Tina, thank you for that question. I'd like to start by expressing my gratitude to the staff and leadership of Murray State University for being such gracious hosts for this event. I'd also like to thank Mr. Ireland for his tenacity in this campaign. That tenacity makes us both stronger candidates. I'd also like to welcome Mr. Mustang."

"Tina, my primary strategy for addressing the deficit is through a wealth tax, which I have discussed with the American people many times. I'd like to ensure that the one percenters, such as Mr. Mustang, pay their fair share. Mr. Mustang likes to portray himself as an everyday common man, but last year he made $1.3 million and paid 4% in taxes. Four percent! I bet there are a lot of single moms that would love to pay 4%, but they aren't as fortunate as Mr. Mustang."

Lionel jumped into the mix with both feet. "What Mr. Mustang is going to tell you is that he made charitable donations that helped lower his tax rate; but what he really did was donate to his own foundation, which conveniently does most of its business out of the country. Now that's a sweet deal!"

Mitch continued the barrage. "He also took two months off for vacation. Two months! How many of you can make $1.3 million while taking two months' vacation?

I think the American people are starting to see the real Elijah Mustang, not some fabricated feel-good story."

The moderator prompted Elijah, "Mr. Mustang, do you have a rebuttal?"

Elijah sighed, turned, and looked directly into the camera. "Is this what you want? Is this what you are looking for in a leader? I was hoping tonight to clearly articulate exactly why I'm running for president, and these two gentlemen just provided the perfect illustration. I am running to give you a choice—a choice that doesn't involve shouting and name-calling and petty arguments. I believe you are looking for something different, and that's what I'm hoping to offer you.

"I will briefly address this tax question. In 2015 I was blessed to earn $1,315,000 through a business that I started with myself and a truck thirty plus years ago. I am also blessed to have started a charity called Promise Ministries, which provides health clinics, homes, churches, and children's facilities for disadvantaged communities in Central and South America. I am very passionate about this charity so I give as much as I can. Last year I gave $1,147,000 to Promise Ministries, as well as to a handful of other charitable organizations.

"I know many of our voters give to charities in their communities and understand that charitable donations are deducted from their income. My tax rate was so low because of my charitable giving. I released my last ten years of returns a few weeks ago, so all this information can be confirmed."

Mitch was unfazed. "Mr. Mustang also lacks the judgment and temperament to be president. He was recently invited to speak to NOPOC, and he so insulted the African-American community that he was disinvited from speaking at dozens of college campuses. I don't think that's what people of color in this country are looking for in a president."

The onslaught against Elijah raged. The topics varied, but the pattern was the same: turning any answer into an opportunity to attack Elijah.

The moderator continued, "Gentlemen, the newest battleground in this country's culture wars involves the LGBT community. There have been historic Supreme Court rulings, controversial state laws, and even debates about where people should go to the bathroom. What is your stance on LGBT rights?"

Mitch was the first to respond. "The LGBT community has my complete support. I have a number of LGBT members on my staff and have a rating of 100% from several LGBT advocacy organizations. Mr. Mustang believes..."

"Mr. Mustang can speak for himself." Elijah finally had enough and decided to chime in before Ireland and McCoy could double-team him again. "In trying to correct what some see as bigotry against the LBGT community, we've simply traded one bigotry for another. Bigotry is defined as intolerance toward those who hold different opinions from oneself. Our national institutions—our governments, courts and media—have decided to be assertive advocates and take sides on matters of conscience, where, by definition, there are always going to be differences of opinion, not differences of fact.

"Foundational principles in our nation are freedom of religion and freedom of speech. We are now picking and choosing whose speech and religion is right and whose is wrong. For example, there are legitimate differences of opinion about the definition of *marriage*. Some believe it should be between a man and a woman, while others argue that same-sex marriage should be legalized. Our institutions have decided that we must accept the same-sex marriage argument. If we disagree, we run the risk of losing our jobs, getting sued, being fined, being labeled as bigots, not being welcomed on college campuses, and being sent to re-education sessions to correct our misguided beliefs.

"Did you ever stop to think, 'What if things change? What if a different group of people assume positions of authority and your belief system becomes out of vogue and you get fired, and ridiculed, and fined?' If I am elected president, I will do everything within my power to restore First Amendment rights to everyone. No one should lose their jobs, get fined, or be marginalized on matters of conscience."

Mitch tried to interject, "Mr. Mustang thinks..."

"I'm not done!" Elijah said assertively enough that both Lionel and Mitch backed down. It was truly a turning point in the debate. One criticism of Elijah was that he was too nice and too mild-mannered to tackle the more difficult responsibilities of the presidency. Those three simple words— "I'm not done!"—stated emphatically—showed the tenacity, strength, and leadership that helped Elijah build his business and his ministry. The debate continued, but the entire tenor changed. Mitch and Lionel became meek; Elijah was bold, clear, and authoritative all the way to his closing statement.

"What you see in these debates…this isn't the real America. In real America, Democrats and Republicans live next door to each other, borrow each other's lawn mower, and break bread together on Friday nights. In real America, blacks, whites, and Latinos share a lunch table bragging about their kids' achievements. In real America, gay and straight people sit next to each other at ball games cheering for their hometown teams. In real America, Christians, Jews, Muslims, and atheists share the same American dream of liberty, opportunity, and freedom. That's the America our candidacy represents. That's the choice we offer you on November 8. We would be honored if you would give us a chance. Thank you."

"Tell me about Level X, Leonard."

Stunned by the question, Leonard looked up from his desk to find Zeke standing in the doorway. He tried his best to deflect, but it wasn't a skill he had mastered. "Level X? Wha...what is Level X?"

"Leonard, this can be as long and as difficult as you want it to be. I'll ask again; tell me about Level X." As Zeke asked the question for the second time, he stepped toward Leonard's desk as two guards entered the office and silently stationed themselves on either side of the doorway. Leonard's heart raced and his breathing shallowed. His response was tempered only by the fact that the guards were members of Greenforce. As Omnia's administrator, Leonard was well aware what Blackforce was capable of, so their absence was a relief.

Leonard swallowed hard, leaned his head back, and bit his lower lip. "Well...I don't really know anything about...what did you call it, Level X?"

"You have caused great harm to our organization. This is obviously your last day of employment with Mouse Trap. You are terminated. These gentlemen will escort you out of the building."

"Yes sir. I understand." Mumbled Leonard.

Leonard rose from his chair and followed one of the guards to the Mouse Trap's entrance, where he surrendered his security credentials. The guards then led him to the front door, where he was left to walk to his vehicle unescorted. "Wow, that's it? That was too easy," he thought. He looked over both shoulders, concerned about what would come next.

68

Papers were strewn throughout the room covering both beds, the desk, dresser, and TV stand. Although it looked like a disorganized mess, Jeremy had an order to the stacks. Produced by a printer and 19 ink cartridges purchased from a local electronics store, Jeremy was building an impressive library. He still had some final work to do to execute the plan he had developed on the 26-hour drive from Bethesda to Rock Springs, Wyoming. Room 24 at the Bison Inn had been his home for the past 11 days. He had requested a room closest to the Wi-Fi router in order to conduct some "business." The front-desk clerk accommodated him with a room directly below, ensuring a strong signal. He could see an end in sight to his plan, but he knew everything had to be accomplished perfectly. The ring of his cell phone brought a welcome respite from his monotonous task.

"Hello, Leonard. How are things going?" Jeremy asked.

"Not so great, Jeremy," Leonard responded nervously. "They found out, Jeremy. They found out *everything*. Level X, our messages, everything."

"Now calm down, Leonard; how do you know…"

"It was Zeke. He came to my office with two Greenforce guys."

"I need some more time, Leonard. I'm getting close to connecting Victor with Wembley, but I just need more time."

"It looks like there's a black SUV following me. That can't be good, can it?"

"There are a lot of SUVs on the road. It's probably nothing."

"It's getting closer, Jeremy! It's right on my tail!"

"OK, Leonard, listen…"

The next sound Jeremy heard was the crashing of metal; then the phone went dead.

69

October 21, 2016

18 Days Until 2016 U. S. Presidential Election

"We're slipping in the polls. Mustang now is actually ahead of both you and McCoy. He's pulling in 40% in some polls. I can't believe you just backed down from him like that." Victor Youngblood was delivering his daily berating of his" boss," Lionel Ireland.

Lionel feebly protested, "I didn't really…"

As Lionel was speaking, Victor's cell phone rang; and, as was his custom, Victor walked away to answer it.

"Zeke, what have you got?"

"We finally got a breakthrough. You remember Leonard Applebaum, the IT guy that works on Omnia?" Zeke asked.

"Yes, I remember Leonard."

"Turns out he's been working with Jeremy for the past several weeks. One of the IT guys turned him in. We found that he had created a rogue section within Omnia to which only Jeremy and Leonard had access."

"*I see,*" Victor remarked intently.

"They have been planning this coup for a while. The best part is that we found Jeremy. He has been logging in to Omnia from a motel room in Rock Springs, Wyoming."

"Wyoming? What's he doing in Wyoming?" Victor asked.

"We intercepted a phone call between Jeremy and Leonard last night. Jeremy is there trying to get information to connect you to Wembley. He thinks he's getting close. What do you want us to do?" Zeke asked.

"Sit tight. I'm heading to Wyoming."

70

Jeremy's piles were complete. He still had some work to do to organize everything on his laptop, but he was satisfied with the progress he had made. Although he put in some long days and nights at Mouse Trap, he couldn't remember a two-week period he had worked so intensely. He didn't really have a routine. He worked until he was too weary to continue; then he slipped into a sliver of one of his beds that wasn't covered in papers and slept. As soon as he was able to wake up, he started the process all over again. He didn't think he had ever been so bone-weary. He hoped it would all be worth it.

Just as he began to doze off, he heard a loud knock on the door followed almost immediately by a loud crash and then a voice. "Put your hands in the air and don't move!" His room quickly filled with police as bright lights flooded in.

A devoted fan of the show "Cops," Jeremy had witnessed this scene play out on TV hundreds of times; but this experience offered him a unique perspective on the apprehension process. It was a perspective he was sure he didn't like.

As Jeremy was led out of the motel room in handcuffs, local media stations were there to capture the proceedings. Within minutes, he was behind bars.

"They found him," Zeke reported.

"*Who* found him?" Victor asked.

"Believe it or not, the Sweetwater County, Wyoming Sheriff's Office apprehended him. He's sitting in their detention center."

Victor chuckled. "The FBI has been looking for two weeks, and Andy and Barney from Mayberry found him! That's great! I'm going to call Gavin and give him a hard time about this one! Make sure he stays in jail until I get there. I have some things I'd like to personally discuss with him before he goes away. I'll be there tomorrow."

71

" . . . **I**t is towns like Rock Springs that are the true backbone of this country."

Victor's rally was held in the Sweetwater Events Complex, home of the annual Sweetwater County Fair, also known as The Big Show, offering rides, concerts, and exhibits around which locals planned their calendar.

Although residents were given short notice about the vice presidential candidate's visit, the crowds still showed up. This was clearly a big deal for little Rock Springs.

"Over the past several weeks, I have traveled throughout this glorious country; but I must say I haven't found a more beautiful place than Sweetwater Country, Wyoming. The only thing more beautiful than the scenery is the people.

I have been so moved by your hospitality and kindness. I hope to visit you again someday soon. God bless you, and God bless the United States of America."

The crowd erupted as their civic pride swelled. They had just hosted what could be the vice president of the United States! Victor stayed around for a while shaking hands, signing autographs, and posing for pictures. He had completed the transition from clandestine kingmaker to public politician. It was even starting to seem authentic.

Victor waved one last time to the crowd and climbed in the back of his SUV to make the short drive into the town of Rock Springs. Following Victor's instructions, his driver pulled up to the Sweetwater County Sheriff's office. Victor got out of the SUV and walked into the facility, where Sheriff Buck Earnest greeted him at the door and led him into the facility. After meeting an excited staff and posing for more pictures, Victor and Sheriff Earnest met privately in the sheriff's office.

"Sheriff, I want to thank you for agreeing to meet with me. My trip to your beautiful county has been beyond my expectations."

"This is a big deal for us. People will be talking about your visit for years to come."

"I have one matter I'd like to discuss with you. One of my former employees was arrested yesterday. His name is Jeremy Prince."

"Yes, I recall. The FBI had an arrest warrant out for him, and we got a tip that he was in town," Sheriff Earnest boasted.

"Jeremy and I worked closely together. I guess you could say that I was somewhat of a mentor to him. I know this is a lot to ask, but do you think I could possibly meet with him? This campaign is all-consuming, and I'm concerned I won't get an opportunity once he enters the legal system. I would I like to have a few words with him."

"He's down the road in the detention center. I don't think it would be a good idea for you to visit him there, but we could arrange for a deputy to bring him here to the office."

"I would be truly indebted to you if you could." Victor replied thankfully.

"It will take a few minutes. I know my staff would appreciate it if you would visit with them and pose for a few more photos."

"Certainly! I will be happy to."

Smiles, handshakes, poses, and autographs consumed the next 30 minutes for Victor until the real object of his visit walked through the side door. Jeremy looked rough. He wore an orange jumpsuit with *Sweetwater County Detention Center* printed on the back. His hands and feet were shackled as he struggled to shuffle through the door. His hair was unkempt, and the bags under his eyes bore witness to his sleep deprivation.

"Would you like to speak privately with Mr. Prince?" Sheriff Earnest asked.

"If it's not too much to ask, that would be appreciated," Victor responded humbly.

"You can meet in my conference room."

The deputy led Jeremy into the conference room and helped him into a chair. Victor took a seat across the table from him. Sheriff Earnest motioned for the deputy to go, leaving Jeremy and Victor alone.

"This is rather symbolic; isn't it, Jeremy? I'm a step away from my ultimate goal, and you could spend the rest of your life behind bars."

"I didn't fully understand what you were capable of, Victor," Jeremy mumbled, his head hanging low.

"Is that a compliment?" Victor asked.

"You probably see it as such," Jeremy said wryly, still not able to bring himself to make eye contact.

"Jeremy, you lack the strategic focus and vision to accomplish great things. You allowed yourself to prioritize meaningless drivel like morals, ethics, and relationships above the ultimate goal."

"I don't regret anything. I still think I made the right decisions."

"And yet the circumstances speak for themselves," Victor boasted. He gestured to Jeremy and spoke with mocking sorrow. "You are sitting here in chains. I am about to walk out this door a free man. In a few weeks I will be the most powerful man in the world, and you will still be in chains."

As Victor spoke, the TV monitor in the conference room powered up and flickered, causing Victor to turn his head. A second later, the screen showed the drone video footage from Senator Wembley's death at the Killpecker Dunes, followed instantly by video from Jeremy's office with Victor speaking the words, "Yes, Jeremy, I killed a United States' senator; and nobody is going to do anything about it." The 20-second video looped back to Wembley's death and then back to Victor's confession, then repeated over and over again.

A shocked Victor asked, "What is this?"

"This…is strategic focus and vision," Jeremy blurted, smiling, his eyes finally rising to meet Victor's.

As Jeremy spoke Sheriff Earnest and three armed deputies entered the conference room.

"Victor Youngblood, you are under arrest for the murder of Grant Wembley." The deputies grabbed his arms and bent him over the table securing his hands with cuffs.

"What!?" A shocked Victor shouted. "The FBI has already discredited this video as a fake! Call them; they will tell you!"

"I actually just got off the phone with FBI Director Thompson. He congratulated us on the arrest."

"That's not possible. He knows me!"

The deputies grabbed Victor's arms as he shouted at Jeremy, "I trusted you Jeremy!"

"Yes, Victor, you did. In fact, trust was my most powerful asset."

As the deputies ushered Victor out of the room, he shouted, "You don't know what you're doing! You don't know who you're dealing with! You are going to regret this!"

The deputies continued the short walk through the office staff, with whom only moments before Victor had posed for pictures, and out to an awaiting police car. All of the proceedings were captured on video by local news media for the world to see.

Sheriff Earnest removed the chains from Jeremy's hands and feet.

"Great job, son," Sheriff Earnest congratulated, extending a hand of thanks. "Everything worked to perfection."

Jeremy's first three days in the Bison Inn were devoted to compiling as much evidence as possible against Victor. Omnia Level X provided Jeremy the opportunity to move Omnia files to his laptop. In addition to the drone footage, Leonard also sent him the video from Jeremy's office, where Victor admitted his role in Senator Wembley's death.

Jeremy arranged a meeting with Sheriff Earnest, who was skeptical at first but quickly found Jeremy's story compelling. The office video also captured Victor's phone call with FBI Director Thompson, making it clear that this was a complicated case, made even more tenuous by Victor's public persona as a vice presidential candidate.

After spending the first few days building the case against Victor, he spent the balance of his time in the Bison Inn orchestrating a sequence of events necessary for his plan to be fully realized.

The *Trapped* application was a treasure trove of information. Jeremy searched the database and found other deaths about which Victor had interacted with the

FBI. He sent this e-mail to Director Thompson's private account:

> *Director Thompson – I worked for Victor Young-blood. I know that you conspired with Victor to ignore the deaths of Roginsky, Sammons, and Wembley. Probably more. I'll be arranging for Victor's arrest soon. All I need for you to do is allow it to happen. If you intervene on his behalf, your involvement will be made public. A Friend.*

Given that Senator Wembley's death occurred in the Killpecker Dunes, Sheriff Earnest knew it was within his jurisdiction to arrest Victor. He just had to get Victor back into the county. That's where Jeremy had a plan, with a little help from a friend.

"Jeremy, this is kinda fun!" Leonard exclaimed, walking into the conference room.

"Leonard, this is awesome fun! Sheriff, this is my friend Leonard Applebaum. He works with me and made much of this possible."

"Nice to meet you, Mr. Applebaum," Sheriff Earnest responded.

Both Jeremy and Leonard knew that Blackforce was given the order to "trap" Leonard. Jeremy and Leonard staged the SUV-chase phone call, knowing that Zeke would be listening. They gambled that in the chaos of Victor's being out of Mouse Trap and the frantic search for Jeremy, Zeke wouldn't actually confirm that Blackforce had made the "trap." Their gamble paid off when Leonard joined Jeremy in Rock Springs to put together the final pieces of Jeremy's plan.

"Did everything else go OK?" Jeremy asked.

"Yep. Everything's done," Leonard replied.

In fully digesting the breadth of carnage Mouse Trap had caused, Jeremy assessed his realistic options. The corruption involved every government agency up through the FBI and all the way to the White House. Hundreds of major U. S. corporations were implicated. Both political parties were involved. He couldn't just turn over the *Trapped* file to the authorities because any honest investigation would lead back to the authorities themselves. Therefore, he decided to peel the onion one layer at a time. Victor had to be first. Once he was out of the way, others would understand that if Victor could be captured, there was nowhere they could hide.

Jeremy had a series of e-mails in the queue that Leonard was instructed to send upon Victor's arrest.

> *Zeke – It's all over. Victor was arrested today for the murder of Senator Wembley. Mouse Trap is no more. I know Mouse Trap has provided you great wealth, but it has also been at a great price. You will be held accountable for your actions. Jeremy*

This e-mail went to the global distribution list of everyone at Mouse Trap:

> *Members of Mouse Trap – Effective immediately, Mouse Trap is closed. Greenforce has been instructed to clear the building and you will not be allowed to return. There will be no additional communication.*

This e-mail went to Andrei Ovchenko, head of Blackforce:

> *Mr. Ovchenko – Victor Youngblood has been arrested. Mouse Trap is closed for good. The services of Blackforce will be no longer needed. Thanks to Mr. Youngblood's meticulous documentation of Blackforce activities, each mission your organization undertook is recorded on video. You and the members of Blackforce should consider leaving the country.*

The e-mail was unsigned.

"Leonard, what do you say we go grab a burger? I hear they have a great cafe just down the street."

"Sounds good," Leonard concurred.

Sheriff Earnest interjected, "Let me grab my hat, and I'll go with you guys. I'm buying."

72

"Hey, Grandpa, do you remember a crazier election season that this one?" Emily Everman asked her Grandfather, Bronson.

Bronson chuckled and then answered, "Let's see; one vice presidential candidate murdered, another arrested for committing the murder, and an independent candidate who is leading in all of the polls. I'd have to say that this is one for the record books."

"See, I told you guys back in the spring that this was all one big conspiracy," Maggie interjected.

"It's still not a conspiracy!" a frustrated Jake bellowed.

Bronson decided to take charge. "OK, everyone; it's time for the quadrennial Bronson family election. Edith has printed ballots for each voting-age family member.

That's nine this year with Cameron and Emily being old enough to vote for the first time."

"The ballots do include Elijah Mustang, don't they?" Cameron asked excitedly.

"Yes, they include all three candidates," Edith responded. "Record your vote, and then put your ballot in this bucket."

Each family member dutifully completed a ballot.

"OK, I'll tally the results," Edith announced.

"If anyone voted for Ireland, you oughta just go ahead and make your reservation at the asylum," Brad bellowed.

"We have a winner," Edith announced. "Let's start at the bottom. We have two votes for Lionel Ireland."

"Seriously? Two of you actually voted for that guy?!" Brad exclaimed.

"We have three votes for Mitch McCoy. That means the winner of the Everman family election is Elijah Mustang with four out of nine votes.

"Yes!" Cameron approved.

"We'll know in three days who the real winner is. Don't forget to vote!" Bronson urged.

73

The leadership team decided weeks in advance that they wanted a momentous election eve celebration to cap off Elijah's historic run for the presidency. The plan was to rent the Knoxville Civic Coliseum for Elijah to make one last speech to his supporters. The Coliseum had a capacity of just over 7,000. Elijah laughed at the prospect that thousands of people would actually show up to hear him speak.

As Elijah's popularity soared, so did the interest in his final campaign stop. Although admission to the event was free, tickets were distributed to determine crowd size. The 7,000 tickets went quickly and even started selling on the secondary market through ticket scalpers.

As Elijah's campaign gained momentum, the leadership team upgraded the event a few weeks into the campaign to Thompson Boling Arena, home of the Tennessee Volunteers basketball teams. With a capacity of 21,000, it was triple the size of the Civic Coliseum.

After Elijah's electric debate performance and the crash of the Ireland campaign, ticket demand again surged. A donor stepped in and footed the $1.2 million price tag to rent cavernous Neyland Stadium for an evening. Home to the Tennessee Volunteers football team, Neyland was among the largest stadiums in the country with a capacity of over 100,000.

Much to Elijah's shock, over 90,000 people had assembled on this night before the election to show support for their unconventional candidate. As Elijah stood backstage, a flood of emotion began to overwhelm him. What pushed him over the edge was a stirring rendition of "God Bless the USA" that had filled the massive stadium with tens of thousands of people singing along.

Walking toward a backstage corner, Elijah dropped to one knee, then both, as a small puddle began to form from the tears streaming down his face. Scheduled to take the stage in less than ten minutes, he began praying.

He felt a hand on his shoulder as he looked up and saw Jethro kneel beside him. Then another hand and another and another as his entire leadership team had formed a circle of prayer around their friend.

Pastor Roberts began to pray out loud, "Father, I lift up my friend to you and ask that you give him strength, wisdom and clarity. We believe you have called him for this purpose on this night in this stadium. We believe you have called him for such a time as this. In Jesus' name I pray. Amen."

"Amen," the assemblage echoed.

Elijah rose to his feet, steely eyed, and purposefully walked toward the stage. "I'm ready" were the only words he spoke.

"Ladies and gentlemen, this has already been a historic night; but the best is yet to come. Our final speaker tonight is the reason we have assembled." The crowd began to cheer. "He has given us hope that our country can really be saved. He gave me strict instructions to avoid flowery introductions; so I'll simply say, ladies and gentlemen, Elijah Mustang."

The crowd rose to their feet with thunderous applause. Chants of *USA* filled the stadium for what seemed like forever. Signs were held up throughout the stadium with the phrase *I'm not done!*—the de facto campaign slogan after Elijah's debate performance. Finally, the crowd calmed down enough that Elijah could speak. He skipped the pleasantries and "thank yous" and got down to business.

"Eight Saturdays a year, this stadium is filled to capacity as the Tennessee Volunteers take the field. They run through the *T* with The Pride of the Southland Marching Band playing "Rocky Top." It is truly a spectacle to see.

There are 100,000 people in the stands watching 22 players on the field. When things on the field are going well, the crowd cheers. When things are going poorly, the crowd becomes dejected. The mood in the stands is dictated by what those 22 men do.

"That sounds a lot like where we are as a country. We have 300 million people who watch a few hundred in Washington actually in the game. We allow those few people to determine our country's direction. While most of us are never going to come onto this field and play quarterback, the beauty of our political system is that we are allowed to get into that game. Every one of us is called onto the field.

"Accountant, we need you! Electrician, get in the game! Plumber, baker, artist, pastor, teacher, engineer, custodian, scientist, salesman, doctor, nurse, and truck driver—its time you entered the fray.

"You see, this movement has never been about a single man. This has never been about me. Some of you are holding signs that say *I'm not done*. I hope you mean that—that *you're* not done. That you are going to use this experience as a springboard to launch into action.

"I don't know how the vote is going to go tomorrow; but it almost doesn't matter, *at least it shouldn't matter*. Tomorrow isn't the end of the process; it's the beginning. It's the beginning of your taking back control of your country. Wednesday morning when the voting machines are returned to their closets, the pollsters put away their computers, and the networks convert their studios back to normal, you are just getting started.

"Stay engaged. Run for school board or city council. Run for statewide office. Write your congressman. *Be* your congressman! Make a difference!

"Beyond the emotion you are feeling tonight, there's something more lasting going on inside you. A feeling of inspiration that you know things not only need to be different but WILL BE different. Take that feeling and inspire others. Keep this going! Because YOU'RE NOT DONE!"

74

November 8, 2016
2016 U. S. Presidential Election Day

"Here you go, Dad." Rachel placed the omelet on Elijah's plate.

"Still bacon, provolone cheese, and jalapeno peppers?" Shelly asked.

"Is there another kind?" Elijah teased.

Of all the places Elijah could be on this Election Day, into which he had poured so much energy, he chose to be at home. Joining him were his three daughters, two sons-in-law, and his dog Clyde. "How are you feeling today, Dad? Nervous? Excited? Scared?" Kathi asked.

Elijah paused for a moment, obviously in deep thought, then looked to his family and simply said, "Blessed."

∮

Pre-election polls had been all over the map. Political prognostication was difficult enough with two candidates; throw in a third and anything could happen. Predicting the popular vote was one thing; getting the state-by-state electoral vote was proving to be next to impossible. Each candidate's ultimate goal was to receive 270 electoral votes to secure the White House.

The general consensus was that Elijah would win several states, particularly in the South. Mitch McCoy would sweep the coasts. Even with his unbelievably bad fortune with running mates, most predicted that Lionel would at least win a few states, most likely in the middle of the country.

As polls began closing, both McCoy and Elijah had states in their column. Elijah won Alabama, Georgia, Indiana, Kentucky, Mississippi, and his home state of Tennessee. He also pulled off surprising wins in the battleground states of Ohio, Pennsylvania, and Florida.

McCoy won Connecticut, Delaware, Maine, Illinois, Massachusetts, New Hampshire, New York, and New Jersey.

In the early-reporting states, Ireland only pulled off a victory in Virginia.

By 10 p.m. EST, the outcome was just as murky as when the day started. McCoy and Elijah were neck and neck in the electoral vote. The only certainty was that Lionel Ireland had no mathematical chance to reach the magic number of 270.

As results from the Midwestern states were tallied, the picture became clearer. Elijah won Louisiana,
Missouri, Nebraska, North Dakota, and South Dakota.
When Texas, the state with the largest number of electoral votes, also went for Elijah, it sealed the fate of
Mitch McCoy who, like Lionel Ireland, had no path to
270 votes.

By 2 a.m. EST, the political number crunchers had
concluded that the State of Nevada held all of the cards
for the 2016 presidential election. If Elijah could pull off
a win in the Silver State, he'd record 274 electoral votes
and would be the next president of the United States. If
either McCoy or Ireland won Nevada, Elijah would be at
268, two votes short.

As Nevada's votes came in, it was clear the tally was
going to be close. In the end, the totals were Mitch
McCoy - 347,698; Lionel Ireland - 273,886; Elijah Mus-
tang - 325,487. On the wave of high voter turnout in
Clark County, home to Las Vegas, Mitch McCoy secured
Nevada's six electoral votes.

At the close of Election Day 2016, the electoral vote
count was Lionel Ireland - 49; Mitch McCoy – 221; Elijah
Mustang – 268.

After four debates, hundreds of speeches, thousands
of miles traveled, billions of dollars spent, and one murder, nobody won 270 electoral votes and consequently
nobody won the 2016 presidential election.

75

Jeremy and Leonard spent the next several weeks dispositioning Mouse Trap resources, a task that proved to be much more complicated than anticipated. They enlisted the help of a friend who worked as a finance manager in Mouse Trap. Their friend provided eye-opening insight into the intricate web that Victor had created.

Mouse Trap entities held large percentages of major corporations; real estate holdings measuring in the hundreds of square miles; and significant natural resources including coal, oil, and natural gas. When the tally began reaching in the hundreds of billions of dollars, they decided to enlist the FBI's help. Even if they didn't totally trust the Bureau, they at least wanted that kind of wealth out of their hands.

They also provided the Bureau with the *Trapped* file's full content. They wondered if it would even be opened.

Jeremy sent one final text to CivDis that simply stated, "Disband." Cedar Lassiter spent the next four hours poring through his maps app trying to find a place called *Disband.*

Jeremy and Leonard also agreed that Omnia needed to be destroyed. It was a concentration of data that should not be stored in one place. They agreed that Leonard would break all the links and reformat all of Omnia's drives. It was a task that Leonard could pull off...almost. He felt that he had satisfied the spirit of the agreement with Jeremy by just powering down Omnia. He kept the data stored safely in a server farm outside Salt Lake City...just in case.

76

January 6, 2017

C ongress set aside January 6, 2017, as the day the Electoral College met to cast its votes for president. Elijah fell two electoral votes short of winning, mirroring Election Day results

According to the U.S. Constitution, if no candidate receives the required 270 electoral votes, the House of Representatives elects the president from the three candidates who received the most electoral votes. In this voting process each state's congressional delegation casts a single vote.

After the House of Representatives voted, the tally for each candidate was as follows: Mustang – 7 states; Ireland – 17 states; Mitch McCoy – 26 states.

After much debate the prevailing sentiment among the congressmen was that they knew what they were getting with Mitch McCoy. Elijah Mustang was just too much of a wild card and too risky. They concluded that neither Elijah Mustang, nor the people of the United States, really understood what it took to run the country.

The 45th president of the United States would be Woodrow Mitchell McCoy.

While the forces of Victor Youngblood, The Council, Omnia and Blackforce were defeated, the forces of deeply entrenched Washington politicians proved to be invincible.

❦

"Hey, Dad, we got an e-mail from Quality Plumbing. They said the ball valves aren't going to be in until Tuesday."

"Tell them that's not acceptable. We need them at least by Monday!"

After a brief investigation, Rosita and Walter Prince were cleared of any wrongdoing and released with apologies from the Bureau. Jeremy moved back to Abingdon to work with his mom and dad at the hardware store. Being the fourth-generation Prince to work at the store had a renewed appeal.

Chip, the front desk clerk, stuck his head in the office. "Hey Jeremy, there's a guy out front to see you."

"Who is it?"

"I don't know, but he's a stocky older guy. He's got like a weird accent; and get this, he's wearing an eyepatch."

77

I t was a six-hour drive from the Bolivian capital of La Paz to the rural region in the State of Beni, where they set up camp. After half a day on site, the truck was mostly offloaded with food, water and medical supplies for the Bolivian people who made the impoverished region home.

A group of children had climbed into the back of the truck and were tearing open the final three boxes, which contained toys and children's books.

"Hang on, don't open those yet!" Tyler Edison chided.

"It's OK. They're for the children," Elijah replied.

The day after Elijah announced he was running for president, Tyler's positive profile was again published online. The day after that, Tyler was told his services were no longer needed at the National News Service.

After some soul searching, Tyler decided to do a freelance project chronicling the real Elijah Mustang. He followed Elijah to speaking events, was invited to sit in on leadership team meetings, and got a behind-the-scenes view of his historic run for the White House. Tyler felt the story wasn't complete without accompanying Elijah on one of his Promise Ministries' mission trips.

To stay in touch with the outside world, Tyler brought along a satellite phone that was currently holding his attention.

"Well, the House voted. Want to know the results?"

"Not really."

"Really? After all the work you put in, you don't want to know?"

"Not really."

A little girl named Belen climbed into Elijah's lap, gazed into his eyes, and asked him to *leer* (Spanish for *read*). Elijah smiled and opened the book to the first page.

Tyler insisted, "Well, I think you need to know. I'm sorry to be the one to tell you, but...you lost."

Elijah shook his head, glanced up from the book and simply said, "No I didn't."

Here's what's coming next!

Manipulated: Book Two – Rise of the Mustangs (working title) is planned for late 2018.

Manipulated: Book Three – Declaration of Independence (working title) is planned for late 2019 and will focus on the 2020 presidential campaign.

Please stay in touch at www.johnfordclayton.com for book release updates and much more.